TRINITY

by

Luke Romyn

Published by Luke Romyn
Paperback Edition
Cover illustration by Luke Romyn © 2016

Edited by Chuck David.

If you are interested in more writing by Luke Romyn, be sure to visit
http://www.lukeromyn.com

Dedicated to my dear friend, Richard Watz.

Fighting the good fight.

Acknowledgements

Huge thanks go out to editing team: Chuck David, Karen Hansen, Sarah Dougherty, Claude Bouchard, Joanne Chance, and Kendra Williams.

Thanks to my dogs. You guys make walking worthwhile.

And all of my readers. Yes, you. You are the reason for all the tears. Keep making me cry.

Remember to keep up to date with all my writing at **http://www.lukeromyn.com**

CHAPTER I

Crying eyes rarely see.

Chance stared at the tiny coffin. One hand shook fiercely as her fingertips stretched out toward the lid, but before she could touch the wood, another racking sob overwhelmed her. The priest stood awkwardly in the empty church, seemingly unsure how to console the single mother.

It had been Greg's idea to move to the city. His career was destined to take off in New York; he had felt sure of it. His certainty was almost annoying. Two weeks later, a Yellow Cab had run him down as he crossed the road, killing him almost instantly.

Almost. Such a big word.

Chance thought she would never recover from the loss of her soulmate, but she had fought on for baby Cameron, knowing she needed to remain strong if she wanted to raise a child on her own in a world where Yellow Cabs lurked around every corner, waiting to tear dreams to shreds.

If only she had known.

SIDS, they called it. Such a traumatic experience should never be shrunken into an acronym.

Baby Cameron's tiny fingers had failed to twitch, and his beautiful lips had remained sealed, never to breathe again. Chance's heart had torn from her chest at that moment, when she had stared down into the crib and seen her beloved child, a part of her soul, resting like a stone doll.

Chance reached out again, stroking the varnished wood of the coffin lid. The tiny box felt horribly real. The texture of it beneath the tips of her fingers was smooth, the lacquer flawless, the timber cold. She wanted to hurl the lid away and crawl in alongside her child.

The priest's words floated out hollowly through the empty pews, a somber reminder of all the friends Chance had made since arriving in Brooklyn. A lone child herself, her parents had passed away in a car accident a decade before, leaving her as the last of her line. Greg's family had always despised Chance for reasons she never understood. Even so, she had hoped they might turn up to say farewell to their grandchild.

Never before had Chance felt so utterly alone.

The service concluded. The priest offered empty condolences, and then shuffled beyond the altar, shadowed by his two altar boys, leaving Chance to trolley the coffin outside to the waiting hearse. Those forty-six steps were the longest walk of her life.

The two funeral directors drove her to the gravesite and lowered the coffin into the ground. To Chance, the men looked somewhat bored, but the void inside her refused to allow anything more than the smallest coal of anger to flare.

She stayed by the gravesite for hours, long after the two men had filled the hole with dirt and walked away.

Sometime after midnight, Chance arrived home in a taxi. Her eyes burned, and her throat felt raw, but that did not stop Chance from cracking open a bottle of whiskey and downing it straight. The fire from the liquor barely warmed her, and she slumped down on the couch she used to share with her husband, its coarse woolen covering scraping her skin like a thousand tiny claws. Her soulless eyes stared at nothing.

Minutes, maybe hours passed. Her daze only cracked when she heard footsteps approaching from behind.

Initially, Chance failed to react to the sound. By the time understanding filtered through her misery, a thick, hairy arm wrapped around her throat, an uncaged anaconda, crushing off the air from her lungs. She slapped and clawed, all to no avail. Her attacker was viciously efficient. The last sound she heard was an emotionless grunt in her left ear. Darkness swamped her, along with the cold terror of not knowing what was about to happen to her body.

Chance awoke to a dull ache in her head, her body placed on cold stone tiling, bound hand and foot with duct tape. Glancing around, her head snapping left and right, her breathing erratic, she recognized the familiar surroundings of her basement.

"Ah, you're awake," a deep voice whispered from the shadows.

"Who are you?" Chance demanded, panic threading her tone.

"We are here to unburden you."

"*We?* Who is with you?"

The unseen speaker seemed to consider the question for a moment. "We are alone, just as you are alone." The speaker paused. "And you are so very alone, aren't you?"

Chance fought to gather her thoughts. "You need to let me go. You don't want to do this."

"We have to."

A figure stepped from the shadows, a hulking brute of a man bearing scars up and down both arms. Half the intruder's face puckered with scar tissue from a horrendous burn, as though someone had pressed his face against a glowing red-hot grill. Chance shuddered at the image, but the monster offered no reaction. Reaching behind his back, he pulled a long carving knife from the belt of his pants.

Chance tried to squirm away, but the hulking man snatched at her bound feet and dragged her back. Too late, Chance realized the man's intentions and began to scream.

"Nothing personal, lady," he grunted.

The hulking figure lunged down almost casually and thrust his knife into Chance's chest. The blade bent slightly when the tip dug into the tiles beneath her spine. Collecting himself, the towering figure shrugged and strolled from the basement, leaving a trail of bloody footprints in his wake.

A choking sensation filled Chance. She coughed heavily, spurts of blood erupting from her lips. The room began to close in around her, blindness clawing its way over her eyes. She wheezed, and shadows enveloped her completely.

Then the floor dropped.

CHAPTER II

Chance slammed hard against the ground.

She leaped up and stared around, wild-eyed. Her hand raced to the knife in her chest, only to find the blade had vanished, her skin revealing no evidence of injury. Her blouse remained unblemished, barely creased, no trace of blood splashed across the silk.

"What the hell...?" she murmured, surprised to find her voice had returned and her throat didn't hurt from the bruising.

Streetlights glowed with an orange tinge. One across the way flickered like erratic Morse code. The houses, all red and yellow brick and double story, looked odd and out of place with her memory of Brooklyn. Even the trees looked odd, and the air... it *smelled* different. After several moments of gawping, Chance felt certain the street was one she had never seen before. In fact, as she looked around, she received the distinct impression she was no longer in New York. The roads and buildings appeared more like... Chicago? But how had she traveled here from Brooklyn?

A bus flew by, blowing her long skirt around like a leaf in the breeze. Chance rubbed her hair, and then pulled it in front of her face. It was no longer mousey brown, nor was it curly. Somehow, in the space of a few moments, her hair had transformed into straight black locks.

Chance's brain felt like mashed potatoes. She swam through confusion, trying to piece together some sense of what had happened. The longer she stood still, the more familiar the street appeared. After five minutes, she realized where she was.

"This is Grand Avenue," she muttered. "How did I not recognize it?"

Looking down, she now remembered the skirt was one of her favorites, same for the blouse. The personality of the woman who had been stabbed began to fade into a dreamlike mush, replaced by the realization those memories did not belong to her. Chance had never been married to a man named Greg. And at no time had she ever been pregnant. Yet the loss of the baby named Cameron still felt like a wound in her chest, as real as the blade that had slid between her ribs.

Hailing a taxi with a shaking hand, Chance climbed in and told the driver the address of her home on Madison Street. The studio apartment was far from the Brooklyn house she had stepped into earlier, but for the moment, Chance could not imagine any place she would rather be. The memory of the executioner's knife lingered, and she could still smell the brute's breath in her hair. Lifeblood seemed to leak from her breast, as though part of her soul were dripping through her skin.

Upon arriving home, Chance practically banged on the elevator buttons all the way up to her sixth-floor apartment. She didn't run down the hallway, but she definitely rushed. When she reached the entrance to her unit, she found the door unlocked and resting ajar as though she had strolled out without a care in the world. Chance couldn't close it fast enough behind her. She fastened all three locks and the safety chain before flicking a glance through the peephole, half-expecting to see the man with burn scars covering half his face on the other side.

The hallway remained empty.

Allowing a shuddering breath to escape her lips, Chance backed into the studio. Darkness filled the apartment, and she slapped the wall to flick on the light.

An arm wrapped around her neck, and Chance screamed. The intruder's arm clamped tight around her throat. Familiar pressure started to build. She scratched and clawed, but again to no avail. Midnight swamped her, and with it, the knowledge of what was waiting for her upon awakening. Before she blacked out, she felt her attacker's slimy tongue lick the right side of her face from chin to earlobe like a giant slug.

Consciousness, when it came, arrived carrying a cart full of dread. Chance felt all her weight dangling from her wrists, but instead of opening her eyes, she merely listened, trying to ascertain where her attacker might be.

"We know you're awake," murmured a sibilant voice, one totally unlike the tone of the scarred killer.

It was all Chance could do not to shriek. Her body tensed despite her efforts to remain limp.

Footfalls approached. They clacked on the tiling like goat hooves, slowly clip-clopping closer. Eventually, Chance could bear the tension no longer. Her eyes snapped open.

A cadaverous man stood before her, a curved blade in his left hand. He licked his lips. His skin was pockmarked, almost green in pallor. Fresh scabs formed a mysterious design across his cheeks and forehead, making Chance wonder what drugs the intruder was hooked on. Maybe, if she could figure that out, she might know how best to communicate with him.

"Welcome," he hissed.

Chance screamed, but her voice failed to penetrate the duct tape covering her mouth. Despite the horror raging from her eyes, only muffled whimpers murmured through the studio.

Twisting, Chance found her hands duct taped together, slung over the hook from which her single potted plant usually dangled. She yanked and hauled, but the hook was bolted into the brickwork too securely for her to snap it loose.

The cadaverous man stepped close and pressed the flat of his blade against Chance's cheek. The steel felt like ice, and she tried to scream again. He smiled, but the expression never reached his eyes. With a sudden jab, he stabbed the tip of the knife into her eyeball.

Chance howled. Fire erupted through her brain. The intruder stepped back and watched her flop like a fish on a line. His expression reflected one of casual amusement, a light grin dancing across his lips, his eyes wide with rapture.

Eventually, he stepped in close, pressing her body flat against the wall in the same movement. His long tongue flickered out, sliding up her face, licking the juices from her damaged eye.

The pock-faced man slithered back and regarded her once more. Chance tried to kick out, but he parried her blows effortlessly, amusement warming his hollow features.

"My, aren't you a feisty one."

Without warning, the man slashed the blade across her belly. Chance felt pressure, but no pain. A sloshing sound followed by a noise like wet fish slapping on the floor made her look down. Intestines dangled from her abdominal cavity to the floor. She had a moment to wonder how the man's knife could be so sharp before he stepped close once more. The blade impaled her remaining eye, plunging everything into darkness.

CHAPTER III

The bed sheets felt scratchy.

Chance awoke and screamed, the sound long and piercing. Hands grabbed her, pushing her down.

"I need a doctor in here!"

"Get off me!" Chance howled.

"It's okay, Chance, we're here to help."

The sound of her own name brought with it partial relief, but she still bucked and thrashed. Something encircled her biceps and wrists, additional restraints snapping tight around her ankles.

"He killed me!"

"Nobody killed you, Chance. You've been here the whole time."

With a tremendous thrust of her hips, Chance hurled the body away from her. The man in blue skidded across the floor, but swiftly regained his footing and leaped back toward her.

"Wait there, Stephen," another voice, calm and measured, ordered.

Chance turned toward the newcomer, a middle-aged man wearing glasses and a long white coat. The man held his hands up beseechingly toward her.

"What's happened this time, Chance?"

"He killed me. They both did." She was all too aware of the spit spraying from her gums, but Chance felt unable to do anything about it in her panicked state.

"Only two this time?" The newcomer glanced outside the door. "I need a two milliliter syringe of Diazepam." Chance heard footsteps rush away. The man in the white coat looked back at her. "Nobody killed you, Chance. Everything is fine. You're still here in the hospital; you never left your bed. It's just another episode."

"*Episode?* What are you talking about? Who the hell are you?"

The man in the white coat frowned slightly. "I'm Doctor Smith, Chance. You know me."

Through the haze clouding her memory, the name seemed to resonate. Chance paused her thrashing and stared up at the doctor, for the first time recognizing his features.

"What's happening to me?"

A woman dressed in a clinical white lab coat appeared carrying a stainless steel tray. Doctor Smith lifted a syringe from the tray and analyzed the dosage before squeezing the plunger slightly. A tiny squirt of liquid sprayed from the tip of the needle.

"You'll feel better in a moment, Chance."

"Wait!" Chance pleaded as the doctor moved to grasp her upper arm.

Smith paused. "You need this."

Blowing out a pensive breath, Chance collected herself. "I'll be calm, just don't jab me with that thing."

"That's what she said," muttered a voice to Chance's left.

Glancing over, Chance saw a large lump of a figure sitting up in a bed several yards away. Leather straps hung limply from three locations running down its side, and Chance suddenly understood what held her to the bed. In the semi-darkness, it was impossible to make out any of the bed's resident's features.

"Be quiet, Jarvis," the doctor ordered.

"Hey, if that shrieking sissy don't want a dose, I'll be more than happy to take it."

"I'll be calm," Chance promised. "Please don't inject me."

Doctor Smith appeared doubtful, and held the syringe for some time, fingering the plunger, seemingly debating whether he should use it or not. Chance took several deep breaths, calming herself the best she could. Eventually, she offered him a tentative smile.

"I had a nightmare, that's all."

The doctor scowled once more, apparently unconvinced, but he placed the syringe back down on the stainless steel tray and nodded to the nurse. The woman scurried away without a word.

"That must have been one hell of a dream."

Chance fought to bring her mind to the moment. She could recall the cold blade slipping into her eyeball, the slug-like tongue slurping up its juices. The recollection made her want to scream again. Nothing could feel so real without an element of truth behind it. The knife had felt more tangible than the rough sheets upon which she lay. And then there was the scarred killer; the knife slicing so smoothly into her abdomen. His scent still lingered upon the edges of her memory, fighting for recognition.

"It definitely *felt* real."

"Do you want to talk about it?" Doctor Smith asked.

"Did it involve sex?" inquired a boisterous voice from the neighboring bed. "I could do me a good sex dream once in a while."

"Enough of that, Jarvis."

"You could help me have one of them dreams, Doc."

Doctor Smith looked unimpressed. "Do I have to tape your mouth shut?"

"Ooh. Fifty Shades, eh?"

"Let me talk to Chance for a while, okay?"

Chance heard a loud *humph*, followed by an enormous weight shifting against squeaky springs. When she looked over, Jarvis had rolled to her left side, facing out the small window, staring at the sky.

"So, what happened in these dreams?" Doctor Smith asked.

Chance licked her lips. "Where exactly am I?"

The doctor sighed and sat on the edge of the beyond Chance's reach. "This is the Mount Sina. Refuge."

"An asylum?"

"We prefer not to use that term."

"But it *is* an asylum," Chance insisted.

Doctor Smith regarded her for some time. "Why don't you tell me about your dream, Chance?"

Blinking several times, Chance fought down the impulse to shriek. She didn't feel crazy, but if she started to act nuts, this guy would simply dose her up with medication and stroll out the door.

"I was murdered. Twice."

Doctor Smith nodded as though this were the most ordinary thing in the world. "How were you killed? Was it the same way each time?"

"The first time… I was in New York – Brooklyn, I think. I had just come from burying my baby." She shuddered at the thought of baby Cameron. Tears began to well.

"I was unaware you had ever been a parent," said the doctor casually, jotting notes down on a clipboard the nurse handed him.

"I never have," Chance replied. "That's the thing. I had all these memories of a life I'd never lived and…." She trailed off. "My husband's name was Greg."

"Husband?"

"In the dream." She paused for so long she expected Doctor Smith to prompt her to begin talking, but he sat calmly, waiting for her to start again. "After I buried my baby, I went home and was attacked." Chance glossed over the assault. The reality of the moment was still too real for her to relive in significant detail, but she outlined the bare facts. When she finished talking, Doctor Smith stared at her, his expression thoughtful.

"So, you're telling me that, in your dream, you were female?"

The question stabbed into Chance in much the same way the cadaverous man's blade had. Chance's throat dried up, and she blinked several times. "What's that got to do with anything?"

Once again, the doctor appeared thoughtful. Finally, he called out, "Jarvis, do me a favor and roll toward us, would you? I know you're not asleep."

Chance stared to her left, toward the lumpish silhouette in the bed there. It slowly shuffled around until the person there faced her. A nearby lamp clicked on, and light washed over the figure's face, revealing the features. Blue eyes stared out from above a lumberjack's beard. Chance shrieked.

"Well, you sound like a girl," grumbled Jarvis.

"No, no, no, no, no, no, no, no, no." Chance repeated the begging litany over and over, as though to echo it would make the horrific revelation untrue.

As with when she had awoken on the street in Brooklyn, memories trickled in, slowly gathering momentum like grains of rice pouring through an ever-widening gap in a sack.

"Do you have any idea why you always think you're a woman in your dreams, Chance?" Doctor Smith murmured, slicing into the edge of his thoughts.

Chance wanted to tear at her hair – at *his* hair! The restraints prevented his arms from moving, however, so Chance merely uttered a low moan, something so primal that the doctor actually stepped away from the bed.

"I think he's about to shit hisself," muttered Jarvis.

"Shut up!" Chance snarled.

"Okay, maybe not," the bulky figure reversed amiably.

"I need you to take a deep breath and calm down," stated Doctor Smith, "or else I'm going to be forced to sedate you."

"They died! I died! Don't you understand that?"

"All right."

The doctor motioned for the nurse to return. She hurried over, still carrying the stainless steel tray, her rubber-soled shoes squeaking on the tile floor. Doctor Smith collected the syringe from the tray and examined it. This time, Chance couldn't control the scream welling up inside. It erupted like vocal vomit, echoing from the spotless walls of the asylum.

The prick was tiny. Hardly noticeable at all. A warm blanket enveloped Chance, and suddenly everything was okay. So what if he were a man? Who cared that he had died?

The bedsheets no longer felt scratchy.

* * * *

A hand clamped down hard over his mouth.

Chance awoke in an instant, his heart pounding. The palm smelled of crayon and mint leaves, an oddly familiar scent. Darkness filled the ward, refusing to allow Chance to identify his attacker.

He struggled hard, his legs snapping the leather bindings at his ankles taut. But the restraints on his bed refused to release, and the hand pushed down forcefully. Not as physically dominant as the scarred brute he had encountered previously, more a wiry kind of strength.

"Shut up, bitch," a voice hissed in his ear.

Breathing slowly, Chance flexed his arms against the bindings. For the first time, he realized his arms were no longer at his sides; they stretched above his head. As to the fastenings themselves, something seemed different about their composition. For a start, the bindings on the hospital bed had felt padded and, despite their restrictions, nominally comfortable. Whatever held him now was coarse and cut into the flesh of his wrists and ankles. His biceps were no longer restricted, but that didn't mean he could move any better. Each wrist pulled toward an opposing bedpost. The same treatment had been devised for his ankles, pulling his legs apart, so that from above, his body would look like a human-sized X on the mattress.

"What's going on?" hissed Chance. "Where's Doctor Smith?"

"Do I look like a doctor to you?" snarled his tormentor. The tone was coarse, guttural. Yet the speaker sounded young, possibly a teenager.

"I can't…." Chance strained to see, but couldn't even make out the attacker's silhouette. "I can't see you."

A light flicked on, and Chance squeezed his eyes shut instinctively against the glare.

"You escaped us last night, but we've got you now."

Images of the cadaverous murderer flitted through Chance's mind. He fought to see against the blindingly bright light, tears streaming down his cheeks as his eyes struggled to focus. Finally, his pupils adjusted enough for him to make out the figure standing over him.

"You're a woman!" he blurted out.

The person was indeed female. Slender and muscular, Chance's tormentor appeared to have spent hours in the gym to stay fit, not bulky. The woman sneered down at him, her blonde hair bound in a tight ponytail, her face clear of makeup. Her beauty was astonishing to behold. This woman could hold her own on any catwalk in the world, at least in Chance's estimation.

Even as he gawped, however, Chance realized his mistake. The beauty snarled, her visage abruptly contorting into that of a beast. Wrath tore apart the calm façade she wore, and she punched down repeatedly into Chance's stomach. Each hit knocked more wind out of him, but it wasn't until the eighth blow that Chance realized the woman held something in her striking hand. When she paused, he glimpsed what the object was and tried to yell for help, but his lungs felt tight. Something was filling his throat, and Chance coughed, crimson liquid spraying past his lips. An oddly familiar sensation, it took a moment for Chance to realize he had suffered a similar fate at the hands of the scarred killer.

The woman grinned, the expression cold and hard. She wiped the implement she gripped, a corkscrew, on the dress Chance wore, leaving long bloody smears on the light blue material, and then tossed the tool aside. It made a dull *thunk* on the timber floor.

Dress?

Memories lingered close to the surface, but Chance's fear and pain swamped their weak attempts to break loose. There would be no understanding of the life he had stepped into this time.

"We'll see you in Hell, bitch," snarled the woman.

Chance thought she might leave, but his killer leaned closer, peering into his eyes as he fought for breath. She appeared to be inhaling his terror-stricken gasps, examining each moment he fought for life.

The memories surged forth once more, and just as Chance felt his life beginning to fade, a name popped into his mind.

Susan Crestwell.

* * * *

Chance tore loose from the dark moorings and wrenched himself up from the bed. At least he tried. The leashes holding him down refused to budge, no matter how hard he strained against them.

A scream still lingered in the room. Chance had no delusions about where it had come from. His throat felt raw with the effort his unconscious self must have thrown into hollering terror. The room was lit, though not as brightly as the room he had so recently slipped from. Looking around frantically, Chance saw he was back in the asylum.

"Who the hell is Susan Crestwell?" grumbled a voice to his left.

Looking over, Chance saw the lumpy form of Jarvis sitting up in bed, a book in his left hand. *One Flew Over the Cuckoo's Nest.* Chance blinked at the irony of the moment, the nightmare he had so recently lived through fading like a tiny trickle of water escaping a bathtub.

"You heard that?" Chance asked.

"The whole damn wing heard you, buddy."

As if to affirm what the bulky man said, rushing footsteps echoed in the corridor outside the room. Two doctors – Doctor Smith and another man in a flowing white coat who Chance didn't recognize – raced in, followed closely by a trio of nurses and two bulky male orderlies.

Remembering the injection that had put him under previously, Chance hurried to lift his hands in surrender, only to find the action impossible, blocked by the leather restraints at his wrists and biceps.

"Wait!" he pleaded.

Doctor Smith paused. The syringe was already in his hand, ready to plunge down. "What is it, Chance? Why are you hollering as if you're trying to wake the dead?"

"I had a nightmare, that's all."

The doctor stared at him, his expression unreadable through his glasses. The tension seemed to ease in his arm and the doctor appeared to relax somewhat. Doctor Smith glanced at the other physician and nodded slightly. The second man withdrew, taking two of the nurses with him, leaving only a single nurse and two orderlies behind.

"What's going on, Chance? Another death?"

Chance blew out a heavy breath. "This time, I was murdered by a woman."

The doctor stepped close, but remained beyond Chance's reach. "I don't want to keep dosing you, you know that, right? I mean, during your lucid stages, there seems little reason to keep you in this place. But your psychotic episodes grow increasingly worse, despite your therapy."

Sucking in deep breaths, Chance battled to control the racehorse in his chest. He fought to think of something that might make him sound rational, anything to keep the doctor's syringe at bay. "How did I get here? I mean originally."

"You can't remember?" Doctor Smith's brows narrowed above the wire-framed glasses he wore. "How far back can you recall?"

Chance blinked several times, his mind fighting to recover any shred of memory. "I can't remember anything from before when you jabbed me with the needle. I mean, the dream about the two women getting killed and me then waking up is still there, but anything before that is lost to me."

"The most recent time I jabbed you, you mean?"

"There's been more than once?" Chance's mouth ran dry. "How long have I been here?"

Doctor Smith appeared uncomfortable. "We prefer not to discuss patient stay durations, you know that."

Jarvis cut in. "A long time, from what they say."

"They? Who's they?" Chance demanded, highly aware of how strangled his voice sounded.

"That's enough, Jarvis." Doctor Smith frowned over Chance, toward Jarvis's bed. "Where in the world did you get that book?"

Jarvis motioned toward the ceiling. "A little birdy dropped it out of the sky. Excellent book, though. It's giving me lots of tips."

For a moment, the doctor scowled at the hulking figure, but then he shook his head dismissively, apparently choosing to keep his fight constrained to one patient for the time being. "Now, Chance, what are we to do with you? I know you're not mentally impaired, quite intelligent from all reports, but if you keep disrupting the ward, I'll have no choice other than to move you to the solitary wing."

"Her name was Susan Crestwell," Chance murmured, as though trying to keep the name alive before the memory faded.

"What?" Doctor Smith's face suddenly paled, and he blinked several times. He peered down at Chance. "Whose name?"

Chance swallowed. "The woman who was murdered this time. Her name was Susan Crestwell."

For several moments, the doctor looked completely flummoxed. His mouth opened and closed like a hooked salmon drowning on air. Eventually, he collected himself, turning abruptly and hustling from the room. The nurse glanced at his retreating form, then back at Chance, over at Jarvis, and finally followed in the doctor's wake. The two orderlies appeared equally uncertain, but soon shrugged and wandered off.

"What did you say?" Jarvis asked.

Stunned, Chance murmured, "All I told him was her name."

"That's one hell of a name."

Chance heard pages rustling and glanced over to see Jarvis reading his book once more.

CHAPTER IV

Chance rubbed his wrists.

The leather restraints hadn't rubbed them raw, but the tightness of the bonds had imprinted his skin, leaving the sensation of the looping bands long after Doctor Smith had unbuckled them.

Release had not been easily earned. After Chance's recent bouts of psychosis, the staff walked warily around his bed. Only Jarvis seemed untroubled about sharing the room with him. Perhaps that was why the hulking man was his roommate. Over the three days since Chance's memory had been scrubbed clean, the pair had struck up an interesting and companionable relationship. Jarvis seemed to take nothing seriously, flirting with both male and female staff without any real intention, more as a way to relieve the tedium of confinement to their room for sixteen hours a day – or so it seemed. The remaining eight hours were split between therapy — sometimes group, at other times one-on-one — and time on the grounds. Chance had yet to approach any of the other 'crazies', as Jarvis called their fellow Ward Z patients.

Chance couldn't remember anything from before that first awakening. His memories seemed crowded out by the three murders, cutting off anything prior. Apparently, this had not been the first time he had claimed to slip into the minds of women being killed. The main difference, this time, had been the revelation of the woman's name. Never before had he recalled the name of one of the imaginary victims, and in Jarvis's highly vocal estimation, it meant Chance was slipping deeper into whatever delusion clawed at his sanity.

Jarvis was subtle like that.

Despite the bulky patient's occasional creepy sexual innuendos, Chance was warming to his roommate. Lucky for him, since they were the only two occupying the stark-white room. According to Jarvis, there were a dozen rooms identical to theirs in this ward.

Ward Z, as it was called, was home for some of the slightly more deranged individuals residing in Mount Sinai Mental Refuge. They weren't the worst of the worst, but they teetered on the brink of insanity's fathomless chasm.

"Tell me something, Jarvis," Chance began. The two were sitting at the small table off to the side of their room, close to the window, steel mesh prohibiting them from reaching the glass. Outside, the sun shone brightly in a cloudless sky. "If this is Ward Z, does that mean there's an entire alphabet of wards before you arrive here?" He envisioned a monstrous building, filled to capacity with people suffering various mental ailments over twenty-six wards, each one with twelve rooms containing either two or four patients.

Jarvis barked out a short laugh. "Hah! You'd think so, wouldn't you? No, there are four wards — Alpha, Gamma, Sigma, and Zeta. Some asshole probably thought he was being smart when he named them, but didn't take into account that crazy people aren't always… well, you know… *smart*. Anywho, at some point, the confusion must have just become too much, and they just named the wards by standard letters. I guess the guys trying to eat their own poop had trouble understanding the difference between one swirly Greek letter and the next."

"But we never leave our own wards, do we?"

Jarvis squinted evasively. "On occasion. Sometimes, people have guests and need to be taken to the visitor center. Maybe one or two wandered off in the wrong direction when nobody was looking. I don't know. All I know is we sleep in Ward Z. Happy?"

"You don't seem… I don't know how to say it."

"I don't seem nuts?" Jarvis snorted, and a large chunk of snot blew from his right nostril, landing on the armrest of his chair. He picked up the green glob, studied it briefly, and then placed it under the seat as though hiding a piece of treasure. "I don't think so, but the judge sure did."

"Judge?" asked Chance nervously.

"I didn't kill no one, don't worry. But I did technically have what the docs called a 'severe psychotic break from reality'. Apparently, cops found me chasing squirrels around Central Park with no pants on. I don't know if I was trying to eat them or fuck them, alls I remember is waking up in hospital — not this one: the Manhattan Psychiatric Center.

They had me strapped down the same way you were the other day, but my straps were actually handcuffs. Apparently, I managed to break their regular restraints. Also managed to pop a couple of cops in the mouth — broke one guy's jaw in three places, apparently." Jarvis studied his sledgehammer-like right fist, an expression not unlike pride creasing his features. "So, I went to court, and then ended up here."

The enormity of significance comprised in that final sentence left them silent for several moments. Jarvis picked up his book. Chance stared at the ceiling. He wondered how he had come to be in this place; the doctors had told him it was due to episodes such as those he recalled, but Chance found himself curious as to the exact details. They refused to inform him of anything beyond the bare bones of his past, claiming he needed to recall things in his own time if he were to ever hope to make a full recovery.

"When did you first see me, Jarvis? What was I doing?"

"Crapping your pants."

"Great. Thanks. Maybe something a little more informative?"

Jarvis sighed heavily and placed his book aside. He seemed to think about the question for a moment before answering. Finally, he said, "The first time I saw you was the first time you saw me, my boy."

"What do you mean?"

"Exactly what I said. When you woke up was the first day I arrived in Ward Z. Before that I was… it doesn't matter right now."

Chance swallowed deeply and frowned. "Who was in here before you?"

"What am I, the asylum genie? Am I supposed to know everything that goes on in here?" He picked up his book again and made as if to read.

"Jarvis, please. This is important to me. Have you heard how long I might have been in here?"

The big man sighed. "Maybe three months. That's what I heard, anyway."

"Who from?" Chance knew he was pushing his luck, but felt driven to try.

"A nurse. Fat one. Loved my attentions. And don't ask me for a name because I don't have one. Now, is that all?"

Wrestling down the panic that fought to break loose from his breast, Chance contemplated how many times he might have envisioned people being murdered in those three months. The ones he could remember had been so vivid, even though the details now seemed frayed and flimsy, like gossamer curtains after a hurricane. No wonder he had ended up in a place like Mount Sinai Mental Refuge. Simply thinking about the potential horrors made him want to curl up into a ball on the bed.

"How long until we're allowed outside?" he asked Jarvis.

The large man glanced away from his book and out through the nearest window. Patients weren't allowed wrist watches or any other device that might indicate the passage of time, but Jarvis had a knack for being able to estimate time simply by looking at the sunlight.

"Another hour or so." He looked back at his book. "I wonder what I'd look like with long hair."

Chance frowned. "Are you reading about the Indian in that story?"

"His name is Chief Bromden."

"Why do you want to look like him?" asked Chance nervously, remembering the infamous scene in the movie, where Jack Nicholson ended up being smothered by a pillow. How he recalled something so inane and yet could not recollect his life before a few days ago remained a mystery.

Jarvis shrugged again. "Something to do, I guess. Maybe I could be like Rapunzel and grow my hair long enough to make a rope, so I could climb out the window and escape."

"We're on the ground floor."

"Won't have to grow it too long then, will I?"

Chance chuckled softly and felt the tension begin to lift from him. Jarvis had a knack for that. There seemed an easy camaraderie between them that stretched longer than a few days. The big man had that effect on most who passed within the radius of his charm.

"Whoa!" said Jarvis suddenly. "Hold on there, Tiger. That's a first. Are you okay?"

"What are you talking about?"

"You laughed. That's the first time I've heard a sound like that come out of your mouth. You might have a fever or something. Do you want me to call a doctor?"

Chance smiled wryly. "Ha ha. Hilarious."

"I'm serious, man. If you get any sourer, we might have to name this Ward Misery Guts instead of Ward Z. So you've imagined a few dames getting murdered; it's not the end of the world."

A dagger of ice slid between Chance's ribs. If only the meds could convince him the visions hadn't been real.

Footsteps approached, rubber soles squeaking on the linoleum floor. Doctor Smith entered the room cautiously, like a cat that had previously been chased off by a junkyard dog. He stared hard at Chance, eyes guarded behind his wire-framed glasses. A second figure followed him, this man's face cold and hard, his strong jaw jutting out.

"I smell bacon," muttered Jarvis.

Chance flicked a glance over. "What do you mean?"

Jarvis nodded toward the newcomer. "Guy's a cop. Maybe even a fed."

Chance looked back, this time noting the man's crisp gray suit and clean white shirt. His charcoal tie formed a tight double Windsor knot. On his right hand, he wore a silver ring with a flat blue stone in it. It wasn't a precious stone; this looked to be plain, yet startling against the simplicity of the silver setting.

"Sorry to interrupt you, gentlemen," said Doctor Smith softly.

"You should be sorry," muttered Jarvis, burying his nose in his book once more. "I'm trying my best to read."

The doctor glanced at the cover of Jarvis's book and scowled. "You really need to tell me how you managed to get your hands on that."

"A little sucky-sucky goes a long way, Doc," Jarvis replied, not looking up. "Just you remember that."

Shaking his head, Doctor Smith murmured an apology to his companion. The man's expression failed to change, his cold eyes refusing to move from Chance's face. Chance, in return, felt his cheeks burn under the scrutiny.

"Jarvis, why don't you take your book out into the grounds so we can talk privately with Chance?" suggested Doctor Smith, more an order than a request. "If anyone stops you, tell them I gave my permission."

Jarvis grumbled incoherently, but eventually rose from the bed and shuffled from the room.

"Chance, this is a friend of mine from college," began the doctor. "His name is –"

"I'm Special Agent Broachford," interrupted the man, unfolding a badge and holding it out for Chance to examine.

"Yes, of course," muttered Doctor Smith. "Now, Chance, you mentioned a name the other day when you woke up. Do you recall what that was?"

"Um, wasn't it Susan something?"

"Susan Crestwell," bellowed Jarvis from the doorway, making Chance jolt slightly. Doctor Smith glowered toward the now-empty entryway. Jarvis's slippers scuffed away down the hall.

"Uh, yeah, that was it," Chance said. "What about it?"

Doctor Smith glanced at Special Agent Broachford. The fed scowled down at Chance as though determining his credibility.

"That name has not been released to the press," the man said, his voice like ice. "How do you know it?"

"I… er… what are you talking about?"

"Susan Crestwell was murdered. How is it that you, a patient locked in a mental hospital, have managed to find this out before anyone outside of law enforcement?"

Chance's fragile sanity seemed to be crumbling around him. Had he somehow slipped into another level of psychosis without noticing? It had happened before; why should this time be any different?

"She can't be real," he croaked, his throat suddenly dry.

"She was." Reaching into his inside suit pocket, Special Agent Broachford pulled forth a four by six photo and held it out toward Chance. Doctor Smith raised his hand as if to object, but he was too late to prevent the action. His hand wilted back to his side.

Chance peered at the picture, at the image of the smiling blonde woman holding a chubby infant on her knee. The pair was surrounded by snow – this photo could have been taken mere months ago.

"I've never seen her before in my life," said Chance.

The agent nodded, his eyes narrowing. "That's right, you view through their eyes, don't you. How convenient."

Something hardened within Chance. "I wouldn't call it convenient to have to live through other people's murders. Horrific is the word that comes to mind. What do you want?"

"This is Susan Crestwell. And she was murdered exactly when Dennis –"

"Uh, Doctor Smith, if you don't mind, Special Agent Broachford."

The fed glared at Doctor Smith. "Right." He turned back to Chance. "From the Medical Examiner's report, Susan Crestwell was murdered almost exactly when you woke up screaming. How is it that you managed to know that?"

Chance's throat went dry. "Um, Doctor, could I please have a drink of water."

"Nervous?" pressed Special Agent Broachford.

"Well, I'm not exactly singing choir songs," Chance snapped. He glanced at the doctor, who was near the door calling out to one of the nurses for Chance's water. Looking back at the agent, he pondered the man's question for a moment longer. "What about the other women?"

Special Agent Broachford cocked his head. "What other women?"

"There were other incidents. I saw other women killed – at least two of them. People here say there were former cases, but I don't recall them. Nobody seems to know why."

Special Agent Broachford turned just as Doctor Smith returned to the conversation. "Is this correct?"

"What?" asked the doctor.

"This man claims to have witnessed other murders. Is he telling the truth?"

"Well, only he knows for sure. But he definitely showed signs of de-realization. This could be caused by a psychotic break brought about due to trauma in his past."

"What trauma?" Chance demanded.

Doctor Smith closed his eyes, and Chance could almost hear the man cursing himself. When he opened them again, his expression held a hint of sympathy, or perhaps something else.

"I've explained this to you before, Chance. We cannot discuss what you don't remember; you need to recall everything in your own time. To do so prematurely could cause irreparable damage to your psyche."

Special Agent Broachford analyzed them both, and Chance received the impression he was weighing up what to ask next. He didn't seem the type to care about Chance's psyche, but the possibility he might lose valuable information if his principal source in this case dove headlong into the deep end of the insanity pool seemed to give him pause.

"What can you tell me about these other two women?"

Chance took a deep breath. "The first one had just lost her baby. She was from… New York – Brooklyn, I think. I don't know her name."

The agent was jotting down notes on a pad. "What was the child's name?"

"Um." Chance scraped through the tortured vestiges of his memory. The recollection of the knife plunging through his breastbone brought with it a wave of nausea. He looked around for somewhere to puke should the need arise. When nothing presented itself, he swallowed the sickening sensation down. "It was a boy. Carl – no, Cameron. The husband was Greg. He was killed by a Yellow Cab."

"Good details." The agent scribbled them down. "What about the other woman? You said there were two, right?"

"She...." The image of the cadaverous killer licking his slimy tongue up Chance's cheek returned. Chance shuddered, his skin exploding in goosebumps. "She lived in Chicago. In a small apartment. A studio, I think." Chance closed his eyes as he fought to recall details, but the sensation of the blade piercing his eyeball consumed everything else. "She was wearing a skirt and blouse. He hung her up like a fish, and then gutted her. He also blinded her."

The vomit, when it exploded, came with no warning. Chance heard a curse from Special Agent Broachford as unidentifiable chunks of partially digested food rained down on his shiny black shoes.

"Nice," hissed the man, stepping back.

"I think that's enough for today," said Doctor Smith, stepping forward.

"Wait," demanded Chance, holding up a hand. He slowly wiped his lips and sucked in a breath before continuing. "The first killer was huge and scarred badly, as if by acid or fire. The second killer was scrawny. He looked either diseased, or perhaps he was a drug addict, scabs all over his pocked cheeks. And scrawny. But somehow still strong." The arm that had clamped around Chance's throat had felt like a vice.

Special Agent Broachford nodded while he wrote down the details. "Very interesting."

"Why are you asking me about all of this?" probed Chance. "I mean, what does the FBI have to do with my hallucinations?"

For the first time since meeting him, Special Agent Broachford appeared somewhat uncomfortable. He stared at his notepad for several moments, as though that might magically produce an appropriate answer.

"I am delegated to a section of the Bureau that occasionally deals with unexplained phenomena. We utilize psychics on a regular basis to help us solve investigations."

Chance frowned. "You're Mulder?"

Special Agent Broachford closed his eyes and shook his head slowly. "I most certainly am not *Mulder*. There are no aliens or ghosts in my investigations. However, we are known to use tools outside the norm to solve otherwise unsolvable cases. On several occasions, the use of psychics led us to otherwise unattainable information; facts that helped not only solve cases, but save lives."

"So, you think I'm psychic?" Chance snorted and grinned weakly, but his heart hammered.

"I don't know what to think. Not yet." Special Agent Broachford fixed Chance with his stony glare. "But the name Susan Crestwell is not exactly common, and yet you seem to have pulled it out of thin air. You haven't left this facility, had no access to outside media, but you know some guy out there killed her."

"No, not a guy."

"Excuse me?"

"Susan's killer was a woman. She...." He fought to recall something. Anything. "Her hands smelled like crayons... and mint leaves."

Special Agent Broachford added this note to his pad. "Anything else?"

"I think she was pretty."

"A pretty killer. That's interesting."

Chance swallowed and closed his eyes. "There's a lot there that seems to be hiding. I try to reach for it, and it pulls away."

"Well, if you think of anything else, give me a call." He went to hand Chance a card, paused, and then passed it to Doctor Smith instead.

"Why do you think this is happening to me?" Chance asked.

Special Agent Broachford glanced at the doctor. A silent message seemed to pass between the two, perhaps something they had discussed earlier.

"In my experience, anything can activate what people consider 'psychic' abilities. In some, they have it from birth. In others, physical trauma, such as a car accident, triggers something inside them, which suddenly gears up into overdrive. Nobody even comes close to understanding the human mind, and charlatans make such matters seem even more implausible. But I have seen events that defy explanation, leading me to believe there are things we cannot see, and probably can't rationalize. Maybe one day there will be a groundbreaking discovery that explains how the human mind works. Until that day, however, I will use the tools that come across my doorstep in any way that might help to save lives." He stared hard at Chance. "And I think you might be one such tool."

"Oh, great. You're a tool," muttered Jarvis, walking through the doorway, munching on a waffle.

"Where did you get that?" demanded Doctor Smith.

"Do you really want to know, Doc?"

Smith seemed to think about it for a moment. "No, I guess not," he conceded. "Are we done here, Special Agent Broachford?"

Broachford nodded. "I guess so. Contact me if you have any more… insights."

Chance made as if to tip an imaginary hat, thought twice about it, and eventually ended up making a weird half-salute. Special Agent Broachford frowned at him, his expression clearly showing his lack of comprehension, before finally turning and striding purposefully from the room. Doctor Smith followed hurriedly in his wake.

Jarvis stood, leaning against the wall, reading his book. Ostensibly, he was ignoring Chance, but Chance sensed the big man was merely waiting for him to talk, to fill him in on why the FBI had been here.

"I need to get out of here," muttered Chance. "Do you think they'd be pissed if I went out on the grounds early?"

"Nah. Just tell them that Doctor Smith said it was okay."

"But he didn't."

"Didn't what?"

"He didn't...." Chance trailed away, unsure if Jarvis was taunting him or sincerely confused. "I think I'll just go."

"Good. I've read the same paragraph three times while you insist on interrupting me." Jarvis buried his nose in the book once more.

Chance drifted out into the corridor. Despite wandering these halls for several weeks since his reawakening, he still occasionally ended up turned around. They all appeared identical; long white corridors that turned into more long white corridors. The fluorescent tubes above his head, recessed into the ceiling and shaded by foggy plastic, buzzed like bees in a hive. At any moment, he feared they might explode in a hail of glass.

Chance turned right and paused. The new corridor was nothing like the previous one. In fact, this hallway was not a hallway at all. It was a huge library. The ceiling soared high above his head; he counted four stories. Books lined the walls, perched on shelves carved from polished mahogany. A beautiful curling staircase with a white railing accessed balcony levels, each laden with further shelves of books. Study nooks, desks and chairs carved from the same wood as the shelves and filled with seated students or other researchers, dotted the floor between bookshelves. Green lamp covers contrasted beautifully with the polished wood desks. The entire place smelled of grandeur and knowledge, and Chance wondered how such a wondrous place could be secreted away within an asylum.

"You're late," snarled a quiet voice behind him.

Chance turned and spotted a tiny bespectacled woman in her fifties hurrying toward him. In her short arms, she carried several large books, the stack reaching almost to her chin. She dumped these into Chance's arms.

"Return these to their locations, and then come back to the front desk. It's been a madhouse around here today."

"Madhouse? What?"

The bespectacled old woman turned and scurried away, leaving Chance gaping with an armload of books. He looked left, looked right, and then dumped the books on the nearest desk.

"I'm getting out of here," he mumbled.

Turning, Chance sought the exit to the room, the corridor through which he had initially entered. No matter where he looked, however, nothing appeared familiar. The only entrance to the library remained a large set of timber double-doors, intricately carved with brass handles. Chance blinked several times, and then rushed toward the doors, pulling them open and hastening through.

Sand appeared suddenly beneath his feet, and he fell onto a beach.

Gathering himself and rising, Chance brushed sand from his clothing. Sun scorched him from above while the beach scrunched between his toes. A seagull, white and gray, squawked loudly and picked up a French fry near Chance's feet before flapping its wings and escaping with its prize. The smell of salt hung heavily in the air.

A hand clamped down hard on his shoulder. "What are you doing out here?"

Chance spun around. The beach vanished in an instant, replaced with a sterile corridor. The familiar surrounds of the asylum greeted his eyes, crushing him with its reality. Terror swamped him as he peered around, wide-eyed. The hand belonged to an orderly he did not know, a hulking man who looked capable of bending steel bars.

"What just happened?" Chance whispered.

The orderly peered at him, his eyes narrow. "You've been standing there for almost a minute, staring at the wall."

"A minute?" Surely it had been longer than that.

"Can you find your way back to your room?"

"I'm from Ward Z. My room...." Chance couldn't remember his room number.

"Ward Z? How did you get into Sigma? Who is your doctor?"

"Doctor Smith."

For a moment, the orderly seemed unsure of what to do. Finally, the man guided Chance's elbow with a surprisingly gentle grasp. "Let's get you home, okay?"

"Hardly my home," grunted Chance, pulling his elbow away. Then he realized how petulant he sounded. "But I would appreciate a little assistance."

The orderly stared at him for a moment, and Chance received the distinct impression the man was waiting for him to wig out. For a couple of seconds, Chance thought of doing it just to shock the man, but decided to refrain. The last thing he needed right now was to be doped up on Diazepam. Perhaps the patients from Ward Z were expected to be a little out there, or maybe the man recognized Chance. Perhaps his reputation preceded him. Whatever the reason, the orderly led Chance through the building.

Unlike his journey here, the route did not consist of only corridors and hallways; the return trip led them outside, into the grounds. But to get outside, they needed to pass through three checkpoints, two of which required a security card to access. Once outside, Chance looked around at the high stone walls topped with razor wire encompassing the perimeter of the grounds. Chain-link fences crowned with barbed wire separated different sectors, their spikes gleaming in the morning sun. Again, they needed to pass through another two checkpoints along the journey.

"How did I get through all this?" Chance asked, astonished.

"You tell me," grunted the orderly. "Someone's going to be in a whole lot of trouble if they find out you made it out of your ward, but it won't be me."

Their journey continued, and Chance found himself astonished at the breadth of the grounds. The orderly led him unerringly toward a building at the far end of the estate, completely separate from the structure they had just left.

"What's that?" he asked, pointing toward the three-storied building.

"Ward Z."

Chance frowned and flicked a glance between the new structure and the building they had recently exited. Ward Z appeared older, or at least dingier. What had once been pristine white stone was now stained gray with mold. Perhaps the rest of the sanitarium had recently been sandblasted, with Ward Z being left apart. Regardless, the air of neglect was apparent, hanging over the structure like a foreboding cloud.

There were several hedges near the building, though none obscured it from direct view. Chance assumed this was for security reasons; nobody could hide in plain sight.

The sun burned down on him, and Chance glanced up. He might not be as efficient as Jarvis when telling the time via the sun's position in the sky, but he could discern high noon as well as anyone. Pausing mid-stride, he gawped at the fact hours had passed since he'd vanished from his room in Ward Z. Hours during which he'd somehow managed to slip through walls and avoid security measures with ease. Yet, according to his guide, he'd only been staring at the wall for a minute. Where had he been for the rest of the time?

The orderly shoved him in the back. It wasn't a hard shove, but it was enough to get Chance moving once more. His rubber-soled, lace-free shoes trod silently along the paved pathway through the sparse garden. This was not the garden patients were allowed to roam around – that was located at the back of Ward Z. This was more a glorified lawn with a few clumps of bushes to make it resemble something other than a prison. The high perimeter walls detracted from the mediocre effort, reducing the building's appearance to something akin to a low-rent convalescent home.

"What are you going to tell the doctor?" Chance asked.

"I'm not going to tell him anything. If you say something, that's up to you. But don't be surprised if nobody believes you managed to walk all the way over to Ward S unchallenged. Chances are you'll be sedated and locked up in the padded cell."

"Padded cell? You mean those things actually exist?"

The orderly chuckled. "You must be new here."

"I've apparently been here for months. I can only remember the last few days, though."

"Few days? How does that work?"

"You tell me, and we'll both know," replied Chance, grimacing.

"You hardly seem cra – I mean… uh… unwell. At least, not bad enough to be in Ward Z. Sigma, maybe. But not Z."

"I don't think I am that bad. Not always, anyway, but I have these spells, and I… I lose time. I also see things. Horrible things." Chance assessed the orderly. "Nobody else seems to want to mention crazy around here. I ask them what happened to me, and they all look ready to jump out a window to avoid answering. How long have you had this job?"

The orderly scratched his neck. "Not long, really. My uncle is James Rogers; in fact, I'm named after him, but people call me Jimmy."

"Pleased to meet you." Chance extended his hand, but the young man peered at it as though the limb were infected. Maybe he thought insanity was contagious.

"Uh, that's okay. We're not supposed to… you know."

Chance dropped his hand and kept walking. "Sure, I know. So who is James Rogers in the grand scheme of things?"

Jimmy gawped at him. "He's… well, his granddaddy practically built this place with his own two hands back in nineteen hundred and something."

"Wouldn't that make him your great granddaddy?"

Jimmy blinked several times. "Well, I guess."

"Sounds like an extraordinary man. So that's how you got your job here, right?"

"Huh?" Jimmy frowned at him for a moment and then his expression cleared. "Oh, yeah. I mean, they never would have looked at me otherwise."

"I can't imagine why."

"Are you making fun of me?"

Chance shook his head innocently.

"It's not a bad job. Pay's good, as long as you can handle the weirdos – uh, no offense."

"None taken. I'm not sure I can handle the weirdos in this place, either. Let me know if you see any."

Jimmy chuckled. "Are you sure you're a patient here?"

"Unfortunately. Unless you want to walk me out the front gate."

"Not today. Say, what's your name?"

"I'm Chance."

The change in Jimmy's demeanor was immediate. All friendliness vanished in an instant. "You're the guy who sees people dying?"

"Yeah. I told you that, didn't I?"

Jimmy chewed over this new realization. "I'd better get you back real quick. They'll be looking for you."

The two hurried along the path and through another security checkpoint. This checkpoint was tighter than in the previous building, with bag scanners and metal detectors in place. The security guards stared at Chance curiously when they saw his hospital garments, but when Jimmy chose to offer them no explanation, Chance followed his lead.

Ward Z looked immediately familiar beyond the checkpoint. The architecture was distinctive, as was the atmosphere. The squeaky linoleum seemed to chant to Chance as he shuffled along the corridor, welcoming him home. The stark white walls felt like they emanated a chill, and the high ceilings seemed to look down on him with condemnation. Everything about this place, after having stepped beyond its power, felt offensive to the senses. Abruptly, Chance wondered how many screams the walls had absorbed. He knew a few of his own had echoed from the plaster.

"I can find my own way from here, Jimmy. Thanks."

The orderly appeared unsure. On one hand, Jimmy no doubt feared that if he let Chance go ahead on his own, he might wander off again and cause a scene, which might implicate Jimmy and get him in trouble with his superiors. On the other hand, if he led Chance into the ward and someone asked where they had come from, Jimmy might also be implicated in a drama not of his own making.

"Are you sure?" Jimmy asked, looking around. Whether he sought someone to pass Chance off to or feared someone might walk around a corner and witness them together remained unclear.

"My room's just down here. I promise."

"Well… okay. But don't tell anyone I just cut you loose, all right?"

The fact they had passed several security checkpoints and been seen together by around a dozen people didn't seem to register in Jimmy's mind. All he feared was that between the point they separated, and when Chance reentered his room, there might be a cataclysm in which he could be implicated. The orderly scurried away. Chance watched him flee with a sense of wry amusement. Once alone in the corridor, however, all humor fled.

How in the world had he ended up in that other ward?

Even if he believed he had wandered off in a fugue state, that still didn't explain the innumerable checkpoints he had somehow slipped past without issue. There seemed no way.

And what were these most recent visions of, anyway? They weren't laden with the gore of his previous episodes, but they hardly seemed consistent with the memories of the man he hoped he might have been. Chance hated books, so why he would have ever been in a library made no sense. And why the beach?

It had all felt so real. The sun's warmth had crisped the skin of his cheeks. The seagull… could it have been some kind of omen? He reached the doorway to his room and turned to enter.

A fist smashed into his nose, knocking Chance from his feet. The hard floor cracked against the back of his skull and the world swirled. Blood filled his mouth and oozed down the back of his nasal passage into his throat.

"What…?" Chance moaned.

Jarvis loomed over him, a manic look plastered across his face. His mouth stretched into a rictus grin, and his eyes seemed to be screaming. The big man was wearing no pants.

"Code 4! Code 4!" a voice hollered, away to Chance's left.

Footfalls slapped the tiles. Jarvis's meaty paws clutched the front of Chance's hospital pajamas and lifted him effortlessly from the floor. Blood dripped from his torn lips and battered nose, splatting onto the white linoleum.

"Jarvis. Wait."

"You stole her, didn't you?" the giant man bellowed. Spit sprayed all over Chance's face. He had no idea to whom Jarvis referred. "Give her back to me!"

Blue-shirted orderlies slammed into Jarvis, but they might as well have thrown themselves against Ward Z's concrete walls. A massive paw clamped around Chance's throat, half encircling it. Jarvis squeezed, and Chance felt his windpipe squash shut. He battered and clawed at the giant hand, but to no avail.

A needle jabbed. A plunger pushed.

Chance had no way of knowing what concoction the staff used on Jarvis. He doubted it would be something as mundane as Diazepam. Whatever it was, it hit the big man like a sock full of pennies. First, the sausage-like fingers loosened, allowing

Chance to steal a breath. Then, Jarvis's knees buckled. He released Chance and fell face down on the floor with a loud *smack.*

Someone dragged Chance aside, and then bodies in blue were grabbing Jarvis. Chance noted some of them were none too gentle about hauling the big man up and moving him back to his bed. One unlucky contender acquired the inauspicious job of pulling Jarvis's discarded pajama pants back on before they strapped him to his bed, elbows, ankles, and wrists.

"What just happened?" asked Chance, rising slowly to his feet.

One of the orderlies looked him up and down before answering. "This one was mild compared to some of his other episodes. One time, he –"

The man cut off whatever he was about to disclose and hustled away. Chance looked where the man's attention had snapped and noted Doctor Smith approaching. The doctor looked harrowed and disheveled, as though he had only recently risen from bed – or simply hadn't slept for some time. His gray-flecked hair stuck up in clumps, and dark circles hugged his lower lids.

"What is going on here?" he demanded.

"The – er – patient had an episode, Doctor," explained one of the orderlies, a man Chance couldn't remember seeing before.

"Who sedated him?"

"Nurse Ripley, sir."

Doctor Smith nodded, apparently satisfied. "Was anyone injured?"

"This patient was struck."

Doctor Smith gave Chance a cursory examination, eventually handing him a gauze patch and advising him to hold it to his nose until the bleeding stopped. "Why don't you get into bed, Chance?"

"It's the middle of the day!"

"What?" Doctor Smith glanced toward the window. "Oh, yes, of course. Perhaps a walk in the grounds, then. Let the staff know if you feel dizzy or nauseous. Perhaps mingling with the other patients for a while will help you get over this incident."

Chance had seen some of the other patients, but had never spoken to them – outside of group therapy, that was. At least he couldn't recall having talked to them socially. There remained the possibility that, in his former life, he had regaled these people with all kinds of tales of fun and frivolity. Right now, however, he had no idea who any of them were. They remained strangers in an asylum, and as such, he was somewhat timid around them.

With a sigh, Chance headed toward the rear of Ward Z. The patient garden beckoned, a place dramatically different from the interconnecting lawn between buildings he had seen when returning from his unintentional visit to Ward Sigma.

There was a security checkpoint here, but the guard barely looked up from his magazine. Patients were allowed through during this part of the day; his only true concern, as far as

Chance could make out, was that they didn't try to take furniture from the ward outside. Chance strode through, dumping his blood-soaked gauze in the trash as he passed the desk. The guard glowered at him, but said nothing.

The back garden was the image of tranquility its designers had intended. But it was a tainted peace, like a printed photograph of a beautiful sunset with mold on the back of the paper. Nothing directly offensive greeted Chance's eyes, but the fragrance of the blooms smelled too sickly, and the dry grass crackled like broken glass beneath his rubber-soled sneakers.

Looking around, Chance saw a dozen or so other people occupied the area. Some appeared doped to the gills on medication, blank gazes gawping at nothing, while other patients glared at him menacingly, daring him to breach their bubble of sanctuary. Only one person stood alone, over by the chrysanthemums in the corner of the triangular garden. A woman, her hair chopped short and uneven, as though hacked away with a kitchen knife, stared at a flower cupped in her hand. A bee buzzed down and landed on the stamen, but the woman didn't flinch, she merely watched the creature, a strange smile tilting the edges of her mouth. Chance felt drawn to this unusual figure and strode across the crackly lawn toward her.

"Hello," he said once he reached her side.

She looked up and smiled. "Hello, Chance."

"Oh. Do you know me?"

The woman giggled. "Silly man." The bee took flight, and she watched it go, a look of bemused wonder creasing her features. "Silly Mr. Ripley."

His heart thudded in his chest. Was that really his last name?

"What's your name?" he asked.

"Did it happen again?" There was no worry in her tone, no amusement, no anger. It was a simple question, but to Chance, it carried so much more.

"I can't remember much before the last few days. Were we friends?"

She tilted her head. "I suppose so. When you could be bothered to stay here."

"You mean in the garden?"

"No, silly." She spread her arms wide. "Here."

"Ward Z?"

The woman gave him a bemused look. "In the asylum," she whispered.

"Where did I go?"

"Oh, you know." She picked another flower and looked around expectantly, as though hoping another bee might land.

"I have no idea."

She held a finger to her lips. "Shh!"

Chance stood, wondering and waiting. The woman remained frozen like a statue in the corner of the yard, her eyes flitting left and right, searching for something in the still air. Chance waited, occasionally glancing toward the orderlies scattered about the garden. Three were near the far wall, talking among themselves, while another two stood near the steps leading back into Ward Z. Nobody seemed to think the woman was doing anything exceptionally odd. Then again, this place *was* full of crazy people.

"What are we waiting for?" Chance asked in a hushed tone.

"Nothing at all. I just wanted you to shut up." She giggled, the sound like glass tinkling. Despite himself, Chance laughed. Catching on the awkwardness of the moment, his laughter petered out, and within moments became a faded memory.

"Always so serious, Chance. You'll give yourself cancer." The woman threw aside the two flowers she held and pulled a third from its stalk.

"What's your name?" Chance asked for a second time.

"I'm tempted not to tell you."

"If you did that, I wouldn't be able to call you."

"On the telephone?" she asked, her lips smirking.

Chance shrugged. "Why not? Hell, we're all crazy anyway; why not call each other on the phone?" He mimicked punching a number into a cell phone and held it up to his ear, grinning.

All humor vanished from the woman's face. She flung the flower to the ground. "I'm not crazy." The statement came as a low growl.

Chance dropped his hand to his side. "Of course not, I didn't mean –"

"Yes, you did. You think I'm the same as all these other people. The same as *you*. Well, I'm not. I shouldn't be in here, all right? But they won't listen. Nobody listens."

Glancing at her hands, Chance saw them both clenched into fists so tight the nails were slicing into the skin of her palms. Blood dripped down into the garden bed, spattering the white petals of the chrysanthemums.

"I'm sorry," Chance murmured, his tone cautious.

"Sorry? *Sorry?* Jesus, David. What the hell does sorry even mean, huh? Does that stop you sleeping with her?"

Chance held his hands up before him as if to placate her. "Wait. What? Who's David?"

"Don't play dumb. Where's…?" She glanced away, her eyes focused on nothing.

Chance took the opportunity to look around at the orderlies again. Two were watching intently, but none had reacted. Perhaps such behavior was a regular thing with this woman. He began to back away slowly.

"Oh, hello, Chance." Her tone returned to the soft lilt she'd adopted when Chance had first approached.

"You know me now?"

"Don't be silly." She pulled yet another flower loose and stared at it.

Chance stood silently for a moment, trying to understand what he had just witnessed. The woman seemed profoundly odd – but what should he expect of someone in this place? Jarvis was a prime example. The big man had flipped out in a way Chance would have previously thought impossible. Jarvis had always seemed quite calm and deliberate, nothing like the psychopath into which he had morphed. Looking around the garden, Chance wondered how many of these other patients were liable to explode without warning.

"What's your name?" he asked the woman. "I forgot it when I had one of my… spells."

A look of sympathy erupted on her features. "Oh, poor Chance. It happened again? My name is Betsy. Betsy Burrows."

"Thank you, Betsy," replied Chance. He chose his next words carefully. "Do you know how long I've been here?"

"Oh, months and months. It's so hard to keep track of time in here; they won't let us keep calendars or clocks. Are you still seeing the women?"

"You know about them?"

"Of course. Here, sit down."

Chance looked for a chair or bench, but Betsy merely folded her legs and dropped to the grass. She still held one of the chrysanthemums in her bloody hand. He joined her, looking around self-consciously as he did. Nobody seemed to care.

"Was it three again?"

Chance's throat dried up. "You mean it's been three before?"

Betsy reached over and stroked his cheek with her left hand. Chance felt the blood on her palm smear across his skin. Betsy seemed not to notice, or care. "It's always three, silly. At least, that's what you claimed. I never saw them myself." She shrugged, as though this were a minor matter. "You sometimes cried while describing the horror of it all. Other times…."

"What happened the other times?" Chance demanded.

Her eyes fixed to his, the gaze intense. "You seemed thrilled by it." She giggled shrilly. "You can be scary sometimes."

"Really?" Chance's heart pounded in his chest. "How many do you suppose there've been?"

"How many? Dozens, I guess. I never actually kept count. Did you see my flower?"

Chance flicked a glance toward the blood-smeared white flower. "It's very nice. Do you come here often? I mean, to this part of the garden," he amended, realizing how foolish the statement sounded.

"Where else is there?" Betsy asked, frowning.

"Well, there's...." He trailed away as he looked around. There were a few other bushes, but nothing blooming with flowers. As it was, the buds on Betsy's chrysanthemum shrub were dwindling, though there appeared to be a vast quantity of broken stalks. "I guess there's nowhere. Tell me, are we friends, Betsy?"

"You don't judge me," she replied, as though this were response enough.

"Do other people judge you?"

She shrugged. "They think I killed her, but I didn't. Even the judge believed me." She looked around the garden at the other patients. "But *they* don't trust me. I can see it in their eyes."

Chance desperately wanted to ask what Betsy was referring to, but knew that to do so was to walk a precarious line between the peaceful woman before him and the screaming wretch into which she had transformed. No, he needed to steer clear of that mania. Whoever she had been accused of killing could remain a mystery, at least for the time being.

"Do you know anything about my life before I entered this place, Betsy? I honestly remember nothing before a few days ago."

Betsy seemed to think about it for a moment. "You were a painter."

"Really? I – well, I guess that might make sense." Chance tried to envision himself sitting before an easel, but failed.

"Or maybe you were an actor." She lifted her chin high and stared up at the cloudless sky. "Hold on, I think you told me you were an engineer."

Chance's hopes fizzled. "You don't really know, do you?"

Betsy shook her head. "No, not really. But you could have been any of those things."

"I guess."

Chance scratched his throat. The stubble there was really beginning to itch. Patients weren't allowed razors; he would need to organize a shave through the asylum's barber. He looked at Betsy's hair, wondering why it looked so ragged and chopped. Even if she'd done so herself, how had she managed to lay her hands on the equipment necessary?

Betsy noticed him looking. "Do you like my hair?"

"Um, yeah. It looks great."

She smiled thinly. "The last time you saw me, you said it looked like I'd put my head in a blender."

"I did, huh?" Chance stared at Betsy's mop of unruly hair chunks. "Maybe I was a little harsh."

"Do you think so? I appreciated your honesty. So few people in this place are honest."

"Well, there's honesty, and there's honesty," Chance replied, thinking swiftly. "How did you cut your hair, anyway? They won't even let me shave on my own."

"I work in the garden." Another wistful smile flitted across her lips. "At least I used to until I cut my hair with a pair of pruning shears. They worried that I might use them on someone else next time." She shrugged. "As if I'd do something that stupid."

Chance looked around the garden at all the bloomless shrubs. He looked back at the chrysanthemums, at the dozens of empty stalks.

"Why did you leave this bush for last?" he asked.

She looked up, her eyes slightly wider in surprise. Blinking several times, she gripped one of the few remaining blooms and twisted it loose.

"Oma always loved the white ones," she said, as though it explained everything.

"Oma? Who is Oma?"

"It's Dutch for grandmother. Oma always loved the white petals." Betsy's face suddenly became savage, and she crushed the flower in her bloody palm.

"Oh," said Chance. More than one piece slipped into place. The denial of guilt, the obsession with the flowers. Aware he was treading a tightrope, but inclined to dip to curiosity anyway, Chance asked, "Where is Oma now?"

Betsy flung the flower to the ground. "Don't play stupid, Chance. It doesn't become you." Gone were the whimsical tone and dreamy gaze, replaced with a look of intense focus and a sharp, business-like manner.

"She's who they claim you killed, right?"

A frantic expression danced across Betsy's face, consumed once more by the visage of a woman in control. "And who did you kill to wind up in here, Chance? You always insist you are the one witnessing the crimes; how many of them are memories, committed by your own hand?"

The question slid like a dagger between his ribs, and Chance staggered back under the weight of the accusation. It wasn't like he hadn't contemplated the possibility, at least in some small way, but to hear it spoken by another made the prospect all the more tangible.

"I didn't kill them." Was it a statement or a plea? "I can't have. I was in here."

"Were you?" Betsy peered around for a moment, staring up at the blue sky. A faint smile flitted across her lips. Finally, she looked back and waggled a finger at him. "That's thin, and you know it, dearie. Those might be repressed memories slipping out from your subconscious, replaying before your eyes to torment your already tortured conscience. You are one of the smartest people I've met in here, Chance, and yet you argue against the simplest solution."

"You know it's not true," argued Chance. Despite himself, his tone sounded desperate.

Betsy's eyes widened. "Oh, really? Do tell."

"If you thought I were a killer, you wouldn't be talking to me."

She smiled widely. "Perhaps I like to converse with my own kind, Chance. Maybe, in this place, we're the top of the food chain." She glared around, her eyes narrow. "Who shall be our next prey? Which one of these cattle will fall to our designs? Here, you choose."

Pausing, Chance analyzed her. "You're mocking me."

"Am I?" Betsy stood straight once more. Chance followed her lead, brushing loose blades of grass from the rump of his pants. She reached over and twisted loose another flower. "Maybe I am. Things get so boring in here. They won't even let me watch TV; did you know that? Doctor Hallowell says it might push my regression to the fore. Stupid man. As if I'm suffering from regression. I'm perfectly in control of all my faculties, thank you very much."

"Did you kill her?" Chance asked, suddenly desperate to know.

"Nobody in Ward Z is a killer, you know that." Her eyes met his, the lids hooded. "Not even you, apparently. This place is for those in purgatory. The ones who don't fit in with the lightweights in Sigma, but aren't bad enough for Ward Alpha."

"Ward Alpha?"

Her expression softened, once more becoming gentle. "Stay away from Ward A, Chance. Even you, for all your hardiness, won't come back from there intact." She tittered softly. "Not that any in here are very intact."

"I couldn't get in there, even if I wanted to."

Betsy's eyes widened. "In where?"

"Into Ward A," he explained, frowning.

"Where is that?"

Chance stared at her. Was it all an act, or was Betsy so entirely displaced from reality that she could flit between personalities the way another might slip on a different outfit? If it was all an act, it was definitely a convincing one.

"Don't worry. That's a lovely flower."

Betsy glanced down at her hand. The newest broken bloom lay coated in drying blood, just like the last one. She frowned down at it.

"How did that get there?" she mused. She flung it away as though it were diseased.

"Don't you like the flowers anymore?" Chance asked.

Without warning, Betsy lurched toward him and gripped the lapels of his pajamas with an astonishingly robust grip. Her eyes were wide, but appeared clear of lunacy for the first time since he'd met her.

"Beware of Nothingman, Chance," she hissed. "He is coming for you."

An orderly approached. "All right. Time for sessions."

Chance glanced back at Betsy, his eyes widening. She slowly released his shirt and stepped back, a confused expression plastered across her features.

"Goodbye, Chance," she whispered before scurrying away.

Chance watched her go, wondering which face had been her true one.

CHAPTER V

"Sorry about… you know," muttered Jarvis.

The big man rubbed his wrists. The manacles that had eventually confined him to his bed had not been leather. The staff of Mount Sinai Mental Refuge had learned from past mistakes and possessed metal cuffs for instances where exceptionally powerful patients became uncontrollable. Jarvis's bed might have regular leather restraints, but that was only because it was a regular bed, designed with the leather shackles already in place. There were few occasions, apparently, when such flimsy fetters proved strong enough to contain the rampaging mountain. Luckily, according to staff, Jarvis rarely fell into such fits. And they didn't tend to last longer than a day.

"Which are you referring to," asked Chance, "the punch or seeing you without pants?"

Jarvis chuckled softly. "Probably both. How's the nose?"

"Fine. I barely had trouble breathing last night at all. Your snoring, on the other hand…."

"I don't snore," Jarvis grunted.

For a moment, Chance remained silent, glancing toward the door as if to assure himself of the exit before sitting opposite Jarvis at the table in the far corner of their room. The table was circular, lacking any sharp edges, its central leg bolted to the floor to prevent anyone from using it as a weapon. The stainless steel stools were similarly attached to the concrete. Chance wondered how many violent incidents had occurred before the management agreed the extra cost was worth the increased safety it would provide. Maybe it was an insurance issue. Large companies tended to work that way.

That thought brought with it another idea. Who was paying for Chance to be here? Was this a government-funded institution, or did Chance have some unknown benefactor in the real world? Was there a Mrs. Ripley out there somewhere – did he have a wife? If so, did she worry about him, trapped within the imposing gray walls of the Mount Sinai Mental Refuge?

Too many questions lay unanswered. Perhaps the next time they allowed Chance out into the garden, he might be able to chat with Betsy once more. She seemed to know more than she let on – or at least more than Chance knew.

"Hey, Jarvis," he began. "Do you know a woman named Betsy?"

"Plays with flowers? Sure, heard of her. Why?"

"What's her story?"

"Same as the rest of us, buddy. The bitch is crazy."

Chance screwed up his face and waved his hand as though trying to swat the comment away. "She seemed to know a lot about me." He fought to recall something of worth. "She remembered my name, for instance."

"So do I. It's Chance. Big deal."

"My *last* name."

"Is it Tsar?" asked Jarvis.

"Tsar? Why would it be Tsar?"

"Then you'd be Chance Tsar. Get it? Chances Are." The big man began guffawing as though he had just mouthed the funniest wisecrack in the history of the world.

Chance waited until the laughter subsided. He had to wait longer than he anticipated, but made do, pleased that Jarvis was still wearing pants and not punching him in the face.

"Finished?" he finally asked.

Jarvis swiped tears from his eyes with a meaty paw. "You have to admit, that was funny."

"Sure. It was hilarious. But how could Betsy have known my last name? Did I ever talk about her to you before? It seems we had some kind of… connection."

"What, like you fucked her?"

Chance shook his head in dismay. "I can't talk to you." He stood up.

"How do you know it really was your name?"

Pausing in his stride, Chance turned. "What do you mean?"

Jarvis shrugged. "How do you know she's telling the truth? She could say you were a former sweatshop worker named Lao Ball, and you wouldn't know better."

Despite his glimmering hope, Chance couldn't deny the accuracy of Jarvis's statement. He knew nothing about this woman or her truthfulness. She definitely wasn't on the stable end of the scale – not that there was one in Ward Z. The few patients Chance had met so far seemed three steps away from living full time in a padded cell. But Chance was desperate for answers.

"Are you sure you don't know anything else about me?"

"I told you, man. The first time I saw you was when they wheeled me in and you were strapped to that bed. I asked to be put in another room, by the way."

"That's good to know," muttered Chance.

"Look, I don't know anything about the dame," said Jarvis, his tone repentant. "For all I know, she was telling you the truth. What did she tell you your last name was?"

Chance slid back onto the metal stool. "She said it was Ripley. Chance Ripley."

"That's a cool name." Jarvis appeared thoughtful. "You might have been a porn star with a name like that."

"Why do I bother?" Chance muttered.

"What else did she say?"

"I don't know. She rambled on about some stuff. Told me not to go into Ward Alpha."

"Well, duh. Everyone knows that. Ward A is like… I don't know, a cesspool for the mentally ill. That's where Howard Mason ended up, and we all know how nuts that guy was." Jarvis shuddered. "Seriously, from what I've heard, going there would make this place look like a never-ending picnic." His eyes grew distant. "Mmm. I miss picnics."

A thought suddenly occurred to Chance. "Where were you before you ended up in this room with me, Jarvis?"

"I was in Sigma. That's for those who need full time care, but aren't considered a danger to others."

"What happened?"

"I lost control and hit an orderly named Jimmy. Nice guy, as far as I can recall. No idea what got into me to hit him. Then again, I never know what the hell is going on when that happens. They were talking about organizing a specialist, something to do with epilepsy, but my insurance doesn't cover that kind of expense. So, I'm stuck in here. Lucky you, huh?"

"It could be worse."

"In here? Sure. You could be stuck with someone who *never* wears pants. At least I wear mine most of the time. While you're awake, anyways."

"You're a funny guy," said Chance, a wry grin stretching his features.

"I do my best to liven up the situation."

They sat in companionable silence for some time. Jarvis stared out the barred window while Chance chewed over what he wanted to say next. How much could he trust the big man? Jarvis seemed to take nothing seriously, which was a good thing, considering the nature of what Chance wanted to discuss. But the trust he would be putting in the man would be tremendous; Chance wasn't sure he could do such a thing. Finally, with a huff, he dove into the unknown.

"I had another spell," he muttered.

Jarvis frowned. "Really? I was under the impression that you are rather… um… vocal when they happen. I never noticed."

"It was when I left the room yesterday. I was walking the corridors, and then suddenly I was in a library."

"We don't have a library here." Jarvis's expression had become deadly serious. "At least not one the patients can access."

"I know. It was…." Chance fought to remember. "Magnificent is the only word I can think of to describe it. A woman came over, threw a pile of books into my arms, and told me to put them on the shelves. I tried to leave, but when I walked through the doors, I fell onto a beach. Then a hand grabbed me, and I was back here. But not here in Ward Z; I was over in the main building – in Ward Sigma. An orderly had found me wandering around lost and brought me back here. I think he was worried about getting in trouble because he didn't tell anyone I wasn't supposed to be there."

"There's no way you could get over to that building, not past all the checkpoints."

"I know. But I swear it happened. The orderly's name was… Jimmy, I think."

"That's the guy I hit over in Sigma. How in the world did you make it over there?"

"I have no idea," replied Chance. "All I remember is walking through corridors, all of which looked identical, and then I was in the library with that old crone giving me books and ordering me around."

Jarvis pondered the story for a moment, his expression deadly serious. "What did that fed want from you?"

Chance shrugged. "He said he was part of some division of the FBI that dealt with paranormal stuff."

"Like Mulder?"

"Exactly what I said!"

"Did he take what you told him seriously?"

Chance dropped his gaze, pondering the possibility. "He seemed to write down a lot of notes, more than someone merely going through the motions of an investigation. Asked me a lot of questions, too."

Jarvis scratched his hairy chin. "I hate this beard. Wish they'd give us a razor."

"Yeah, me too." Just the thought of it made Chance want to scratch his cheek. He pushed the impulse aside. "What are you thinking?"

"I'm thinking I want to shave this beard."

Chance rolled his eyes. "I mean beyond that."

"Shave my balls?"

"I'm talking about the guy from the FBI!" Chance snapped.

"Oh, right." Jarvis stopped scratching. "Sounds like he might think there's something behind what you're seeing. I mean, weirder things have happened, right? I've heard of cops using psychics to solve cases before; maybe that's all that's wrong with you."

Chance suddenly felt ill. "But that would mean I see these murders through the eyes of the actual victims." He paused. "It would mean these women actually died, and pretty horrifically."

"You've gone pale," said Jarvis conversationally. "Are you going to puke? Do you want a bucket?"

"Do you have one?"

Jarvis glanced around. "No."

Chance sucked in several breaths, fighting off the sensation with an effort. "What do I do? Do I try to contact this agent to tell him… what? I was in a library, and then on the beach? I doubt he'll appreciate the information."

"What if they're women about to be killed?" Jarvis shoved a sausage-like finger up his nose and dug around for a moment, finally giving up his search, a look of disappointment creasing his face.

Chance blinked several times. "I never thought of that."

"Well, there you go."

"But what about the third woman. From what I've heard, these visions of mine always come in threes."

"Maybe you shouldn't worry about what you don't know and concentrate on what you do know. Weird shit happened, and you walked through walls or teleported or some other nonsense. You stepped into the body of a librarian, and then a woman on the beach. Do you know what beach?"

Chance thought back. "I saw a pier. It might have been Santa Monica."

"What about the library?"

Chance shook his head. "No idea. Although it did look fancier than most libraries I've been into. Maybe if I saw a photo."

"So, the way I see it, you've got two choices. You can mope around here, worrying that something might happen, or you can tell the doc to get in contact with Special Agent Fuzzypants and advise him about what's going on."

"It's pretty thin." Chance grimaced. "Do you really think he'll buy it?"

"Did he tell you to only call if you had something thick for him?" Jarvis scowled and glanced away. "Wait, that doesn't sound right." He looked up, his expression turning lecherous. "Or maybe it does."

Chance shook his head. The larger man broke the façade and chuckled darkly. "Hey, I'm just trying to lighten the mood, you know?"

"Not the right time, Jarvis." Chance glanced around at the white walls. "And this definitely isn't the place."

"All right, so what are you going to do?"

Chance sighed and stood. "Any idea where Doctor Smith would be at this time of day?"

* * * *

"What kind of library?" Special Agent Broachford asked.

Darkness lurked beyond the first unbarred window Chance had seen since waking from his visions into the nightmare of reality. Jarvis had been snoring too loudly back in their room, so Doctor Smith had allowed the interview to be conducted in his office. Suggestions of a straightjacket had been thrown around – Chance suspected it had been more from the doctor worrying about his personal property than any real security issue – but eventually Broachford had become frustrated and barked at the doctor, ending the discussion. The brief exchange had reminded Chance these men had known each other before either had chosen their individual career path.

"The library was elegant; it had a lot of timber carvings," Chance replied. "Four floors high, desks and study areas aligned into all the open spaces."

"Okay, I'll check it out." He scratched something down on his pad. "What about the woman. Any clue who she was? A name would be great."

Chance shook his head. "Not at this time, I'm afraid. I can't even remember what she was wearing. The old woman was crotchety, though."

"Crotchety old female librarian doesn't narrow it down much. The second scene you described; you think it might be Santa Monica?"

"I saw a long pier with what looked like a Ferris wheel on it. I can only think of Pacific Park in Santa Monica. Is there another like it?"

Special Agent Broachford appeared thoughtful. "There's Steel Pier in Atlantic City, but from memory, they don't have a Ferris wheel. Pleasure Pier on Galveston Island down in Texas, on the other hand, has a Ferris wheel – at least it did when I went there as a boy." He rubbed his face as he thought. "But I don't believe they 're open until the spring."

"Why not?"

Special Agent Broachford snapped his gaze up. "I have no idea." He collected his pad once more and stared at it, gathering his thoughts. "I'll look into it, but the sound of your description might indeed run with Santa Monica. The library, on the other hand…."

"What about it?"

"The term, 'needle in a haystack' comes to mind. A four-floor library decked out with carved timber could be in any major city. The Bureau won't justify the hours needed to search for something on such scant information." He shook his head and muttered, "I'm only holding onto this case by the skin of my teeth as it is."

"Why?"

Special Agent Broachford glanced up as though Chance had slapped him. At that moment, the wall of division slid back between them. Chance was a patient in an asylum. A crazy man. For Broachford to divulge information to such an individual was surely way beyond protocol.

"Forget I said that."

For several heartbeats, Chance glared at him, considering the challenge yearning to explode from his mouth, only to cave in right when it seemed the words would tear loose of their own volition.

"Yeah, sure."

"All right." Special Agent Broachford flipped the notepad closed and placed it in the breast pocket of his pressed white shirt. He clicked the pen once and slotted it in alongside the pad before standing and buttoning his jacket. He motioned toward the office door, where the orderly on the other side of the glass pane nodded in turn and twisted the handle, allowing them out.

The man in blue motioned for Chance to stand up. Chance half-expected to be frisked in the off chance he'd managed to pilfer something from Doctor Smith's office, but the orderly merely indicated for him to leave the room. As they reached the door, Special Agent Broachford's voice rang out, halting them. Chance turned.

"I just want you to know, I'm taking everything you tell me seriously."

Chance thought about it for a moment. "Why?"

Special Agent Broachford appeared lost for a reply. He regarded the bare timber desk, scanning the leather inlay as though it might hold the answer. Eventually, he looked back up and met Chance's gaze.

"Let's just say I don't have much choice."

Chance held his gaze for a moment. Then, without another word, he turned and walked away.

CHAPTER VI

A fist slammed into his gut.

Chance reeled back, gasping for breath, stumbling over a fallen lamp and sprawling awkwardly against the cold tiling. He held up a warding hand. "Please," he begged. "Stop."

"You lying bitch! How could you?"

Chance's memory felt fuzzy. He had no idea how he had come to this place, nor why it seemed as if he were floating beneath the surface of his skin, like a body immersed in water sloshing around inside a moving vehicle. He tried to stand and discovered he couldn't. Instead, of its own volition, his body shuffled backward on the floor.

Gradually, the fog lifted from his mind and a semblance of clarity began to seep in. This wasn't his form, yet it didn't feel like one of his visions either. This was something else entirely, like watching a movie through the eyes of a character. He felt no pain, no emotions, had no memories of the person whose body he inhabited. He could tell by the diamond-encrusted wedding ring on the warding hand she held up that the victim was a woman. However, that seemed the only similarity to his other visions. Some deep sense inside told Chance this wasn't happening in the present; it had already occurred, and as such the results were beyond alteration. For some reason, his mind had latched onto this thread and was now forcing him to relive the moment. Perhaps here lay an answer to the many questions dogging his mind. All he could do was hold on and hope for illumination.

A man towered over the prone woman, one foot planted on either side of her waist. The unknown man leaned down, grabbing her by the hair with his left hand, punching her again with the right, this time in the head, just above the brow. The scene hazed, her eyes filling with blood. A stinging sensation arose from her forehead. The man's ring had cut her.

"Look what you made me do," he hissed, releasing her.

"This isn't you," she wept. "It's the drugs." Something in the familiarity of her tone suggested she knew the man well.

"What do you know? I'll fucking kill you, you sanctimonious bitch," the man growled.

Chance fought to glimpse a face, but the woman's head was cowed and her eyes filled with crimson. As the scene faded from view, all Chance could hear was weeping.

* * * *

Doug Broachford sighed and closed the door.

The apartment looked empty without her touch. The little things he had taken for granted before seemed monumental now, though he couldn't place what they might have been. The place smelled different. Clean, but different. Doug couldn't figure out what it was, despite going through every scent in the grocery store aisle.

He pulled his FBI badge from his jacket pocket and placed it reverentially on the dining table. With a soft grunt, he unbuckled the holster from his right hip and dropped it beside the leather badge wallet. All he could think of was a long-overdue shower.

The water scalded his flesh, but Doug ignored the discomfort. After spending time in that asylum, impulse compelled him to try to remove the taint clinging to his body. He scoured his skin with the washcloth, the scented liquid soap not seeming to help at all.

Finally giving up, Doug snapped off the faucet, cutting the water instantly. After drying his body and hair with a towel, he dressed in comfortable sweatpants and a t-shirt, and then entered the kitchen. Perusing the selection of frozen meals in his freezer, he chose apricot chicken and stabbed the packed three times with a clean fork before placing it in the microwave. He didn't need to check the box for a cooking time.

One second before the bell chimed, Doug pressed the button and removed the piping hot packet. He tore off the film lid, scraped the contents onto a clean dish and, after grabbing a can of lime iced-tea from the refrigerator, strolled into the living room.

Doug ate his meal in silence. There was no television in the house, and he despised the clamor of most music, so he kept his own company and ate his simple meal methodically. Too many years in the military had left habits ingrained so deeply they were unlikely to wear away. Within moments, the food was completely gone, and the dish racked in the dishwasher.

Grabbing his laptop, Doug sat at his desk and turned it on. Once the computer had booted up, he navigated to the internet and began searching.

So many libraries. Opulent and brimming with compressed knowledge. Page after page flicked through his browser, all to little avail. After an hour, he felt ready to give up, but then an image flicked onto his screen that made the agent pause.

A spiral staircase.

Many of the libraries he had virtually visited had possessed similar stairways, but none possessed the ornate white steps and railing that Chance Ripley had described on his spiraling flight of stairs. This library also boasted four floors, and study desks similar to those Chance had told him of, complete with the green lamp covers. He checked the description he had jotted down in his pad. Everything slipped into line with the account he had been given, but Doug still refused to be dragged in too far. If his job as an agent had taught him anything, it was to keep an open mind, but also demand absolute proof before committing. He kept researching the library details, finally looking up who the head librarian was. It turned out to be a man named Chilton Sladek, previously a law professor at Berkley. His staff of seventeen included four female interns and a mixed contingent of permanent staff.

Doug picked up his cell phone, but then paused. Looking at his watch, he swore softly and put the phone back down. It was close to ten; no way anyone would still be there. After more searching, however, he found the personal phone number for the former professor-turned-librarian and rang it without compunction.

Three rings and an answer.

"Hello?"

"Yes, hello. Is this Chilton Sladek?"

"That's correct. To whom am I speaking?"

"I'm Special Agent Broachford from the FBI. I need details on members of your staff as quickly as possible."

A pause. *"What is this in regards to?"*

Damn. Legal Professor. Doug could almost hear the roadblocks slamming into place within the man's mind. This was not going to be easy.

"This is about a murder case."

"You know I can't give out personal information over the phone, Special Agent Broachford. If you would like to come down to the library tomorrow, we could make an appointment and, if my staff are willing, you can meet them individually, and they can provide their own details. If they refuse, you will need a court order."

Doug swiftly did the math in his head. "It will take me at least twelve hours to drive to where you are. Probably more."

"Surely there are other agents closer who you can rely on."

"Right." Doug paused, imagining trying to call on another agent to chase up his psychic lead. "I'll get back to you on that. Is there any information you can give me? Do you perhaps have a young woman on staff who works under an older lady wearing glasses?"

The derisive snort was all the answer he needed. *"Please don't call me on my personal number again; I prefer to leave work-related business for hours when I am actually being paid. Good evening."*

The line cut off, leaving Doug frustrated and staring at his cell phone. Eventually, he flung the phone away. It landed on the couch, and then bounced off, settling with a soft thump on the carpet. Drawing several deep breaths, Broachford marched over and picked it up, wiped the screen on his sleeve, and then placed it carefully on the side table.

Walking into the kitchen, Doug moved to the cupboards above the refrigerator, opened up the right door and reached in. After a moment of fumbling, he found the glass pipe coated in a thin layer of dust. He felt his lighter beside it. He placed the pipe and lighter on the counter with a half sneer, stared at them for a moment, and then grabbed a tumbler glass from another cupboard. Dashing in some ice from the freezer, he half-filled the tumbler with scotch and grabbed the pipe, walking back into the living room.

The old chair groaned under his weight as he sat down. One day he would buy a new one, but not this week. Probably not this month. The scotch sat on the side table beside his cell phone, and Doug once again stared at the pipe, disgust plastered across his face. He made as if to smash the pipe on the armrest of the chair, but at the last moment halted, picking it up instead. His fist clenched so tightly around the implement that a part of his mind feared he might shatter it – another part thought he would deserve the punishment such pain would bring. The pipe ended up resting beside the tumbler of scotch.

Rising again, Doug walked to where his badge lay beside his holstered gun. For a moment, he seemed uncertain between the two, but eventually picked up the wallet. Behind the badge was a small pocket out of which he produced a tiny bag filled with crystal rocks. The wallet dropped back to the table, the badge staring blankly up at the ceiling.

Doug returned to the living room. Part of him groaned in time with the armchair as he wilted into it. The pipe somehow returned to his hand. A habit he'd struggled to forget came fresh to his mind as he packed the pipe and brought the flame to the glass ball.

He sucked greedily on the tube. Euphoria hit and, for a moment, he blacked out. Coming back with a rush like a freight train, Doug's eyelids stretched wide, and he gasped. He despised himself and loved himself at that moment, wanting to fling his body through the window, yet having never felt so in touch with life.

Reaching for the glass of scotch, his shaking fingers almost knocked the tumbler from the table. He paused and clenched his hand into a fist until the tremors faded. Finally, he managed to lift the glass and took a deep swallow, his senses tingling as the chilled liquid flowed down his throat.

As he exhaled, remnant vapors escaped from between his lips like a ghost, and he almost wept. Memories flooded in on him, but Doug batted them away like a knight clashing against shadows. After a moment, the attack subsided, leaving only the burning desire to make things right.

He would avenge her, even though it would likely cost him his career.

CHAPTER VII

"Looky, looky."

The hauntingly familiar voice chilled Chance's blood. At first, he struggled to place where he knew the voice from, but his heart knew panic moments before his mind recognized why. He turned to face the voice, filled with dread. A hand swiped across his cheek, the movement almost sensual, but he knew there was no allure intended. The palm smelled like mint and crayons.

Chance tried to move, but his body refused to respond. He felt trapped within his own skin, a prisoner inside treasonous flesh.

"Having trouble?" the voice asked.

He still couldn't see the speaker, but he knew who it was. Any moment now, the sinuous figure of the third killer would saunter into view, her beauty beguiling and deadly, ready to shred his life.

Chance's mind began to blur. Memories not his own started to seep in, congealing what he knew into a gluey mess. He was aware that a woman… what about the woman? Where was he? The room seemed familiar, but at first, he couldn't place why. Slowly, like treacle through a keyhole, knowledge seeped into his consciousness.

This was his home. He lived here – had always lived here since his parents had died. That chair over there, he remembered the leg had cracked and almost broken....

What was he talking about? He was not a he. This... all of this made no sense.

"Gloria. My name is Gloria," Chance mouthed aloud.

"I know," replied the other voice.

A woman, sensuous and beautiful, stepped into view, and Chance gasped.

"What have you done to me?"

The beautiful woman smirked. "Curare. It is a wondrous drug. Used by South American Indians for hunting. Occasionally, I adopt it for my own kind of hunting."

The knife appeared in her hand as if summoned by magic. She gripped it in a familiar fashion, as if the weapon were an extension of her being. The blade ran almost the length of her forearm and glimmered in the low light. Its serrated edge curved up to a wicked tip, almost seeming to smile at him. Chance imagined the blade stroking flesh and screamed.

The woman slammed the butt of the knife into Chance's throat, cutting the scream short. He choked and coughed, fighting to retain some sense of self within the chaos of memories and terror swirling through his mind. One moment he was the librarian, and the next he was Chance Ripley from Ward Z.

"Which is real?" he whispered.

The woman paused. For some time, she stared at him, her eyes wide.

"Who are you?" she finally hissed.

"What?" Chance gasped.

"Who are you?" she screamed into his face. "Get out of her! She's mine!"

The knife plunged down. Chance sensed the impact in his chest, but felt no pain. The curare had an effect this killer never intended. His body felt like it had been filled with Novocain. He could feel the blade, but nothing hurt. The urge to laugh fought for dominance, but down that path crept the fetid claws of insanity, waiting to hook in and never let go.

"She's mine!"

The frenzied gaze seared beyond the eyes of Gloria-the-librarian, straight into Chance's soul.

"It's you!" the killer screamed, stumbling backward.

Death clouded Chance's vision, swirling like dark shrouds of fabric, mummifying his thoughts until the world vanished completely.

CHAPTER VIII

Chance didn't scream.

He woke as if rising from a deep slumber, despite the horror of the vision from which he'd fled. His heart thudded in his chest, but a secondary awareness lingered, and he knew that to yell within the asylum would risk being restrained or drugged again. There remained a possibility his memories had faded as a result of the medicines designed to calm his mind, and right now he needed to retain every facet of his identity that he could.

The killer had seen him within the flesh of the woman named Gloria. Of that, he held no doubt. The recognition in her gaze had been unmistakable. But where had she recognized him from? The wrath had been worse. She hadn't been trying to kill Gloria; that knife had been aimed at Chance's heart. He couldn't even begin to imagine how such a thing was possible. All Chance knew was that to lose his memories now would leave him more exposed than he could possibly afford. The idea of one of those killers hunting him while he remained blissfully ignorant terrified him even more than the concept of the woman knowing who he was.

He tested his body, half-expecting it to remain immobile under the effects of curare. Nothing impaired his movement, however, and he rose from the bed without issue. Jarvis was in the shower, bellowing out a Madonna hit from around 1983 as though he were singing for his life on American Idol. Chance silently urged the big man to hurry up; he desperately needed a shower to cleanse the taint of the vision.

Chance no longer held delusions that the visions were dreams. He had dreams all the time, even in the asylum; the atrocities he witnessed were nothing like them. No, these forays into another life – or lives – left his mind shredded in ways that had nothing to do with imagination. The sensations felt all too real to be mere mental creations, no matter how unstable his mind might be.

That agent had believed him. The fact a man from the FBI actually took him seriously left Chance with a singular lifeline to cling to. Why the man trusted him left Chance baffled. Were their positions exchanged, Chance doubted he would have been lured into such a strange web of delusions. But Agent Broachford had reacted as though Chance's words were canon, and as such, it gave Chance hope he might not have slipped too far away from sanity.

What was sanity, anyway? It was the way society believed things should be, not necessarily founded in reality. No doubt, visionaries and geniuses from the past had been deemed insane. The first person to imagine the world was not flat, for instance. Or the first follower of Christ. Even the man who had initially thought it might be a good idea to eat a chicken's egg.

"Seriously, that thing just came out of the bird's butt. Now you're going to stick it in your mouth?"

On another day, the thought might have made Chance giggle, or at least split a grin, but today was not that day. The visions allowed him to glimpse what lay through Death's door, and he had awoken knowing it would probably not be his last time. Even if he weren't already declared insane, such knowledge might be enough to tip him over the edge. He needed to use all his mental resources to hold himself together, if only for the time being.

The shower cut off, and after several moments, Jarvis strolled out with a towel stretched around his waist. "Awake, are you? Well, you can't complain about my snoring anymore, not after your damn monolog last night."

"What are you talking about?" asked Chance, hurriedly sitting up in bed.

"I don't know what you were saying, but it was obvious you weren't happy. Did you have another one of your vision things?"

"Something like that," murmured Chance. "I need a shower." He rose from the bed and entered the bathroom. The mirror remained steamed from Jarvis's shower, and Chance leaned over to wipe it clean with the palm of his hand.

Within the reflection, the face of the female killer glowered at him. She suddenly lunged. Chance yelped and stumbled backward, tripping over the low step and falling into the shower cubicle. Miraculously, he managed to avoid cracking his head on the tiled base, but he remained immobile, staring up at the now-vacant mirror.

Jarvis poked his head inside the bathroom, looked around, and then down to where Chance lay huddled on the floor of the shower.

"That's not how that thing works, you know," he said casually.

Chance pointed up at the mirror, finding his voice had abandoned him. Jarvis glanced at the reflection and jumped.

"Argh!" he screamed, before calming almost immediately. "Oh, it's okay. It's just me." He rubbed his hairy chin. "I really need a shave. I look like a lumberjack"

Chance rose to his feet hesitantly. "There's nothing else there?"

Jarvis looked all around the reflection. "What else is there supposed to be?"

"There was a… I don't know."

"Well, there's nothing there now, so prepare to be amazed."

Jarvis turned and left Chance alone with an empty mirror.

* * * *

"Tell me, Chance, what do you believe is happening to you?"

Doctor Smith's voice was calm and without any semblance of judgment. Chance feared his judgment, though, perhaps more than anything else… other than the murderers, of course. This man's decisions could change the course of Chance's life forever.

"I have no idea what's happening."

He looked around the circle. Group therapy. The faces seated near him were mostly strangers, though apparently they had all met before in this exact same setting. Each one of them was a patient, everyone except the doctor. Some appeared worse than others – Betsy, for instance, seemed completely lost in another realm of reality. She clutched at invisible vapors, seemingly unaware of the rest of the group. A man three seats to Chance's left continuously mumbled words incoherently. Another man seated almost directly opposite stared at Chance with stretched unblinking eyes. Chance couldn't tell if the man saw him at all, or was fixated on something none of the others could distinguish. Jarvis appeared to be napping. His head hung back, and his mouth gaped open.

"But what do you *think* might be happening," the doctor persisted.

Chance lowered his gaze and stared at the linoleum floor. "I think I might be seeing victims. Actual victims, not imaginary ones. I don't know how it's happening, but they are too real." He looked up. "As real as anyone in this room. And they are… I think they're calling out to me for help, even though they don't know it."

"Why would they call out to *you*?"

He shook his head. "That doesn't make much sense. I'm just a guy. Someone too far away. Maybe I am the only one they can reach. God knows it's not because I can save them."

"Why can't you save them?"

The question flummoxed Chance. For a time, he simply stared at the cracked linoleum and wondered how long it had been since the flooring had been laid.

"I'm stuck in here. To help them, I would need to be out there in the real world."

Doctor Smith seemed to choose his next question carefully. "If you were out there, in the 'real world' as you call it, how would you save them? What would be different?"

"Nothing," interrupted Betsy loudly, causing Chance to jump slightly. Nobody else seemed to react, so he settled back down, feeling rather foolish.

The door suddenly banged open. Jarvis snapped awake with a strangled burp. Betsy ignored the sound, seemingly obsessed with touching colors nobody else could see. Doctor Smith stood up abruptly, the clipboard he had been resting on his lap clattering to the linoleum.

Special Agent Broachford stormed into the room. A patient, a man Chance didn't know, cringed in his chair, urine soaking his pants and dripping to the linoleum beneath his chair. A nurse trailed behind the FBI agent, two beefy orderlies awaiting instructions for how to react.

"Did you see it?" demanded the agent, staring at Chance.

"Doug, what are you –" began Doctor Smith. Broachford cut him off with a glare.

"Did you see it?" he repeated.

Chance stood on shaky legs. "Do you mean Gloria?"

Special Agent Broachford froze as if he'd hit a wall. "What about the others?"

"What others?" asked Chance, frowning.

Broachford grabbed him by the arm and marched him from the room. The nurse sputtered arguments, but Doctor Smith waved her to silence, quietly counselling her and the orderlies that everything would be okay. Before the door slammed shut, Chance heard the orderlies advising the patients to return to their rooms. Chairs scraped, and feet shuffled on the linoleum.

Halfway down the corridor, Chance snatched his arm out of Broachford's grip. The agent glared at him, but Chance returned the stare with equal vehemence.

"What's going on?"

Special Agent Broachford licked his lips and glanced around before speaking. "Three more women were killed last night. One worked in a bakery on Scotch Avenue in Chicago. The second, a woman named Chelsea Bordelow, lived in Santa Monica – just like you predicted. And Gloria Wright was an assistant librarian at the Iowa State Law Library. Who did it?"

Chance tried to calm his pounding heart and focus his mind on what he had seen. "Gloria's killer was a woman; the same one I told you about before. The other two… I have no idea."

The agent snarled silently and slapped his hand against the wall, the most emotion Chance had seen from the man.

"I might be wrong," began Chance, "but is this more than just another case for you, Special Agent Broachford?"

The man glared at him, his red-rimmed eyes fighting hard to focus. For an instant, just an instant, Chance wondered which of them should truly be the patient in this place. A blink, and the moment passed.

"I am treating this case exactly the same as every other one. Just because some things don't make sense doesn't mean they aren't true." He paused, apparently trying to gather his thoughts. "Can we go outside? Is that allowed?"

"You just stormed into a group therapy session in a secure mental ward, and you're worried about taking a stroll?"

"Good point," said Broachford. He glanced around, rubbing his mouth. "How do we get out of here?"

Chance pointed along the corridor. "Down there and to the right."

"Let's go."

Leading the way through the mazelike warrens of Ward Z, Chance finally made it to the security checkpoint opening out to the back garden. The security at the checkpoint stopped him.

"No access outside until eleven, you know that."

"He's with me," grunted Broachford, flashing his badge.

"That's nice," replied the security guard, a man with the squarest jaw Chance had ever seen. "But unless one of the doctors or directors signs off on it, he's not going anywhere."

"Wait!" called a voice. Doctor Smith sprinted down the corridor behind them. He reached their side in moments, but had to pause, heaving in air. "They're fine," he gasped to the security. The man nodded and waved them out the exit.

Once outside, however, Doctor Smith took on an entirely different tone. "What do you think you're doing?" he snapped at Special Agent Broachford. "I brought you in because I thought it might help you with your… case. I did not expect you to turn my hospital upside down in the course of your crusade."

"There have been another three murders."

Doctor Smith looked troubled. "You surely can't think Chance had anything to do with them."

"I don't know what to think anymore. All I know is these bastards are picking off women at will, and the only one to have any kind of insight is your patient."

"Chance can't even leave the hospital."

"But he can make it to a phone, am I right? Perhaps these people are working with him in some sick game that gets them off. Why? I don't know yet, but then again, I'm not crazy."

"Are you sure?" muttered Chance.

Special Agent Broachford snatched his throat in a grip like an eagle's talon. "I don't have time for your bullshit, you fucking psycho."

Chance bucked and fought against the powerful grip. "You said you believed me," he managed to wheeze.

Broachford's gaze seemed to focus. He visibly struggled to reel back in whatever rage fought to break loose and released Chance. "I'm sorry."

"If that happens again," said Doctor Smith, his voice ominously soft, "you will no longer be welcome here. Is that understood?"

The agent appeared repentant, his gaze aimed toward the ground. "Got it."

"And I will call to make a complaint to your superiors."

Broachford's eyes snapped up. "Don't do that!" The words were halfway between a plea and an order. Chance doubted the man himself even knew which.

"All right, then. You may continue your questioning, but I suggest you pull yourself together."

Grimacing, Broachford returned his gaze to Chance. "*Are* you for real?"

Chance shrugged. "These things are happening to me. I don't know why or how; they just are. Part of me wants to know why, but a greater part only wants them to go away. But I can't ignore them, not while women are dying. I'm feeling their fear as they die. Each time a life is snuffed out, I endure the terror and pain they undergo gazing into the features of their killers. You cannot imagine what that's like to suffer through. And now it's even worse."

Broachford's gaze narrowed, his notepad suddenly flashing into his hand. "What's changed now?"

Even the birds beyond the garden walls seemed to silence in the face of Chance's unspoken response, waiting in bated tension.

"She could… see me."

"Who? Gloria?"

Chance shook his head. "The female killer. She saw *me* inside Gloria."

Broachford turned to Doctor Smith. "What does that even mean?"

"How should I know?"

"Well, this is your field of expertise, isn't it? The human mind, the psyche; surely something like this has crossed your desk in the past."

"If not for the case facts that the patient identifies, despite having no way of knowing, I would say he was suffering from acute dissociative schizophrenia. The fact that his projection, or one of them, has turned upon him, means he has an issue of self-loathing, likely from his childhood, which is now starting to resurface."

"But he *does* know those facts, Doctor." Special Agent Broachford looked away, his expression musing. "What can that possibly mean? He predicted where two of these murders would occur. If he's not involved with the killers, there has to be some other connection, most likely of a psychic variety."

"My profession does not accept such a conclusion," Doctor Smith concluded. His expression turned thoughtful. "That being said, there is someone I know who does specialize in such phenomena."

"What's his name?" asked Special Agent Broachford.

"*Her* name is Doctor Sylvia Petrov."

Broachford's eyes narrowed. "A Russian?"

"Emigrated here during the Cold War. She is one of the most respected doctors in the field of parapsychology."

"A field your profession frowns upon."

Chance watched the debate silently, like a fan at a tennis match, his head turning from left to right and back again. It seemed the two disputants had forgotten he existed.

"Can she help me?" he asked unexpectedly. Both men cut off their debate to look at him. "This woman, can she help me?"

Doctor Smith blinked several times. "I'm not sure, Chance. As it is, I'm still not convinced you aren't suffering an ailment which regular treatment can eventually remedy, or at least minimize." He glanced at Special Agent Broachford. "But as my former schoolmate here has suggested, there are too many factors for which there are no explanations, and I must admit I find myself at a crossroads. All my training flinches away from the idea of bringing in what many in my profession would claim to be a charlatan, despite her high academic credentials. If lives weren't at stake, I would never consider such a thing."

"But lives *are* at stake here, Dennis."

The doctor winced at the sound of his first name. "I am acutely aware of that, Special Agent Broachford. As such, I am willing to try to contact her."

"When will that be?" asked Broachford.

"Due to recent events, I took the liberty of researching where Dr. Petrov was on the chance we needed her expertise. She is currently visiting New York City. Once we are finished here, I will call her, and ask if she'll be willing to hear our situation out."

Broachford nodded once, shortly, smartly. "All right, then. Go."

Doctor Smith scowled at the agent for a moment, and then turned and left the two alone in the garden. Chance frowned at Special Agent Broachford. The guy was a bit of an ass – more so than Chance had initially imagined. That he was desperate to solve this case was evident. Whether for career advancement or some other reason remained to be seen.

"What else can you tell me?" demanded Broachford, rounding on Chance once more.

Chance bit back the retort begging to burst loose from his lips. He was in no position to enter into open rebellion with the FBI agent – hell, he was barely higher than a prison inmate on the food chain these days. For all he knew, he *was* guilty of some crime. The thought caused a sick sensation to swish around his guts. Had he done something other than behave slightly loony to earn his place in Ward Z?

"I have no idea what to tell you," Chance said eventually. He glanced around the garden, noticing how lonely the place appeared. "These things come on me without warning; I have no control over what I see or when. If I could tell you –"

He paused. Recollection of when he entered the bathroom and wiped away the steam from the mirror returned with horrific vividness. It must have shown on his face.

"What is it?"

"I… I saw the killer, the woman."

"Yes, I know," replied Broachford, rolling his eyes. "You've already told me."

"No, I saw her when I was awake. In my own bathroom – or at least the bathroom in my hospital room."

Broachford frowned and stepped closer. "What are you saying?"

"She was looking out at me from the mirror. It was like she'd been waiting for me to turn up or something." Chance ran a hand through his hair and scratched the back of his head. The feeling of sickness returned. "It was like she could see me through the mirror." He paused, and his eyes grew wide. "Or if she was looking out from inside me and all I saw was her reflection."

"What in the world are you talking about?"

"Imagine, just for a second, that I am somehow tapping into the thoughts of these killers."

Broachford looked far from convinced. "But you said you're looking out through the eyes of the victims." He pulled out his notebook and flipped it open, read a section, and then flipped to another page. "Actually, you stated that you were inside the victims' bodies, living through them. Their memories become your own, and the torture being done to them is being done to you."

"But what if the positioning was because I couldn't enter the bodies of the killers?" Chance paused, gathering his thoughts. "What if they're the ones who are linked? Three killers all attached to each other. What if they're drawing me to them, like magnets?"

"So the three random serial killers are actually linked, acting as one. Is that what you're saying?"

"It sounds insane," muttered Chance.

"Look around you." Broachford placed his notebook back into his pocket. He seemed to chew over what Chance had suggested for a moment. "Then by her saying she knew who you were, it was because she'd managed to latch onto you somehow. What do you think that will mean in the long term?"

Chance shrugged. "They're killers. It doesn't take much deductive reasoning, does it?" He chuckled nervously, but Broachford merely stared at him straight faced. Chance's mirth slowly petered out, leaving the two standing in awkward silence.

"I need to get out of here," muttered Chance. The realization emerged so suddenly that Chance had voiced it before he realized what he had said.

The statement seemed to smack Broachford in the face. "You're kidding, right?"

Chance thought about it, and then shook his head. "I have no choice. They know I can identify them. These people are fanatical; a little thing like guards and fences won't stop them. And there's another reason."

"What's that?" asked Broachford, his eyes narrowing.

"I can't stop them from in here."

The agent actually took a step backward. For a moment, he seemed to reappraise Chance. He glanced about to make sure they were still alone, and then leaned in conspiratorially.

"Why do *you* want to catch them?"

"I can't explain it. It's like something is scratching around inside my head. But I know they'll never leave me alone until they catch me and kill me. I've died four times already at the hands of these bastards. Apparently, it has been more times than that, but that's all I can remember." He sighed heavily. "What are my other options? I can sit here and wait for them to come to me, or I can get out there."

"You are in a center for the *criminally* insane; you know that, right? It's little more than a prison, no matter what they label it. Essentially, you're talking about breaking out of jail."

Chance's throat dried up in an instant. "What?"

"I guess you didn't know. Now, before you ask, I have no idea what you did to end up in here. The hospital refused to tell me in case I divulged it to you. Apparently, part of the treatment is letting patients work out their issues on their own. But yes, this is a place designed for criminals. And you're discussing escaping with a federal officer."

"Oh," Chance murmured. "Oops."

"That being said...." Broachford scrunched his brows together as he stared hard at Chance. "Were you actually out there, in the world beyond these walls, would you be able to track them down better?"

Chance shrugged. "Maybe."

The agent glanced around. "Let me see what I can organize."

"You think you can arrange my release?"

"Not legally, no."

The cogs in Chance's mind clicked into high speed. "Are you saying what I think you're saying?"

Special Agent Broachford stepped in close to Chance. There was something within his gaze, something Chance couldn't pinpoint, but it unsettled him.

"Let's get one thing straight: if I do this, it isn't for you. I don't care if you rot in here for the rest of your life. What I do care about is catching these murderers and bringing them to justice. If I can use you for that, it's a price I'm willing to pay."

"But won't that get you in trouble?" Even as the question slipped from his lips, Chance realized how ridiculous it sounded.

Broachford's eyes appeared slightly unfocused. "Someone has to find these people. If I can't do it from within the lines, I guess I'll have to take alternative measures."

The response was hardly something Chance expected to hear from a federal agent, and he peered at Broachford, still unsure if the man was on the level. The memory of the screaming killer staring at him from within the mirror returned, and he swallowed slowly. He needed to get free of this place, or he would be like a pig in a pen, waiting for slaughter.

"Okay." The reply came from within him, but Chance could not believe he had uttered it.

This couldn't possibly end well.

CHAPTER IX

Oh yeah, she was definitely Russian.

The woman looked robust enough to drag a plow through a frozen paddock, and Chance wondered absently if she had ever competed as a powerlifter. He would have bet good money on her winning gold.

"Doctor Smith tells me you have visions."

In contrast to her physique, the doctor's voice was soft and calm. Chance blinked several times, focusing his thoughts.

"Um, yeah." He proceeded to tell her of the visions he could recall, right up to the appearance in the mirror.

Doctor Petrov raised an eyebrow. "This woman saw you?"

"Apparently."

"Do you think she was alive?"

Chance paused. The idea had never occurred to him before. "Why wouldn't she be alive?"

"Sometimes spirits are known to play havoc with people, particularly on the Sixth Plane."

Chance scowled at her. The pair sat in the linoleum-floored room generally set aside for group therapy sessions. Without the circle of other patients, he felt horrifically alone and exposed.

"What's the Sixth Plane?"

"A hypothetical realm of existence. Some have proposed that those who have refused to pass over to the other side inhabit it." She paused and gave him a measured stare. "But there are also others, supposedly."

"What others?"

The large woman peered over the rim of her half-moon glasses at him. "Some of my contemporaries have suggested demons exist there, though I have never personally encountered any proof of such allegations." Her accent clung to every word, but her English was flawless. "Those I am referring to are people with cerebral keys who can unlock this realm, either consciously or unconsciously."

"Like me?" asked Chance.

"Possibly. There also remains the high chance you are schizophrenic, as Doctor Smith has suggested. The line between the two is thin, and hard to differentiate. As such, for centuries, people with real psychic ability have suffered persecution when their only crime was being able to tap into a higher plane of existence that others could not see. You are lucky Doctor Smith has an open mind; most psychiatrists would medicate you and ignore the underlying issue."

"And what is the underlying issue?"

The large woman stared at him for some time, her icy blue eyes peering beyond his surface, peeling away layers of protection, leaving him feeling bare and exposed. "What you have described is a singularly unique experience. I have heard of people spirit walking before, but to be drawn to the victims and not the killers leaves me pondering the reasons. Perhaps you are linked with these victims in some way that makes you subconsciously desire to protect them. Or maybe you are drawn to witness their deaths."

The memory of what Special Agent Broachford had suggested, that he was a criminal locked up here for a reason, combined with what the doctor suggested, leaving Chance shaken. "I don't remember these women."

"Are you sure? There is nothing about them that seems familiar?" Once again, her gaze left him feeling like a morsel beneath the leer of a hawk.

Chance began to sweat. His mouth ran dry, his throat like sandpaper. His mind battled to break loose, to flee from the icy judgment of the parapsychologist. But it remained trapped beneath that startling gaze, locked in the nightmare that Chance lived and breathed. Placing her pen and clipboard down on the table, she leaned in closer, her eyes seeming not to blink, to gaze beyond all his barriers and into his soul.

"Leave me alone," Chance hissed.

His head felt like a pressure cooker ready to explode. As the force built to bursting point, his eyes began to water, tears streaming down his cheeks.

"It is all right to cry," murmured Doctor Petrov, misunderstanding his reaction. Perhaps she wasn't so perceptive.

"No," he grunted.

The bubble popped. Chance screamed, a short burst of anguish escaping from between his teeth.

The lights exploded.

Glass rained down like razor-sharp snowflakes, the shattered tubes scattering, tinkling like a million bells as they spread across the linoleum. The room fell into shadows, a single band of sunlight streaming through the barred window. Not a single shard of glass touched either Chance or Doctor Petrov.

She snapped back in her chair, her eyes wide. For a moment, as the glass tinkled down, the large woman sat motionless, staring at him. Her power was gone – if it had ever existed in the first place – and the pressure within Chance's mind began to ease. He let out a harsh, shuddering breath and wiped the tears from his eyes.

"What did you do?" he asked. His voice sounded choked.

"Me? Absolutely nothing," Doctor Petrov murmured. "You, however, you are very interesting."

She peered at him intently through the dim illumination of the thin ray of sunlight from the far window. There was curiosity within that gaze, and Chance couldn't help but sense there was something else, an emotion he couldn't immediately pinpoint. After a moment, it came to him, but when it did, he wished he had remained ignorant of it.

It was hunger.

* * * *

"Like… they blew up?"

Chance nodded. "I'm not sure what happened. It seemed like she was trying to get a reaction out of me, but when that happened, she got scared."

"I'm not surprised," grunted Jarvis, picking up his book once more. The title of his latest paperback was *1984,* by George Orwell. "I would have shit my pants."

Frowning, Chance stood up from the table and paced around the room. It was almost time for lights-out in the ward, and soon the orderlies would be moving from room to room to secure the doors. Before he had discovered the asylum was designated for the criminally insane, Chance hadn't thought much of this security precaution, but looking back now, he wondered how he had never put the evidence together.

"Jarvis," he began, turning back to the giant man, "did you know this place was for the criminally insane?"

Jarvis put the book down on the table, scowled at him, and then burst out laughing. "You didn't?"

"Well, I guess it was a little naïve. No need to laugh about it, though. It's not like they plaster it on the walls or anything."

"A little naive?" Jarvis kept chortling. A thin line of snot dribbled from his right nostril, but he didn't react. "Why do you think there are bars on every window? And did you think the razor wire was to keep pigeons out?"

"Why didn't you tell me?"

"I would never have thought anyone could *not* see it. Remember, I told you about Ward Alpha being full of the seriously insane people, the ones likely to eat your face. And I also said that I was in here on a court order; they don't do that for non-criminals."

"Do you…." Chance's voice grew small. "Do you have any idea what I did?"

"You stole a sweater from a Brazilian milkmaid."

Chance blinked several times. "What?"

"How the hell would I know what you did? I'm barely able to keep track of my own damn brain in this place with all the meds they keep giving me. They must be truly desperate for me to keep my pants on, I tell you." He picked up *1984* and began reading again.

"Do you think I killed someone?"

Jarvis huffed and put his book down for a third time. "I've told you before, they don't keep the killers in here. They're over in Ward Alpha. Therefore, that's off the table. Now, all you have to do is whittle through the thousands of other possible crazy things you might have done to come up with a solution. In the meantime, you can shut up and let me read."

The big man stood, towering over Chance, and strode to his bed. Kicking off his slippers, Jarvis clambered onto the hospital bed, which groaned under his weight. He rolled to face the wall and hauled the blankets up over his shoulder, effectively ending the conversation. Chance stared at the bulky blanket fortress for some time before moving to his own bed and climbing in. His leg kicked one of the leather straps, and the buckle rattled dully, reminding him of his blindness to his situation. Free people did not usually require restraints.

Lying on the bed, Chance stared at the chalky white ceiling, lost in his thoughts. A tenuous plan began to unravel in his mind, a way to escape, but just as swiftly, he dashed it to pieces. Another, and then another formed, only to meet the same fate as the first.

Ghostly echoes of the three killers surfaced to whisper to him. These weren't actual visitations, thankfully; they were mere memories of the brutal murderers. He wondered how the three were connected. Were they actually operating from the Sixth Plane as Doctor Sylvia Petrov had speculated, or were they phantasms of his distraught mind, creations that had nothing to do with reality and everything to do with insanity?

He shook the notion away. There had been no way he could know the details of Special Agent Broachford's case while being locked away in here. He had known names and places, details a man in his position had no way of knowing. Of course, nothing he'd passed on had been of use, but the fact he could divine evidence no other living person had access to made Chance wonder what was happening to him.

Or had he always been this way?

What if he had been born with this gift-curse? He tried to imagine growing up as an infant, seeing people dying or in terror. How had he not ended up in an asylum before now?

Perhaps he had. Maybe he had been in here for most of his life, and that was why they didn't want to give him any details. To know you were locked up for a lifetime due to a curse you had no control over would be enough to send anyone further over the edge, wouldn't it? Maybe that was why he couldn't remember the horrors of his past; it was his mind's way of protecting itself –shutting out everything that might cause it harm, including memories.

Had he killed people in his madness? Had he stabbed innocents to death while trying to escape the horrors echoing within his own mind? He recalled the first awakening in the hospital bed, the manic terror that had enveloped him upon stepping from one reality to another. Slipping from the brink of death into a body he hadn't known had been like waking up with the grasping talons of a demon raking across his skin.

"I have to get out of this place," he muttered.

"And how are you going to do that?" demanded Jarvis, rolling over.

"Oh, sorry. I didn't mean to say that out loud."

"Well, you did. And now you've piqued my curiosity. Don't look at me like that; I know how to use fancy words too, you know. So how do you plan on escaping this shithole?"

An orderly stepped into the room, and Chance froze, sure the man had heard them talking.

"Lights out now, guys," the man said. He used a card swipe to cut off the main lighting, leaving only dull floor lights to illuminate their way to the bathroom. The door to the hallway closed and locked with a rattle.

Chance blew out a breath he hadn't realized he'd been holding. "That was close," he whispered.

Jarvis snorted loudly. "Are you kidding me? Those guys wouldn't care if you were planning to burn this place to the ground. They're minimum wage earners; barely more than security guards in medical uniforms. So tell me about this plan."

"I don't have a plan."

"Oh, come on. I heard your tone. That was the sound of desperation; you're serious about getting out of here. So, out with it, what's the plan?"

"I wish I could tell you differently, but I can't think of a way out of here, no matter what I come up with. Without the right information, even if I find a set of keys, I'll be running around in circles."

"You mean *we*."

Chance frowned through the gloom, unable to make out more than Jarvis's bulky silhouette. "What are you saying?"

"I'm coming with you."

"Oh no," protested Chance. "That'll be too dangerous."

"Are you calling me fat?"

"Wait… what? No."

Jarvis's earthy chuckle filled the darkness. Finally, it petered out. "I need to get out of here, Chance. This place is eating me up inside; I can feel it. Eventually, I'll just be a husk banging my head against the wall like Peterson was doing in the garden the other day."

"Who is Peterson?"

"The guy with a big lump on his head," Jarvis responded, as if that answered everything. "Nobody knows what broke him. One day he just started bashing his head against the concrete as though he thought he might smash his way free. By the time the orderlies reacted, he had a bulge the size of a tennis ball above his right eye, pissing out blood everywhere. I don't want to end up like that."

Chance didn't want to divulge the fact he might be able to procure the assistance of Special Agent Broachford. Such an admission would inevitably result in scorn from Jarvis, who would likely call him all kinds of foolish names for trusting the agent.

"Well, what do you propose?" Chance asked.

He heard Jarvis's bedsprings creak as the big man leaned closer. "I can get us architectural plans of this place, of the whole asylum."

"What?" Chance hissed. "How?"

"The same person who's been getting me my books. But it'll cost you."

Chance immediately remembered Jarvis's explanation of how he had obtained said books. "I'm not going to suck a penis."

"Good to know. But this won't require that."

"Oh." Chance's mind became a whirlwind. Part of him rejoiced at the possibility they might be able to get their hands on a map of the grounds, potentially finding a weak point through which to escape. Another part trembled at the thought of being hunted; on the run until they were either caught or died. "What *will* it require?"

"Money," replied Jarvis bluntly. "A lot of it, too. More than I can get my hands on."

"You mean you've been planning this?"

The big man nodded in the shadows.

"But why? I thought you were in here for chasing squirrels with no pants on."

"There might have been one or two other minor indiscretions," Jarvis admitted.

Chance squinted through the gloom, straining to see Jarvis's expression. From the tone of his voice, he sounded uncomfortable, but that might easily have been stifled mirth.

"What did you do?" Chance demanded.

For a time, only silence filled the room. Chance refused to break it, allowing the pressure to grow.

"Okay, I shot a cop."

"*What*? When were you going to tell me?"

Chance sensed more than saw the giant shrug.

"It never came up."

"You're asking me to escape with you, yet you hold something like that back? Can you imagine the manhunt for someone who shot a cop?"

"I think the hunt will be big enough whether you take me or not, buddy."

Something in Jarvis's tone made Chance pause. "What are you talking about? I thought you said you didn't know what I was in here for."

"And I don't," Jarvis confessed. "What I do know is what a lot of the other patients in Ward Z are in here for. None of them are angels, not a single one. These people might not be sociopaths or child killers, but they're not goodie-two-shoes upset about the stock market, either. Ponsonby, in the room next door, deliberately drove a car into a restaurant full of people during dinner time. Apparently, it was a miracle none of them died. One man will never walk again, though, and a woman miscarried three days later. Several broken bones and thousands of dollars in damages later, he ends up in here. Want to know why he did it? His cat told him the people eating there were consuming human body parts."

"Shit," murmured Chance.

"And it don't end there. A woman named Kathleen Belafonte – you might have seen her at the canteen, the chubby one with bright red hair – set fire to a school because some kids pulled faces at her from the school bus. Obviously, something else was going on in her life, but from what I heard, she tried to secure the external doors with bike locks. Luckily, the fire department had bolt cutters, and everyone escaped, but the whole building went up in smoke, completely reduced to ashes."

A fist of ice gripped Chance's stomach and refused to let go. He feared that if he moved, he might piss the bed, so he sat motionless on top of his sheets, praying the sensation would pass.

"So, my dear roommate, if these other patients have committed such atrocities, what do you think *you* did to end up in here?"

The vocalization of what he feared most jolted Chance. He leaped from the bed and sprinted to the bathroom. The dull illumination of the lights set low on the walls allowed him to skip across the floor without incident, and he almost made it to the toilet before the contents of his stomach erupted. As it was, he slipped on his own vomit and fell to his knees. Taking no time to pause, he crawled to the rim of the porcelain bowl and emptied the rest of his stomach contents into the toilet. When he finished, he expected to hear the laughter of the buffoon who shared the room with him, but Jarvis remained silent. For some reason, his silence made the truth of his statements all the worse.

Chance cleaned himself up as best he could, and then wiped down the floor. A small pile of paper lay in the bottom of the toilet bowl by the time he had finished. Burping softly, he moved to the sink, rinsed out his mouth, and then brushed his teeth as well.

As he reentered the room and headed for his bed, Chance felt grateful for the first time that so little light permeated the gloom. At least Jarvis couldn't see the shame plastered across his features. Or his fear.

The tightness in his gut remained, despite him having emptied his stomach. A tugging, gnawing sensation, like worms burrowing themselves into his brain, also refused to leave him. He was a criminal. Somewhere between the ranks of chewing-gum shoplifter and axe-wielding psychopath. If only he could remember what he'd done. But the fog clouding his memory refused to part, not allowing even a glimmer of the truth to shine through. As far as Chance's mind was concerned, his life began mere weeks ago. His time before that awakening could yield any number of difficult questions to which he might not want answers.

"All right. How do we get the money to pay for the plans?" he asked.

"Two words: blow jobs."

Chance sighed heavily. "Well, that's not going to happen."

Jarvis chuckled, the sound slightly ominous in the darkness. "Just trying to lift the mood. No, we need the help of someone on the outside. My list of friends is rather small, especially after what happened before I came in here. That means it's up to you."

"I can't remember anyone."

"That doesn't mean they don't remember you, does it? Perhaps if you ask the friendly Doctor Smith, he might let you peek at the list of people allowed to contact you in here."

Chance shook his head, and then remembered that Jarvis probably couldn't see him. "Doctor Smith won't even think about doing anything like that. He keeps hoping that my brain's going to slip into gear and start working again if he leaves me alone for long enough."

"Lucky you," grumbled Jarvis. "They've got me swallowing second-hand suppositories. The damn things taste like shit."

It took Chance a moment to realize his roommate was joking. "That's sick."

Jarvis's rumbling laughter bellowed out. "I've got a spare one here if you don't believe me."

"I'll pass." He paused, uncertain of how much he could trust the large man. "But I might know someone who can help us."

Jarvis's mirth cut off as if sliced by a knife. "Who?"

"I can't tell you. The fewer people who know what's going on, the better."

"So, you don't trust me?" There was a half growl in Jarvis's accusation, leaving Chance recalling how hard the man could punch.

"Imagine if you have one of your pants free episodes again and somehow blurt it out. It wouldn't be your fault, but we'd still be screwed."

For a time, Jarvis remained silent. "All right," he finally conceded. "But we're going to need it soon. My guy isn't what you would call the patient type, and apparently, the admin is already searching for the lost plans. We have a few days. A week at most. Think about it, and let me know."

As the big man rolled over, Chance wondered how much Special Agent Broachford would be willing to help him. The memory of the agent's expression, the near-fanatical determination in his eyes, clearly showed that the lines between right and wrong were blurring for Broachford, whom Chance suspected typically lived by the book. But would Broachford be willing to slip him some money the next time they met? Chance doubted it.

What other choice was there, though? He could rot in here, waiting for the day when one of the three killers managed to reach him. And they would; these three clearly didn't operate within the normal constraints of society. They would either wade through the staff, leaving a trail of bodies in their wake, or slither through the gaps in security, disguised as patients or even potentially as doctors. They would find Chance, and then he would die for the last time.

He was their one loose thread, the only person who could expose them.

CHAPTER X

Icy fingers traced patterns across his cheek.

Chance awoke with a start. He looked up, or rather *out*.

Gravity kicked in, and he suddenly realized he was not lying down… *or* standing. Somehow, he dangled from his ankles, a thin rope cutting into his skin. A city sprawled out in front of his eyes, upside down, the twinkling lights like so many scattered dreams. The vista might have been dazzling were he not hanging so precariously. As it was, breath caught in his lungs, and he fought down the urge to scream.

Memories battled for supremacy within him. On one front, Chance remembered he was an inmate at the Mount Sinai Mental Refuge. On another, he knew he was a schoolteacher from East L.A. He taught English and Math to twelve-year-olds.

A moment later, Chance realized he couldn't have screamed, even if he had wanted to. The tautness of duct tape tugged at his cheeks, and half a heartbeat later, he realized that his wrists were similarly bound. He tilted his head and viewed the ground so far below through eyes stretched wide in terror.

The pavement would have been invisible if not for the orange glow of the streetlights.

Cold fingers stroked his face once more, and Chance spun his head to the right, immediately wishing he hadn't. The cadaverous features of the second killer leered at him, fresh scabs peeling from his gaunt, pockmarked cheeks. Up close, the man's skin shone with a greenish tinge, leaving an impression of taint and disease. A wicked grin stretched the killer's cheeks as he peered straight into Chance's eyes.

"Well, well, well," the walking corpse breathed. "She said it was so, but I didn't believe her. I can see you in there, though, beyond the husk. Don't ask me how – this connection is still a mystery to me. Perhaps the others understand, but I am a simple man."

The killer's breath smelled of peanuts. Usually, this wouldn't have bothered Chance, but such a mundane scent within so horrendous a visage set him even more on edge. He yearned to gnash and fight, but every attempt at movement cut the line around his ankles deeper into his flesh. The killer seemed to sense his discomfort and looked up, grimacing almost apologetically as he did.

"It was all I could find, I'm afraid. The nylon cord is supposed to be used for clotheslines or similar, not for stringing up wannabe Hollywood starlets who teach during the day to make ends meet." He peered closer, gazing deep into Chance's irises, teetering on the edge of the rooftop. "But you're not a Hollywood starlet, are you. You're an intruder. An interloper on the scene. Who are you?"

The killer moved to tear lose the duct tape sealing Chance's lips, but suddenly paused. His head tilted to the left as if listening to something.

"Nobody can hear her up here," he hissed, barely loud enough for Chance to understand. Another pause. The killer's brows narrowed and a look of intense annoyance flashed across his face. He glanced back at Chance, then away once more. "We need to know who it is," the cadaverous man muttered. "It's too dangerous to leave whoever it is out there while they can identify us."

Again, some kind of exchange appeared to take place. The killer snarled silently, but said nothing, merely glared at Chance once more.

"Fine." He stared back at Chance, his expression hateful. "She told me to tell you we're coming."

Without warning, a blade appeared in the man's hand. With a swipe, he cut the line at Chance's feet.

The ground that had seemed so far away rushed up with terrifying speed, and Chance screamed into the tape.

* * * *

The ground hit him with the force of a Mack truck speeding down the freeway.

Strangely enough, the impact didn't kill him. In fact, as Chance gingerly reached out through his body, every moment an agonizing crawl across a frozen lake where he expected to plunge into the icy embrace of death, he sensed no injuries. There wasn't even a glimmer of pain. Had he been paralyzed? The itch on the sole of his left foot made him think such a possibility was unlikely.

Lifting his head, Chance peered around. He laid in the middle of a pumpkin patch, fields spreading out all around him. A rickety barn swayed in the light breeze half a football field's length away, and beyond that stood a farmhouse, white paint peeling from the clapboard siding. A screen door hung askew, suspended by a single hinge, and the porch steps had rotted through in the center.

"How did you get here?" hissed a voice.

Startled, Chance twisted around. A small girl, perhaps no more than eight-years-old, stood nearby. Chance wondered how she could have crept up on him. Where could she have been hiding in the vast nothingness of the pumpkin patch?

"Where am I?" Chance asked.

The girl clutched a tattered cloth doll in her left hand. In her right was a broken red crayon. Upon the ground at her feet was an open coloring book, the image of a woman etched black upon white. Scrawling red crayon covered the page, haphazard and spreading way beyond the lines. Her clothing was little more than threadbare rags, and her skin was caked with dirt.

"This is my place." The voice was that of a child, but the undercurrent tones were much more mature.

Chance rose slowly to his feet, but suddenly paused. He stood only as tall as the little girl did. Looking down at his body, he saw he was still dressed in Ward Z pajamas, but these appeared only big enough to fit a child. He plucked at the cotton, wondering at the roughness of the material beneath his fingertips. This place had the feel of a dream, but the reality and solidness of the ground beneath his feet, the sensation of the fabric, the light breeze against his cheeks, all gave the moment a jarring realness. He swallowed, deliberately tasting the spit sliding down his throat. If not for the young girl's scrutiny, he would have pinched himself.

"You're not supposed to be here."

"How did I get here?" he asked, looking around.

The girl glared at him and refused to answer. Chance looked closer, noting the dark purple bruises hidden beneath the earthen smudges.

"Are you hurt?" he asked.

"Always." The word was barely more than a whisper. Her gaze shifted, and fear slipped into her expression. "He is coming."

"Who?"

The girl lifted her free hand, the one not holding the rag doll, and pointed toward the creaking barn. Chance peered as she pointed, noting that the structure looked much larger than when he had first noticed it. A figure emerged, shoving its way through doors that now stretched high into the sky. The silhouette was that of a man, but one of gargantuan proportions. A giant filled the doorway. With a casual wrench, the figure tore loose one of the doors and flung it away into the breeze.

The wind must have picked up without Chance noticing, because the enlarged barn door, a wooden construction that could have roofed a dozen car spaces, flipped and curled away into the sky, gone in seconds. Stinging rain whipped against Chance's cheeks, and thunderous clouds bunched overhead, ready to unleash angry torrents.

"Don't let him take me."

The tiny voice whispered in Chance's ear. He spun to see the girl now stood right beside him. She reached out with her right hand, the one not clutching the dolly, and gripped his left palm.

"Who is that?" Chance asked, fear drenching his voice.

"Nothingman."

The towering figure stomped forward, and the ground shuddered. Chance saw the giant's foot sink deep into the soil, the very ground seeming to scream at such violation.

"Run," Chance hissed.

He tugged the little girl, and the two tore off through the rows of pumpkins. The giant roared, and the earth rumbled with its pursuit. The two sprinted for all they were worth, but soon Chance found himself gasping for breath. Glancing behind them, he discovered they hadn't moved a single yard from where he had woken. The one the girl had called Nothingman loomed above their heads, his upraised fist seeming to scrape the clouds.

"Remember me," the little girl hissed in Chance's ear.

The fist plunged down.

Chance awoke, sweat-drenched, and trembling. He stared out, forcing his eyes to focus. The familiar surrounds of the asylum greeted his gaze, barely lit by the dim glow of the safety lights. Chance found himself grateful for the scene, certainly for the first time he could remember. The memory of the girl's hand remained with him; her tiny palm still seemed to grasp his own. He raised his hand up in the darkness as if to affirm she no longer existed and sucked in a slow, deep breath. It seemed an age since he'd remembered to breathe. The inhalation caught in his throat, however, as a lingering scent hit his nostrils.

Chance glanced around the room, his heart thundering. No shadows moved, and nothing seemed untoward, yet the smell remained. After a moment, he raised his hand to his nose and sniffed.

It smelled of crayons and mint leaves.

CHAPTER XI

The crystals glittered in the light radiating from the kitchen.

It wasn't a glamorous glitter, not like diamonds, but the contents of the small plastic bag were worth more than all the diamonds in the world to Special Agent Doug Broachford. Part of him, the career FBI agent, yearned to rush to the bathroom and flush the drugs down the toilet. But a greater part knew he never would. The beast had its claws in him once more, riding his back like an insane monkey.

Doug had thought he had conquered his enemy, rendered it an ugly little piece of his history, but with her death, all the pangs had returned with a vengeance. It was like a deep hunger of the soul. How had he ever managed to defeat such a dogged stalker? The answer was simple: *she* had been by his side. Everything back then had held more meaning. Life had been worth fighting for. Now, the world seemed reduced to shades of ash. Only one purpose held meaning, and that didn't require him to be careful with his health. If anything, the drugs helped blunt the pain long enough for him to deal with everyday niceties without the overwhelming urge to start screaming and never stop.

A part of Doug's mind lingered on the thought. Something about such a release of control appealed to him, to step into the mouth of madness and let go. Perhaps he would end up alongside Chance in the hospital for the criminally insane. He licked his lips, knowing that journey wasn't as farfetched as he tried to make himself believe.

The pipe seemed to materialize in his hand. Doug couldn't remember bringing it with him into the living room, yet here it was, along with the butane lighter. He tipped a few crystals in, sealed the bag, raised the lighter, but then paused. The trigger of the lighter, shaped much like a blowtorch, itched beneath his index finger, but Doug fought the urge. He licked his lips and stared at the glass pipe. He longed to hurl the tool away, to smash it against the wall, but his arm remained locked, immobile.

The phone rang, its shrill insistence shattering the silence of the apartment. Doug jumped, almost dropping the lighter. Collecting himself, he placed the pipe down carefully on the coffee table, along with the lighter. Rising from the couch, he lurched into the kitchen on unsteady legs.

"Hello?"

"Doug, it's me, Doctor Smith."

"What can I do for you, Dennis?" replied Doug. He glanced back at the coffee table as if to affirm his prize still waited for him.

"There has been another… incident."

Doug's eyes narrowed. "Has he seen another murder?"

"I believe so, but he'll only talk to you."

"I'll be there first thing tomorrow.

"Good." Doctor Smith paused.

"What is it, Dennis?" Doug coaxed.

"I could lose my medical license for this; you know that, right?"

"And I could get thrown out of the Bureau. What's your point?"

Doug could almost hear the man wringing his hands on the other end of the line.

"When I contacted you, it was because of Gloria Wright. We both knew her, and I worried that this patient might have somehow hurt her. I never expected this to be an ongoing thing, nor did I expect you to buy into the whole psychic angle. I brought Doctor Petrov into the fold in an attempt to expose the patient's delusions, not enable them further. But things just seem to be getting worse."

"He knows something, Dennis. You don't see the case facts I have access to. If you did, you would see that the coincidences are too accurate to be lucky guesses. So, without internet, television, radio, or phone access, tell me how a patient in your secure ward is somehow accessing such information. For God's sake, he practically predicted who two of the victims would be."

Doctor Smith paused. He seemed to be contemplating something. *"I'm putting an end to this,"* he said finally. *"You'll have one more interview, but beyond that, you'll require a court order to speak to any of my patients. I need to concentrate on their rehabilitation, and distractions, such as your case, don't help anyone."*

"They help me," Doug growled. "They help the victims."

Doctor Smith paused again, seemingly unsure how to respond. *"Be that as it may, my concern is for the patients of Mount Sinai Mental Refuge. After tomorrow, you will need to find your answers elsewhere."*

The phone went dead. Doug stared at it for some time before finally nodding and placing the handset down on the kitchen cabinet.

"Maybe there's another option," he murmured.

The siren call from the living room became impossible to resist. With a wrenching moan, Doug trudged toward his only escape.

CHAPTER XII

"Stay away from Ward Alpha."

Chance jolted and spun around.

"Oh. Hello, Betsy." The garden seemed to still around them. Betsy glared at him with a piercing gaze, unblinking and unflinching. "What can I do for you?"

"I know what you're planning."

"Planning?" Chance frowned. "What are you talking about?"

For a moment, Betsy appeared confused. She ran a hand through her chopped hair, her fingers clutching at strands, and then stretching wide as though trying to escape a cramp.

"No, it's there," she murmured. "You'll die in there. Or worse."

"I can assure you, Betsy, I have no plans to go to Ward A. From what I've heard, it's not a very nice place."

"Don't condescend, you philistine." Betsy's voice suddenly adopted a cultured tone. "I know what I know." But the expression of confidence faded, leaving a lonely child. "Or do I?" She looked around as though noticing for the first time that they stood in a garden. She reached down and plucked some grass from the lawn. She studied it the way one might read a newspaper. "They scream when I pluck them, did you know that?" She looked up at him. "Or maybe you can hear them."

Chance shook his head. "I can't hear them."

She smiled. "You're lucky." She reached down and tore loose another clump. "The flowers are worse." She looked around. "But I can't seem to find any."

"Maybe you plucked them all."

Betsy suddenly looked distraught. "Why would you say such a horrible thing?"

"Um… sorry."

"I should think so." She blew the clump of grass from her palm as though it were fairy dust. Her expression turned to one of disgust when the grass clippings merely flopped back to the lawn instead of taking flight. "Stupid grass," she muttered.

After a moment, right when Chance was wondering how he might extricate himself from the situation without making a scene, Betsy raised her gaze once more. "Why are you going to go to Ward A?"

"I'm not. I never said I would."

"Oh, yes you did. It's written all over…." She trailed off and swiped a hand down the front of his face. It was a clumsy movement, like a drowsy kitten trying to act like a tiger. "I'm going to miss you when I'm dead."

"That's great. Now, if you could excuse me."

Betsy shook her head. "No, I don't think I will."

"Um, pardon?"

"You can't go. Not until I've finished."

"Finished what?" asked Chance.

"What I started, silly."

Chance looked around the garden. About twenty other patients lingered, most too withdrawn or doped up on medication to converse with. None paid any attention to Chance and Betsy, giving him no excuse to break off this discourse. He wished Jarvis were here.

"What have you started, Betsy?"

He knew the question was a mistake, yet the words slipped from his lips before he could call them back.

"Where are my flowers?" She looked around, worried.

"They're growing as we speak," Chance hedged.

She bent and tore up more grass. "Trinity is coming for you. You know that, don't you?"

Chance's throat tightened in an instant. For several moments, he couldn't find his voice and simply gawped like a drowning mouse. "Who is Trinity?" he finally asked, his voice barely above a whisper.

Betsy looked at him, her gaze level, void of any madness. "The three killers." She held up her hand, the grass tumbling back to the lawn. Three fingers pointed to the air. "Bull. Siren. Pestilence. They are coming for you." Her eyes flitted toward the high walls. "You won't be safe here… but you already know that. That's why you're going to escape. But you can't go through Ward Alpha, Chance. You won't survive, despite what they promise you."

"Who will promise me?"

"The ones you trust. I can't see faces." Her gaze drifted, losing focus. "Where are my flowers?"

"Tell me more about the killers," Chance pleaded desperately.

"What killers?"

Whatever connection Betsy had held to her strange gift had slipped beyond her grasp, along with her ability to think along rational lines. Her information left Chance cold. He knew it indicated something around his looming escape attempt, but from what Jarvis had mentioned, they wouldn't need to go anywhere near Ward Alpha.

"Ripley," one of the orderlies called to him. It had become common knowledge that he now knew his last name. "You have a visitor."

Chance nodded and bid Betsy goodbye. She waved vaguely and stared at the remnants of the torn grass in her hand as though it contained all the answers in the world.

* * * *

"You'd better have something useful."

"Well, hello to you, too," replied Chance snarkily.

Special Agent Broachford glared at him. Dark circles hung under the agent's eyes. There appeared something fanatical in his gaze, and it was all Chance could do to hold the man's stare. Finally, Broachford broke contact and wiped his mouth. "What happened?"

Chance thought back to the murder, the one committed by the killer Betsy had referred to as Pestilence. He wondered if he should tell the agent about how the man had been able to see Chance within the woman he had captured. After a moment's consideration, he decided to keep his story as simple as possible.

"She was hanging upside down, tied at the ankles, from a roof. It was in Los Angeles."

"How do you know?" asked Special Agent Broachford, scribbling down in his pad.

Chance shrugged. "I just recognized it – or rather she did."

"So you can access the memories of the victims?"

"To a point," Chance admitted, looking at the agent strangely. "But I already told you that." Broachford blinked, nodded hastily, and bid him continue. "This time, I knew what was going on, so I fought to remain myself. If I don't, I end up immersed in the victim, and it makes things a lot worse."

"But you would have had a lot more information for me. You might have been able to tell me where this woman lived or what she did for a job, maybe even her name; it would have narrowed the search down immensely."

"She could see the city lights. I doubt many high-rise buildings in LA can claim such a view. From memory, apart from downtown, the city is more sprawling than skyscrapers."

Broachford scribbled the information down. "All right, what happened next?"

"He cut the rope, and I fell… I mean *she* fell."

The agent looked up from his pad. "That's it? He didn't say anything?"

Chance glanced away, unwilling to disclose how Pestilence had recognized him. "Not that I can recall."

Special Agent Broachford peered at him for some time. Chance forced himself to meet the man's gaze, but was unable to hold it for long.

"What are you holding back?"

"I don't know what you're talking about," replied Chance, shaking his head.

"He did say something, didn't he? What was it?"

Chance's shoulders slumped, and he huffed. "He was able to see me. The real me. Inside the woman." He recalled the cadaverous killer's reaction. "It seemed like he was talking to someone else, but there was no one there. Crazy, I know. Lock me up." Chance looked around melodramatically. "Oops. Too late."

The agent's stoic demeanor failed to crack. "Hilarious." He looked at his notepad for some time and chewed on the end of his pen. Finally, he seemed to come to some conclusion. "What if they can communicate telepathically?"

"What do you mean?"

"Three people are killed almost exactly at the same time. For such coordination, they would need to communicate. Intelligent killers, such as the three we're dealing with, wouldn't hazard something so traceable as regular phone lines. And the internet has paths that can be followed, no matter how careful you are. What if these three are killing at prescribed times chosen via mental telepathy?" The agent gazed hard at Chance as though he might know the answer. "Do you think that's possible?"

"So their random killings aren't so random?"

"Maybe not."

Chance considered this possibility over for some time. The fear such killers might be after him had been bad enough, but the knowledge they possessed otherworldly abilities threatened to unnerve him completely. In retrospect, he should have suspected such a thing was possible. They could see his consciousness beneath the physical surfaces of their victims. How long until they discovered where he was hiding? Betsy's warning about the walls of the asylum not being secure against such killers returned to haunt him.

"Can you help me escape?" he asked suddenly.

Their previous conversation around this had yet to reemerge, but Chance was feeling exposed. He presumed Broachford might have had second thoughts about what he'd promised, but the need to escape this place before the hunters arrived pushed Chance to raise the awkward question when he might otherwise have remained silent.

Special Agent Broachford paused in his note scribbling, closed his pad, and then placed it and his pen in the breast pocket of his shirt. As he pulled aside his charcoal-colored jacket, Chance noticed a small ink stain on the bottom corner of his pocket and wondered how a seemingly fastidious man had left home bearing such an obvious blemish to his appearance. The agent cast a cautious glance around them. Two orderlies remained near the door on the other side of the room, but their distance seemed safe, their preoccupation apparent from raised snippets of conversation.

"What do you need?"

"A thousand dollars," Chance hissed without pause.

The agent stared at him, his expression unreadable. "What for?"

"A contact has blueprints of this place."

"Pretty steep. What happens when you get these plans? What's the strategy then?"

"I'm not sure," Chance admitted. "I guess we'll find a way out, and then see you on the outside."

"Just like that, huh?"

"Obviously not. I'm sure other eventualities will arise. But at this stage, it's the only idea we've been able to come up with."

"Who is this *we*?" Broachford demanded.

Chance cursed silently. "I've had to ask someone for help. He knows a guy –"

"I'm sure he does," cut in the agent. "Jesus Christ. You're going to end up putting me in jail." He stood to leave.

"Wait!" said Chance, rising and grabbing Broachford on the arm. An orderly moved to intervene, but the agent waved him back.

"Get your hand off me."

Chance dropped his hand and stepped back, but he refused to lower his gaze.

"I can't help you," Special Agent Broachford appraised finally. "If, by some miracle, you manage to find your way out of here, call the division of the Bureau in New York from a payphone, and ask for me by name. Do *not* give them your name, no matter what they ask. Likewise, do not mention that it has anything to do with the case, or rather *cases*, we have discussed. Nobody at the Bureau believes that these murders are connected in any way."

"So what do I tell them?"

Broachford appeared to consider for a moment. "Tell the operator that you are my brother-in-law, Frank Grafton." Saying the name seemed to pain the agent. "Tell them that you need to talk about your sister… Sarah."

"Who is Sarah?"

Broachford pursed his lips and waved a hand dismissively. "That doesn't matter right now. What is important is that it's probably the only statement that will get you patched directly through to me wherever I am. From there, we'll try to work out some kind of strategy that will keep you from getting caught immediately. At least until we find these bastards."

"Trinity. They're called Trinity."

"How do you know that? One of your visions?"

Chance shook his head. "Let's just say you're not the only one who gets to keep a few secrets." The last thing Chance wanted to do was implicate Betsy in this mess. The poor woman had enough issues without the incessant grinding

Special Agent Broachford's questioning would undoubtedly induce. A sudden memory pounced into the forefront, and Chance wondered how he hadn't recalled it earlier. "I did have a vision, though. One completely different to all the others."

"What was it?" demanded Broachford.

Chance's brow clenched as he fought to recall the odd vision. "It was more dreamlike than anything else I can recall, but I don't think it was a dream." The smell of mint leaves and crayons returned to him. "I met a young girl in the midst of a pumpkin field. She carried a doll; it looked handmade." He paused, thinking. "Something came after us, a giant she called… what was it? Nothingness?" Chance furrowed his brow. "No… Nothingman." He nodded, certain of the name. "He was like an enormous shadow, and he smashed me into the ground. Then I woke up."

Special Agent Broachford had retrieved his pad and was scribbling notes once more. "Any idea who the little girl was?"

Chance licked his lips. "I can't be sure, but –"

"This interview is to be terminated immediately."

Chance looked up as Special Agent Broachford surged to his feet. "On whose authority?"

A short, pudgy figure in an ill-fitting suit waddled into the room. To Chance, the man appeared to have tried extremely hard to find a wardrobe that made him look distinguished and had failed miserably. The suit might have been fashionable a couple of decades previous, but had died deservedly with the end of the nineties. His polished black leather shoes looked two sizes too large, leaving the impression the squat figure wore flippers instead of dress shoes.

"On mine," stated the man, adjusting his horn-rimmed glasses.

"And who exactly are you?"

"I am Mister Ripley's attorney."

Broachford turned to Chance, who shrugged. "I don't know."

"It's true," admitted Doctor Smith, hurrying into the room. The doctor appeared flustered. His glasses sat slightly askew on his nose as though he'd rushed to put them on. He struggled into his white coat, pulling it up over his shoulders. "This is Reginald Blake, Chance's attorney. We have been out of communication for some time, but –"

"But since I heard my client was being questioned without my knowledge by a federal agent, I rushed here to ensure his constitutional rights were not being infringed upon." He slapped a faux-leather briefcase onto the stainless steel table in what Chance felt sure was supposed to be an act of dominance. Special Agent Broachford didn't even blink. "So are they?"

"Are they what?" asked Broachford.

The little man puffed himself up like a toad. "Are you infringing on my client's right to counsel?"

"We were simply having a conversation." Broachford flashed daggers at Doctor Smith, who promptly dropped his gaze. It seemed obvious who had tipped off the attorney, but Chance couldn't imagine why. Was there some friction between Broachford and Smith that he didn't know about?

"A conversation that is now finished," stated Mister Blake.

"Wait. I…." Chance trailed away. He had no idea what he wanted to say. Three sets of eyes turned to him, and for the first time since waking in this place, Chance felt some modicum of power. Yet in that same moment, he felt powerless. What could he say that might be of worth, that might alter the reality before him?

In the end, Broachford saved him from his discomfort. "We'll talk later, Chance. Just remember what I told you." After throwing another venomous glance at the doctor and attorney, Special Agent Broachford stormed from the room.

"Well, that was close," said Reginald Blake.

"Close to what, exactly?" asked Chance, his eyes narrowing.

"Well, close to you being questioned about –" He glanced at Doctor Smith, who shook his head. "Well, stuff, I guess."

"Right. Stuff. Yeah, that stuff is pretty darn dangerous, isn't it?"

Doctor Smith stepped in closer. "Chance, I know you think we're overzealous with what we conceal from you, but your mind has closed your memories off for a reason. Pushing yourself to remember too soon would be like a person in physical rehabilitation trying to walk before their legs had mended. It might well do much more damage than healing."

"But in the meantime, here I am wandering around like an idiot with no memories. The one person who was claiming to help me, a man you brought in here, Doctor Smith, just got shunted out like a leper. What next? Are you going to fill me up with drugs and sit me at a window like some of the patients here?"

"Calm down, Chance."

From the corner of his eye, Chance noticed the two orderlies edging closer. The volume of his voice suddenly became apparent to him. He had been close to shouting. Forcing himself to take a deep breath, Chance held his hands up in a placating motion.

"Okay, I'm calm." He looked at them with an expression he hoped was open and pleading. "You have no idea what it's like being locked in here with no memories. You might think you do, but unless you live through it, there's no way you could understand."

"That's fair enough, Chance."

Chance turned to the attorney. "So what's your story? Did I hire you myself or did someone procure your services in my stead?"

Reginald Blake glanced at the doctor, who appeared reluctant to give permission. After a moment's pause, however, Doctor Smith gave in. "Keep it simple, though. No details."

"I was hired by someone else."

The revelation felt like a cold wave surging over Chance. Who was out there in the real world that might still care for him? Did he have a family worried about his wellbeing, or was his benefactor someone else, perhaps somebody involved in whatever crime he was accused of committing.

"Apparently that somebody doesn't want me talking to the Feds."

"They are concerned about your legal welfare while in this… hospital. The fact you were railroaded in that farce of a trial –"

"That's enough, Mister Blake," cut in the doctor.

"He doesn't even deserve to know he might still be innocent? It was all I could do to get him committed here instead of sentenced to Rikers Island for the short term, then probably on to Sing Sing for the rest of his life."

"I said that's enough," repeated Doctor Smith, his voice stern. "I didn't impede you doing your job, so I would appreciate it if you returned the courtesy. Now, is there anything else you need to discuss with your client before you leave? If not, I suggest we conclude your business here and let the patient head off to group therapy."

"Shame it's not *grope* therapy, huh, Chance?" Reginald Blake winked and nudged Chance with his elbow.

"You obviously haven't met my roommate," Chance muttered, shifting away from the strange man. He could quite easily imagine Reginald Blake running down the road, chasing after an ambulance. A thought occurred to him. "How do I get in contact with you if I need… anything?"

Blake turned to Doctor Smith, who said, "I can contact Mister Blake's office if you need to talk to him about your legal case. Anything else will be best left outside these walls while your treatment takes place."

"Of course, of course," Reginald Blake agreed. He stepped in and threw his arm around Chance's shoulders. It felt like an octopus had just latched onto him. Just as Chance was about to crawl out of the lecherous grip of the man, he felt something scratch under the collar of his pajamas. He frowned, but made no other outward sign that he had noticed whatever it was the lawyer had slipped him. He could feel it resting on his shoulder, a piece of cardboard judging by its texture.

The attorney picked up his briefcase and, after throwing Chance a less-than-subtle wink, he followed Doctor Smith from the room. Chance waited until he felt satisfied both they and the orderlies had moved down the corridor before reaching inside his pajama top and feeling around for whatever Reginald Blake had left there. A moment later, he plucked a business card from beneath the collar of the shirt. It was a simple affair, nowhere near as ostentatious as Chance would have imagined the little toad creating for himself. He must have paid someone else to design it for him.

REGINALD BLAKE
ATTORNEY AT LAW
New York. New York.

At the bottom of the card an email address and phone number were printed in bold text. Perhaps Mister Blake was used to requiring ways to get around such issues as being unable to contact his clients. He looked like the kind of man used to peddling to bottom feeders. Did that mean Chance was a bottom feeder as well? The thought made his stomach churn.

He could have been anything before entering this place. Even Blake had admitted he had almost ended up going to Rikers Island. What crime could he have committed that he would face such a sentence, yet avoid him being committed to Ward Alpha with the dangerous criminals? From what Chance had heard, nobody in Ward Z had been accused of murder. Some had tried, but none had succeeded.

Chance moved to his bedside. A single book lay there, a gift from Jarvis that Chance had yet to begin reading. It was some fantasy about a man with leprosy transported to another world, where the power of his white gold wedding ring made him into a hero… or something. Chance hadn't thus far perused much past the synopsis and perhaps a dozen pages. But it provided a handy hiding place for the newly-acquired business card. He slipped it into the center of the book and closed it again, leaving it on the simple stainless steel bedside table. A quick glance would have the searcher believing it was nothing more than a bookmark. Or so Chance hoped.

As he walked from the room on his way to group therapy, Chance couldn't shake the fear that his former life might have seen him involved in something much worse than anything he had previously considered.

* * * *

"You Ripley?"

Chance looked up from his bed, where he had been trying hard to get into the storyline of the book Jarvis had given him. An orderly stood in the doorway. The man looked cold, someone used to dishing out punishment. Most of the orderlies were employed because they could handle physical situations, but few acted as if they enjoyed hurting the patients. This guy appeared the type not only able to handle breaking a few bones, but also looked like he might relish the opportunity. Chance nodded at him uncertainly.

"Someone wants to see you."

"Who might that be?"

The man's eyes glowered. "Get up."

Chance knew better than to argue with one such as this. Bruises and broken bones were easily explained when dealing with crazy people. While such instances were rare in Ward Z, the orderlies here were still fallible. Every person had their breaking point. Chance doubted this man's would be difficult to reach. He rose from his bed and shuffled over to where the thuggish orderly stood.

"Where are we going?"

"You'll see," grunted the man.

The two walked through the corridors of Ward Z without conversation. Chance occasionally looked over at the orderly, but the man ignored him except to shove him in the center of the back from time to time when he deemed Chance was proceeding too slowly. This wasn't a deliberate move on

Chance's part, but the rising dread he was experiencing must have transferred to his feet, making them trail through imaginary sludge.

The path the orderly took was different from any Chance had traveled before, even when Jimmy from Ward S had returned him from his strange wandering. One thing he did notice was the strange lack of security cameras along their route. Eventually, the pair reached a security checkpoint leading out of Ward Z's building. The guard there barely looked up, swiftly glancing back to his magazine when he saw who was guiding Chance. The short path across to the main structure left Chance feeling filled with anxiety.

"Why does this person want to see me?" Chance ventured.

"You'll see," grunted the orderly for a second time.

"Can't wait."

This, at least, garnered a snorting chuckle from the man. Chance looked over and grinned uncertainly. "What's so funny?"

"I'm just wondering if he will let you leave, is all. You use that lip on him, I doubt you'll ever see Ward Z again."

Chance's heart fluttered. As they entered the new building, he tried to take note of their direction, but in the end, he didn't need to pay attention at all. Their path was dead straight down a corridor interspersed with three security junctures where the corridor split off to the left and right while continuing straight. All junctures were blocked by heavy barred doors, requiring them to be buzzed through by guards sitting on the other side of security cameras, each sealed within thick steel boxes in the corners of the square intersection.

From his previous venture, Chance knew that the section to his left was Ward Sigma, the less secure ward, even though the way he had exited from there seemed different to their current path. He pointed to his right at one security point.

"Is that Ward Alpha?"

Again, this elicited a chuckle from his escort, but the man said nothing. He didn't need to. Such a response left no doubt that the ward Chance had indicated wasn't Alpha, which meant it could only be Gamma. The information in itself didn't concern Chance, but it did raise awareness of where their ultimate destination would likely be.

"Shit," he muttered.

"Figured it out, have you?"

Now it was Chance's turn to ignore his traveling companion. Fear gnawed at his guts with every forward step. Any indication he might be slowing returned the shunting fist to his lower back. Finally, they reached another checkpoint, more secure than any they had passed so far. It was comprised of three barred gates, each one released individually by whoever the controller or controllers beyond the cameras were. The concept was simple; you might get past one, possibly even two, but the chances of making it through the three gates without authorization were minimal. They exited the central building, and Chance froze.

He had expected a mirror of the path between the main building and Ward Z beyond the final gate, but he was markedly shocked by what he saw. Cement lay between the path and the walls. Chance could see the original path within the rest of the gray stone, indicating that perhaps there had once been a lawn laid here, but it had since been torn up and replaced. He wondered what kind of event had forced such a drastic change. The surrounding gray walls remained the same height as those surrounding Ward Z, around three times the height of a tall man, but atop these wasn't just a singular row of razor wire, but rather a six-foot-high chain-linked fence. At the peak of the fence were several spiral coils of razor wire, each barb like the tooth of a shark, ready to shred anyone foolish enough to try to clamber over them. At each corner, too, were guard towers the likes of which Chance had seen in prison photos. Within each tower stood a guard in full riot uniform, holding a high-powered rifle.

"First time to Alpha, eh?" snarled the orderly. "Might be you end up here for good if you upset Mister Mason."

"Is he the warden?"

The thuggish man snorted. "There's no warden here. It's a hospital, remember? We got a director, but that don't mean he's in charge." He refused to comment beyond that, despite Chance's imploring. All Chance received was yet another shove, this one more forceful than those previous.

The new building loomed above them. It mirrored Ward Z, but emanated a sense of foreboding far beyond the weathered structure to which Chance was growing accustomed. It felt as though the screams of the ill had soaked into the stones, leaving them oozing with malice. Betsy's warning returned to Chance, and he halted in place.

"I don't want to go in there."

"It ain't like you've got a lot of choice in the matter, is it? Get moving."

The man made to shove Chance once again, but this time, Chance dug in his heels and refused to shift. He became immobile, immutable as stone. The look of surprise on his escort's face showed how effective his resistance had been, but the orderly didn't hesitate for long.

Leaning in close, the blue-clad orderly whispered in Chance's ear. "You can walk in here, or I can get a half dozen men to drag you in; it's your choice."

"I'm not supposed to go in there," Chance replied, his eyes glued to the open doorway. The bland architrave blended with the equally bare stone around it. A metal gate glinted in the shadows in the entryway beyond the doorframe, indicating the first of what Chance felt sure were a multitude of security checkpoints.

"Today you are."

Betsy's warning screamed through his mind, and Chance's legs locked. All multitude of horrors reared up in his mind's eye, the least of which were the three killers he was slowly coming to relate to as Trinity.

The orderly punched Chance just below the rib cage, straight into his kidney. It was a short jab, probably to disguise it from the surveillance cameras, but it still felt like a hammer had clocked him from behind. Agony roared up his left side, and Chance's knees buckled.

"What are you doing?" he gasped through the pain.

The orderly remained calm. "Are you going to move now?"

This brute could beat him to death in minutes; Chance didn't doubt it for a moment. It would be chalked up as a death in custody, a crazy man who had killed himself. Nobody would really care, not even his sleazeball lawyer. And in that action, Betsy would be proven correct.

Sucking in a deep breath, Chance threw a malicious glance toward his attacker and stood. A reluctant step forward led to another, and then another. Soon he was walking steadily once more, straight through the doorway, pausing only when they reached the metal gate. The orderly waved at the camera, and the barred gate buzzed. They pushed through and waited while the first gate swung shut and the second buzzed open. To his right, behind a security grill, a security guard wielding a shotgun glared at him with lifeless eyes. The second gate clanged open, only to reveal a third door, this one constructed of solid steel. The orderly waited once more while this door buzzed open, and then pushed Chance through.

"Who is Mister Mason?" Chance asked again.

The orderly hissed at him to shut up and glanced around. Chance's gaze narrowed. The lurking suspicion that this man was working outside the boundaries of the institution grew stronger with each passing moment. Whoever this Mister Mason was, he had nothing to do with the regular running of the asylum.

As they wandered through the corridors of Ward A, Chance noted that the building itself mirrored Ward Z almost perfectly. But whereas Zeta was all polished tile and calming colors, Ward A held a proliferation of steel bars and metal doors. Each room was locked off from the corridor, and no patients wandered the halls. They passed a few other workers, each with eyes as hollow as Chance's escort. None of them said a word. At several junctions, Chance heard screams echoing out from rooms, but the orderly didn't flinch. He seemed as used to the sound of tortured thoughts as another person might be to birdsong.

Reaching the end of one corridor, Chance found himself faced with a staircase leading down. He glanced at his escort, who grunted and nodded toward the stairs. Reluctantly, and with the memory of the stinging kidney blow flitting through his mind, Chance began to descend.

Adrenaline seemed to have replaced the blood pumping through his veins, and his hands trembled. Chance clenched them into fists and kept walking. He wondered if Ward Z had a basement, convinced he'd never ventured down there, yet even this certainty felt hesitant. Still, when he reached the bottom of the stairs, he had no idea what to expect.

What waited beyond the door was definitely not what he had imagined.

Lights covered with burgundy shades dotted the timber-paneled walls. Looking down towards his feet, Chance noted that expensive-looking granite tiles covered the floor instead of the dull concrete of the floor above. Delicate cornices edged the plastered ceiling, adding a simple touch of opulence.

For the briefest of moments, Chance feared he had stepped from reality into one of his visions. A fist shoved into the small of his back, however, propelling him forward down the corridor

"What is all this?" Chance hazarded.

His escort seemed to chew over the question. "Best you don't ask that sort of stuff and focus on the reason why you're here."

"What is that reason?"

Again, a pause. "You'll know soon enough."

They walked down the strangely opulent corridor, and Chance soon saw an open doorway approaching on their left. He glanced at the orderly, but the man's expression remained impassive. When they reached the door, Chance noted that it had been framed with polished timber, the door itself crafted from rosewood.

A monstrously burly man stood inside the doorway. He towered at least seven-feet-tall, his skin so black he seemed carved from ebony. Chance noted that his escort swallowed deeply.

"I've brought him."

The ebony giant gazed at them with eyes so black they seemed to have no pupils. The gaze hollowed Chance, and he felt himself cringing despite every effort to stand firm under the man's scrutiny. The silence burned; the absence of any reaction made Chance want to scream at the man, but he knew to do so would make the orderly's previous kidney punch seem like a lollipop at the park. This giant could squash his head like a grape with a single enormous paw.

"Let him in," called a voice from deeper inside the room. The voice was soft, almost feeble, and a small wheeze accompanied it. A slight cough followed, and the orderly scurried away, his task apparently complete.

The giant stepped sideways, allowing Chance to enter. He paused just inside the doorway, peering around the stunning room. To call it elegant was to do the room a disservice. Surrounding the walls were polished bookshelves filled with hundreds of tomes, between which either hung framed artwork or statuettes carved from solid marble. Plush carpet covered the floor, in the middle of which sat a hospital bed, the back slightly inclined, machines beeping softly around it. A decrepit figure lay on the bed, oxygen tubes inserted into his nostrils, partially disguising his face, but Chance recognized him nonetheless.

"Oh, Jesus."

He turned to flee, but the giant had silently moved behind him. It was like running into a brick wall. Chance tumbled to the ground, his fall cushioned somewhat by the burgundy carpet.

"Get… up."

The wheezy voice retained authority, and Chance rose slowly to his feet. He paused for a moment, and then turned to face the bed again.

Pestilence glared up at him from the sheets. With difficulty, Chance forced himself to meet the man's stare.

Silence hung between them, broken only by the faint beeping of machinery and the soft wheezing of the figure's collapsed lungs, Chance frowned. Closer scrutiny revealed that, while remarkably similar to the killer he knew as Pestilence, this man could not possibly be the butcher Chance cowered from in his dreams. Distinct differences, such as this man's advanced age, became increasingly apparent.

"Who are you?" Chance asked eventually.

A low growl emitted from behind him, but the ancient figure waved the protest away, and the giant returned to silence.

"I am Howard Mason."

The name sounded ridiculously familiar, and not because the orderly had mentioned it earlier. Chance fumbled around with his syrup-infused memory, desperately scraping for clues. Finally, the answer snapped to the fore, and his jaw literally dropped.

"The Billionaire Cannibal?"

"That is what the newspapers named me," the old man wheezed.

"I thought you were sent to the gas chamber back in...." He fumbled for the year, but the memory faded away.

"Amazing what lawyers can do for you these days. Especially when provided with unlimited funds. They extradited me from California to New York due to an earlier incident." He sucked in air. "As you may or may not know, this state no longer has the death penalty." Breath whistling softly, the figure motioned with his right index finger. "Come closer."

Despite his instincts to flee the room, a task undoubtedly impossible with the ebony behemoth blocking the doorway, Chance shuffled closer to the bed, stopping barely outside grasping distance. The withered old man smiled.

"It is pleasing to see I can still invoke such trepidation," he gasped. "But don't worry; you're quite safe for now."

"For now?"

The man's eyes narrowed, and Chance saw echoes of dark cruelty lingering within. "It all depends on how this meeting ends."

Time seemed to freeze in that one moment. Chance could hear the rhythmic beeping of the machines surrounding the hospital bed, the faint hiss of the oxygen tubes inserted into Howard Mason's nose, the strained inhalations of the dying man lying beneath a single blue sheet. Oddly enough, his mind swayed to the bookshelves, and he wondered what titles the man possessed. A specific volume caught his eye, causing Chance to blink several times.

"One Flew Over The Cuckoo's Nest," he murmured.

"Are you a fan?"

Chance's gaze returned to Mason's face. "A friend was reading it recently."

"I know."

Blocks seemed to tumble through Chance's mind, eventually falling into place. "Jarvis works for you?"

"Your roommate used to reside here, in Ward Alpha." The old man sucked in a breath. "But he wanted a way out. I provided it to him."

"He said he came from Sigma and only ended up in Ward Z because he hit an orderly."

The sunken figure gave a tiny shrug. "Would you admit to bludgeoning a man so severely that police were unable to immediately identify the body?" Wheeze. "From what I recall, they took several weeks."

Chance held a hand up to his mouth. "Oh my God."

"Now, you have seen a glimpse of what Ward Alpha is like from the inside. Trust me, apart from my own demesne, this ward is even worse than it appears. If you don't agree to what I ask, you'll find that out for yourself."

"What do you mean?"

"I have heard rumors of your abilities. It is said you have seen certain crimes, even to the point that the FBI have visited to talk to you about them." Eyes the color of storm clouds narrowed. "It is said that you have watched my son."

There it was. Chance had guessed it from the moment he had realized Mason was not one of the Trinity killers.

"Your son is Pestilence." Chance croaked the statement. The words tore from his throat unwillingly, as though they clung on to the flesh, refusing to let go.

Howard Mason seemed unperturbed. "I call him by a different name, but yes."

The admission was simple. The man seemed to hold no qualms about Chance's insinuations; he merely absorbed them and continued. Then again, Chance supposed Mason, a monster in his own right, would hardly be perturbed by the news that his son was following in his footsteps.

Though his recollection of his own life remained a mystery, for some reason, Chance was able to recall the history of the Billionaire Cannibal. It was as if they were etched upon his memory. Perhaps the horror of the man's deeds had made them unforgettable.

Howard Mason, this living corpse, had been convicted of killing and eating several influential people, rumored by some to be his competitors. Not their entire bodies, merely tidbits selected carefully from the remains. The story had been so horrific, a gentleman from the upper echelon of society falling from grace so drastically – the chattering classes had followed the case with fascination.

"What do you want from me?" croaked Chance, his throat dry.

"I want you to save my son."

The statement was unassuming, as plain as if he'd asked Chance to check his mail while he was out of town. But the reality wasn't so simple. Far from it.

"What do you mean?" He asked the question mostly to delay answering. Such a strange request needed time to process.

Howard Mason seemed to guess at Chance's reasoning, but chose not to challenge him. "I do not want my heir trudging down the same road I did. He should get the help I decided not to use and live out his life in the real world, not in an institution such as this one."

"Oh boy," murmured Chance.

The withered man sighed heavily. "So what is your answer?"

"What do you expect me to do from in here?"

"Your friend, Jarvis –"

"You mean the man you planted in my room."

"The very same," replied Mason calmly. "And if you interrupt me again, I will have Wylis there snap your left arm."

Chance looked over his shoulder and saw the dark giant glowering at him, a suggestion of eagerness glinting in his eyes.

"So, Jarvis told me you are preparing to escape from this place. Such an endeavor is not impossible, though to accomplish it you will require various tools. I was hoping to provide these tools to you anonymously, thus keeping my involvement a secret, but it seems you were unable to obtain the paltry price I asked for the institution's blueprints."

"Paltry? I would have trouble getting that on the outside, let alone in here."

"Nevertheless, you have forced me to show my hand." He sucked in a wheezy breath. "There will no doubt be repercussions against me, but I will deal with those when they come. What is more important at this time is the future of my son."

"What about the other two?"

The old man's eyes narrowed. "To whom are you referring?"

"You don't know? Three of them seem to be working together, killing women concertedly, seemingly at random."

"Nothing in life is random," mused the old man. His gaze snapped up, his gray eyes stormy. "Why do you think I committed the crimes I did?"

The question caught Chance off guard. "I wouldn't have a clue."

"Take a guess."

"They were in your way?"

Mason scoffed lightly. "That is probably the most ignorant thing you could have said," he wheezed. "Look deeper. If you can't figure out my reasoning, there is no way you'll be smart enough to track down my son."

Chance pondered the issue, brutally aware of the leashed silverback lurking close behind him. Wylis would no doubt relish tearing Chance limb from limb simply for the hell of it. All he needed was permission. Chance pushed the thought aside and concentrated on Mason's question.

Howard Mason, the Billionaire Cannibal, had lived up to his reputation of being a business carnivore. Those he had killed had been business rivals, but he hadn't merely killed them, he had eaten portions of each victim. Seven people had died before the police had discovered Mason's den where he had lured the victims: the basement of an innocuous house in the woods, near New Jersey's Eagle Rock Reservation.

In retrospect, it seemed easy to put the pieces of the crimes together and point the finger at Howard Mason, but at the time, such a notion appeared impossible. In fact, almost all those investigating the case had felt confident Mason would end up being a victim as well. His security had beefed up, ending with a veritable army of contractors paid to keep him safe. An unintended issue, or so it had seemed at the time, had been that the police could not communicate with him for anything; his lawyers blocked them at every turn under the pretense of protecting his privacy. As such, Howard Mason became almost invisible, his movements rarely known.

But why would he eat his victims? And not in their entirety either, only selected parts. For each person he butchered, he retained a single memento, a tiny portion of their body, which he ate raw. This intelligent and seemingly logical man had committed heinous acts, but for the life of him, Chance couldn't figure out why. How did you rationalize such things? The withered figure glared up at him through those stormy eyes, eyes full of cunning, waiting for Chance to respond.

Then the answer struck him. It was such a brutally simple reason that Chance initially could not believe it was true, but deeper analysis could find no fault with the logic. After all, why else did people consume food?

"You were trying to absorb their power." He spoke the answer softly, almost shyly, waiting for the man to laugh at him derisively.

But Howard Mason didn't laugh. He nodded weakly from the bed, an expression not unlike fascination creasing his visage. Chance suddenly felt like a bug beneath the microscope of a small child, and wondered what the bed-ridden figure might have done to him were he in better physical shape. Would Chance have become victim number eight? Was he, even now, contemplating ordering his enormous lackey to hold him down while Mason carved off a slice of Chance pie?

"In essence, I was attempting to fill myself with portions of their souls." The withered old man acknowledged the matter briskly, a statement of fact, not anything out of the ordinary. "I will not bore you with the details of why I selected the body parts I did, but rest assured each was chosen for a particular purpose. My son, on the other hand, has no purpose to his savagery – at least none I can discern."

Chance thought about it for a moment. "He's being led. Someone else is choosing the victims."

The old man's eyes crinkled. "You are definitely smarter than you appear. That is exactly what I believe as well. Now, whether it is the one called Siren, or whether it is Bull, is yet to be discovered. Which do you suppose?"

"You certainly have done your homework. I guess Jarvis has been a real wellspring of information." Chance's mind raced. "I would be inclined to think it was Siren, but…."

The old man's head tilted. "You have doubts?"

Chance didn't want to talk about the dream he'd had, with the young girl seeming so vulnerable. This creature did not deserve to know all the cards he held.

"What if they're all being deceived?" The statement was more to put Mason off what he truly thought, but the moment the words slipped past his lips, Chance gasped at the potential. "I mean… what if there's another player?"

A look flitted across Howard Mason's face that Chance could only describe as hunger. The expression was gone in an instant, but it left Chance feeling that this man would have loved the idea of controlling three killers such as Trinity. Howard Mason might be crippled, but he could never be underestimated.

"That is an interesting concept," mused Mason, his features adopting an unimpressed air. The memory of the hungry expression remained with Chance, refusing to dissipate. "So, if there is such a person, how will you pry my son from their grasp?"

"I...." He paused. "How in the world am I supposed to do such a thing?"

"You need to figure that out quickly if you hope to ever leave this ward."

"You can't kill me!" Chance protested, all too aware of the dominating presence behind him.

"I can, and I will if I so choose. But we are not talking about murder. Remember how I told you that I manipulated your friend Jarvis out of this ward?" He wheezed several times, apparently excited. "What makes you think the reverse is so impossible?" Above the nasal tubes, the old man's gray eyes twinkled maliciously. "How long would you survive in Ward A, Mister Ripley?"

The memory of Betsy's warning echoed through his mind. "Not long," he murmured.

"No, not long at all. Even less time without the protection of one such as I." He chuckled, the sound like dry leaves rustling. "So, what will it be? How will you save my son?"

"Perhaps…." Chance stared at the carpet, his mind racing. "What if I somehow turned them all against each other?" He had no idea how, or even *if*, such a possibility existed, but he wasn't about to admit that here.

"Good. That is good," the old man wheezed. "A chaotic nest is easier to pilfer from. How would you manage it?"

Chance almost swore aloud but caught himself at the last moment. "Well…." Possibilities, each as implausible as the one before it, flitted through his mind until one finally stuck. It seemed flimsy, but definitely worth a try. "If I somehow find Siren, then perhaps, with your help, I can convince her that Pestil – I mean your son – is looking to branch off on his own."

"Why her?" asked Mason, scowling.

"Bull seems too unpredictable. On the one hand, he might be more gullible, but he is also more likely to react violently, without giving me a chance to talk. He might try to track down your son instead of communicating with his partner – or leader if there is one. No, Siren is cunning. She will take the information we feed her and run with it on her own. She will search out the truth of what she discovers before reacting." Chance rubbed his chin thoughtfully. "Yes, she's a hunter. It might work."

"And if she finds him and kills him instead?"

Chance held his hands out wide. "There are no guarantees in this world."

"Not good enough," Howard Mason wheezed. "Let me tell you what will happen if my son dies. I have people out there, not reputable people, nor even professionals. They call themselves *Masonites.* Some would class these people as cultists, fans of my work. They are, for the foremost part, mindless in their devotion, but if word reaches me that my son has expired, the results would be dire."

"What are you saying, exactly?"

"They would eat you, Mister Ripley."

Chance's mind fought to refute what it had just heard; there was no way it could be true. But the humor shining from Howard Mason's eyes glowed all too real. For the first time, Chance glanced at Mason's teeth and noticed they were the only part of him not tainted by the ravages of time, as though they were his most prized possessions.

"I guess I have no other option than to help you, do I?"

"Did you think I would invite you here to offer you options? No, you are now my tool, an instrument through which I might manipulate the world beyond these walls. My son must be protected at all costs, even if it means your own life. Understand that a swift death will prove much less painful than what my Masonites will provide." Another rasping breath. "In return, I will give you plans of the asylum and grounds. I will also make available whatever tools you require to escape, though I do trust your strategy will involve something more intelligent than shooting people or digging under the walls. From your files, I have discovered that your previous life provided you with more than enough experience to escape without too much difficulty."

"My files? You mean you saw them?"

"Of course I saw them." Mason grinned sharkishly. "I probably know more about your life at present than you do. Correct?"

"What did I do to land myself in here?"

The old man shook his head. "Oh no, not that easily. Everything is for sale in Mount Sinai, but certain information is priceless. This is such a thing, and I think I will hold onto it for a time when you might be better positioned to pay."

Frustration tore through Chance. "Why are you doing this?" he asked suddenly. "You don't seem the sentimental type to me. If you really cared about your son, you would have never done the things you did."

"This is true." Howard Mason took several deep breaths, his eyes fixed on Chance. "Let us just say that my reasons are my own, and the reasons behind them are not fleeting. If you think to outlast me, to escape from within these walls, and then wait for my demise, know that my offer is not without a time limit. You are not to know that limit, but when it expires, you will discover all too well how devoted my followers truly are. They will track you to the ends of the Earth and feed on your body, most likely before they kill you. Imagine that, Mister Ripley, and keep the thought with you once you travel from this room. Now, leave."

A massive paw dropped onto Chance's shoulder, propelling him out through the doorway. The timber door closed behind him with an echoing thud. Squeaking footsteps approached, and from the far end of the corridor came the unnamed orderly, as though he had been waiting there the entire time.

"Good doggie," murmured Chance, too softly for the man to hear.

The orderly glanced at the closed door. "You done?"

Looking back at the door, Chance felt a sudden wave of nausea wash over him. "I have a feeling I'm only just beginning."

CHAPTER XIII

"I have the plans."

Chance lifted his gaze and glared at Jarvis. The big man scowled, but eventually dropped his eyes. "How many times do I have to apologize?"

"Betraying me to somebody who used to eat people isn't a thing you just apologize for, Jarvis."

A haunted look came over Jarvis's face. "I had to get out of that place. You've seen Alpha, you know what it's like. I would have done anything to get out. At least here I can hold onto what's left of my sanity; in there I would have become a corpse." He looked up and met Chance's gaze. "I never knew you, had no idea what I was signing up for. Mason can get anything for a price, but sometimes that price isn't pleasant. You were some nameless guy I had to provide information on. Why wouldn't I do it?"

"That's supposed to make me feel better?"

Jarvis shrugged. "At least I'm honest."

"It's impossible for me to tell if you're honest about anything anymore, Jarvis. Hell, how am I supposed to trust anybody in this place? Even the doctors might be in on it."

"More than likely," Jarvis agreed with a nod. "You've met Mason; the idea of limitations doesn't exactly apply to him, does it?"

"No," Chance agreed reluctantly. He licked his lips and walked over to the table, sitting down. He yearned to storm out of the room, but it was too early to go roaming the corridors. "How did you meet him?"

Jarvis sauntered over and slumped into the chair opposite Chance. "I was in Alpha for a month or so – time is impossible to tell in that hellhole; it might have been a week – and I'd just been attacked for the third time."

"Someone attacked *you*?" Chance exclaimed, staring at Jarvis's bulk.

"You do understand the term insane, right?"

"Good point."

Jarvis swiped a hand across his mouth, and his view turned inward. "I won't tell you what they did to me, but it was the final straw. I knew I'd rather die than live in there another day. So I asked the orderly I told you about, Jimmy, if he could do anything to help. He said he'd see what he could do." Jarvis smiled grimly. "Like I said, he's a nice guy."

"Wait, I met Jimmy in Sigma."

Jarvis nodded. "That was the other part of my bargain. I promised to keep an eye on you. In return, I was transferred here, and Jimmy, for his services, was reassigned to Sigma."

"Was anything you told me about your time here before we met truthful?"

"A little. I did hit Jimmy, but that was in Ward A. In fact, that's how we met. He never held a grudge, and we ended up getting along famously." He shrugged his enormous shoulders. "As well as two guys like us could, I guess."

Chance sighed heavily and stared at his feet. For a long time, he said nothing, but eventually, he lifted his gaze and stared at the big man once more. "So what's this about the plans?"

A smile flitted across Jarvis's lips. Chance frowned darkly, and he reverted to a somber seriousness. "They arrived about an hour ago, while you were asleep."

"From Mason?"

"Initially, yes. I didn't recognize the man who slipped it under the door, but he was dressed as a cleaner."

Chance glanced at the doorway. There were possibly another twenty minutes before the orderlies arrived to open the ward doors.

"Let's have a look."

The plans proved to be much smaller than Chance had anticipated. The paper that Jarvis supplied was only A4, a photocopy of the original blueprint. As such, finer details were impossible to decipher, as were any of the writings. What they were left with was a generalized floorplan. Far from what he had expected, but still better than nothing. For ten minutes, Chance examined the paper without comment.

"There might be a way."

"Through the sewers?" asked Jarvis.

"What?" Chance looked at the map again. "Where are the sewers?"

"Aren't there always sewers?"

Chance stared at the big man, finally shaking his head when he realized the question was serious. "No, we won't be going through the sewers."

"Then how will we escape?"

Chance gave him a tight grin. "I'll let you know."

* * * *

"You survived."

Betsy was tearing apart a single leaf, taking her time with it.

"Are you surprised?" Chance asked.

"Yes," she replied bluntly. "You weren't supposed to." She dropped the leaf and looked around on the lawn for another. "But that is your talent, isn't it?"

"What do you mean?" Chance glanced around, trying to appear casual, but feeling like he was failing miserably. He wondered how many of the orderlies dotted around were in the employ of Howard Mason.

"You don't fit into…." She appeared to struggle to find the words to use. "It's impossible to predict the outcome of anything you become involved in. You're like lightning."

"I don't feel like lightning."

"Oh, but you are, silly." Betsy spotted another leaf and pounced on it. With infinite delicacy, she began to tear along the lines of the leaf's veins. "Lightning can kill, but it can also cleanse. What kind of lightning will you be this time around, I wonder." She paused her tearing and looked up into his eyes. "Did you and Jarvis make up?"

Chance contemplated asking how she knew they'd been fighting, but figured it would take too long. "I guess so."

She nodded and resumed tearing the leaf into strands. "That's good. He needs you. More than you know."

"What for?"

"How would I know?" Betsy asked, casting him an askew glance. "Seriously, Chance. Sometimes you say the weirdest things."

Something flickered in the corner of Chance's vision, and he turned. Nothing out of the ordinary seemed to be there, yet Chance couldn't shake the feeling he had just missed something.

"Hey, what's up?"

Chance looked back around and saw Jarvis approaching. "Oh, I was just talking with Betsy."

"Where is she?" Jarvis asked, gazing around.

Chance turned back, but Betsy had vanished, leaving him alone with Jarvis on the edge of the garden. He looked everywhere, but the woman was nowhere to be seen.

"You all right?" Jarvis asked hesitantly.

"She was right here," Chance assured him, stabbing his hand toward where Betsy had been standing. "Surely you must have seen her."

Jarvis shook his head. "You were standing here alone the whole time. I thought you were enjoying the sun or –" he lowered his voice conspiratorially, "— thinking about the plan. A plan you haven't really told me about, by the way."

"You've already betrayed me once, Jarvis. I'm not likely to tell you too much from now on, okay?"

"Well, that makes sense." The big man hardly seemed offended.

"I'm not even going to ask if you're still reporting back to Howard Mason on my movements." Despite his words, Chance paused expectantly.

"I would lie to you, but there seems little point. Anyway, he hasn't asked me for anything since your meeting; perhaps he knows you won't relay any information to me."

Chance peered around at the other patients and orderlies scattered throughout the garden. Part of him hoped to see Betsy wandering among their ranks, but the mysterious woman remained nowhere to be seen. "Or maybe he has other sources."

"No doubt. You never heard of Mason in here because he didn't want you to know. His reach extends throughout the asylum and beyond."

"Then why doesn't he break himself out?"

Jarvis shrugged. "He probably could if he wanted to, but you imagine the manhunt. And then there's the fact he's almost dead. Perhaps he likes controlling people."

"I think he does," Chance agreed, recalling the hunger in the old man's eyes. "Maybe such manipulation is another form of cannibalism." He looked around once more. "Are you sure you never saw Betsy?"

"Sure as shit stains sheets," grunted Jarvis, picking his nose. "As a matter of fact, I haven't seen her for ages. Are you sure it was her? I mean, there are other women in here, not just the flower child."

"No, it was her. Remind me to ask Doctor Smith when we have therapy."

"Speaking of which..." Jarvis nodded toward the orderlies, who were quietly ushering patients back toward the building.

Chance grimaced. Sitting through something as tedious as group therapy gnawed at him like teeth on a bone. Suddenly, an image of Howard Mason's ridiculously perfect teeth chewing the meat off the thigh of one of his contemporaries flashed through Chance's mind. Chance shuddered.

"What have I gotten myself into?" he muttered.

"You've made a deal with the Devil, just like me," Jarvis mused. The two began walking toward the beckoning doorway. "All you can hope is to escape with your soul intact."

* * * *

"Excuse me, Doctor. But do you know where Betsy Burrows is?"

Therapy had proceeded almost exactly as Chance had expected. Lots of words were flung around the group, much like feces being hurled between chimpanzees. Some of the words stuck, most just made a mess.

Doctor Smith stared at him. "How do *you* know Betsy Burrows?"

Chance shrugged. "We talk sometimes."

"Do you remember beyond your amnesia?"

"No." Pausing, Chance glanced around, wondering if something was happening without his knowledge. The other patients were shuffling out of the room, leaving the two of them alone. Nothing seemed amiss. "What are you talking about, Doctor?"

"I'm not sure how much I can safely discuss with you, Chance. You need to fill me in a bit more before I can disclose anything about Betsy. You're saying you've had conversations with her since your memory block, is that correct?"

"Yeah, sure. Out in the garden. What's wrong with that?"

"And what did the two of you discuss? Anything out of the ordinary?"

"Pretty much everything was out of the ordinary." Chance walked over and sat down on one of the chairs scattered as the group left. "I have a feeling we might be here for some time."

Doctor Smith sat opposite him. "I need specifics here, Chance. Was Betsy one of the women you saw killed?"

"Of course not! She's one of the other patients here. We talk sometimes. She seems to know me from before… I forgot everything, I guess."

Doctor Smith's eyes peered into him, but the man's expression remained unreadable. "What did she claim to know about you?"

"She was the one who told me my last name." Chance scratched his head. "She also knew about the women I saw killed."

Doctor Smith wrote something down on his clipboard. Chance couldn't read what it said.

"She told me about her grandmother," Chance continued. "She called her Oma. Apparently, the old woman liked chrysanthemums. I figured that had something to do with her always tearing loose the flowers."

"There are no chrysanthemum bushes here."

"But I'm sure…." Chance recalled the white flowers spattered with Betsy's blood. "It doesn't matter. What's all this about anyway, Doctor? All I asked is if you knew where she was."

Doctor Smith peered at him over his wire-framed glasses. "Betsy Burrows has been in a coma for some weeks, Chance. She's locked away from the general population in the emergency medical wing. There's no way you could have seen her since the onset of your amnesia."

For several moments, Chance stared at the Doctor, waiting for some kind of punchline. When nothing came, he scowled at the man. "That's not true. I've seen her out in the garden at least three or four times."

"Are you sure she wasn't one of your hallucinations?"

"Wha – no, she was as real as you are."

Doctor Smith looked back at his clipboard. "How long since you took any medication, Chance? I know it's been given to you, but I also know a nurse discovered one of your tablets sitting in the bottom of your toilet bowl."

"I…." He contemplated lying and then thought better of it. "They make my head fuzzy. Right now I need to remain clear-headed."

"And do you believe you are thinking clearly, Chance? You have been having conversations with a woman you definitely cannot have seen. How many other things have you done that could not possibly have happened?"

Chance rubbed a hand through his hair; the memory of wandering the corridors only to end up in Ward Sigma returned to haunt him. Had he really met Howard Mason, or had that been a hallucination, too? Suddenly, Chance desperately needed to see the hospital plans, to feel the grittiness of the paper in his hands.

"Can I leave, Doctor?"

Doctor Smith plainly did not want him to go, but it appeared he could find no reason to make him stay. "Yes, okay, but you're to begin taking your medication again immediately. I don't want to have to give it to you intravenously."

“Sure, no problem.” Chance would have to find a better hiding spot for his unused pills. Perhaps Jarvis would swallow them in recompense for spying on his activities.

Chance stood up to leave, but the world tilted. He snatched at the back of the chair, steadying himself.

“Are you all right, Chance?” The doctor’s words sounded like they were echoing down a long hallway.

“Yes, I’m –”

The floor whooshed up, but before Chance felt any impact, a door opened, and he stepped through.

For several moments, he stood motionless, unsure of what had just happened. He turned and glanced over his shoulder. A street, bathed in midmorning sunlight, stretched beyond the frame of a door. He had never seen the setting before – at least not that he knew of.

“Is everything all right, Doctor Petrov?”

He turned back. A man, his face vaguely familiar, was staring at Chance.

“Are you talking to me?” asked Chance.

The man nodded, a slight frown creasing his brows. “Unless there’s another Sylvia Petrov in here.” The man stepped forward and offered his hand. Chance shook it uncertainly. “I trust you didn’t have any trouble finding the place.”

“Sylvia Petrov,” Chance murmured. “The parapsychologist.”

He recalled the large Russian woman who had discussed the Sixth Plane with him. For him to have slipped into her consciousness seemed far from coincidental.

"Are you sure you're all right?" the man asked. He was a slim man in his early thirties wearing slacks and a white shirt hanging loose outside the pants. The man's dark hair receded somewhat, but rather than try to conceal it, he swept the remaining strands straight back, as though proclaiming his baldness for the world to see. The familiarity of his appearance refused to flee, no matter what Chance did to fight it. He, or rather Sylvia, knew this person, but Chance couldn't place where from.

"I… no, I'm sorry," replied Chance. "I had no trouble finding the place, Mister…?"

"It's me. Warren." He peered at her closely. "Are you having one of your psychic episodes?"

The surprise of discovering the stoic woman might possess psychic abilities rocked Chance, but he fought hard to keep the astonishment from his face.

"Something like that."

"Well, come inside and have some iced tea. That always relieves the headaches you suffer after such visions, am I right? I have the kind you like, with peach."

"That would be pleasant."

Chance hated peach iced tea.

He followed the man named Warren through the house, down a corridor, and into a kitchen. The room was a simple affair, with a wooden table surrounded by four chairs off to the left, a four-burner dropped into the cooktop, an oven beneath it. The fridge was mid-sized, the variety you might find in an apartment – or the house of a man who lived alone. Warren moved to it and removed a large porcelain jug. He filled two glasses with ice from the freezer, and then filled them with peach iced tea.

"Please sit," the man requested. "I need to know about the man you saw in the psychiatric hospital. Chance Ripley, wasn't it?"

Chance's ears instantly perked up. "What about him?"

The man frowned. "You sounded excited on the phone, telling me he might be the one you have been searching for."

Taking the proffered glass of iced tea, Chance sipped it, more to delay answering than anything. "What else did I say?"

"You claimed he could slip into the Sixth Plane without narcotics – at least you thought that was the case. Has something changed?"

Chance shook his head slowly. "No, that all seems to remain the same."

Something suddenly tugged on his consciousness and the world swirled. Nausea swamped Chance, and he gripped the edge of the table, battling to contain a strong sense of vertigo.

"Say nothing more, Warren!" The words tore from Chance's lips, or rather the lips of Sylvia Petrov, without his control. "He has taken over my consciousness. I cannot hold him back. Even now, he regains control –"

The dizziness faded, and Chance straightened in the chair. The man named Warren stared at him, open-mouthed, and

Chance wondered how much of a physical transformation had taken place. Not of skin, clearly, but of countenance and bearing. Judging by the man's reaction, it was a noticeable change. Warren stood up swiftly and held the jug in front of him as if for protection.

Chance held up his hands in what he hoped was a sign of surrender. "Hey, it's okay. I don't know how this has happened." The words that slipped from his lips were tinged with a Russian accent. "I fell over, and then I was standing in your doorway."

Warren's eyes narrowed. "Yet you didn't tell me who you were. You sought to deceive me."

"Not intentionally." Chance slowly stood. The chair scraped on the wooden floor. "Okay, maybe intentionally. But I had no idea who you were, or if I could trust you."

"Leave Doctor Petrov now," he pleaded. "She is innocent, and doesn't deserve to be treated in such a way."

"I wish I could," Chance assured him. "But it's not that simple. I have no control over this… phenomenon. It pulls me whichever way it wants, and I have no say. Usually, I end up in other people's bodies, but other things have also happened."

"What other things?" asked Warren, placing the jug down on the countertop.

Chance wasn't sure he could trust this man, but the need to discuss his problems overwhelmed any sense of caution. "I walked through walls."

"You *what*?"

Chance sighed. "Well, not exactly that. I was walking down a maze of corridors, and suddenly found myself in a library in another city. I no sooner found my bearings, and then I was standing on a beach. Finally, I was deposited in a ward I could have never reached on my own, passing through checkpoints and security gates."

"You phantom walked?"

"I don't know. Is that what you call it?"

Warren's caution seemed to lower slightly. "What you are currently doing at this moment is called *psychic* walking. It is possible for those who can reach the Sixth Plane. In the most simplistic terms, your spirit reaches out and possesses another's body for a short period of time. Your approach to the art is cumbersome and brutish, as unacceptable as rape in the case where such invasion is intentional." His eyes narrowed. "But in this instance, I do not think you are to blame. Your spirit is flitting out on its own accord and latching onto certain people – usually, the victims of murder – shortly before they are killed. I suppose such an absence of being could be described as a blessing." He seemed to chew over the problem. Finally, his eyes lifted, his face set with grim determination. "And if that is the case, if you truly are not in control, Doctor Petrov would want me to find out as much information as possible about what you are experiencing."

"So what's this phantom walking? You indicated that it was different to psychic walking."

The man stared at him for some time. "Please, sit."

Chance slipped back into the chair at the table. Warren came over hesitantly, and when Chance didn't lurch up to attack him, the man sat down opposite him.

"Well?" Chance asked. "I'm not sure how much time I'll have here."

"Phantom walking is when your entire physical form reaches the Sixth Plane. Very few people in history have accomplished such a feat, and yet, if what you tell me is true, you seem to have done it without intention."

"It's not very good if I somehow wander into the wrong area of the asylum, you know. There are some pretty rotten people in there." The memory of Howard Mason's teeth flitted through his mind. "The kind who like to eat people."

Warren's face blanched. "Dear Lord."

"Exactly. So, is there a way I can control this ability?"

Blowing out a heavy breath, Warren continued. "Who would know? Perhaps Sylvia could tell you if another phantom walker exists on the planet, but she has never mentioned it to me. Maybe you should try to organize another meeting with her in the hospital."

"Yeah, sure. After I've possessed her body, I'm confident she'll just love to come at my beck and call."

"Don't fret about that. Although from her side, I have no doubt she feels this is an invasion, she will ultimately understand the scientific possibilities of studying your case further. If you truly have no control over this latent talent, you can hardly be held accountable, can you?"

"You don't know many women, do you, Warren?"

A shadow flitted from the corner of Chance's vision. He turned to look, but a hand grabbed him by the hair and banged his face on the kitchen table. A short cry sounded, and when Chance lifted his dazed head, he saw a knife had been plunged through the center of Warren's chest. Blood bubbled from the man's mouth.

"Is this her?" murmured a deep voice. Bull.

Chance turned to his right, Sylvia's right, and saw the hulking man, his face scarred with the memory of a horrendous burn. Blood splattered up his right arm, and flecks of crimson dotted his right cheek. Finally, Bull nodded, as if responding to a statement only he could hear. Lunging forward, he grabbed Chance by Sylvia's hair once more and effortlessly lifted him from the chair. With a tremendous hurl, Bull launched Sylvia's body through the air to crash headfirst into the fridge. The door crumpled under the impact.

"You should not be messing with us, little man."

In his dazed state, it took Chance a moment to realize the scarred killer was referring to him. "What do you mean?"

"We know you have talked. FBI asked you questions, and you gave them answers."

Fight him.

The plea emanated from within Chance, and it took him a moment to realize the appeal came from Sylvia Petrov herself.

I don't know how, Chance protested.

Sylvia Petrov faded, leaving him alone on the floor, staring up at Bull. The brutish figure leaned down, gripped the knife jutting from Warren's chest, and wrenched it clear.

"Every person you come close to will die," grunted Bull. "And you will eventually give yourself up to us to save them." His eyes gleamed. "You will have no choice."

The big man stepped closer. Chance scurried backward on the tiling, but only ended up in the corner of the kitchen with nowhere to go. His heart – Sylvia's heart – pounded in his chest.

A presence formed in his mind. At first, Chance couldn't recognize who it was, but then the unmistakable tinge of Sylvia wafted through. If possible, his heart beat even faster. A horrendous headache formed between his brows. It tore at the inside of his cranium, the pain a shackled beast turning feral, gnashing and howling, fighting to break loose. Chance screamed, and the sound echoed through his skull.

Bull lunged down. The bloodied knife plunged toward Chance's chest.

Time slowed. It could only have been for the briefest of heartbeats, but clarity shone through the scene with stunning vividness. Chance's hand came up, his palm out. The knife tip touched his ribs.

Bull hurtled backward. The scarred man flew through the air, toward the front door, finally crashing to the ground, stunned. The knife clattered away, beyond his reach. For a moment, the two stared at each other, both stunned, eyes wide.

"It *is* you," he murmured.

The big man leaped to his feet and sprinted out the front door.

Without pause, the scene changed. Chance was sitting in a chair, and upon looking around, saw he was back in Doctor Smith's office. The doctor himself was standing over Chance, a concerned expression plastered across his face.

"How long was I away?" Chance gasped.

"Away where?" asked the doctor. "You tripped over, and I helped you to sit. What are you talking about?"

Chance blew out a long breath, gathered his thoughts, and then said, "You need to call Doctor Sylvia Petrov." He thought about it, realizing a flaw in his reasoning. "If her cell phone doesn't answer, send the police around to her friend Warren's house immediately."

Doctor Smith held up a placating hand. "Hold on for a moment, Chance. What's going on?"

"One of the Trinity killers just tried to murder her. I'm pretty sure he managed to kill Warren. I managed to scare the killer off, but he might return to finish the job. Every second you stare at me like that could be a second less she has to live. *Call her now!*"

Chance's last phrase was pronounced so forcefully that Doctor Smith barely hesitated. He nodded and pulled a cell phone from his pocket. Rummaging through his list of phone contacts, the doctor finally paused and pressed call.

"Yes, Doctor Petrov, is that…?" Doctor Smith paused, listening. Chance thought he could hear sobbing on the other end of the line. The doctor glanced up at Chance, his expression worried. "Okay, I understand. Have you called the police?" Another pause as she answered. Doctor Smith nodded several times. "All right, I'll… yes, I'll tell him that. Is there anything else I can do? Should I call an ambulance? No? Uh huh, I can hear them now. Goodbye, Doctor Petrov."

"What did she say?" asked Chance once he'd hung up.

Doctor Smith breathed a heavy sigh and ran a hand through his hair, sitting down in the chair opposite Chance. He stared at the phone for several moments, his eyes blinking rapidly. Eventually, he looked up, his expression bemused.

"Doctor Petrov has asked me to thank you… for saving her life."

CHAPTER XIV

"Doctor Petrov is under protective custody." Doctor Smith paused, looking around the garden. "I don't suppose you've had a chat with Betsy lately, have you?"

Chance huffed lightly. "Not since you told me she was in a coma."

"Would you like to visit her?"

Cautiously, Chance turned. He studied the doctor, searching for any sign of deceit, but the man appeared genuine. "Why would you let me see her?"

Smith shrugged. "It can't really hurt, can it?" But something in his expression stated there was an underlying reason, something the doctor wasn't relaying.

Contemplating the potential benefits, Chance eventually nodded. "Sure, I'd like to go and say hi. Why not?" In his mind, he yearned to see the physical form of the woman he had spoken to if only to confirm that the doctor was not lying.

Doctor Smith led Chance through Ward Z, through to the connecting garden, and then into the main building. At the junction between Sigma and Gamma, the doctor turned right, leading them into Ward G.

"Is this the hospital ward?" Chance asked.

Doctor Smith nodded. "The entire facility is technically a hospital, but here is where we keep those in need of permanent physical care."

Chance yearned to bring up Howard Mason, the living corpse lying in the basement of Ward A, but decided to keep that card close to his chest. Who knew what would happen if he disclosed what was transpiring over there? Doctor Smith seemed like he was on the level... for the most part. Letting him know that a lunatic partial to devouring human body parts was living in the lap of luxury in the midst of the most secure ward in the institute would likely send him investigating. Such an investigation could not possibly end well for the doctor. Not to mention what might happen to Chance for divulging the information in the first place.

He peered into the rooms as they passed, noting the heavy machinery around most beds, bulky and noisy contraptions, nothing like the sophisticated and near-noiseless contraptions surrounding Howard Mason. These were functional machines designed to monitor and assist those who needed it most. Some of the patients peered out curiously as Chance passed. Differing expressions creased their features, most weak and in pain, some blank and cold, while others, a quiet few, stared out vehemently, violence apparent in their natures. On two occasions, Chance saw the restraint straps on the sides of the hospital beds had been put to use, detaining thrashing men.

Chance and the doctor remained silent during the walk. Doctor Smith wore an expression of quiet dignity while striding past the rooms, though Chance sensed a trickle of sorrow weeping from the man. He was a healer, and to be in the midst of so much pain he could not treat left him feeling somewhat lost. Perhaps Chance was assuming things, but after weeks of therapy with the man, he was beginning to get a sense of him, of what drove him to follow the career path he did. Doctor Smith was intelligent and caring, fully capable of a job that undoubtedly paid much more than an asylum could ever hope to provide. No, he was here for his own reasons, and those reasons remained a mystery.

"In here, Chance."

Chance had been so locked in his own thoughts he hadn't realized the doctor had stopped. The man indicated a room, a single bed within it. Cautiously, feeling as timid as a cat, Chance approached the bed. Betsy laid unconscious on the mattress. A ventilator tube vanished down her throat, her chest rising and falling in time with the soft beep emanating from the machine to which it was attached. The other machinery around her bed seemed minimal compared to some of the rooms they had passed on the journey here. A heart monitor was attached to the tip of her index finger, the display sitting on wheels beside her bed, rhythmic blips flickering across the screen.

Slowly, as if afraid to wake her, Chance approached the bed. Betsy's hair was no longer chopped short; the dark curls framing her face made her appear more serene. Chance pulled over a chair and sat beside the bed, hesitantly reaching toward Betsy's hand. He paused, looked back over his shoulder as if to gain permission from Doctor Smith. The doctor nodded, and he reached forward once more, his fingers finally gripping Betsy's.

"Um, hi –"

There was no sensation of movement. One moment, Chance sat beside the bed, but the next he was on a high mountaintop, standing upon a flat rocky platform. Snow coated the ground, blanketing every surface in a thick white layer, yet Chance felt no chill. No warmth, either, he noticed. Clouds licked the sky, seemingly within reach, and Chance yearned to stretch out toward them, but he found his hand gripped by something else. Turning, he looked into the tawny gaze of the woman beside whose bed he had just been sitting.

"Betsy?" he breathed.

The yellowish-brown eyes crinkled, and for the first time, Chance saw no madness within them. "I knew you would come."

"How…? What's going on?"

"You're in here with me," said Betsy. "This is so much easier than me trying to travel through the fog to speak to you. Much less confusing too, without all that extra baggage."

"Baggage?"

"The insanity I dragged around when I was alive." She chuckled. "Well, I guess I'm still alive, for now at least, but when I visited you out there, tapped into your mind, I drew all my bad habits along with me. The Betsy Burrows you know is a rather confused young lass, I must confess. I'm amazed I was able to tell you all that I did."

"You mean about Ward Alpha? Well, you could have been a bit clearer about that."

She shrugged. "In the end, I doubt it would have made any difference. That man wanted to get his claws into you, one way or another. At least you survived the encounter."

"Are you… psychic?"

Betsy giggled. "Not in the slightest. At least I don't think I am. But in here," she waved a hand around, "well, the rules seem different. It's like I can glimpse through windows from the street on a foggy night."

"What about when you visited me in the garden?"

She shook her head. "I wasn't visiting you, Chance. You were drawing me out. At least I assume it was you. And don't even think of asking me how you did it. One moment I was alone and sane, and the next I'd be crazy Betsy once again, rambling about flowers and other nonsense." A small chuckle escaped, but it sounded heavily laced with sorrow. "I tried to tell you what I'd seen through those windows, but my words always came out jumbled and incoherent."

"Is there anything else you've seen? Anything you can tell me now?"

Betsy peered towards the horizon. Chance followed her gaze, ignoring the drop so close to where he stood. The sky seemed unmarred, but on closer inspection, he saw something hovering in the distance. At first, it looked like a singular dot in the sky, but after a moment, it split into three separate smudges.

"What are they?" he asked.

"Trinity." Betsy's voice was soft, bereft of any emotion. "They're drawn to you. Whenever you slip into this realm, they will race toward you, no matter how far the distance."

Chance squinted. "How can they hover in the air like that?"

"It's not air, silly." She lifted their hands, their fingers still entwined. "No more than this is flesh. They manipulate this world to fit their purposes. I think it is an innate skill, something they may not even be conscious of."

"What do you mean?"

"I don't think they realize we see them like this. Wherever they are in the world, they just feel a pull toward you and hunger to reach you by whatever means possible. This," she indicated the rapidly approaching figures, "is how we see them on the Sixth Plane."

"You know of the Sixth Plane?" Chance gasped. "Does that mean it's real?"

Betsy giggled and leaned in close. "Where do you think you're standing?"

Chance glanced around. Everything seemed ridiculously tangible to his eyes; he had expected something more nebulous. "What is the Sixth Plane? Doctor Petrov touched on it, but I don't think she has a clear understanding of what this place truly is."

"You might as well ask me what makes up the sun," replied Betsy. "I only know what I've seen. Just think that your consciousness has taken a step sideways into a realm where anything is possible if you know how to manipulate your environment."

"So I could make them fall from the sky?"

Betsy shrugged. "Try it and find out."

Facing the three approaching dots, Chance focused his thoughts, channeling every fiber of energy, willing Trinity to crash into the valley a mile below. He strained for all he was worth, sweat – or the equivalent of sweat – beading on his forehead, but to no avail.

"Are you done?"

Chance turned toward her. "I guess. How do I do it?"

Betsy's giggle lightened the air. "You're asking me? I don't even know how I ended up here. One minute I walked toward the garden, the next I was locked in my own creation."

"But you told me you see windows."

"Things appear from time to time. I don't know how long I've been here, but it feels like years. Once every few months, a vision will appear, like a smudge in the air. Sometimes, like when I'm with you in the garden, it's quite clear. Unfortunately, it seems the translation from my side to yours ends up scrambled. I blame you." She tittered playfully. "The other visions are like a smudged crayon drawing at the bottom of a muddy puddle. I saw you entering Ward A, a huge shadow hanging over you, like a dark cloud, or death, and I knew you'd be in danger."

"But what do we do about *them*?" Chance asked, pointing. The three figures had halved the distance. He could now see that each sported a huge set of black wings.

"I have no idea," Betsy responded. She looked around. "But I think their connection is to you, not me. If you escape, their tethers will snap, and they'll hold no power here."

"That's one hell of an assumption." Chance bit his lower lip, thinking. "So what do I do? Is it like a dream, where if I jump off I'll wake up before I hit the ground?"

Betsy peered over the edge of the craggy lip. Her lip curled. "If that's something you want to risk, go for it."

"You don't sound too confident."

"I'm not. It seems like a stupid thing to do."

Chance threw his hands in the air. "What other option do I have?" He peered desperately toward the three figures. They were so close now that he could see they were not even human. The three appeared reptilian, dark scales covering them from their heads to their long whip-like tails. Their faces resembled those of lizards or snakes, each with jet black eyes. Soulless eyes. They bore arms and legs like a human, but the arms seemed longer, the same length as the legs – better for chasing down prey by running on all fours, Chance guessed.

"Are they a representation of what they think they are, or what I imagine them to be?" asked Chance.

Betsy frowned. "I have no idea. But if it is as I surmised, they have no actual knowledge of being here and are merely drawn to you telepathically. It would seem, then, that their appearances derive from… you."

"There must be a way I can use that." Chance murmured. He peered around, searching for some kind of escape. Not even the semblance of a path led from the stone platform. But why would it if this were all a creation of his mind?

He turned slowly, peering back at Betsy. This wasn't a creation of his mind, but of hers. She had been here ever since falling into her coma, and as such, he had no control over what was going on.

"You need to get us out of here, Betsy."

Her gaze clouded. Chance received the distinct impression she could no longer see him, that she was peering at something else, far away. Soon, her eyes snapped back into focus, and she gave out a small gasp.

"What happened?" Chance demanded.

She looked him up and down as though unsure if he were real or not. "Take the pants."

"What pants?" he asked with a frown.

"You won't want to, but you'll have to. If you don't, you'll be caught, and it will all be for nothing."

"I don't know what you're talking about, Betsy."

The mention of her name seemed to clear her mind a bit. "I saw… one of the windows I told you about. Don't ask me what it means."

"Okay, fine," Chance acceded. "But right now you need to do something about them!"

"What are you talking about?"

Chance glanced back toward Trinity; the beasts were now so close he could hear their stertorous breathing rasping in and out of their beak-like maws.

"This is your creation, not mine. I'm just a visitor."

Betsy blinked several times and looked around once more. "I don't know...."

"You have to try, or they will kill us both. I can't do anything here, even if I knew how to. This is your world, your creation."

"How...?"

"Just do it!" Chance was practically shouting. The whooshing of the beasts' wings drew ever closer. He could almost hear them hissing in his ears.

"But Chance, I didn't arrive on this mountain until I saw you."

The words sunk icy daggers into Chance's flesh. He had assumed that Betsy had been atop the mountain the entire time, never imagining he had been the one to drag *her* consciousness here.

Time was up, he had no more to waste on suppositions. He didn't even glance at the trio of killers approaching, didn't look over at Betsy. Without another word, Chance sprinted toward the edge of the rocky platform and leaped off.

Chance skidded face-first across the white tiles beside Betsy's bed. He heard Doctor Smith cry out in surprise. Footsteps rushed to his side. Before his shock had receded, hands were helping him to stand. Heaving in a deep breath, Chance peered around.

"Is this the real world?" he gasped.

Doctor Smith loomed in front of his face. Hands pushed him down into a chair. The doctor flashed a light into his eyes and asked what had just happened.

"I was speaking to Betsy," Chance murmured.

The doctor pocketed the penlight. He motioned to a nurse to bring over a chair, and then sat opposite Chance. "What are you talking about?"

"I held her hand, and then we were together." He looked over at the bed, at the poor comatose figure with her head propped up by pillows and a tube running down her throat. "She's alive in there. She's on the Sixth Plane. We met on a mountaintop and… Trinity came for us."

"Trinity?" You mean the three killers?"

Chance nodded. "It all happened so quickly. I didn't have time to think; I just reacted. I jumped off a cliff and ended up back here."

Doctor Smith leaned in close. "But is here where you think it is?"

Chance peered at the man quizzically. Before he could form a question, the doctor gripped him, his fingers stretching and wrapping all the way around Chance's chest like surging roots. They crushed his arms to his sides, squeezed the air from his lungs. The doctor stood, lifting Chance effortlessly from the chair, his feet dangling several inches above the tiling.

"You cannot escape us so easily," the doctor hissed.

Beyond him, Chance saw the nurse twitch and morph into the figure of Siren. The orderly standing near the door blurred, becoming Bull, hulking and hideously scarred.

Sores spread across the doctor's cheeks, becoming the third killer. Chance heaved and thrashed, to no avail. Pestilence gripped him, still wearing the doctor's white coat.

"We know where you hide. Mount Sinai Mental Refuge will offer no refuge. We are coming."

Pestilence's mouth opened impossibly wide. His perfect teeth, so similar to those of his father, morphed into sharpened fangs. With a viper-fast strike, he chomped over Chance's head.

CHAPTER XV

A veil parted.

Chance's scream had hardly left his mouth before he realized the world had changed once more. No longer was he in the hospital ward. In fact, nothing about the scene appeared familiar. He blinked several times and looked around. Hundreds of strangers surrounded him, but only a few paid him any attention, their expressions curious, but unwilling to become involved.

"What in the world…?" Chance murmured.

The sun had set, replaced by a skyline of neon stars. What time had it been when he'd visited Betsy? Chance took in the bright lights and huge flashing billboards affixed to towering skyscrapers. Yellow Cabs honked and bustled through traffic. Away to his left a man in a superhero suit waved to passers-by to come and have a photo with him.

"First time in Times Square?" a voice asked.

Chance jumped around, his eyes wide. A cop stood several feet away, his expression curious. His hand rested casually on his belt, close to his gun, but far enough away to have been a typical stance. The man was probably in his early forties, though his gray hair aged him significantly.

"Times Square?" Chance murmured, glancing around once more. He looked down at his body, expecting to see an unfamiliar form wearing a dress, perhaps heels. But the figure he saw was his own, still sporting the hospital garb he was now so used to. The same rubber-soled shoes covered his feet. "How in the world did I get here?"

"Not sure, bud. I heard you scream and turned around, and you were there." He looked Chance up and down. "Interesting costume. Who are you supposed to be?"

Chance glanced over at the superhero, noting that several others were similarly costumed. Some were dressed as cartoon characters; others appeared to be from video games.

"I'm… Jack Nicholson. From *One Flew Over the Cuckoo's Nest.*"

The cop frowned, and then shrugged. "Hey, at least you're original. Try to keep the screaming to a minimum, though, okay. It tends to put the tourists on edge." The man looked around the square. "I've seen some of these guys for years." He pointed toward a figure in a dingy red costume. "Keep an eye on Mexican Spiderman over there; he tends to get a bit territorial with you new guys. And those two Minions are anything but happy-go-lucky."

"Thanks for the advice," Chance murmured.

"And don't harass the tourists too much. Read the signs around the place regarding how you lot are supposed to behave, and we won't have a problem."

"I'll do that."

The cop looked him up and down once more. "Hey, what was that character's name, the one you're portraying?"

"Uh.... You know what? I forget." Chance felt a stupid grin stretching his lips, a combination of embarrassment and fear of being caught out. "It'll come to me later, though."

Eyes narrowing, the cop nodded slowly. "Sure it will. See you later."

Chance turned and walked away, fighting hard to control the urge to run. He could feel the police officer's eyes burning into his back, but he fought hard to remain as calm as possible. For a moment, he contemplated playing up to the bystanders, as the other character players were, but after noticing a few odd looks in his direction, he decided such a move wasn't in his best interests. Instead, he tried his best to meld with the crowd of onlookers, meandering through large groups until he felt sure he'd slipped beyond the curious cop's sightline.

Looking around, Chance rubbed his chin. How in the world had he arrived here in his own body? For he had no doubt it was his body. Apart from the hospital garb, he still had the tag around his wrist identifying him as a patient. His hands were his, the fingernails as familiar as his reflection in a mirror. That said, he turned to the nearest window and glimpsed his reflection, confirming what he had already deduced. His own tired and worried eyes stared back at him from the glass.

Part of him hoped he might somehow shift back to the safety of the asylum. The real world held too many unknowns for the moment. But such thinking was foolish. He had been planning to escape anyway; this happenstance had merely expedited the process.

Special Agent Broachford had offered to help him. He tried to remember what the man had told him to do if he managed to escape.

"I need to call the FBI," Chance murmured. "What was the name he gave me? It was his brother-in-law. Frank… something."

Great. That would surely hold up under scrutiny. Was it Frank Broachford? No, that didn't sound right.

As he pondered the question, another part of Chance's mind worried about how to make the call in the first place. Would the FBI accept it if he reversed the charges? Did such calls even exist anymore? It had been so long since Chance had used a payphone that he honestly had no idea. He turned around, watching the character actors for some time, wondering if he could possibly emulate one of them long enough to earn sufficient money for a phone call. Finally, he shook his head. His costume sucked, his acting sucked, and from what he could tell, tourists were avoiding the oddly-garbed people anyway, staring at them from a safe distance, far enough away to retreat should one approach them to request money for the photo they just took.

Above all, one worry floated through his consciousness like a cloud of noxious vapors. Was Chance likely to vanish from here and end up someplace else without warning? He had no control over whatever powers he seemed to be exhibiting.

Would he suddenly transport to the bottom of the ocean without meaning to? Just the thought made him sick to his stomach.

Keep moving. One step after another.

First, he needed to acquire some clothes that made him stand out a bit less. He had no idea how far from Manhattan the asylum had been. If the call went out that a patient had escaped from a secure mental facility somewhere close to the city, no doubt the officer who had been so full of advice would come gunning for him with all his boys in blue hot on his tail.

Chance crossed the street and ducked down an alley. Usually the last place he would venture, the darkened side street cloaked him, allowing him a moment of sanctuary. Where could he acquire some other clothes?

He didn't see the legs.

The next thing he knew, he tripped over the splayed-out limbs in the dark and tumbled to the alley's greasy pavement. A low groan emitted from the owner of the legs, a man's voice, and Chance scurried around, swiftly rising to his feet, prepared to flee at a moment's notice. The moaning altered, becoming incoherent grumbling, and Chance realized the speaker was drunk. Nearly comatose, from the sound of it. Soon, the muttering faded, and the alley became quiet once more. Focusing his eyes, the outline of the figure slowly became distinguishable in the shadows. He sat, slumped between trash bags, which explained the rancid odor originating from the area.

Chance looked from the shadowed figure to his hospital bedclothes and then back again, grimacing as he did. The prospect didn't appeal to him, but neither did the idea of being captured and hauled back to the asylum.

The thought of the asylum dragged with it a memory of Betsy, ostensibly from mere moments ago.

The pants.

She had told him to take the pants.

Had these been the pants Betsy had referred to? Deep down, despite yearning for it not to be so, Chance knew they were. He squatted down beside the figure.

"Hey, buddy," Chance muttered, nudging the man's leg with his knuckles. The last thing he wanted was to get the smell on his palms.

The comatose figure grunted and shifted to the side. Chance huffed and stood, wondering what to do.

"I tell you what," he eventually said. "I'll give you these fancy, *clean* clothes in exchange for what you're wearing. How's that sound?"

The man farted in his sleep.

Nodding grimly, Chance muttered, "I'll take that as a yes."

Bending down, he began to warily remove the man's clothes.

Several moments later, Chance stood in his new outfit, trying his best not to gag. The bum hadn't been wearing any shoes, so Chance had kept his slippers from the hospital. To make them look more in mesh with his disguise, he bent down and rubbed some grime from the pavement over the white material, eventually doing a passable job of destroying any semblance of cleanliness. He daubed a few smudges of filth on his face and neck, all the while reminding himself it was this or the risk of returning to the asylum.

Miserable and reeking, Chance wandered out of the alley and back onto the street, hoping he might now at least be able to move with some degree of covertness. People tended to ignore the homeless, especially ones in as sad a condition of shabbiness as Chance portrayed. Partly there was the fear these lost souls would approach them and ask for money if they paid them the slightest morsel of attention, but worse, they might have to acknowledge a problem with their neatly ordered society. God forbid people be treated like people.

"Are you all right?"

Chance closed his eyes and cursed silently. Served him right for doubting the strength of human compassion. Looking up, he saw an older gentleman standing nearby, concern etched upon his features.

"Yeah, fine," Chance grunted, trying to sound like a street dweller.

"I run the homeless shelter a few blocks from here. Do you need somewhere to stay tonight?"

Sighing, Chance shrugged. "Sure, I guess." At least, it would give him somewhere out of the public eye where he might be able to plan some kind of strategy.

The Samaritan turned out to be a man named Wentworth Haggins, and the 'few blocks' stretched out into around nine.

Chance felt grateful with each step that he'd retained the hospital slippers.

"It's not much," said Wentworth upon arrival, his tone almost apologetic, "but you can have a hot meal and sleep on a mattress for the night. You're lucky, in a way; most evenings see this place full by seven, but for some reason tonight everyone seems to be busy elsewhere."

Probably in an alley getting their clothes stolen, thought Chance. Aloud, he said, "I'm grateful for anything you can do for me."

Wentworth stared at him for a moment. "You don't seem like our regulars. There's something about you that I can't quite place." He chuckled. "But as the Bible says, 'Judge not, lest ye be judged.'"

"Sounds good to me," replied Chance.

Nothing indicated the door was access to a homeless shelter. Chance wondered if that had something to do with the city bylaws, or whether they intended to make the place less intimidating to those they hoped to attract. For all Chance knew, Wentworth was a serial killer luring him into a trap. The thought weighed heavily on him as he stepped through the doorway.

If Chance had been expecting some kind of gimp dungeon, he was sorely disappointed. The door led through to an open entry hall with a set of stairs on the right-hand side. Wentworth led the way up the stairs, and at the top, Chance heard a low murmur of conversation.

"My wife and I live downstairs," said Wentworth, "so please respect our privacy. But if you have any problems, just press the buzzer on the wall, and one of us will come up to help. You'll see it when we get inside; it's clearly marked."

The old man led Chance to the only door on the second floor and opened it without preamble. Chance followed him into the room, and all conversation ceased as if interrupted by a thunderclap. A group of seven sat at a long table, and all turned to look at Chance as he shuffled in after Wentworth. Chance felt like the new kid at school standing up in front of the class.

"Sorry to interrupt everyone," Wentworth said, "but we have a newcomer tonight. This is... oh my, I don't believe I asked your name. How rude of me."

"I'm... uh... Jack."

Wentworth nodded amiably. "Everyone, this is Jack."

A few grunts responded, but nothing exceptionally welcoming thundered out. Conversations renewed and the group began eating again. For the first time, Chance saw that everyone had a plate in front of them. Some possessed bowls of soup, whereas others had mashed potatoes or rice with what looked to be gravy smeared over the top.

"Take a seat, Jack. There's one over there beside Lawrence. I'll go downstairs and see Mrs. Haggins to wrangle you up some food. How's that sound?"

Despite the meager nature of the meals, Chance's stomach growled at the prospect. "Thank you. That would be great."

Sitting down at the table, Chance nodded toward the other diners. They came in various states of disarray and cleanliness, but he noted that none seemed as disheveled in appearance as he did. Quiet conversations continued, none of which included Chance, so he simply sat back and waited for his food.

"So who the hell are you really?"

Glancing up, Chance noticed the talker was directing the question at him. The speaker was a tremendously large black woman, cleanly dressed, sporting an explosive afro. A large backpack sat beside her, bulging at the seams, close at hand. Her eyes were clear, and she appeared free of any intoxicants, but that made the malice in her gaze all the worse.

"I'm Jack."

She sniffed loudly, apparently unconvinced. "That so, is it?" Her eyes glowered. "Why are you wearing Slim Jimmy's gear? I'd notice the smell anywhere."

Chatter ceased, and everyone turned to hear the answer. Chance had no idea if everyone at the table knew the man named 'Slim Jimmy', but they seemed to know the woman talking, and from the looks of things, she had garnered a serious amount of respect.

"Oh… um. These are my clothes."

She shook her head. "Nuh-uh. That shirt is definitely Jimmy's. That bloodstain on the sleeve there is the one he got last week when he tried to break into that liquor shop up on 48th Street. It's even got the tear in the material. I patched him up myself."

"Ah." This had not been on the list of eventualities Chance had planned for.

The large woman stood up. "Did you kill 'im?" Her fists were clenched.

"No! He's fine."

"So you stole his clothes."

Chance cursed inwardly. "I would prefer to say that Jimmy and I came to an agreement. I swapped him what I was wearing."

"You swapped him? For that? You're shitting me."

"Not at all. I needed to…." Chance didn't know what to say. He feared a lie would be transparent to this hulking figure, a woman who lived by her wits on the street and was clearly a no bullshit sort of girl. "I was trying to avoid notice, if you know what I mean."

The woman's eyes narrowed, but surprisingly, the statement seemed to mellow her somewhat. She sat back in her chair, absent-mindedly stroked her backpack as if to check it was still there, and then nodded begrudgingly. "I think everyone at this table knows what you mean. So, you swear Slim Jimmy is still alive."

"He was rotten drunk when I left him, but still breathing."

She chuckled darkly. "That sounds like him." She picked up her fork and resumed eating. "I'll check on him tomorrow. If you're lying –"

"I'm not," Chance assured her.

"All right, then." She eyed him one more time, and then turned to her right, murmuring something to the woman sitting beside her. The older woman smiled thinly and nodded.

"Don't worry about Keisha," assured a voice beside Chance. He turned and saw the man named Lawrence, a short, balding fellow with a round face. "She tries to look out for us all. I think she feels like she's our mother or something." Lawrence slurped a spoonful of green soup; it looked like pea. "Who are you hiding from?"

Chance had begun to think the probing was over. "Just stuff, I guess. You know."

Lawrence looked up at him, his weathered face reminding Chance of an old tortoise. "No, I don't. That's why I asked."

"My old life."

"What about it?" Lawrence persisted.

"Well… I needed to get away from it. One thing led to another, the next thing I know, I'm standing in that alley with Slim Jimmy."

"Did you kill someone?"

Chance glanced around the table. Nobody else seemed to be listening. "No, I ran into…." What *had* he run into? Another dimension? "There was some trouble with people to whom I owed money. They found me, but I didn't have their money, so I was running from them. Happy?"

"Rarely," Lawrence replied, taking another loud slurp. "To whom, huh. Where'd you learn how to talk so fancy? You a rich kid looking to see what it's like slumming it? Fancy-looking haircut and all."

Chance blinked several times. He might not be able to recall how old he was, but he knew he definitely wasn't a kid. And his haircut? "How about you mind your own fucking business," he snapped.

Lawrence chuckled. "That's the first time you've sounded like one of us since walking through that door."

A straw-haired mousy woman entered, carrying a bowl of soup in one hand and a plate with some bread on it in the other. Wentworth Haggins followed close behind, his hand on her shoulder, marking her as Mrs. Haggins. She placed the food down in front of Chase with a tight smile.

"I'm sorry, but this is all we have left." She glanced at Wentworth. "I didn't expect any more visitors, so I dished out extra to the rest of the group."

"And it was much appreciated, Mrs. H," bellowed Keisha, wiping gravy from her chin. Wentworth's wife smiled embarrassedly and excused herself.

Chance picked up a spoon and began sipping the soup quietly – pea, as he'd predicted – occasionally dipping a thick slice of bread into it to soak up the juice. The soup was watery and the bread bland, but it filled his stomach, and for that, Chance felt grateful.

"There's a cot bed over there when you're ready for sleep," Wentworth advised Chance as he wiped the last traces of soup with a tiny crust of bread. He discovered a pattern of a flying blue sparrow hidden on the bottom of the bowl. Chance nodded to the older man and thanked him. Wentworth smiled and followed his wife from the room.

The meal finished up swiftly, and those around the table all gathered their plates and cutlery and rinsed them off in a large rectangular container filled with soapy water in the corner beyond the table. Gradually, they meandered off to what Chance guessed were previously claimed bunks. He slipped over to rinse his dishes, and then crept to the one remaining cot, closest to the door.

"Turn off the light, new guy," grunted Keisha.

Rising once more, Chance flicked off the switch located a few paces to his right beside the door, and then dropped back onto the cot, which groaned under his weight. He paused, holding his breath, and when the canvas bed didn't collapse, he exhaled a sigh of relief and stared into the dark, certain he wouldn't be able to drop off to sleep.

Moments later, he was snoring softly.

CHAPTER XVI

The shuffling of several feet cut through his dream.

The edges of the memory hazed almost immediately, and as Chance sat up, he felt the remainder slipping from his grasp like breath through his fingers. By the time he sat fully and looked around, Chance barely recalled even having a dream.

The rest of the group was leaving. The thin blankets had been stripped from their cots and piled in a corner, and the guests were heading past Chance's cot toward the stairs. He looked around groggily, wiping the sleep from his eyes.

"Wake up, new guy," Keisha snarled. "Rules is rules."

"What rules?"

"We leave before they wake up; it's always the way. Nothing worse than having to tell unwanted visitors to leave, is there? If they have to do that every day, chances are our little oasis here will dry up for good. So we dump our dirty blankets over there and get out before the welcome disappears."

"Did you make up that rule?" Chance asked.

Keisha glowered down at him. "And what if I did?"

"Seems like a good rule. I'll just go pee and then –"

She shook her head. “Nope. I just cleaned up in there and I ain’t going in to wipe up your splashes. Next time, wake up earlier and get in line.”

“Oh,” said Chance, rising. “Where are you heading today?”

“Why?” Her steely gaze burned into him.

“I… don’t really know what I’m doing out there, is all.”

“Didn’t think your plan through too far, did you?”

He shrugged. “There was no plan. I just ended up where I ended up without warning, and now I’m not really sure where to go. There are a couple of things I need to do, but to do them I will need some help.”

“What’s in it for me?”

Chance looked down at his filthy clothing, his only possessions in the whole world. “I don’t have anything to give you.”

“Guess you’ll have to owe me one, then.”

“Thank you,” Chance gushed.

“Don’t thank me yet, handsome. You’ve got no idea what I might ask for. Now, strip your bed and let’s get going.”

Chance tore off the bedclothes and suddenly understood why the group did such an act. The sheets were stained from the garments he wore. He grimaced as he threw the blanket into the corner, embarrassed to have soiled the bedding in such a way. Sucking the feeling down, Chance wandered out after the large woman, feeling like a gnat in the shadow of a mountain. All right, perhaps not so dramatic, but standing behind Keisha made him realize how large the woman truly was. How did someone get so big eating only soup and rice?

Keisha led Chance out to early-morning Manhattan. She didn't speak to him, but occasionally she did nod or otherwise acknowledge someone on the street. Not the ones wearing suits or carrying briefcases, Chance noted; more those who lurked in shadows, the ones at whom he feared to stare. They might have merely been other street urchins, but Chance doubted it.

"Where are we going?" Chance asked.

"I have to introduce you to someone. No doubt you'll want more favors, and I ain't got none to give. But the person I'm taking you to might."

Chance thought about the spare change he needed to call the FBI. Such a thing was hardly the kind of favor that needed a special meeting. Keisha's impassive visage didn't allow him to voice such an argument, however, so Chance merely strolled along in her wake, wondering what drama he was about to wander into next.

"Down there," Keisha ordered, indicating an alley barely wide enough for the two of them to pass through together. Chance paused.

"Aren't you coming with me?"

She refused to meet his eyes. "She wants to meet you alone."

"Wait? *Who* wants to meet me?"

"Word came in the night. Figured you wouldn't follow me if I told you, and I didn't want to have to drag you here unwillingly. But now you're here, you ain't got no choice."

Chance peered down the narrow walkway. He couldn't see anything beyond fifty feet.

"Who is this person you expect me to go and see?"

Keisha glanced left and right as if concerned someone would overhear them. "She's someone you need to show respect to, or you probably won't walk out of there again. We all tread warily around her, so mind that you do too." Keisha paused. "Don't say anything about the way she looks; she tends to get a bit sensitive about it."

Chance considered fleeing. He held no doubt that he could outrun the overweight Keisha, but the memory of those she had nodded to on their way here returned to trouble him. There had been something knowing in their silent exchanges, as though Keisha had wanted the slithery figures to recognize Chance. How far would he make it before someone stopped him, one way or another?

"Nothing else you want to tell me?" he asked.

Keisha refused to meet his eyes. "I'll wait here for you."

"*If* I make it out, right?"

She refused to answer. Chance shook his head, turned back to the walkway, and straightened his shoulders before stepping into the shadows.

The alley was straight, with high buildings rising into the clouds on either side, making Chance feel like he was walking at the bottom of an abyss. No doors or windows appeared as he wandered down, no means of escape should someone want to attack him. But nobody attacked him. The way seemed clear and remarkably clean for such an apparently vacant backstreet, making Chance wonder who cleaned it and why.

A single door awaited him at the end of the alley. Glancing back over his shoulder, Chance saw Keisha's silhouette blocking his exit, apparently peering back at him, though he couldn't be sure. The door beckoned, and he returned his gaze to it. Old paint, dark red in color, peeled from the timber. It reminded him of blood. On the right was a timeworn knob, the kind one saw on ancient church doors, black and cast from wrought iron. In the center of the door was a similarly crafted iron knocker in the shape of a grinning devil's face. The ring of the knocker dangled from between its clenched teeth.

Reaching out, Chance gripped the knocker with a sweaty palm and banged it once. The sound bounced off the walls of the alleyway. He waited, not knowing what to expect. Footsteps approached. A lock clacked open, and the door creaked inward. Chance stepped back, half expecting something horrific to leap out and attack him.

"Hello, darling."

Chance frowned, completely at odds as to how to respond. A woman towered before him; at least it appeared to be a woman. After a moment of review, however, Chance realized the figure was actually the tallest drag queen he had ever seen. Dressed in a floral mini skirt and glittering gold crop top, the Nigerian must have stood at least seven-feet-tall. Long wavy curls cascaded down over the daunting figure's shoulders, framing a face that appeared to have been blasted with both barrels of a makeup shotgun.

"What the…? Who are you?"

"My name is Kandi Flawless, darling. And you are Chance Ripley." She smiled, and Chance noticed crimson lipstick on his… no, *her*… teeth. "So, now that we're acquainted, won't you step into my parlor?"

"Said the Spider to the Fly," Chance murmured.

"Nowhere near as dramatic, I'm afraid, dear," Kandi promised him.

Chance felt his hands shaking and clenched them into fists before stepping through the doorway. Kandi closed the door behind him, the thick wood booming ominously, like a trap snapping shut.

In contrast to the flamboyant figure and the creepy doorway, however, the room he entered appeared positively bland. A single table sat in the center, two chairs facing each other on either side. Beyond it was a small kitchenette. A closed door lay at the far end of the space.

"What do you want?" asked Chance.

"I want you to relax, dear. I'm not here to eat you." Chance had a feeling that a praying mantis would have assured him of exactly the same thing had he blithely wandered into its lair. "Would you like some tea?"

"Tea? You asked me here for tea? No, something –" Chance froze. "How do you know my name? I told the people at the shelter that my name was Jack."

"You thought of Jack Nicholson since your friend in the asylum was reading *One Flew Over the Cuckoo's Nest*, I know."

Chance became uncomfortably aware that this towering figure dressed as a woman was currently standing between him and the only exit from this place. "I think I will have some tea."

Kandi smirked, her ruby red lips stretching tight. "You can't run out unless I unlock the door." She lifted a key high, dangling it in front of his eyes, and then promptly dropped it down the front of her top, between her padded theatrical breasts. "Of course, you could try to get the key on your own."

Considering Kandi's chest sat slightly higher than Chance's eyes, he doubted his chances of such an acquisition. He sighed and strolled over to the table, slumping down into one of the chairs. "Happy?"

"Infinitely." Kandi strolled over to the kitchenette and lifted a cup from the counter top. She passed the steaming teacup to Chance. "Two sugars, right?"

"How did you know?"

Kandi shrugged. "Lucky guess, sweetie." She picked up her own cup and sat opposite him. "Now, down to business."

Chance sat the tea on the table and leaned forward. "That'd be great."

"I haven't poisoned it."

Glancing back at the cup, Chance grimaced. He hated the idea of drinking a beverage prepared by someone so odd who he did not know and definitely didn't trust.

Kandi huffed, reached over, picked up his cup, and took a swift sip before placing it back on the table. "Satisfied?"

Chance eyed the lipstick stain on the edge of the white porcelain. Finally, he gave in, lifted the cup to his lips and took a small sip. He placed it back on its saucer with a soft *tink* and shrugged.

"Very nice tea," he admitted.

Kandi smiled thinly, but the action failed to reach her dark brown eyes. "So, how do you plan on stopping Trinity?"

Chance knew he shouldn't have been shocked, but he was. Had he been sipping tea, he would have either choked on it or sprayed liquid across the table. As it was, he stared hard at Kandi, acutely aware of how fast he was breathing.

"Whose side are you on?" he asked, his eyes narrow.

"I'm on my own side, as always. But for the purposes of argument, let's say I am against the three killers doing in women across the country."

"So, are you some kind of psychic?" he asked, hoping to delay answering outright.

Kandi shook her head, making a soft *tsk* noise as she did. "What an inadequate phrasing. I am much more than that, as are you, but to save time, yes I am psychic. Now, quit stalling and tell me what I want to know."

"Don't you already know?"

"Actually, no. And that tells me that you have no idea what to do. Tell me how you escaped from the asylum. One moment you were there, and the next you were… elsewhere. It was a most unusual sensation."

Chance fought to keep the surprise from his face. "How long have you been watching me?"

"Long enough."

He nodded slowly. "I think the term is spirit walking."

Kandi raised a single eyebrow, her only reaction. "Have you done this before that you know of?"

"Only once," Chance admitted.

The tall drag queen traced her forefinger over her bottom lip, a look of intense concentration etched upon her face. "You shouldn't be able to do that."

"I'd argue with you, but I have no idea how any of this works." An idea came to him. "Do you know? I mean, do you know all of it? How I came to be in the asylum, and why I can see the things I see." Hope thrummed through his voice, along with the fear that his hopes might be dashed.

"I could remind you, but the question emerges as to whether I *should*." Even seated, the immense height of the dark-skinned crossdresser was daunting. "You have accomplished more in the month since you lost your memories than any of the time before it. To refresh your memory might bring with it the lackadaisical qualities you displayed before your amnesia."

"Don't I deserve to know?"

"*Deserve*?" Kandi chuckled darkly, but there was no humor in her tone. "Did those women deserve to be tortured and humiliated before dying in terror? Deserve has nothing to do with this situation, my dear. What we have here is a case of what is our best course of action. In all the futures I have seen, only one has shown me a scenario where you succeed, and in *that* future, you don't remember a thing. It is what drives you on, pushing you to discover answers. If I simply give them to you, you will still try, but the burning need within will have faded, and you will die."

"Wait, you've seen the future?"

"*Futures*, deary. Please do try to keep up." She paused and huffed slightly. "Think of every decision as a road down which you might or might not travel. And every decision beyond that has a similar crossroads. Consequently, after a mere day of decisions, you would be left with thousands of roads down which you might or might not have traveled. Multiply this by months and we're looking at millions, possibly billions of possible futures. From this point in time, all of these futures are possible, and as a seer, it is feasible for me to travel down them… to a point."

"And you only saw *one* where I succeed?"

Kandi smiled grimly. "Puts things in perspective for you, doesn't it? Do you still wish to know about your past?"

Chance shook his head numbly, unable to voice what he felt.

"Now that you understand the scope of things, perhaps you will be a tad more forthcoming with your answers, hmm?"

Chance nodded, his head bobbing like a puppet on a string. Within it, his mind felt like mashed potatoes. He had known his task would be difficult, but had never put serious thought into how momentously challenging it would prove. Always, he had been moving forward, never having much time to ponder the details.

"So," continued Kandi, "what's your next step?"

"I was planning on calling the FBI."

The towering figure shook her head. Bangle-sized earrings jangled with the motion. "Bad idea."

"But... I have a contact there who promised to help me. Special Agent Broachford is also hunting the killers."

"Oh, that one." Kandi seemed to think about it. "How do you plan on contacting him?"

"Don't you know?"

"I'm not omnipotent, dear. I am not a god. Much like yourself, I have a few skills that I can call upon from time to time. Unlike yourself, I have some small amount of control over these skills. However, that doesn't mean I know what every eventuality is all of the time. Some destinies are immutable, as intractable as minerals within stone, whereas others are sand upon the beach, washing to and fro with each passing wave."

"I thought you said they were roads."

Dark eyes glared at him across the table. "How do you step into the bodies of these victims?"

"Sorry?" asked Chance, frowning at the sudden change in conversation.

"I'll tell you how. Your talent resonates with that of the killers. You are more like them than you know, and as such, you slip from your own mind into that of the women about to be murdered. Explain the sensation."

"I... well, I'm not sure –"

Kandi slapped a palm twice the size of Chance's on the table. Chance jumped slightly. "It is a part of you, and as such you don't question it. Imagine riding a train. From the inside of the carriage, you see seats and baggage racks, perhaps some doors. It is a vastly different experience than an observer looking at the vehicle as it rushes by at the station. Such is the way of my talent. I look at it from the inside viewing out and am sometimes unable to describe the sensation as it might look from the outside. So, tell me about this federal agent."

Chance blew out an anxious breath. "What is there to tell? He seems committed to hunting down these people."

"Would you say more intent than a regular cop should be?"

"Possibly," replied Chance with a shrug. Then he recalled the near-fanatical look he had witnessed in Broachford's eyes from time to time. "Actually, yes, I would say that."

"Interesting," mused Kandi, her eyes gazing elsewhere. "This is that one. I never thought they could be connected."

"Thought *what* could be connected?"

Her gaze snapped back to him. "Futures, deary. I saw one glimpse, and then a separate one and never imagined they might be linked. It's all very frustrating." She sighed. "But enough of all the schoolroom nonsense. Time is of the essence, no pun intended. So, Special Agent Broachford is the one you want to contact, yes? And to do so, you need to…." She paused, thinking. "You need to communicate with the FBI here in New York."

Kandi rose from the chair and took two steps to the kitchen cabinet. Opening a drawer, she pulled out a disposable cellphone and slid it across the table to Chance. "Keep it. Throw it away if the need arises, I don't care. I have a drawer full of them. Call the FBI now and give them the message he told you. Do you remember it?"

Chance picked up the phone and looked at it. "Uh… no. Something about his brother in law, I think."

"His brother-in-law's name is Frank Grafton." She held up a hand. "Stop. Do not ask me how I know; it should be obvious by now." Chance closed his mouth. "You are to say that you're Frank Grafton and give them the number of the cellphone I just gave you for Broachford to call back. You want to talk about your sister, Sarah, okay?"

"Um, okay. Where's the number for…?" Kandi slipped a piece of paper across the table with a number written on it. He didn't see where she had materialized the paper from, but at this stage Chance hardly felt surprised.

"You're like David Copperfield in a sparkly dress, aren't you?" he muttered.

"If only it were all smoke and mirrors, dear. Maybe then I'd be able to sleep at night."

Chance punched the number into the phone and waited. The line began to ring, and after three trills, a woman answered.

"Office of the Federal Bureau of Investigation, New York. How may I direct your call?"

"Um, Special Agent Broachford, please."

"What is your call in relation to, sir?"

"I'm his brother-in-law. My name is…." His mind went blank. Kandi slipped another piece of paper across the table to him. Chance hurriedly read it. "I'm Frank Grafton, his brother-in-law. I need to talk about my sister, Sarah."

The operator seemed to be either writing his details down or typing it on a computer. *"Your message will be passed on. What number can he contact you on?"*

Chance relayed the cell phone number. The operator thanked him, and then the line went dead. Chance thumbed the end call button and sat back, letting out a tense breath in the process.

"Why so stressed?" asked Kandi. "All you did was make a call."

"I guess. I just hate those kinds of things."

"Obviously." Kandi stood and collected Chance's barely-touched tea. She moved to the sink and tipped it out. "Would you like me to make you another cup?"

"No thanks," replied Chance with a tight grin.

"Okay then, sweetie. Time for you to go."

Chance stood, the chair scraping back on the linoleum. Strangely, he felt reluctant to leave. Despite Kandi's strangeness, he sensed a connection through their talents, a link he had not been able to conceive with any other human being since waking in the hospital. For once, here was a person who understood, even if only slightly, what he was going through. Others might have claimed to believe him, but none had lived the life, none had felt the deaths.

"Can you train me how to use my... talents?" he asked suddenly.

Kandi stared at him straight-faced for several moments, and then burst out laughing. The echoes of mirth bounced off the walls, and Chance smiled faintly. Eventually, the humor petered out, and Kandi wiped the tears from her cheeks.

"Oh, dear boy. You're going to make me mess up my makeup here." She wiped more tears, a streak of mascara smearing across her cheek.

"I'll take that as a no, then."

"How do you propose I teach you? Should we sit here and push our mental powers against each other, back and forth? Or should it be an entirely literary exercise? I could write down what you're supposed to do, and you could memorize how to control a talent of which I have absolutely no idea the extent." She stared at him, all traces of mirth gone. "You might as well ask me to train a squirrel how to be a fish. Just because we both have talents that ordinary people couldn't understand doesn't mean our skills are identical."

"But, surely you could teach me something."

Kandi rose from her chair and patted him on the back. "Here's the only advice I can give you: Don't die. There is more at stake here than you realize."

"What does that even mean?"

"To give away too much would be to taint you against the possibility of success, dear. You walk from this door with a myriad of crossroads before you. Let's pray you choose the right paths."

Chance cursed under his breath as Kandi led him to the door. She opened it, exposing the long alley, Keisha's silhouette still outlined at the end. "My girl will help you as much as she can. Please don't get her killed."

Mouth dry, Chance stepped out into the alley once more. As the door clicked shut behind him, he checked the cell phone in his grimy pocket and sighed. All he could hope was that Special Agent Broachford was faring better than he was.

* * * *

Doug exhaled.

Gaseous fumes, almost blue in color, drifted into the air. He watched them for a minute until the rush hit him. Then he swayed back on the couch, unable to think. The world faded away in that instant of adrenaline. It wasn't so much a euphoric hit, such as he had heard heroine could provide. The meth seemed to pull him together, dragging all the fragile pieces of his soul in and making him solid once more.

Several minutes – or perhaps several hours – later, he came back to a semblance of himself. The presence of the drug still lingered, a troll beneath the bridge of his demeanor, but he could function now, and few would notice he was under the influence of anything… *if* he managed to act normally.

The phone rang. His heart leaped into his throat, and Doug stared hard at his cell on the end of the couch. Gritting his teeth, he shifted over and picked it up.

"Hello?" He paused and listened. If his heart had been able to beat faster, it would have exploded. "Frank Grafton, you say? Do you have his number? Okay, thanks." He hung up.

Doug scratched his cheek, eventually pulling his hand away when the sensation became compulsive. Either his brother-in-law had decided to start talking to him again, or Chance Ripley had beaten his keepers at the asylum.

The television had been bleating frantically about a patient escaping from a high security criminal mental ward, and curiously – or perhaps not – Dennis had called maybe an hour after the story broke. His message had been simple: 'Call me', but Doug had been fixated on other things, and honestly knew nothing of what he supposed might be happening. Well, almost nothing.

Now, Chance had decided to contact him. In his heightened state, Doug's paranoia began to kick in, and he wondered if his phone might have been tapped. Could he securely call out without worrying about his own people kicking in his door? Blowing out a breath, he pulled his hand away from his cheek, where he had unknowingly begun to scratch the skin once more.

Pushing aside his anxiety, Doug tapped in the number the FBI operator had provided and placed the phone to his ear. It rang several times. Doug was about to hang up when someone answered.

"Hello?" a timid voice queried.

"This is Special Agent Doug Broachford from the FBI. No names, but is this who I think it might be?"

"Yeah, it's me. I need help."

"Where are you?"

The speaker answered, and Doug's brows raised in surprise. "That's close to Times Square. How in the world did you manage…? Wait, don't answer that. There's a Denny's near to where you are. Wait for me there."

"That might be a problem."

Doug's eyes narrowed. "What do you mean?"

"I'm dressed as a homeless person."

"Smart move," said Doug. "Good way to fly under the radar. All right, wait for me outside Denny's. I'll be there in thirty minutes."

"Okay."

Doug ended the call.

Unclenching his jaw with an effort, he collected his drug paraphernalia and moved to the stove, hiding everything inside. The last time the stove had been used was when Sarah was still alive. He stared at it sadly for a moment, remembering. Eventually, he turned, grabbed his keys from the kitchen table, and marched out the front door.

CHAPTER XVII

Sarah stared at the television screen, horrified at the news of yet another murdered woman, this time in Dallas, Texas. The police report, while lacking details, stated that the killer's methods retained similar characteristics to several murders in other states, leading police to believe there might be a serial killer involved.

Grimacing, Sarah stood up and walked over to the television screen. Part of her wondered if Doug was still chasing the man he believed had killed her, or whether his grieving had finally passed. She shook her head grimly. No, that one was more tenacious than a pit bull when it came to a case. It had been part of what had attracted her to him in the beginning. She sighed and swept her hand through her short blond hair, remembering.

The drugs had never been a problem, at least not according to Doug. He had hidden them from her, but she'd found them each time. He had stated that they helped him focus on cases, helped him to put away the bad guys. Slowly, so damn slowly, he had slipped down the slope, never knowing that he was becoming one of those 'bad guys' in the process. It hadn't been until he'd been gripping her by the throat, out of his mind on methamphetamine, that Sarah had realized he would never change. She needed to get out or die; it was that simple.

But where did one go to flee from the FBI? Doug was, for all his faults, one hell of an investigator. She could run, but he would find her. There was no doubt. She needed something final, something that took him off her heels once and for all.

Doug's office was always unlocked. Sarah had no problem gaining access to his files, rummaging through them until she came upon his most recent cases, a series of murders he claimed were all connected. That one thing that would keep him away for good was if he thought those he was already seeking had killed her. Nothing would distract him from hunting them down. While he was diverted, she could quietly slip into the shadows. Eventually, she would need to leave the country. Probably somewhere nice like Canada. Even that, however, didn't seem far enough away.

Living with an FBI agent for over a decade had bestowed certain skills upon Sarah. One was how to punch a woman without leaving noticeable bruising. Another was how to plan a crime from the point of a criminal. He talked about his cases enough that sometimes Sarah thought she was living through them herself.

The hardest part had been seducing the mortician.

Doug had been under the assumption Sarah was visiting her brother, Frank. In reality, she had been taking a week to set up the slightly obese son of one of the most prestigious funeral directors in Ohio. At least that's what their business card claimed. There wasn't enough soap in all the world to wash away the taint of what she had allowed that man to do to her – or rather to the dark haired girl he thought was named Jessica. When the man had finally slipped into his apnea-riddled sleep, Sarah had slipped out of bed and out of his life, taking with her the body of a woman who bore a passing resemblance to her.

The phone call to Doug had been almost as difficult as the affair. She still remembered the screaming; it had left her voice hoarse for days afterward. After that, all she'd had to do was mimic one of the murder scenes she'd copied from Doug's files and burn the body in such a way as to make it unidentifiable.

The memory of bashing out the corpse's teeth with a hammer and the heat from the blazing car doused in gasoline still woke her some nights. The burning flesh had smelled disgustingly similar to frying pork. But the alternative was to die at the hands of a psychopath who claimed to love her.

Sarah sighed and rose from the couch. A cool breeze caressed her neck, and she turned, frowning slightly at the open window. As she crossed the floor towards it, she glimpsed a figure step out of the shadows from the corner of her eye.

Too late.

The behemoth gripped her with one hand on the back of her neck and smashed her face into the top pane of the window. Glass shattered, its edges slicing her like a dozen razors. The intruder pulled her back, spun her around, and head-butted her full in the face. Sarah saw stars and collapsed to the ground. The giant man towered over her. Through her daze, Sarah noticed his face was puckered and scarred.

"It's because of you that she's suffering," grunted the man.

"Who?" murmured Sarah. She received the distinct impression the behemoth was not talking to her, despite him glaring directly into her eyes.

* * * *

A knife appeared in Bull's hand. He sliced it across Sarah's face, and Chance screamed. Again and again, the monster repeated the act, until her skin hung in ribbons. Eventually, he seemed to tire. Leaning down, he gripped her hair with his left hand, hauling her to her feet. The man peered deep into hollow, lifeless eyes.

"Tell your friend in the FBI this is what we did to his wife."

The knife plunged into Sarah's stomach.

* * * *

Chance woke up screaming.

"What is it, Chance?"

Chance looked up into the one set of eyes he really didn't want to see at the moment. Doug Broachford peered down at him, concern etched upon his features. Even in his panic, however, Chance noticed the agent was also high.

Sarah's memories lingered within Chance, the times this man had beaten her while in such a state, a history of hurting her so badly that she had faked her own death in an attempt to escape him.

Glancing across the table at Denny's, Chance saw Keisha peering at him oddly. "I thought you was just having a nap. Then you started mumbling all that stuff."

"What stuff?" Broachford demanded.

"Nothing!" Chance gasped, quickly calming himself. "It was… nothing."

"You saw something, didn't you?"

Chance swallowed several times, fighting hard to lessen the memory of Doug Broachford choking Sarah, of him slapping her and calling her a whining bitch. On the other hand, the agent knew Chance had seen something, and there would be no pretending it was just a dream now. Doug would see right through such a ruse, Sarah's memories assured him of that.

"Another woman was killed. Bull murdered her before I could find out who or where she was. He said… he told me they were killing her because of me… and you."

"Me?" demanded Broachford. "How do they know about me?"

"Hell, I don't even know who you are," Keisha muttered. Broachford ignored her, sliding instead into the booth beside her, opposite Chance. "Oh, feel free to make yourself at home."

Chance glanced around at the inside of the restaurant. "I thought I was supposed to meet you outside."

"You were," cut in Keisha, "but then you started acting all weird and this guy turned up and told me to bring you inside with him. Didn't *ask*, mind you, but told me to do it, like I was some damn dog."

Broachford made a shushing noise in her direction without taking his eyes from Chance. "Why would the killer mention me, Chance?"

"Oh, you did not shush me," snarled Keisha. "Get the hell out of my way." The large woman bustled out of the booth, shoving Special Agent Broachford out of her way in the process. He stood up impatiently to let her pass. She turned back toward Chance. "I'll wait for you outside, Jack, but only because you-know-who asked me to, okay?" Shouldering her backpack, Keisha stormed out of the diner.

Broachford barely gave her exit any notice. Sliding back into the booth opposite Chance, he demanded, "Well?"

"Well what?" Chance asked."

"Why did that bastard mention me?"

"I think they know you're working with me." Chance picked up the menu, desperate to divert the conversation. "I'm hungry."

"I'm not," replied Broachford, pushing Chance's menu back down to the table. "How would they know something like that?"

Chance rubbed a hand through his grimy hair and pondered the issue. "Maybe… I don't know. They might be able to…." His eyes stretched wide. "What if the doorway opens both ways?"

"What do you mean?"

"What if they're able to see what I'm doing the same way I can see from the perspective of their victims?" His heart started to thump in his chest. "What if, even now, they're eavesdropping on our conversation?" Searching deep inside, he couldn't find any indication of another presence. But what would such a thing feel like? "How in the world would we ever fight such a thing?" he murmured.

Broachford sat back in his booth seat, his gaze distracted. For some time, he seemed to contemplate the problem. Finally, he blew out a breath and returned his scrutiny to Chance. "I'm not sure, but we're going to have to try. For Sarah's sake, if nothing else."

Chance's throat tightened. He couldn't have replied, even if he'd wanted to.

* * * *

"Try this."

Chance took the proffered clothes, a simple blue shirt and blue jeans, and offered thanks to Special Agent Broachford. He felt awkward, standing in the man's apartment on the outskirts of New York City, knowing the history of the place. Broachford had demanded he call him Doug, for appearances' sake, if nothing else, but the FBI was so ingrained in the man that Chance couldn't shake the impulse to refer to him by title. And again, that history didn't leave Chance feeling chummy.

"Now, go and have a shower. You smell. Watch the hot water, though; it tends to be a little temperamental." He glanced toward the living room. "I need to keep an eye on this woman you insisted had to come with us, to make sure she doesn't pilfer any of my silverware if nothing else."

The statement was uttered casually, apparently intended to lighten the mood, but Chance couldn't shake the remembrance of this man choking and abusing Sarah while under the influence of meth. The excuses had been many, as had been the tears, but there remained beneath the surface of Doug Broachford a monster almost as dark as those he had vowed to hunt down. Chance grimaced at the remark and entered the bathroom, closing the door behind him. He locked himself in and breathed a soft sigh of relief.

Events were taking on a life of their own, whisking Chance along in their wake, giving him little time to catch his breath, let alone control what was occurring. Shaking his head, he slowly peeled off the grimy shirt and threw it on the floor, where it landed with a slap like a wet fish. He wanted to douse the thing in kerosene and set it on fire, but instead he dropped his trousers and stepped into the shower, flicking on the faucet as he closed the door.

Realization of his stupidity hit at the same moment as the water touched his skin. Scalding liquid, like the juice of Mount Doom, cascaded over him, and Chance yowled. Slamming open the glass door, he leaped out. Glancing in the rapidly steaming mirror, he saw his skin was red beneath the grime, but luckily, it hadn't blistered.

"I told you it was touchy," the voice of Broachford called from the other room.

Chance wanted to bawl at the man, to blame him for the fact his flesh felt charbroiled, but he controlled his anger and said nothing. Tentatively, he reached inside the shower and smacked the faucet. A moment later, icy water began to stream out of the showerhead, squirting onto the blue and white tiling. Chance contemplated adjusting the heat once more, but after his scalding, he chose not to risk the pain. A little cold water never hurt anyone, he reasoned. Apart from those who died of hyperthermia, of course.

He stepped in.

The water was colder than cold. Splatters of liquid ice rained down on him, causing breath to freeze in his lungs. Determined to clean the filth from his skin, Chance ducked his head beneath the flow, gasping as his chest constricted. He grabbed the bar of soap and, as swiftly as possible, worked it into a lather. Several times, he reached tentatively toward the hot faucet, but then retreated, unwilling to suffer another scorching. In the end, the shower was functional and swift. He scraped his skin raw with a combination of soap and washcloth, finishing with a scrub through his hair using about a third of the bottle of shampoo. Conditioner was not an option. When he finally stumbled from the glass cubicle, shivering and gasping, Chance wasn't sure if he felt more alive or dead.

After drying himself, he donned the clothes Doug had given him. Without any other shoes, he pulled the hospital slip-ons back onto his feet. They wouldn't do him much good if he wanted to go jogging for long periods, but for walking around, they seemed fine. When he looked in the long mirror behind the door, he paused. This was the most human he could remember himself looking since awaking in the hospital. Strangely, he felt tears threatening, his throat tightening beyond his control. Looking away, he swiped a hand across his eyes, opened the door, and walked out through the bedroom and into the living room.

"Do you have a trash bag or something I can put those dirty clothes into?" he asked, waving vaguely back at the bathroom.

"Leave them," replied Broachford dismissively. He turned to Keisha. "Would you like to shower, too?" The query was automatic, not something born of genuine concern for her well-being. Keisha shook her head, her cold gaze reply enough. "All right, then," continued the agent. "I guess we had better get down to business."

"And what business is that?" Chance asked. Despite his efforts, he found himself unable to keep an edge of anger from his tone.

Broachford seemed to notice it, and his eyes narrowed. "The business of stopping the killers who murdered my wife." He made no effort to shield his reasons anymore. Perhaps the knowledge they were all in this together created a bond within the tense agent's strained mind. "Do you know where they might be?"

Chance licked his lips. "My last vision...." He remembered Sarah, Broachford's estranged wife, being butchered. The memory flicked to earlier, when she had been watching television. "Was there a murder in Dallas?"

"There are always murders in Texas."

"I mean one that fits the profile of our killers. It couldn't have been Bull, but one of the other two might have been down there."

"How do you know it couldn't have been Bull?" demanded Broachford, his gaze narrow.

Because he was busy killing your ex-wife.

"I have a feeling he was elsewhere, that's all," Chance said hurriedly.

Broachford sat down at the table opposite Keisha. The agent motioned for Chance to join them, and he sat beside the large woman. When he looked up at Broachford, Chance searched for the monster who had harangued his wife to the point where she felt desperate enough to fake her own death, setting him on this path of vendetta. The monster seemed absent this day, however; all he found was an intensely focused man, asking for his help.

"What support can the FBI offer us?" Chance asked finally.

"You're an escaped felon. I'm a somewhat dubious agent who has pursued this case long after my seniors told me to let it go."

"Wait, you mean you're not officially assigned to this case?"

"My wife was killed by these people, Chance. There is no way the FBI would allow me to be officially involved. My visits to the asylum were chalked up as me going to see my brother-in-law at his house in Connecticut. Any probing beyond the surface would have exposed how flimsy my story was, but I had no choice at the time. You were my only lead."

"Were you ever involved in a unit investigating psychic phenomena?"

Broachford shook his head briskly. "It was the only way to gain your trust."

Chance cursed softly. "No wonder you were so willing to help me get out of Mount Sinai."

The weary agent scrutinized Chance. "You never did tell me how you escaped."

Keisha seemed to appraise him from the side, and Chance wondered what was going through her mind. Unusually reticent, the large woman appeared happy to sit back and listen. Perhaps she was under orders from Kandi Flawless to observe from a quiet distance and report anything of worth. She certainly wasn't here out of any personal interest, that was for certain.

"I walked out," Chance replied. "And not a single person saw me."

"That's impossible. I saw the security in that place. There was no way you were getting out without one hell of a scheme or assistance from the outside. So out with it."

"No," Chance replied, his voice like stone. "I'm done taking orders. If you want to help me, that's fine. But I'm not your dog."

The agent sneered. "You came to me, remember? Those clothes you're wearing are mine. All it will take is a phone call, and you'll be whisked straight back to your lovely little room in Ward Z. Actually, they might feel the need to ramp up your security and dump your escaping ass straight into Ward Alpha with all the child killers and rapists. How long will you survive in there, I wonder?"

The threat was supposed to intimidate Chance. Before his vision through Sarah's eyes, he might have been cowed, but now when he looked upon Special Agent Broachford, he didn't see a dominant figure of iron will, only the hateful bully who enjoyed beating women while high.

"What about when I tell them you're a drug addict?" The question was stated softly, but it cut through the air like a dagger. He saw Broachford glance at Keisha, guilt flaming across his features, then swiftly replaced by rage.

"What the fuck do you think you're talking about?" snarled the agent. "I'm as clean as they come."

Chance shrugged. "If by 'they' you mean junkies, maybe you're right. You know I'm telling the truth, just like you know it'll only take a piss test to ruin your entire life." Their eyes met, and Chance felt a small flush of victory. "Don't ever threaten me again, okay?"

Wrath flashed behind Broachford's eyes, but he reigned in his emotions expertly. After a moment of silent confrontation, the FBI agent merely nodded, his eyes never leaving Chance's.

"I need to see your files on the murders," said Chance.

"What, all of them?"

"Yes, all of them. I assume you have the records on a laptop or something." He glanced around.

Broachford shook his head. "I distrust technology, especially when dealing with a case I'm not supposed to be within a mile of." The agent stood up and moved to a closet, opened the door, and dragged out a large box. He dropped the box on the table in front of Chance. "Here you go."

Peering inside, Chance saw the container was overladen with cardboard files. "Are you kidding me?"

"Not in the slightest," replied Broachford, with a malicious grin.

"That's just nasty," muttered Keisha.

"You're telling me," Chance muttered. The files had no dust, suggesting Broachford had perused them often. Chance looked up at the agent. "Where should I begin?"

"That depends on what you're looking for."

Chance shrugged. "I just want to know where they might be. Surely there are some patterns to the killings that might indicate where each killer resides."

"You would think so, but no. Most serial killers limit themselves to certain areas – their hunting circle, for want of a better term. But Trinity seems to flit from county to county, state to state. Their killings appear random, but my gut tells me that can't be so. The fact they are so insistent on grouping their three murders together, almost to the hour in some cases, means that they are working to a schedule, but I just can't find the pattern."

Chance could sense the frustration behind Broachford's words, and he gazed hard at the man for several moments, his expression blank. "Don't you have a map with pins in it or something? Maybe then we could see a connection."

Broachford squinted at him. "You do realize I've been investigating this covertly, right? I can't very well claim anonymity if my supervisor turns up on my doorstep and sees a giant fucking map on the wall. I've been warned off this case more than once, and I'm sitting on the edge of unemployment at the first indication of anything sketchy."

"Why would the FBI spy on their own people?"

"You really are raw, huh?" stated Keisha. "Their own people would be the ones they keep closest tabs on; who better to throw a wrench in their works than a mole on the inside?"

Chance nodded slowly. "Okay, so what if they randomly decide to walk in here now and find me?"

"We all go to jail," replied Broachford. "I don't know if you realize this yet, Chance, but you're on the run."

"If only I knew what I had done," Chance muttered.

"Duh!" Keisha said with a snort. "Have you ever heard of this little thing called Google?"

Chance looked between the two of them. "Do you really think it's possible?"

Broachford shrugged. "More than likely. If not for the fear that it might lead them to my door, I might be inclined to look you up on the FBI database. For now, however, we don't have time for any of that. We need to find Trinity."

Grimacing, Chance acceded the point. "Yeah, you're right. Well, since it's been brought up, would the internet prove more helpful at this stage than your archaic box of files? I mean we could sit here for a week and still not find a single fact worth following. It doesn't seem to have helped you too much thus far."

"Those case files are facts around the murders themselves," Broachford acknowledged. "I was never able to obtain profiles on the killers. At this stage, the FBI doesn't even accept that any of them are linked."

"How could that even be possible?" asked Chance. "I mean, we're talking about more than ten murders, right?"

Broachford chuckled mirthlessly. "Try more than fifty."

Chance's eyes bulged in his head. "What? Surely that sort of activity would warrant some kind of task force."

"More than fifty murders across fifty states. Please don't tell me you're so naïve as to not realize how many homicides happen every day in the USA. Fifty killings in half a year? Next to nothing, a drop in the bucket."

"But aren't the scenarios similar? I mean, the ones I can remember mostly had something to do with a knife."

Broachford shrugged. "Knives are definitely less prevalent than guns when it comes to murder; more personal and messy, I guess. But we're still talking several hundred homicides a year, maybe thousands, with knives alone. That dilutes the pool somewhat, but then you mix in all the handgun, shotgun, and rifle murders, blunt weapons, even unarmed physical trauma, and all of a sudden, fifty killings is just another day at the office. Unless they are blatantly similar – and I'm talking signature characteristics such as eating the liver in each case – there are no warning bells to set off. Sure, these are all women killed predominantly with knives, but they aren't all killed in their own homes, some have had body parts consumed, whereas others were left largely untouched. On the surface, there has been no communication between the victims, nothing to –"

"Wait," said Chance, his mind racing. "What do you mean, 'on the surface'?"

The agent peered at him quizzically. "None of them knew each other. They never talked, at least, not that we knew of. That would have set off big alarm bells upon a preliminary investigation. It's basic police work 101. Why is this an issue?"

"What if…?" Chance murmured, more to himself than anyone in the room. He recalled Broachford's wife, Sarah, and how the killers had supposedly found her. Through him. It was through his association with Broachford that they had tracked her down.

Or maybe that had been a secondary issue. Perhaps the only reason they had known about her had been that Chance had met Broachford. This might have provoked them into action, and they had somehow....

"Damn," Chance muttered. The world suddenly seemed a whole lot bigger. "What if Trinity uses their psychic abilities for a lot more than communicating with each other? Perhaps that's how they choose their victims." The memory of the Billionaire Cannibal flashed into his head. "Maybe they are picking victims with latent psychic ability, killing them to... absorb some part of them into themselves." He looked up, his eyes wide. "What if they're making themselves psychically stronger by killing these women?"

Broachford looked thoughtful for some time. "Why only women?"

Chance shook his head slowly. "I'm not sure. Maybe it only works with women. But it can't be a coincidence that one of the killers is the son of Howard Mason."

"*What?*" snapped Broachford. "You never mentioned that before!"

"Oh... shit." Chance sat for some time with his mouth open, unsure what to say. "I forgot to mention it."

"This is the lead we could use, you fool!" Broachford jumped up, ran over to a side table, grabbed his laptop, and swiftly returned. "Mason's son is traceable, God damn it."

Chance contemplated mentioning his meeting with Howard Mason in the basement of Ward Alpha, but then chose to keep the information to himself. The possibility of a horde of Mason-esque cannibals on their heels would surely put a damper on their endeavors. He would let Broachford assume he had simply captured the information in one of his visions.

While the agent tapped away on the laptop, searching for leads on Mason's son, the one Chance thought of as Pestilence, Chance returned to pondering the possibility that the killers were hunting women with psychic ability. The victims probably weren't even aware of their latent talent, possibly writing off their insight as 'female intuition'. He sat back, contemplating what such a revelation might mean. Would it be, such as with Howard Mason, a simple fact of delusion-driven obsession? Or was there some deeper reason behind Trinity's hunting? Did the three killers actually derive something from the women they killed?

Fear gnawed at Chance as he followed the thread of thought. Did Trinity seem stronger since he had first awoken? The fact they had tracked Broachford's wife appeared to indicate so, but Chance was running on precious little information.

"I need to talk to Doctor Sylvia Petrov," he murmured aloud.

"Who's that?" asked Keisha.

Chance snapped his gaze around. The large woman was playing with a thread on her knapsack, seemingly absent-mindedly, but the gaze she turned toward him was startlingly piercing.

"She is a specialist in this kind of thing."

"What kind of thing? The killer kind of thing or the psychic kind of thing?"

"The latter," Chance affirmed.

She nodded, returning her attention to the thread. "Probably a good idea, then."

"How do you know Kandi?" Chance asked suddenly, hoping to divert the subject. "I mean, you two don't seem close, but you're here watching over me for her, right?"

"That's Lawrence," Keisha replied offhandedly. "He's my brother."

The simplicity of the response shocked Chance; he had expected something far more convoluted. To find out the two were simply siblings left him groping for a follow-up question.

"Has he always been, you know, *gifted*?"

Keisha reached up with her thumb and forefinger and rubbed the inside of her nostril. "He's always been damn tall, I'll tell you that. Never could play basketball worth a shit, though. Kept tripping over his own feet. I got no idea how he wears them damn stiletto heels now."

"But you know what he can do, right?"

She looked back at him. "See the future? Yeah, that's what he reckons." The plump woman shrugged. "Never did me no good, though. That bastard won't tell me no lottery numbers or nothing. He can see the end of the world and here I am rummaging through trash for a half-eaten Subway. Now, let me ask you, is that any way to treat your sister?" Her giant afro bobbled as she expressed herself.

"So you're not amazed that your brother can see the future?"

"You grow up with a gigantic asshole who keeps trying to steal your dresses, and the last thing you're likely to worry about is why he can predict what's about to happen. Just kinda got used to it, I guess. Dad was always drunk, and mom was out hookin' to pay for crack, so we hardly had time to ponder the secrets of the universe, if you know what I'm sayin'. Lawrence grew tall, and I grew fat and between the two of us we seemed to get by."

"Surely he could have become rich if he'd chosen to."

Keisha slapped her palm on her thigh, making a loud crack. "That's what I told him. But he was always going on about how fragile the future is and how we couldn't screw with it too much. All I wanted was a house… or ten. Maybe a restaurant. Yeah, that'd be cool."

Chance sat in awe of what he was hearing. As he contemplated her statements, though, he slowly began to understand how Keisha had grown used to her brother's gift. After all, Chance was living a life with similar talents, but for the life of him, he couldn't refer to them as pleasing. Half the time he had no idea what was going on, and the other half he was terrified out of his mind. Perhaps it was the same for Kandi Flawless.

"Connor!" Broachford snarled, punching the air.

Chance jerked around. "What?"

"Connor Mason. Howard Mason's son and sole heir to whatever fortune hasn't been seized by the government.

Which, judging by Howard Mason's business savvy, will still be enough for Scrooge McDuck to take a swan dive off a high board into." He paused, scanning the monitor. "There is almost nothing about him on the internet, which is odd to the extreme, especially considering what his father did. All I found was an old reference from a college in New Jersey."

Chance screwed up his face. "New Jersey? I would have thought the son of a billionaire would have gone somewhere fancier."

"It was Princeton," replied Broachford, his face expressionless.

"Hey, wipe your chin," Keisha suggested, pointing at Chance's face. "Yeah. Uh huh. You got a big dab of ignorance hanging right there." She burst out laughing, her mop-like fro wobbling back and forth.

Shamefaced, Chance felt his cheeks burning. "All right. What did you find on him?"

Broachford shook his head. "Nothing much. This was a small snippet from the chess club that briefly referenced Connor as its captain."

"That's it? What are we supposed to derive from that?"

"Well, we now know that one of the Trinity killers attended Princeton University. And while there might be scant information online about him, there might be tons of solid paperwork about his background and potential contacts left in the records room of the college. Remember, everything online can be tracked from both sides. A man with the connections and money of Howard Mason would have little issue with expunging traces of his family's past. It was only by a fluke happenstance that I stumbled upon the chess club piece. Perhaps whoever cleaned their traces was in a hurry when he did it, and the tidbit slipped through the cracks."

"So, what do we do now?" asked Keisha.

Broachford grimaced. "I can't see any other option than to travel to Princeton and try to gain an interview with the dean. Hopefully, whoever it is will be friendly toward law enforcement.

CHAPTER XVIII

"Could I see your warrant, please?"

Chance fought hard to keep the disappointment from his face, but Broachford didn't miss a beat. "We are talking about a potential serial killer here, Dean Langstrom."

The dean, a woman who seemed carved from steel, raised a single eyebrow. "All the more reason for me to protect our reputation, Agent Broachford."

"It's *Special* Agent, thank you very much."

"How very special for you. Unfortunately, unless you also have a special warrant somewhere between you and your interestingly clad associate," she peered down her nose at Chance, who shuffled his feet nervously, "I will need to remind you that I have an entire wing of legal professors a short walk from where we sit. I'll be more than willing to contact them if that's the course you choose to take."

A manic look flitted through Broachford's eyes. Chance tensed, waiting for some kind of explosion, but it never came.

"Thank you for your time, Dean. Chance, let's go."

The dean snapped her hawkish expression around. "Chance? Chance Ripley?"

"Oh shit," Chance muttered.

"I thought that was you." The dean stood up and stepped around the desk. Broachford slipped in between them.

"Hold on a second. This isn't Chance Ripley. What I said was… we never had a chance."

"Get out of my way, you silly man. Let me look at my nephew."

"Nephew?" Chance echoed, rising uncertainly.

"Yes, my nephew." The dean smothered him in an embrace. Broachford peered at him over the woman's shoulder, but he merely shrugged. The woman eventually stepped back. "I haven't seen you since you were a child. How is your sister?"

"Sister? I… have no idea," replied Chance honestly.

"Are you two still having that ridiculous feud? She always was obstinate. I have never heard of twins being so different."

"Twins?"

"Of course," said the woman. "Don't tell me your sister didn't come to see you after you were committed?"

"You know about that?"

She screwed up her expression. "It was all over the news, my dear."

A knock sounded at the door, and a man promptly entered. Dean Langstrom stopped him with a wave of her hand.

"There'll be no need for that, Trevor. This is my nephew; you know the one. You may leave." The man nodded, turned, and left the office. Once the door had clicked shut, the dean explained. "I told him to interrupt us with a false emergency if you hadn't left after ten minutes." She returned her hawkish examination to Chance. "You look like her, you know."

"Who?"

"Your mother, of course. My sister."

Chance tried to process the information without appearing overwhelmed. First, he had been told he had a sister somewhere, and now this woman was claiming to be his mother's sibling.

"If you heard of my committal," Chance began cautiously, "I have to assume you also heard of my escape."

"Damn it, Chance," snarled Broachford.

Dean Langstrom nodded slowly, her eyes never leaving Chance's. "I saw that on the news. 'Baffling' is the word I believe the reporter used." She rubbed her chin. "Should I even bother to ask how you managed to achieve such a daring getaway? By the way, your hospital photograph hardly does you justice; that's why I took so long to recognize you."

"Well, that's a good thing, I guess." Chance paused, and sucked in a deep breath. "Tell me, do you know why I was committed?"

For the first time, Dean Langstrom appeared disconcerted. "You don't know?"

Chance shook his head.

"Well, isn't that a pickle." A second pause. Finally, she seemed to come to a decision. "You killed your father."

"Oh," murmured Chance weakly.

This was not what he'd been expecting. He blinked several times, wondering if the woman were lying. After all, he knew next to nothing about her. But one look at her indifferent visage left no doubt in his mind; whatever she might be, Dean Langstrom did not seem a petty liar. All that left was the truth of her statement, a statement that Chance knew should have blown him out of the water, but somehow didn't.

"Was there a reason why I killed him? I mean, was it self-defense?" After all, murderers didn't end up in Ward Z, everyone knew that.

"According to the trial, that horrible man abused you and your sister throughout your childhood. He also killed your mother." The clinical way the woman dictated the facts left Chance cold. Bang, bang, and bang. Like three bullets driven into granite.

Chance didn't know his sister, and couldn't recall anything of his mother. Nor could he sense anything similar to emotions for either of them; it was like two strangers had suddenly been inserted into his history, and just as suddenly murdered by another stranger. How should he feel about something like that?

"You had a public defense lawyer," continued the dean, as if the statement explained much more than the words entailed. "A detail I only discovered after the trial. In fact, I only knew you were on trial after the fact, when you had already been committed."

"Why didn't you go see him?" asked Broachford.

"It seemed pointless. The boy needed to heal. It wasn't like we had ever been close; like I said, we hadn't seen each other since Chance was a child. My presence would have surely confused the lad. Besides, I had too much on my plate already."

"I'm sure you did," Chance murmured. "Burying your sister and all."

"Oh no, she was killed years before," replied the woman aloofly. "Your father bashed in her head with a hammer, apparently. He spent some time in a mental ward, possibly the same one to which you were committed. Then, upon his release, he sought you out, and you killed him with a gun." She studied her nails as she spoke. "So, how did you escape Mount Sinai?"

"I walked through the walls," replied Chance coldly. "I guess we'll get going now. You seem to be a busy woman."

Dean Langstrom glanced up. "You can't go yet."

Broachford's eyes narrowed. "Why is that?"

"We have hardly become reacquainted yet. So… how was your rehabilitation?"

Chance didn't reply. Instead, he glanced at the door, remembering the assistant who had entered, and then left. What had Langstrom said to him? Something about knowing who Chance was?

"We have to go," he snapped to Broachford, standing up and indicating the dean. "She's called the cops."

"Seriously?"

"Wait!" demanded Dean Langstrom. "Let me explain."

"Explain what?" Chance snarled. "You need to uphold the reputation of your school? Are you really my aunt?"

Her gaze dropped. "Well… no. But everything else I told you was the truth, I swear."

"Let it go, Chance," Broachford advised, heading for the door. "She's just trying to delay you even more. This bitch is a liar."

"I most certainly am not!" barked Langstrom. "The details of Mister Ripley's case were splattered all over the news for months. And when the police discovered that his sister attended Princeton, well, there was an investigation. Unlike the two of you, they arrived with a warrant and made an absolute mess of our records looking for details as to the whereabouts of your sister. Apparently, she had disappeared, and they needed to know if she was involved in the murder of your father."

"Was she?" asked Chance.

"I am led to believe they never found her. Perhaps she was incarcerated at a later date. She might even have been in that God-forsaken place with you."

The image of Betsy flashed into Chance's mind. Could she have been his sister? The woman knew things about him, personal things. And then there were her abilities. Was the strange woman he'd felt so drawn to his twin?

"Do you remember her name?"

"Of course. Just take a seat while –"

Broachford grabbed him and hustled him out of the room. "Time to go."

"Wait! She might know if the woman I met in Mt. Sinai was my sister."

The agent glanced over his shoulder. Chance followed his gaze. Right before the door slammed shut, he saw the dean furiously dialing on her phone.

"I have a feeling that was a secondary call to let law enforcement know we're fleeing the scene," Broachford muttered. "How long ago do you think she gave that assistant of hers the heads up?"

Chance shrugged. "Ten minutes?"

"Start running."

The two sprinted through the hallowed Princeton halls toward where Broachford had parked his car in the faculty lot. By the time they fled through the exit and out into the grounds, Chance expected to hear sirens wailing in the distance. Only surprised glances greeted them from students who turned at the sound of the double-doors banging open. Broachford waved at him to slow down, and Chance pulled up, nodding apologetically toward those peering at them so oddly.

"We don't want them to ID the car if we can avoid it," Broachford murmured.

The thin gathering slowly turned their attention back to whatever conversations or destinations occupied their focus. By the time the duo made it to Broachford's car, it seemed nobody was paying them much attention. They slid in as covertly as possible. Broachford turned the key and started the engine, slowly reversing and heading toward the exit of the parking lot. When they finally made it back onto the main road, Chance allowed himself a sigh of relief.

"Here they come," Broachford murmured, as though afraid the approaching police cars might hear them.

Four marked police cars passed them heading in the opposite direction. None had lights flashing or sirens blaring, though Chance did note, they were rushing through the thin traffic well above the speed limit. He turned to watch the cars pull into the parking lot of the university.

"Speed up," Chance breathed.

Broachford shook his head and checked the side mirrors. "We don't want to attract attention. The best thing we can do now is meld in with the traffic heading toward the city and hope nobody got a good look at the car or the plate. We'll get home long enough to collect some gear and that Keisha woman… if you want her tagging along. But then we have to go." He looked over at Chance and grimaced. "Looks like we're both fugitives now."

It took a moment for the import of his words to sink in. When Chance finally understood, he murmured a soft, "Oh," and then stared through the windshield, not knowing what else to say. In helping him, Broachford had successfully shattered his career. Dean Langstrom had written down the agent's details upon sighting his badge, and was no doubt currently informing the police who was assisting the psychiatric ward fugitive.

"Won't the cops call ahead?" Chance asked.

Broachford glanced at him sideways, his expression anxious. "Let's hope not."

However, as they approached Broachford's home, the agent suddenly veered off, heading in a different direction. He cursed softly.

"What is it?" Chance asked.

"Two unmarked cars are positioned at the head of my street. No doubt there are more down further." He looked at Chance and rubbed his chin. "Keisha will likely be in custody by now, but they probably won't be able to hold her for long without charging her."

"What about the drugs at your apartment? Won't they be able to pin that on her?"

Broachford's eyes flared wide. For a moment, Chance thought the man might deny the accusation, but part of him seemed to crumple inside. "Probably."

"We should go and see her brother. He needs to know."

"You mean the psychic drag queen?" asked Broachford skeptically. Chance nodded. "They'll probably anticipate that."

"I have a feeling they won't be able to track him down too quickly. Besides, Keisha doesn't seem like the type to crack under pressure. At least not easily."

"If he's all you claim him to be, won't he already know his sister's fate?"

Chance contemplated the possibility. "Maybe. But he might be able to direct us on whatever course we should be taking. I trust him enough for that."

"What about that Russian woman? The doctor. Didn't you want to go and see her?"

Nodding slowly, Chance said, "Soon. To reach her, we need to travel for some time. Kandi is in the center of the city; much easier to find."

"His name is Kandi?" He shrugged. "Why should that surprise me? All right, then. Let's go and see a guy named Kandi."

* * * *

Broachford looked up. And then he looked higher.

"Jesus Christ," the agent muttered.

"Not today, sweetheart." Kandi turned to Chance. "From the look on your face, I am guessing my sister's been arrested? Typical. Don't worry too much, though. I warned her this might be coming."

"You could have warned us," Broachford grunted.

"Honey, I don't even know you. But you're right, I could have warned Chance." Kandi sighed, peering down at Chance. "You know how this shit works, sweetie. If I pluck the wrong thread, the whole web might unravel."

"That's okay; I'm just worried about Keisha."

Kandi shook her head. The voluminous blonde wig she was wearing rustled with the movement. "Don't you worry about that girl. She used to beat the crap out of me when we were kids. A little time in prison will be good exercise for her."

Chance couldn't help but acknowledge the statement. If anything, he felt sorry for the other prisoners.

For a time, the three stood in uncomfortable silence, staring at one another. Eventually, Kandi ushered them over to the kitchen table, and they sat… in uncomfortable silence.

"I'm waiting," murmured Kandi.

Chance sighed. "What do we do next?"

"Well, that didn't smack of desperation at all." The tall man in a dress shook his head slightly. "If I'm to guess correctly, you just failed to obtain information about Connor Mason at the university, right?" Both men nodded, Broachford somewhat reluctantly. "So that means you know you have a twin sister and…." Kandi closed her eyes momentarily, the lids fluttering. "Yes. You should go and see the Russian doctor. The sooner, the better." She fell silent again, her gaze distant. "What in the world is that? Oh –"

Kandi's features suddenly filled with terror, her eyes flared wide and knowing.

"It's not only Trinity." A pause. "So much power!"

A piercing shriek echoed around the apartment, so loud that Chance was forced to press his palms flat against his ears. The cry cut off as abruptly as it had started. Chance looked at Kandi and slapped a hand over his own mouth to stop from crying out.

The tall transvestite's eyes suddenly went blank. He wrapped his broad hands around his skull like a Globetrotter preparing for a dunk. Then, with a tremendous wrench, he snapped his head around. A loud crack sounded, resonating from the walls. Kandi slumped down in the chair, her mouth dropping open and voluminous wig tumbling off. Eventually, the boy called Lawrence toppled to the floor, a thin trickle of blood dribbling from the corner of his painted mouth, with his face on backwards.

Both men surged up from the table. Chance glanced at Broachford. The agent had his gun out, searching for the source of the attack. Eventually, when nothing presented itself, he whispered, "What the hell was that?"

"I'm not sure, but I think we need to get out of here before we say anything else. We don't know who's listening, if you understand me."

"Grab that flannel," Broachford ordered. Chance did as he asked. "Wipe down anything you think either of us might have touched. We can't leave evidence that we were here. The last thing we need at the moment is to be implicated in a murder." He stared at the collapsed figure on the ground, long legs splayed haphazardly like a squashed spider. "Jesus H. Christ."

After Chance had wiped everything down, he nodded to Broachford. The agent holstered his gun, and the two exited the apartment, wiping down the door, its frame, and handles as they left.

* * * *

Special Agent Doug Broachford looked like a man fighting hard to maintain a grip on his sanity. A grip that was slowly but surely slipping.

Chance chose not to speak as the two made their way down the busy Manhattan street. It seemed the wiser option, especially considering Broachford looked ready to whip out his pistol again at the slightest sign of peril.

After three blocks, Broachford finally looked sideways at him. "Do you have any idea what happened back there?"

Chance didn't answer immediately. When he did, his voice was hesitant. "Back in the asylum, I theorized that there might be… someone behind the killings. A mastermind, if you will. It was an unfounded concept, with nothing much to back it other than the fact the murders appeared too well organized for the killers I had met. The female, Siren, appeared the most likely to be the leader, but something about her seemed…."

"What?" Broachford urged.

"It felt almost like… she didn't seem as psychotic as the other two, if that makes any sense."

Broachford shook his head. "No, that makes no sense at all. She has slaughtered innocent women, just the same as the others. Sane people don't do that."

"True, but she seemed more methodical about it, as though she were working toward a final purpose rather than the killings in themselves. She was focused and terrifying, and I'm not saying she didn't enjoy the killing, but she seemed driven by a higher purpose. The Bull is cold, almost completely detached, whereas Pestilence relishes every moment terror is flowing. Neither one would make a good leader. So if it's not Siren leading them, it must be another, as yet unknown, entity."

"And you're telling me this person can… what? Do what we just saw? That guy just snapped his own neck, for God's sake. No, I don't think so. I'm not falling for that. Maybe it was an aneurysm, I don't know."

"Aneurysms don't make people snap their own necks," Chance argued. "Listen, you can't deny what you just saw." Chance remembered hurling Bull away in Sylvia Petrov's home using only his will. "There are powers at play here that neither of us can predict nor exclude. What did she say before it happened?"

Broachford grimaced. "She said it's not only Trinity." He sighed. "I sometimes wish I'd never answered that call from Mount Sinai."

"You and me both," Chance agreed with feeling. "So, if it's not only Trinity, that suggests there is someone else behind the scenes." The vision of the little girl in the pumpkin patch haunted by Nothingman flashed into his mind. "And that someone is powerful enough to manipulate people into acting against their will."

"But if that were truly the case, why use Trinity at all?" argued Broachford. "Why not merely track down your victims and kill them without a trace?"

"Perhaps he can't travel that way. Or maybe he prefers to hide in the shadows, manipulating events." Chance shook his head, and then looked around. He spotted a bar sign hanging crookedly from the wall down a side alley. Suddenly, the urge to take the edge off hit him like a freight train. "You need to buy me a drink."

"Is that right?"

"Yes, that's right." He nodded toward the bar. "That place over there. I just need to get off the streets for a while, to get my head straight and try to figure out what is going on. Maybe we can work on our game plan."

Broachford glanced down the side street at the bar Chance had indicated, his expression unimpressed. The front appeared clean, but dark. The windows were either black glass or covered from the inside. A buzzing neon sign flickered in the window front, indicating that, despite all appearances, the place was open. "I don't know," he muttered.

"It's not like there are going to be any cops lurking in there, right?"

The agent glanced at him sideways. "Cops go into places like that all the time. Usually, they're looking for drug dealers or murderers. Guess which category they'll put you in."

"Oh," Chance murmured, frowning. "Well, it's better than a 7-Eleven. Let's go."

Broachford grudgingly followed him across the street, a Yellow Cab honking lightly at them as they cut in front of him. Chance entered the bar first, and then froze. Broachford smacked into his back.

"I told you it was a shithole," the agent muttered over his shoulder.

The outside proved to be the cleanest thing about the bar. The inside was gloomy and filled with smoke – surprising, considering there were only around twenty people in the place.

A weathered woman with bleached-blond hair leaned crookedly at the end of the bar, her sagging breasts drooping like overripe melons in a top designed for a teenage girl. She looked over at the two newcomers, her cheeks sunken deep into her face. Blackened teeth emerged as she attempted what Chance guessed was a seductive smile. He snapped his gaze away before she decided to approach and offer for them to sample her wares. From the looks of the crone, she would likely fall flat on her face the moment she attempted to leave the sanctuary of her leaning station and walk on her five-inch stilettos.

"Let's just get a drink," Chance suggested. "We're in here now; it'd look weird to turn around and walk out."

"We don't fit in. Look around, we're like two shiny dimes in a bag full of rocks."

"Speak for yourself." Chance muttered.

Broachford was right. Manhattan's darker denizens, those who would never fit in with the office workers in their spotless suits, haunted the place. Most of the customers didn't appear dangerous – well, apart from the hulking figure in the shadowy booth that he couldn't see properly. They seemed broken; discarded husks from a society that only venerated the pristine.

Navigating to the bar, Chance ignored the measuring glance from the dead-eyed barman and ordered two bourbons.

"I don't drink bourbon," Broachford informed him.

"They're both for me."

Broachford ordered a Coors Light and surreptitiously glanced around the room. "I still don't know what we're doing here."

"Neither do I," Chance replied vaguely. His eyes flicked to the hulking figure in the corner booth. He couldn't be sure, but the stranger seemed to be watching them.

Glass clattered onto the bar, snapping Chance's attention back. The three drinks were sitting on the counter top, and the barman was holding out his hand. Chance looked from the drinks to Broachford. "I don't even own a wallet."

Huffing slightly, Broachford thumbed a twenty from his wallet and paid for the drinks. Chance downed one of his bourbons swiftly – too swiftly, in fact. Fire roared down his throat, and he began coughing and wheezing loudly, leaning over.

"Are you all right?" Broachford asked.

"He always was a bit of a pussy," growled a voice.

Chance saw Broachford's hand dart towards his holstered gun, but he didn't draw the weapon. Controlling his coughing with difficulty, Chance slowly stood upright, wiping tears from his eyes. The huge man from the corner booth stood before them, fully visible in the brighter light of the bar. Still, he seemed impossible.

"Jarvis?"

The hulking form swept Chance up in an enormous bear hug. His feet dangled several inches off the floor, and his newly recovered breath whooshed from his lungs.

"Put me down, you big lug," he gasped.

The giant man lowered him to the ground and stood with his hands on his hips, a wide grin stretching his lips. "How are you, my boy? And how did you know I was hiding out here?"

"I didn't," Chance replied, rubbing at his bruised ribs. "How could I?"

"Well –" Jarvis lowered his voice conspiratorially "– I thought you might have used that voodoo magic stuff you can do to search for me."

"Hang on, how are *you* here? How did you escape the asylum?"

Jarvis frowned. "The map. Isn't that why you left it for me?"

"But I was working on a detailed plan. I never even told you about it."

"That's why I escaped through the sewers. I don't know why you didn't do that yourself… or *did* you? Nobody in that place seems to know how you got out. I figured you had followed whatever plan you were devising and left me to my own devices. Bit of a dick move, but hey, I probably would have done the same to…." Jarvis trailed off as his gaze flickered to Broachford. "Hey, isn't that Mulder? What's he doing here?"

Chance nodded. "It's a long story."

"Good. You can buy me a drink while you tell it." The big man sat down on a stool at the bar. The timber groaned under his weight, but amazingly held.

Chance sighed and glanced at Broachford, who shook his head vehemently. Shrugging, Chance sat down on the stool beside Jarvis. "Here," he said, pushing his other bourbon down the bar, "have my second one. I don't think my throat could handle it."

Grinning, Jarvis gulped down the straight bourbon. His face never changed expression. He waved the barkeep to pour them both another one.

"I'm not paying for those," Broachford stated firmly.

"Well, unless Chance has money, I guess they're going to call the cops on us for running out on the check."

Broachford swore softly, and then slid onto the stool beside Chance.

"I guess you've seen something about us on TV."

Jarvis grinned widely. "You're lucky this shithole can't afford a set or else you'd see your two mugs plastered all over the screen. I mean, it's not every day a nutcase and a fed team up on the run, you know. The networks are having a field day with it. Makes it much easier to be me." He chuckled and leaned back, almost tumbling from the stool when he realized it had no backrest.

"Yet you choose to sit with us," muttered Broachford. "Well done, genius."

The grin fell from the giant's lips, replaced with a frown. He glanced around swiftly, but when the barkeep deposited his next drink in front of him, he shrugged and lifted the glass to his lips.

"Bon appetite."

"It's *appétit*, you cretin." Broachford shook his head in disgust. "And we're drinking, not eating. Your statement makes no sense."

Jarvis's eyes narrowed, and he paused midway through lifting the glass to his lips. "Tiny bit cranky there, are we?" He glanced down. "Could it be linked to the reason your hands are shaking? You also seem to be sweating a bit. Now, why is that?"

"What are you trying to say?" growled Broachford.

"You're coming down so hard you're about to crash. Don't deny it; I've spent my share of time around tweakers. If I pulled my cock out right now and told you it was a meth pipe, you'd likely try to smoke it." He chuckled and looked thoughtful. "You definitely have a pretty mouth."

Broachford stood so quickly his stool fell over, landing with a loud clatter on the concrete floor. "I'm not going to sit here and get insulted. When you're ready, Chance, I'll be waiting outside." He threw some notes on the bar and stormed out, shaking the door in its frame.

Once the door had swung shut, Chance turned back to Jarvis. "You did that on purpose."

"Moi? No way."

"Yes way." Chance fingered the glass filled with bourbon. "So when are you going to tell me how you really escaped?"

"I told you, it was through –"

"The sewers. Yeah, right. Except for the fact there are no sewer lines. The maps showed gigantic septic tanks beyond the north wall. I guess whoever designed the place thought ready-made tunnels running beneath the site might be a bad idea." He paused, sucked in a breath. "Was it Mason?"

For a moment, he thought Jarvis might lie, but eventually the giant nodded.

"What did he ask in return?"

"He wanted me to find you."

"Looks like you did that easily enough," muttered Chance.

Jarvis shook his head. "Not at all. I saw all the noise going on about you two and honestly figured I would just lay low for a while. I couldn't believe it when you walked in here."

Chance wondered what had made him want a drink in the middle of the day. He gripped the glass tighter in his hand. "Did Mason order you to kill me?"

"Seriously?" Jarvis broke out in a barking laugh. "If that guy wanted you dead, all he'd have to do is make a phone call. You know that. No, he sent me because he figured I might be the one person you would listen to." He licked his lips, suddenly deadly serious. "He told me to remind you of the promise you made him."

Chance loosened his hold on the glass. He had been ready to hurl it into the giant's face, but now he chose to lift it to his lips and take a deep swig. The bourbon scorched, but he ignored the heat. After a moment, he glanced sideways at the big man.

"Mason wants me to convince his son to stop killing people. Did you know that? That crazy old fuck wants me to find his son, one of the three people killing women for a reason I can't fathom, and convince him to walk away from his evil ways." Chance took another sip of bourbon, grimacing as it slid down his burning throat. "If I don't, or if I somehow screw it up, he's going to set an army of cannibals on my heels. And they're… they're going to eat me alive." He shook his head in wonder, still unable to believe how such a prospect could loom over him.

Jarvis fidgeted awkwardly on his stool. "That's what he told me to remind you."

Chance ran a hand through his hair. "Jesus Christ. What the hell am I supposed to do about that? And to top it all off, I'm teamed up with a junkie fed who –" He cut himself off, remembering to whom he spoke. Jarvis had never proven himself the most trustworthy companion. Telling Jarvis that Broachford's wife had run from his abuse was like handing the man a bullet for a gun that might end up turned upon him at any moment.

"What were you saying about him?" Jarvis asked, his tone low.

"He's fanatical about finding these guys, that's all. I don't think he's taken any drugs since we've been together, but I have been asleep some of the time. As you noticed, though, he's starting to run on fumes. I might not know much about meth, but I have a feeling it's only a matter of time before he snaps."

"Then what?"

Chance shrugged. "For the time being, I need his help. Now that he's wanted for harboring a fugitive, I have to start thinking about a time when I might have to step out on my own."

Jarvis pulled out a pen and turned over one of the cardboard beer coasters. He scribbled a number down on it.

"I got myself one of those disposable phones. Here's the number. Call me when you need help."

Chance took the coaster and peered at it for a moment. Accepting the number practically screamed that he hadn't heard the last of Jarvis. Whatever Howard Mason had actually broken the big man out for would have to remain a mystery for the time being, though. Chance pocketed the number and thanked the giant. Downing the last of his bourbon, he called the barman over and paid the check with Broachford's money. Finally, he patted Jarvis on the shoulder, wished him luck, and then headed for the exit.

Broachford stood some way down the alley, chatting with the weathered prostitute from inside the bar. Chance hadn't even seen the woman leave. At first, the agent didn't notice him, but then the door closed behind him with a bang and Broachford spun around, his eyes guilty.

"What's going on?" asked Chance.

Broachford stalked over to him. "I see your conversation has ended with that buffoon. Did he have any words of wisdom to impart on you?"

"A few," Chance admitted. He nodded toward the old hooker, who was tucking something into her purse. It looked like cash. "What's the story with her?"

"Her?" Broachford glanced back. "She followed me out here and started hassling me for money. I threw her a few notes to get her off my back."

"That's all?"

"What are you suggesting?" Broachford demanded, his gaze narrowing.

"Hey, if you say that's all it was, I have to believe you, right?" He sighed and looked around. "We need to get going. The last I heard, Doctor Sylvia Petrov was under protective custody after Bull attacked her. Do you know anything about that?"

Broachford shook his head. "Why is it so important you see this woman?"

"She might be able to explain what's going on. My phantom walking out of the asylum, the possibility of Trinity hunting people for their psychic abilities, the fact someone might be manipulating the three killers for their own purposes. All of it. If nothing else, she might have the connections we need to track down the killers. If psychics are being hunted, somebody in their circle must have an inkling as to how a murderer might siphon away their energy. It can't be an entirely new idea, surely."

Broachford shrugged. "A lot of the world's population doesn't believe in psychic phenomena. That lowers the suspect pool dramatically. If this professor is as connected as you assume, she might indeed be able to point us in the right direction."

"So is there a way we can find out where she's being held?"

"Sure," agreed Broachford. "All we have to do is find someone who can hack into the FBI database."

* * * *

"This is going to see me end up in Guantanamo, you know that right?"

"More than likely," Broachford agreed. "Just get on with it, Goggles."

"I hate that hacker name, man," the mole-like figure muttered. He continued tapping away at the computer keyboard. His Coke-bottle-glasses slipped to the end of his nose, causing him to pause and push them back up with his forefinger. "Why can't you call me The Crimson Crasher like I asked?"

"Don't blame me for choosing a bad name to hack into the NSA. It's the one that stuck. For the record, I think it's rather appropriate." Broachford paused. "Just to be clear, I don't really care about you, Goggles. If you don't do this for me, Guantanamo will be the last thing you need to worry about. I'll leak your location to the Russians."

Goggles froze and glared up at him, his wide eyes even wider through the magnification of his lenses. "You wouldn't!"

"Yes, I would. You know I would. How much did you end up siphoning away from their drug cartels before you turned state's evidence, anyway?"

"Twenty million and change," Goggles admitted glumly.

"Lucky the FBI changed your identity, then. Isn't it?"

"Not if you're going to turn up whenever you want a favor. Who's that guy, anyway?" Goggles pointed flippantly at Chance. "He don't look like a fed."

"You don't need to know who he is. But it's probably for the best if you don't piss him off."

The eyes behind the glasses widened once more. "Why not?" Goggles whispered.

Broachford lowered his voice ominously. "Let's just say you won't be typing until you learn how to do it with your toes."

Goggles snatched his gaze away from Chance and focused back on the keyboard. Broachford smiled around at Chance, who returned his gaze woodenly. The agent had advised him not to say a word to the former informant lest it ruin their chances of finding Doctor Petrov. Still, Broachford's treatment of the highly-strung man left him feeling disgusted.

"Okay, I'm past their first firewall."

"How many are there?" asked Broachford.

"At a glance, I'd say there are at least seven," replied Goggles. He cracked his knuckles. "Have at you, and unleash the dogs of war."

"It's 'cry havoc'," muttered Chance, forgetting his vow.

"What?" both Broachford and Goggles echoed.

Remembering himself, Chance grunted, "Hurry up," in the gruffest tone he could manage. Goggles jolted and spun back to the keyboard. Broachford glowered at Chance, but said nothing.

For several moments, the three sat in silence, the only sound the clacking of the keyboard, until Goggles proudly announced another firewall had been defeated. But then he paused.

"Uh oh."

"What is it?" Broachford demanded.

"They hid a virus within the firewalls. I disabled it, but in disabling it, I somehow triggered a tracing program." He looked up from the screen. "They're tracking back here, and I can't stop it."

"I thought you were good at this stuff, Goggles!" Broachford snarled.

"It's the goddam FBI, man. You people hire guys like me to do shit like this. It's like trying to fight myself." He peered at the screen. "Hang on. I might not be able to stop it, but I can slow it down with a subroutine."

"Hurry up!"

The tech wiz tapped away at his keyboard like a man possessed. Chance half expected to see smoke rising from the computer as it struggled to process whatever multiple strings of code Goggles forced into it. Chance found himself clenching his sweating hands into fists so tightly his nails were digging deep into the skin of his palms. With effort, he forced himself to relax.

"Another firewall down!"

Neither Chance nor Broachford responded. Chance half-expected sirens to come wailing in through the window of the bedroom. For the moment, however, only birdsong drifted on the afternoon breeze.

"Okay," breathed Goggles. "I've set it on a subroutine loop that will delay it for some time. Hopefully, it'll be long enough for me to crack the other firewalls. That's if they don't have someone waiting to trap me on the other end, of course."

"What if they do?" asked Broachford.

Goggles peered up through his thick spectacles. "Game over, dude."

"Get back to work, then."

The nerdy male, a guy barely out of his teens from the look of him, picked up a blue sippy cup and noisily slurped whatever soda sloshed around inside. He cracked his knuckles dramatically, twiddled his fingers, and then set to work once more.

The wait was interminable. Occasionally, Goggles would call out something in technical gobbledygook that made no sense to Chance, but he found himself nodding as though he knew what a RAM sequencer or a bilateral code transfer was.

"Shit," murmured the hacker.

"What is it?" Broachford demanded.

"They do have someone working against me. I'd bet my balls it's that wannabe, Jester."

Broachford scowled. "Who is Jester?"

"A guy who thinks he's the best." Goggles leaned so close to the monitor Chance feared his glasses might smack against the screen. "Unfortunately, he has yet to be proven wrong. Come at me, bro."

A duel proceeded to take place between the two combatants on a field Chance couldn't even begin to envision. All he could do was watch Goggles' reactions every time he succeeded at something and fist pumped. Alternatively, when he failed, he slapped his desk and swore loudly. Usually in Klingon.

As the duel continued, and the level of soda dropped nearer and nearer to the bottom of Goggles' sippy cup, the fist pumping became less prevalent, and the swearing grew louder. Soon, it became apparent Goggles was losing dramatically. Sweat dripped from the young man's face, splashing onto his keyboard. Finally, Goggles swore louder than ever. He leaped so fast he knocked the swivel chair flying backward. The bespectacled figure dove for the rear of his computer tower, yanking clear the Ethernet cord so hard it snapped the clip with an audible crack.

"What happened?" Broachford demanded. Chance found himself leaning forward.

Goggles ignored the question. Breathing heavily, he stared intently at his monitor. For almost a minute, nothing happened. Goggles sighed and turned to Broachford, ready to answer. Before he could talk, however, his computer monitor flickered with the image of a court jester. Booming laughter filled the bedroom, coming from the computer speakers.

"NOOOOOO!" screamed Goggles, falling to his knees.

"What the hell is going on?" Broachford demanded.

Thick glasses turned toward them, and Chance saw tears dribbling from the young hacker's eyes. "Jester's infiltrated my system. By now, all my files are his – I'll never access them again. The whole computer is fried."

Broachford swore softly and looked over at Chance.

"They'll be coming," said the hacker miserably.

"Wait. Who?"

"You've been with them long enough," sniffled Goggles. "Are you telling me they wouldn't respond to something like this? This is national security shit, man. We're all fucked."

Broachford didn't pause. With one sudden punch, he knocked Goggles out. He spun, grabbed Chance, and surged toward the door. Chance barely had time to gather himself as he was hustled out of the suburban house and back into the car.

"Why did you hit him?" Chance demanded.

"It was the only way to protect him. This way, he can say we broke in and forced him to hack the database for us."

Chance chewed over the information and nodded. "Where are we going?"

"Away from here as swiftly as possible." Broachford glanced around and gunned the engine.

As the despoiled agent's blue Nissan began to pull away from the curb, flashing lights emerged from around the corner, heading directly for them. Broachford cursed and spun the car, but a second black and white blocked the street behind them.

Chance grabbed the door handle and lurched from the car. He made it thirteen steps before one of the cops crashed into him, tackling him to the ground.

Cuffs snicked around Chance's wrists, and the constable read him his rights. Looking around, he saw Broachford standing calmly with his hands above his head, surrendering without a fight. Chance's shoulder cramped, and he wriggled around, trying to release the tension. Sounds of a scuffle broke out, and when he turned back, a cop was on the ground, unconscious. Broachford had his gun trained on the man's head. The three other responding officers had their sidearms unholstered and aimed at the agent.

"Drop them," Broachford ordered. His voice sounded strangely calm amid the tension of the moment. "Otherwise, I'll put at least one hole in his head before you take me down."

The three uniforms appeared uncertain. Broachford unloaded a round into the garden bed near the unconscious officer's head. Three guns clattered to the sidewalk.

"Each of you, take out your cuffs and hook yourself to the man beside you. Then I want you to go over to that lamppost and encircle it. Lock your wrists with the final set of cuffs."

The officers looked at him wrathfully, but Broachford grasped a handful of the unconscious cop's hair and buried the muzzle of his gun into the nape of his neck. The metal was still hot from the recently fired shot. Flesh sizzled, and the man moaned. A moment later, all three officers stood around the post, their wrists secured with handcuffs. Broachford took the unconscious cop's cuffs and secured his hands behind his back.

The agent approached Chance and released his hands with a key from the cop's belt.

"Get in the car," he ordered.

"Wait!" wailed a voice from the house.

Chance and Broachford both turned to see Goggles sprinting awkwardly, as though running were an unknown to the gangly hacker. He reached them huffing and puffing, despite the distance being mere yards.

"What is it?"

"I want to..." wheeze, "come with you."

"No," replied Broachford dispassionately.

Goggles' eyes bugged. "How else will you find whoever it is you're looking for?"

"We'll manage," replied the agent, though his tone sounded doubtful to Chance. "Besides, you said yourself that your equipment is useless."

"I have another setup on the other side of the city."

Chance stepped forward and placed his hand on the young man's shoulder. "You don't want to follow where we're going, trust me."

Something in his tone seemed to sway the young man. "Give me a ride away from here, at least. I can't go to jail, man."

"Get in the car," said Chance. The awkward hacker stumbled over to the back door of the Nissan. Broachford glared at him. "We don't have time to argue," Chance replied to his unspoken comment. "Let's just get away from this place before more cops respond."

Broachford couldn't argue with that. No sirens were wailing in the air yet, but from the babble emitting from the police cruisers' radios, they wouldn't be too far away. Broachford pulled the Nissan away calmly, mounting the curb to drive around the cruiser blocking their path.

"I hope you know what you're doing," the agent muttered.

"Me too."

"Does anyone know why my jaw hurts so much?" mumbled Goggles from the back seat, cradling his chin.

CHAPTER XIX

"Okay, so we've already proven I can't break into the FBI database," said Goggles. "At least not while Jester is defending their fort. But what about if I hack into the phone number database?"

"How is that going to help us?" asked Chance.

Goggles had promised to lead them to a 'secret location'... which turned out to be his cousin's attic.

"We're wasting time here," Broachford snapped.

Goggles held up a hand, like a student asking for permission to talk. Chance nodded at him. "We all need phone numbers, right? Each one is separate and unique, so you could almost say they're a personal identity number. Now, if I can discover which one is linked to this doctor lady, I can find out where she is through triangulation of the phone – if it's turned on, of course."

"But how will you know which one is hers?"

"I discovered that the FBI has their own separate cache of phone numbers that they filter into the system through a complex algorithm, not unlike a code. I broke that code. Now, all I need is the date your doctor went into protective custody, and we'll narrow the field, hopefully ending in a single possible entity. We triangulate the location, and then we have your lady."

"You make it sound simple," Broachford muttered.

"Well, it's not. Not even in the slightest." Goggles adjusted his glasses slightly. "If it were simple, everyone would be doing it." He sat back, a proud smirk stretching his features. "I consider it my grande réussite. That means great achievement."

"Good for you, Goggles." Broachford leaned in close and spun the chair back to face the monitor. "Now, don't tell us. Show us."

"Right." Goggles began typing, swiftly bringing up a coded screen, bereft of anything artistic, merely green numbers on a black background. "When did she go into protection?"

Chance gave him the date, and he began typing in line after line of code. Pages crawled by, each as non-descriptive as the last. Eventually, a second window popped onto the screen. A scrolling mass of numbers and characters exploded on the window, zipping by too fast for the eye to follow.

Goggles sat back and grinned. "My program," he said proudly. "This might take a while."

"Will this set off any alarms?" asked Broachford.

The hacker frowned. "I don't think so. It's crawling through the telephone companies, nothing to do with the federal government, so I can't see why it would trip any alarms. It didn't before."

"How many times have you tried this?" Chance asked.

"Just once. On me."

Chance looked to Broachford. "Maybe you should get the engine running in case we need to escape again."

Broachford glanced at the screen, his expression unimpressed. "I don't see why this woman is so significant."

"If we don't find her, we're looking for three needles in a haystack of about three-hundred-and-twenty million people. Not exactly chicken feed. If you know of a better way to find Trinity, now is your chance to share. Otherwise, it's Goggles and his crazy phonebook algorithm."

Chewing the statement over for a moment, Broachford eventually nodded, albeit begrudgingly. "I'll go get the car started. If, by some miracle, this works, let me know." The agent left the room, his hands in his jacket pockets. Chance heard his feet stomping down the internal staircase, and then the front door opened and closed.

"So… are you really some badass?" asked Goggles hesitantly.

Chance smiled thinly. "I'm not sure what I am."

"I saw your photo on my news feed." He seemed uncertain how to proceed. "They're saying you escaped from an insane asylum."

For a moment, Chance contemplated lying. Eventually, he sighed and dropped down onto the only other chair in the loft. "Do you have a problem with that?"

Goggles blanched and shook his head wildly. "Please don't rape me."

"Huh? Why would I…? I'm not going to do anything to you, Goggles. At this point in my life, you're the closest thing I have to a friend."

An uncomfortable silence descended on the two. After a few minutes, a soft chime sounded from the computer.

"I believe we have a match," said Goggles. He peered closely at the screen. "Wait… this is odd."

"What's odd?"

"It says she's only a few streets down from here."

Chance glanced at the window, thinking. Turning back, he rose from the chair and patted Goggles on the shoulder before writing down the address. He then hurried out the door and down the stairs. Exiting through the front door, he saw Broachford glance around from the front seat of the Nissan. The agent seemed to leap up remarkably swiftly. By the time he had made it to the car, Broachford had walked around to meet him at the passenger door.

"What's up?" Broachford asked.

Chance eyed him suspiciously. Why was he wiping his hands on the front of his slacks? "Goggles found an address. She's a few streets down."

"Maybe we should walk there."

Glancing left and right, Chance looked back at the Nissan. "Is there something wrong with your car?"

Broachford blew out a heavy breath. "Nope. Nothing at all. Let's go."

As the agent skipped back around to the driver's door, Chance opened his side and slid in. The first thing he noticed was the smell. An acrid odor hung heavily in the air, almost metallic in its scent.

"Is something electrical burning?" he asked.

Broachford made a scene of sniffing the air. "I can't smell anything." Turning the key, he revved the motor loudly and smiled. "I'll run the fan for a while to clear it out if you want." He reached forward and flicked the knob for the air conditioning. A loud fan began to blow air into the car, but Chance could still smell the fetid odor.

He stared hard at Broachford. Despite the cold breeze blowing onto him, the agent bore beads of sweat on his brow and cheeks. His eyes appeared unnaturally tense. Chance looked him up and down in disgust.

"You got it from the hooker, didn't you?"

Broachford's face paled. "Let's get going before your professor leaves or something. Who knows, Goggles might have sold us out by now."

"You bought meth from her." Chance shook his head in cold wonder. "Couldn't even last a day, could you?"

Broachford gripped the wheel tightly. "You're insane. I mean literally insane. You should still be in that damn asylum, talking like that." He puffed heavily, glaring at Chance.

"I can't do this with a junkie at my side."

Chance made to open the side door. Broachford reached across and gripped him with both hands, slamming him back in the chair.

"You're not going anywhere, freak."

Chance looked down at the hands holding him, and then up into Broachford's glaring eyes. "Don't touch me," he demanded, the words soft but venomous.

Broachford's tongue darted out to lick his lips. He appeared uncertain at the confidence brewing within Chance.

From Chance's perspective, all he could see was a cowardly man who had once beaten his wife so badly she could find no escape but in death, even if it was only crafted as a ruse.

Slowly, Broachford unclenched his fingers, eventually releasing Chance. "I'm sorry," he whispered.

"Too late."

Chance stepped out of the car and began walking. It was only a few blocks to Doctor Petrov's new home, but he would need to be covert. Or at least as covert as he could manage. Little doubt lingered in his mind that Broachford would try to follow him, and the agent, despite being high on meth, would doubtless be more proficient at clandestine affairs than Chance could ever imagine.

At the first opportunity, he turned right, and then hid beyond the edge of the third house he came to. He waited a long time. As he began to think he was paranoid, he saw the blue Nissan cruise past. Shaking his head, Chance waited a few moments before emerging and stalking off in the direction of the doctor's house. Three more times he had to hide, twice being almost too late. But Broachford never paused in his cruising, never gave any indication he had noticed Chance.

Eventually, Chance neared the address Goggles had given him. Knowing that the FBI would be watching the place,

Chance hopped over the neighbor's fence. A Chihuahua suddenly bolted around the side of the house, yapping like a battery-powered toy in overdrive. Hurriedly, Chance leaped the fence surrounding Doctor Petrov's protective-custody house, barely three steps ahead of the snarling ball of teeth. The ferocious pint-sized canine scratched and clawed at the fence, but Chance ignored it. The back door beckoned, and he stood frozen, staring at the rear porch, wondering what he was going to say. Then, urgency pushed him forward, and he stumbled up the three steps to the door. He raised his hand and knocked twice before stepping back and glancing around nervously.

The door opened, and Doctor Petrov stared at him incredulously. "What in the…?" Her face quickly hardened. "Hurry up and come inside," she urged. "The FBI have a house across the street. Coming around the back might have eluded them for now, but that dog will swiftly draw their attention." She grimaced as she closed the door behind him. "Seeing the inmate who escaped Mount Sinai would likely set off some alarm bells, I think."

"*One* of the men who escaped," Chance corrected her.

She cocked her head. "Excuse me?"

"Jarvis got out too."

The doctor shook her head slowly. "I haven't heard about him. The only person they are reporting on is you." The large woman suddenly stepped in and pecked him on the cheek.

Abashed, Chance peered at her oddly, and then touched his cheek. "What was that for?"

"You saved my life," she replied, shrugging. "It seemed appropriate."

"Okay," replied Chance hesitantly. He contemplated what to say next. "I need your help."

She nodded. "Come with me." Doctor Petrov led him into a living room and bade him sit on the wide couch. "Would you like a beverage?"

Chance fought back the urge to grin. It had been so long since someone had asked him something so formally that he momentarily forgot his situation. "I'll have a beer if you have one."

She shook her head. "Alcohol clouds the mind. As do other stimulants such as caffeine and even sugar."

"I guess I'll need all my faculties clear in the coming conversation, right?"

The doctor nodded grimly.

"A glass of water, then? Thanks."

A moment later, Chance was sipping on some iced water with a slice of lime floating in it. It was surprisingly refreshing, and he smiled and nodded his thanks to his host. She sat down in a single plush chair nearby and gazed at him through her glasses.

"Why don't you tell me where we stand?" Her English, as always, was tinged with a Russian accent, but her enunciation was perfect.

"Well, where to begin?" Chance looked up and met her stare. "I phantom walked out of the asylum."

If he had expected scorn or disbelief, Chance was sorely disappointed. Doctor Petrov merely nodded, a consummate professional, reminding Chance this woman dealt with the paranormal on a daily basis.

"Do you know how you did this?"

Chance shrugged. "No idea. One minute I was there, and the next I was out."

"Hmm." She seemed to think for a moment, steepling her fingers as though she were praying. "Could somebody else have assisted you?"

"What do you mean?"

"What you are talking about is stunningly powerful." She took a sip from her own glass, and then placed it down on a side table and continued. "I know you understand this, or at least think you do, but let me rephrase it in an attempt to put things into greater perspective. What you are talking about is the equivalent of a field mouse deciphering quantum physics."

Chance squinted at her. "How is that even possible?"

She shrugged. "I have no idea. In all my years of study, I have never encountered someone like you, Chance. You have apparently never displayed psychic ability before, yet you are able to tap into terrifyingly powerful aspects of it. To be able to manipulate matter the way you did when inhabiting my body…." She saw him frowning. "You flung the killer away from me, right across the room. That kind of telekinesis is not only rare, but extraordinarily potent. For a start, it wasn't *your* body creating the shockwave that flung him away, but mine. Therefore, you somehow managed to tap into my energy and manipulate it against our attacker. Such a feat is beyond stunning." She shook her head in amazement. "And then you phantom walked out of the asylum. No preparation or meditation, not even drugs. You stepped directly through space. Where did you end up?"

"Times Square."

The doctor's eyes bugged out of her head. "My God."

"Why is that important?"

"The distance you traveled. It's stunning." Rubbing her chin, the Russian doctor mused over the situation, giving Chance a moment to sip his drink. "Back to my original question, though. Could someone have helped you? Someone with special abilities. You might not have even known they were helping."

"There was one person. A woman." Chance proceeded to tell Doctor Petrov about Betsy. "But she was in a coma the entire time. I spoke to her one final time before escaping; I was holding her hand in the hospital, and we somehow transported to the Sixth Plane. Then Trinity came for us, and I thought I fled back to the hospital, but it was all an illusion. Trinity attacked me again, and when I woke up, I was in an alley near Times Square."

"Perhaps this woman, Betsy, helped you to escape."

"She might be my sister." The words had slipped from Chance's mouth before he realized what he was saying. "I met a woman who claimed to know about my past." He didn't need to go into details about what had occurred at Princeton.

"She said I had a twin sister, who might already have been committed. I think that sister is Betsy."

"What leads you to believe that?"

"Well, there's the obvious link between us; how else was I able to communicate with a woman in a coma?"

Doctor Petrov shrugged. Chance knew he hadn't convinced her.

"She also has psychic ability or some semblance of it. Even you think she might have been the reason I was able to escape by phantom walking out of there. The more I think about it, the more I become convinced she's my sister."

"The problem with focusing on a singular point," said the doctor, "is that you can't see the issue from any other angle. You are basing this on a lot of guesswork and speculation. Perhaps this woman, while trapped in her coma, called out to your latent psychic ability in a way that made you respond. Capacity to communicate with her would then come solely from you. Even her assistance in your escape might have been unintentional. Your mind might have merely tapped into her psyche and used her mental energy to propel you beyond the borders of the asylum. You said yourself that you had phantom walked on your own once before; maybe this was merely another episode, multiplied when you panicked and tapped into her soul."

"Wait – what are you talking about?"

She sighed and appeared to gather her thoughts. "There has been speculation among the psychic community that all extrasensory abilities derive from one source: the soul.

Therefore, tapping into a soul might magnify your own abilities. The stronger the soul, the more potent the effect."

"But what would that do to Betsy?"

"I have no idea. As I said, this is pure speculation. There have been no scientific studies on the subject. Any respected parapsychologist who suggested tapping into another person's soul for power would be figuratively burned at the stake." She stared Chance directly in the eye. "For all we know, you're the reason she is in a coma in the first place."

"*What?*" Chance exclaimed.

"Do you know what caused her to fall into the coma?"

"Well… no."

"And how long has she been insensible?"

Frowning, Chance said, "I don't know."

For a long time, he sat silently. Perhaps the doctor was correct and he had been siphoning Betsy's energy for months without even knowing it.

"We need to get in contact with Doctor Smith," he murmured.

"For what reason?"

"Only he can tell us if I'm the cause of Betsy's condition."

"How will that aid you in your current predicament? All it will do is alert authorities to the fact you and I have been in communication. No, for the time being, you must concentrate on the more immediate task of stopping these killers."

Chance stood up and paced over to the window, turning back to face the doctor. "I can't just forget about it."

"There is nothing concrete to indicate she is your sister. Everything we have discussed is pure speculation, without a shred of proof. If you start leaping to conclusions, you will condemn yourself before you know anything. The woman was in an asylum, leading us to believe she was hardly the most mentally attuned being on the face of the planet. You assume she is your relative on the word of a woman you barely met, who practically admitted to trying to delay you for the police. Hardly the most reliable source of information, in my opinion."

"All right. So where do I go from here?"

Suddenly, a commotion erupted behind him. Chance turned and peered out the window, between the curtains. His heart thudded in his chest when he recognized the blue Nissan. A breath later, he saw the source of the disturbance. Special Agent Broachford was face down on the pavement with two men on top of him, attempting to handcuff his writhing form. From the looks of things, the men were not having an easy time of it, reminding Chance of the meth Broachford had taken. Judging from the scene across the road, the stories of superhuman strength derived from the drug appeared terrifyingly accurate. Eventually, however, the sheer body weight of the two agents on top of Broachford's back forced him to remain immobile long enough for them to restrain him with handcuffs.

"What's happening?" breathed Doctor Petrov beside him.

"That's an FBI agent who was helping me. We had a… disagreement before I came here. Looks like he returned to the hacker's place and obtained your address. I don't know who the men wrestling with him are."

"They're also FBI," she said. "Remember I told you about the house across the road? Those men are one of the crews assigned to watch over me."

Chance cursed and looked back out the window. "What if he tells them I'm in here?"

"You need to hide. This house does not provide a wealth of places for such an act, but there is a closet in my office – or what passes for my office these days. Go upstairs and enter the first room on your left. Wait there until I call out to tell you everything is clear."

Taking a second glance through the curtains, Chance saw one of the agents approaching the house. Broachford still lay restrained on the ground, the second agent kneeling on the back of his neck, pinning him, while he spoke hurriedly into his cellphone. In the distance, sirens wailed.

"Upstairs," Petrov demanded. "Now!"

Chance sprinted up the stairs and entered the office as directed. The moment he closed the door, he heard the doctor downstairs open the front door and greet the FBI agent.

"Is everything all right?" she asked. Chance marveled at her calm tone.

"Ma'am, we caught a fugitive lurking out the front of your property. He was involved in the breakout of an escapee from Mount Sinai Mental Refuge, the one our people have previously discussed with you. Have you seen anything unusual? I heard a dog barking next door earlier."

"No, I've seen nothing. Is he dangerous?"

"There's nothing for you to worry about, ma'am. We have no reason to believe this has anything to do with the attempt on your life; it's probably just a freak coincidence. I'll leave you to your afternoon. Thank you for your time."

Chance heard the front door close and waited. Sirens came closer and eventually pulled up out the front of the house. They finally fell silent in a blur of flashing lights. He crept out of the closet and over to the window. A black SUV had parked out front, flashing blue and red lights glowing through its front grill. After a short discussion, two agents lifted Broachford, marched him over to the rear door of the car, and shoved him into the back seat. For a brief time, all four agents stood on the front lawn discussing something Chance had no way of hearing. Finally, they bid farewell to each other, and the original two marched back toward the surveillance house across the road, while the newcomers climbed into the SUV and drove off. Chance exhaled a sigh of relief, misting the window.

Chance turned away from the window, heading toward the office door. As he passed the doctor's desk, however, something in the corner of his eye caught his attention. Pausing, Chance turned, noticing a folder resting there. A photo was paper-clipped to the front of the cardboard.

"What the...?"

He stared at the upside down image of himself. It was not a photo from the asylum, as he might have expected, but a fresher image, one from Times Square where he was still dressed in his hospital attire. Turning the folder around, he flipped the cover open and saw another photo of him beneath it, this time walking the street wearing the drab garb of the hobo named Slim Jimmy. The next image was of him and Jarvis in their hospital room.

The door creaked open. "I think you're in the clear for the moment."

Chance spun around and faced Doctor Petrov. He held up the photos. "What are these?"

Frowning at the folder for a moment, eventually the doctor's shoulders slumped. "After you saved me from the killer, I began to realize how powerful you were. To have flung a fully-grown man across the room while inhabiting my body would have required tremendous psychokinetic strength. I first noticed it when you shattered the light tubes during our hospital meeting, but to do it when away from your physical body...." She shook her head in wonder. "I had you put under surveillance."

"Excuse me?"

"Several nurses answer to me in the hospital, and they reported on many of your unusual dealings. When you vanished, I hired some investigators at great expense. Luckily enough, one picked up your trail almost immediately; that image of you in Times Square was taken from a security camera outside of a bank, I believe. From there, he managed to keep track of you – loosely, but with enough information that I might know what your intentions might be. I concluded that you had no idea what you were doing. Not really, anyway."

"Why would you do such a thing?"

"Part of it was curiosity. But I believe the greater part was that you are physical proof of what I have been trying to study for over two decades." Her tone was reasonable, no hint of tension in anything she said. Nor was there any suggestion of an apology. "You are the equivalent of NASA discovering the existence of aliens, or a historian unveiling the location of Atlantis. I felt the need to study you, to see what you were up to, but I never thought you would appear on my own doorstep."

Chance contemplated her words. Her reasoning seemed rational, but the mere fact she had studied him like some lab rat made the cauldron of his anger simmer. His heart wanted nothing more than to rage at her and storm out of the house, but his brain told him to remain calm and rationalize with the woman who might be able to get a handle on the strange abilities he had awoken. The cold rationality of her tone told him she thought little of her betrayal of trust, if she even recognized it for what it was.

"So, what now?" he asked.

"To be truthful, I'm not sure. One part of me wants to secure you and study you under controlled conditions in a lab. A greater part wonders what would happen if I were to aid you in your quest. You have advanced significantly in your talent since awakening with no memory. Perhaps this is what aids you; something from your past life might have been holding you back, and your clean slate has washed away all constraints. I have seen the aftermath of your power, and can only imagine what you will become when fully developed." She spoke of him with about as much emotion as if he were a strange caterpillar morphing into a butterfly.

"How do I… control this thing?"

A brief frown flitted across her brow. "Well, that's a question for the ages, to be sure. Fear seemed to be the contributing factor when you defended my body. In essence, your mind reacted as though your own life were in danger. Adrenaline would have pumped through my veins, increasing your reactions and physical strength. Your psyche entered fight or flight mode, and you decided to fight. Much to my benefit, I might add." Her green eyes peered at him through her tortoiseshell-framed glasses. "But none of this truly answers your question. I believe that if you stay with me, I might be able to train you."

"What, here?"

"Why not? My house is possibly the last place the authorities would think to look for you. And apart from the FBI, nobody else knows I'm here. Plus, you would have the added protection of federal agents right across the street."

"Do I need to point out that ten minutes ago they arrested my former accomplice on the lawn outside your front door? They will know I'm nearby, and even if they didn't search the place properly, next time, word will filter through and eventually they'll find me. Not to mention what will happen if Broachford blabs about me being here. Let's just say our parting words weren't exactly sweet."

Doctor Petrov exhaled softly, her irritation evident. "You make valid points. Fine, my place is out, which means I can't teach you." A grimace flitted across her features as she contemplated something. Eventually, she looked up, visibly unimpressed with what she was about to propose. "There is another."

"Who?"

"A woman I met following one of the conferences I run around the country. Most who attend are purely scientific, but this person was… different."

"Why do I get the feeling she scared you?"

The doctor nodded slowly. "She claimed to have been testing people with abilities. Nothing beyond that. But her claims were… impressive."

"Impressive? How so?"

"She stated participants' control increased by factors of up to sixty percent. I never investigated beyond the cursory – in fact, it was around the time I was advised of your particular abilities that I became waylaid from any such inquiry." She appeared to ponder something for a moment. "Speaking of which, how long has it been since you witnessed a full triple murder."

"What do you mean?"

"I mean, how long since you saw three women killed? From what Doctor Smith told me, it used to happen quite regularly."

"I…."

The truth was, Chance couldn't recall three women ever being killed together. There had been two, and then the third had happened the day after. But apart from that, there had only been random killings, the closest to tandem being the librarian and the woman from Santa Monica. The more recent attacks seemed directed more toward him.

"I'm not sure."

"Hmm. Interesting." Her green eyes were piercing.

"Do you think it might mean something?"

She shrugged. "It might mean many things. Without evidence, though, I would only be speculating."

Chance let the subject go. "Anyway, more about this woman who might be able to teach me to control this… talent." The last word tore from him. If anything, his abilities felt more like a curse than a gift, but if they could help him solve this mystery, he would need to be able to employ them at will.

"If memory serves me, she was an author. She claimed to be writing a true-life exposé into the world of the paranormal." Doctor Petrov paused. "She spoke of technical points that only one in the scientific or medical field would use in casual conversation, but she claimed no such background. For all intents and purposes, it appeared she was merely a writer."

"There must have been something more about her to unnerve you," said Chance.

The doctor nodded slowly, her expression tense. "I received the impression she was probing me, searching for some kind of mental weakness." She shuddered slightly. "It was a most unpleasant experience."

"Yet you think she'll be able to help me?"

"If her claims are accurate, yes."

"Where can I find her?" Chance asked.

Doctor Petrov pulled a folder from her desk drawer. After rifling through it for a moment, she produced a business card and handed it to Chance. The card was black print on unadorned white cardboard, a simple name and contact number. Under the name, however, was the woman's job title, and the coincidence gave him chills.

The woman's name was Bella Fontaine, and she worked at Princeton University as a lecturer in human psychology.

* * * *

Special Agent Doug Broachford's blue Nissan chugged along the freeway.

Chance had gambled against potential capture to steal the car, but his choices at the time had been limited. It was either risk being spotted by the agents across the road or try to hitchhike to Princeton. Doctor Petrov didn't have a car at the safe house, but as she pointed out, even if she did, the agents would have screamed into action the moment her car appeared in the driveway.

Now he headed back to Princeton, back into the jaws of the lion he had only recently escaped. Would the police be watching the university, he wondered? The odds were minimal, especially given the fact Broachford had been caught miles away, but they might still be lurking. They did expect to be dealing with a crazy man, after all. It wasn't like Chance was supposed to be acting rationally.

A fly buzzed around his head, trapped in the car, and he swatted it away. Moments later, the buzzing returned. He raised his hand to deter the insect, and suddenly the scene around him altered. There was no transition, no blurriness of altering realities. One moment, he was sitting in the car, and the next he stood in the midst of a pumpkin patch.

"Oh shit."

The first thought to shoot through his head was that he had somehow flitted into the subconscious of the little girl he had met here previously, and he glanced around nervously for the entity she had called Nothingman. The second thought was that while he was here, nobody was controlling the blue Nissan.

"You're back."

Between him and a rickety barn, the same barn he had seen in his previous vision, stood the tiny girl covered in grit and bruises. Her left hand clutched her dolly, and her eyes still held the same edge of mistrust, but the glare seemed less harsh this time. Again, the stark reality of this place felt much more than dreamlike, yet the oddness of it could never be real. Looking down at his childlike body, Chance grimaced. Was this going to be a repeat of his last visit here? He glanced up at the barn, a structure of regular proportions for the moment, and saw it was missing one of its doors; the same one Nothingman had flung away during Chance's last visit. Lightly, Chance kicked one of the nearby pumpkins and grimaced as pain spiked through his toe. So real… yet it could not be real. None of it.

"What's going on?" he asked.

The girl's head tilted to the side, her eyes wide and owlish. "You don't know?"

Looking around, he asked, "Where's Nothingman?'

"Everywhere," she whispered. Something in the sound of her voice slipped through his skin, sending shivers down his spine.

"Should we run?"

"Would it make any difference? He always catches us."

"Always? I've only ever been here –"

The statement cut off as a horrendous howl echoed through the sky. Clouds bunched, crowding low and dark, looming in for a better view. Before he knew it, the girl's hand slipped into his.

"He's here," she whispered, terror evident in her tone.

Chance's heart thudded in his chest. He snapped his gaze left and right, searching for the source of the attack. The last time it had emerged from the barn, but now the rickety structure appeared unchanged. Something was happening, though, he could feel it in his soul.

The ground began to tremor. Chance glanced down in time to see thousands of ashen hands rip free from the earth. They clawed blindly at the air above them, a horde of corpse-like appendages seeking purchase on nothing. Well, almost nothing.

Dancing around, away from the orchard of rotten fingers, Chance felt the scraping on his leg cuff too late. The hand grasped him triumphantly and yanked violently downward. One leg remained aboveground while the captured limb sank into the earth so fast Chance did not even have time to scream. His hand tore from that of the little girl. Soil filled his mouth even as he felt his legs splitting apart like a wishbone.

The car horn pierced his eardrums before the vision of headlights punctured his mind. It wasn't night, but the driver screaming toward him was trying anything to gather his attention before they collided. With a gasp, Chance yanked the steering wheel over, hauling the Nissan back to the right side of the road. Angry shouting blurred as the cars snapped past each other, barely a foot separating them.

As soon as he could, Chance pulled over. His door opened, and he spilled out onto the pavement, his entire body shaking. Nausea swept over him, but with an effort, he managed to haul back the urge to vomit. For a time, he merely sat, leaning against the side of the Nissan, calming his thoughts and slowing the trembling of his traumatized body. Between the vision of Nothingman and snapping back to reality, he feared his grip on sanity might be closer than ever to vanishing entirely. Maybe it already had.

Eventually, he rose on shaking legs and stumbled back into the car. Again, he sat without moving for several moments, gathering his wits and summoning enough nerve to twist the key in the ignition once more. He feared reality might break apart at any instant and plummet him down the gullet of another nightmarish fantasy not of his making. The only thing that aided him in shifting into gear and continuing his journey was the hope that maybe, just maybe, the woman waiting at the other end might be able to stave off any further lapses in control.

The rest of the journey to Princeton occurred without incident, but every bump in the road sent panic rushing through Chance, every horn blaring threatened to send him screeching to the side of the road once more. Eventually, he pulled into the parking lot of the university and sat for another ten minutes. The tremor had yet to leave his hands fully, and it was with some effort that he stepped out of the vehicle and considered the buildings.

Chance pulled the business card from his pocket and examined it once more. He contemplated trying to call the number, but if the woman had been alerted to his earlier visit to Princeton, she might lure him into a trap with police. No, it seemed best to find her on his own terms.

Trying his best to act as discreetly as possible, Chance walked directly toward the main building, or at least what he hoped might be the main building, anticipating a primary reception area inside the doors. When he and Broachford had met with the dean, they had avoided the main structure altogether, heading instead toward the offices on the left. He felt like a fool to be stumbling directly into the core building, but could think of no other option. Nobody would suspect him of trying to meet with this Bella Fontaine, whoever that was, and he hoped no alarm bells would ring if he asked for details about her whereabouts.

After some cursory requests for directions, Chance finally found himself walking toward the welcome desk, situated in a stately building on Elm Drive. Unfortunately, it was a decent hike for a man trying his best to remain unnoticed. Unable to do anything about it other than retreating to collect the Nissan, Chance kept his head down and eventually found his way.

"Hello," he said to the friendly-looking woman behind the pale timber desk. She smiled warmly, and he tried his best not to look like a psychopath. "I'm looking for Bella Fontaine." He slipped the business card across the reception desk as if that somehow validated his claim.

The receptionist picked up the slightly tattered card and examined it before placing it back down on the wood. Turning to her computer terminal, the woman tapped something in, and then peered at the screen.

"It seems Ms. Fontaine has only one lecture this week." Chance's heart plummeted. "Luckily for you, it is in about an hour over in the East Pyne Auditorium."

"How do I get there?"

Pulling out a photocopied map, the receptionist drew the course he needed to take through the multitude of buildings to arrive at his destination. Chance gaped at the route, stunned at the sheer scope of the campus. He had imagined a small cluster of buildings and sporting facilities, but the map seemed composed of scores of structures, all with odd sounding names like 'McCormich' or 'Dod'. No doubt, these names meant something to the students and faculty, but to an interloper such as himself, they seemed like a deck of random titles dropped onto green felt cloth.

Chance set off through the university grounds on his way to the East Pyne Auditorium. After many missteps and retreats, he eventually made his way to a stately gothic building. The journey took him close to an hour, and by the time he arrived, all semblance of subtlety had fallen away from his trudging walk. As he ambled up the stairs to the auditorium (turning left instead of right and cursing before backtracking), he wondered what he was going to say to this woman.

Looking up, he saw a line of students assembled outside the door to the hall. He considered slipping past them and into the room, but some semblance of tact remained within him, so he crept to the end of the queue and waited. He didn't have to wait long. Soon, the double doors to the auditorium folded outward, and the students began to file inside.

Once Chance stepped through the doors, he glanced toward the front of the class and froze. Standing before the class, preparing her notes, was one of the most stunning women he had ever seen. Part of his brain refused to believe someone so aesthetically pleasing could possibly hold the answers he desired. His luck simply wasn't that good. A heartbeat later, logic kicked in, and he continued up the stairs, finding a desk at the rear of the auditorium, amongst the topmost tier of the seating rows.

The students opened laptops and gathered writing pads, ready to take down notes. Chance had nothing with him, so he simply stared down towards the burgundy-haired beauty at the front of the class.

Bella Fontaine was young, much younger than he might have anticipated, but she carried herself with a worldliness that belied her years. Despite being only in her late-twenties, possibly early thirties, her confidence shone through her manner. When she cleared her throat, all noise and conversation ceased within moments.

"You are all here today to learn about parapsychology, I presume." Her voice filled the room, soft, yet brimming with self-assurance and authority. Bella peered up at the students filling the auditorium, and she stepped away from the podium, becoming the dominant focus in the room. "Some may question my credentials, as I hold neither a doctorate nor any equivalent degree. I bring this to the fore not to defend myself, but to lay bare that which some of you no doubt know already. There are several here at Princeton who believe my writings are no more than voodoo or witchcraft. They have voiced disdain for the mere fact I have been allowed to speak the few times I have attended as a visiting lecturer." She paused, her light blue eyes scanning the room. For a moment, her gaze seemed to hesitate on Chance, and he fought down the urge to shrink down in his seat. "What I am here to discuss is scorned by modern psychology and chiefly ignored by general science. But the fact this room is almost full gives me hope that maybe there are still some open minds yearning to seize the truth."

She turned back to the podium and picked up a clicker. For the first time, Chance noticed the projector mounted to the ceiling of the auditorium. With a click, Bella Fontaine turned the projector on. An image of a woman strapped to a chair snapped into view on the large white screen hanging on the wall behind the stage. The image appeared old and grainy, and the woman wore an expression of torment. Lank strands of dark hair draped her pale features, her mouth stretched wide in a silent scream.

"This lady's name was Eleanor Stone, and she was possessed by Satan," Bella stated, her tone clinical. "Or so they believed in 1876, around the time this photo was taken." She stared at the picture for a moment. "They tied her to that chair because she claimed to hear the thoughts of others. When questioned, she was able to back up her claims. Exorcism rites at the time saw her tormented and abused to the point where what was left of her was little more than a husk. She died soon after. All records state that her death was due to…." She picked up a sheet of paper and examined it. "'Extreme blood loss due to flagellation.'" Her gaze returned to the crowd. "Not a nice way to go by any means."

She clicked the remote in her hand. Another image, less grainy, but still old, popped up onto the screen. This one showed a man in a straightjacket, his head covered in electronic probes.

"Flash forward to the beginning of the Second World War. Over sixty years have passed, so you would think scientific progress in the field of parapsychology might have shunted ahead, but you would be sadly mistaken. This image is of Benjamin Stokes, an infantryman who awoke one day with the ability to move things simply by thinking about the action. Many of you will recognize this as telekinesis. Instead of treating him as a human with an extraordinary gift, he was locked up in an asylum alongside psychopaths and child killers." Her gaze flitted up toward Chance, and his heart shot into his throat. "A very early form of ECT, or Electroconvulsive Therapy, commonly known as shock therapy, was trialed on Mister Stokes. It fried out his cerebrum, leaving him brain dead for the few remaining years he lived. Needless to say, he never showed signs of telekinesis again."

A third slide appeared on the screen. This one displayed in color, though hardly high definition. A woman was lying flat on a surgical table, her cranium carved open, and her brain exposed. Several doctors stood examining the inside of her skull and her exposed brain.

"Here lies Suzanne Wilkes. In the summer of 1984, Suzanne went to pick up her son from elementary school and during a heated argument with his teacher over poor grades, she somehow set the entire school on fire. Three teachers and a janitor died. Again, Suzanne was committed to a psychological institute, and after numerous fires had broken out in the facility, doctors pronounced her a pyromaniac. Various medications failed – in fact, they seemed to make the outbreaks even more frequent – and eventually, it was decided that Suzanne needed to be lobotomized. Upon examination, doctors found a benign tumor the size of a walnut in her frontal lobe. Whether this was associated with her unusual ability was never documented or speculated upon. She died on the operating table."

Bella Fontaine turned to face the class. "Throughout the ages, psychic abilities have met with scorn, fear, and anger. Even in our modern age, it took a petition from several student bodies for Princeton to permit me to lecture the half dozen times they have allowed. For those of you involved in that, thank you."

For some time, she stood at the desk, rifling through her notes. "Who here has psychic ability?" she eventually asked, looking up. Not a single hand rose. Bella scanned the class, waiting. Still, nobody owned up. "Well, you're all wrong."

A confused murmuring hummed through the crowd. Chance leaned forward, resting his elbows on his knees in an attempt to listen better.

"Every single person has the capacity for some kind of psychic ability. There is nothing different in the brain of an individual with telekinesis than that of a housewife who has never shifted a gram of dust without physically touching it." Rubbing her hands together, she stepped lithely across the short stage. She knew she had them; Chance could see triumph in her gaze. "So, if there is nothing different, it becomes a matter of training the brain to do what you want it to do, correct? Not necessarily. This is not a person training to be a long distance runner. And right there is the crux of the matter. How do you develop an attribute that you cannot sense in the first place? Sometimes an accident will jolt a person's innate abilities. Or a person might be born able to grasp what those around them cannot fathom. But that does not mean those around them lack any mental capacity or differ physically."

A hand rose. A young girl with strawberry-blond hair said, "You mentioned earlier that Suzanne Wilkes had a tumor the size of a walnut in her brain. Could such an anomaly have been the catalyst?"

Bella failed to hide the smile that crept onto her lips. Slowly, she nodded. "Like I said, sometimes it takes an accident to jolt someone into awareness. Perhaps in Suzanne's case, it was the presence of the tumor that unlocked her ability to create fire from nothing. We will probably never know. What we do know is that there are too many documented cases throughout history of people being able to tap into psychic abilities for such paradigms to be needlessly ignored."

She stepped slowly back to the opposite side of the stage. "So, can anyone tell me the possible drawbacks of psychic ability?"

"Being committed," Chance muttered before he realized. The class turned around, peering at him, and he scrunched down in his chair.

"Excuse me, what was that?" asked Bella Fontaine.

"Um." Chance scratched his neck, cursing himself. "Being put in an asylum."

She jabbed a finger at him and nodded. "Exactly." Indicating the image still up on the screen, she said, "Extraordinariness is always regarded with fear or mistrust. If people cannot explain something rationally, they try to box it up in a category that makes sense, whether it be spiritual possession or mental illness."

Despite himself, Chance found himself leaning forward once more. A part of him yearned to call out questions, to interact with the discourse on a much more personal level. The generalized topics of conversation merely whetted his appetite. He yearned to ask why three killers would be trying to siphon the souls of innocent victims. However, to do so would be to expose himself utterly, so he bided his time and listened.

"What about you, Miss Fontaine?' asked a dark-haired male near the front of the class. To Chance, he appeared arrogant and deriding. "What *exceptional* ability do you have?" The question sounded lewd, even from where Chance was sitting. Several students near where the asker sat, most likely his friends, sniggered.

Bella smiled thinly. "Well, for starters, I can spot someone trying to compensate for inadequate genitalia at a thousand paces."

"What did you say about me?" stormed the young man, rising from his seat.

"Whoever said I was talking about you?" replied Bella with a level glare. "Did you read my mind?"

For a moment, the young man blustered. Finally, he turned and gathered his belongings. "I don't need to sit here and listen to this garbage."

"I'm only stating what everyone is thinking," countered Bella. The class laughed openly. "It doesn't take a mind-reader to know that."

The arrogant young man stormed out of the class, followed closely by two companions. Bella waited until the auditorium door banged shut before continuing as if nothing had happened.

Score one for the teacher, mused Chance, impressed.

"There is speculation that people can possess more than one unique ability." Again, Bella Fontaine's glance flitted toward Chance. He felt his cheeks burning, and the urge to flee tore at him, but to rise from his seat would attract the attention of the entire class. "Much like characters from comic books, these people can not only enter minds, but they can phantom walk and manipulate matter at will."

Certainty dropped into Chance's stomach like a leaden milkshake. The comparison of subject material was too similar to be a mere coincidence; Bella Fontaine knew exactly who he was. He began to glance nervously toward the door, half-expecting FBI agents to barge into the auditorium at any moment.

As if sensing his unease, the lecturer abruptly changed subjects. "Throughout history, there are documented incidents involving ordinary people possessing gifts beyond the norm. Tibetan monks have demonstrated psychic or transcendental abilities while deep within a meditative trance. Some have spirit walked or controlled their physical being under extreme stress, similar to the fire walkers of Iron Age India." She sighed.

"But I digress. My point is that these people of apparently mundane character have taught their minds to obey them, despite showing no early indications of psychic ability. So what does this mean for the human race as a whole?" She held her hands wide. "Apparently nothing. If there have been no significant advancements over the centuries that such talents have been evident, why would they alter anything now?"

The question sank into the audience. Bella Fontaine allowed the silence to linger until Chance could hear students shuffling uncomfortably in their seats.

"Think of technology." This seemingly abrupt change in subject matter snapped everyone's attention back to her. "The first general-purpose computer was the ENIAC, or Electronic Numerical Integrator and Computer. It was developed in 1946...." Her eyes rolled around speculatively in her head. "Or thereabouts." A general tittering flitted through the audience. "The ENIAC filled whole rooms and had less computing power than a modern day scientific calculator." She paused to let the fact sink in. "So, in less than a century, we have gone from something like that – " she fished into her pocket and pulled out her cell phone – "to having a device that can access the total history of human knowledge, every video or sound bite ever recorded and made public, scientific formulae and historical documents, in a fraction of a second." She grinned. "And we use it to share selfies."

The crowd laughed. Even Chance found himself grinning at the humor of the statement. At that moment, he glanced around the room, noting how rapt the students seemed in her lecture. Bella gripped their attention because she made it stimulating. *And* believable.

"My studies have led me to believe that the human mind is similar to an intricate lock. With the right manipulation, access can be gained to a near infinite storehouse of abilities. Hopefully, if my funding comes through this year, and they don't laugh in my face, we will be able to expand on these studies. Who knows, one day you might be able to look back and say you attended a guest lecture from the woman who taught the human mind how to destroy cancer cells." She paused. "Imagine if we were able to phantom walk from one location to another at will. What limits could there be to human expansion throughout the universe? Space exploration might become as simple as stepping into another room."

"Sounds like science fiction," muttered a slender girl three rows down from Chance.

Bella nodded. "Perhaps. But some of you might recall the original Star Trek series where they used hand-held communicators that could fit in a pocket and talked face to face across vast distances via large viewing screens. What about the electronic tablets they wrote upon instead of using paper? Back in the sixties, when that program initially aired, such concepts seemed outlandish and unrealistic. Now, a mere fifty years later, these imaginings are an everyday reality that we take for granted. Perhaps our next leap forward lies not in technology, but in the human mind. If nothing else, it bears consideration. But, for now, this is all speculation." She clicked the remote in her hand, and a sketched image of the human brain popped up on the screen. "Who here knows what section of the brain is used most predominantly during telepathic communication?"

The discussion expanded to the more technical aspects of the seminar, but rather than switching off from boredom, Chance found himself rapt in everything the striking woman on the stage had to say. It wasn't so much her physical beauty that captivated him, though that should have been enough. She wove about herself an aura of energy that fascinated him; indeed, it seemed to have a similar influence on the rest of the auditorium. Those not actively engaged in the conversation still leaned forward in their seats, their eyes focused on the poised figure before them. For Chance, he found himself wondering if she cast a silent mental song through the audience. Was this her unique ability, to draw those around her into her charisma in such a way that they became ensnared, much like a fly in honey?

Chance couldn't think of a better way to go.

Eventually, the class ended. Many of the students hung back, lingering within the aura, chatting amongst themselves. Some approached Bella Fontaine directly, asking her questions to which she politely responded. Her face never once showed the slightest irritation at their inquiries, and each time her mouth tilted up in a smile, Chance felt his heart skip a beat.

One by one, they all filed out, finally leaving Chance alone in the large auditorium with the woman he had traveled all this way to meet. Now that the moment had arrived, however, Chance felt himself fumbling over what to say. Would she look at him as if he were an idiot, or worse, a psychopath? She was waiting for him by the podium, not even pretending she hadn't noticed his presence. She stood calmly, peering up at him, and Chance felt awkward and cumbersome, like a bear in a laboratory.

"I'm waiting," she murmured. Her voice carried through the air, up to where he sat, without hindrance. It was as if she had whispered into his ear.

Slowly, awkwardly, Chance rose from his seat. His right thigh caught under the edge of the half-desk. The chair scraped, the sound like nails on a chalkboard, and he winced. Bella's laughter didn't help his discomfort. Like an imbecile, he glanced around as though looking for his belongings, knowing full well he had none. He sensed she knew it too, but she refrained from mentioning it, a blessing for which he silently praised her. Eventually, with no other delaying tactics available, he trudged down the center aisle steps, his head down, refusing to meet her piercing gaze.

"Hi," he said when he reached her side. His mouth felt like it was full of cotton.

"Hi yourself," she replied, an impish grin twisting her lips.

"I'm...." Damn. Who could he say he was? His name had been plastered all over the news stations. If he mentioned it, she might be likely to run screaming from the hall, hollering for the police. "I mean... well...."

"I know who you are, Mister Ripley."

"Oh." The sound was small, weak. He glanced up and saw the amusement in her eyes. "Is that your gift?"

She shook her head. "Not unless by 'gift' you mean answering the telephone. Doctor Petrov called and told me you might be stopping by for a chat."

Chance's cheeks burned. He should have known that. "What else did she say to you?"

Bella shrugged. "Enough." Turning to the podium, she shuffled her papers into a briefcase, collected a laptop and placed it on top, and then snapped the case shut. She looked back at Chance and offered him her elbow. "Should we go?"

He looked at her elbow, up to her face, and then back down to her elbow. Eventually, he linked arms with the mysterious woman and strode with her out of the auditorium.

* * * *

The Nissan remained in the parking lot.

Chance sat in the passenger seat of Bella's Mustang, enjoying the crisp breeze cutting in through his partially opened window. The two hadn't conversed much; Bella hadn't even told him where they were going. All she had stated was that their destination was *safe*. Chance had almost chuckled.

Nowhere was safe, not anymore. He wasn't sure if it ever had been different; his entire memory consisted of confusion and fear in one form or another.

They chatted about mundane things. Chance learned that Bella had been doing seminars at universities around the country pro-bono to expand the public perception of what advanced human potential could truly look like. It wasn't only side-stories for horror and sci-fi junkies, she claimed, but an entirely new gateway for the evolution of the human species. The possibilities were endless.

As Chance listened to her impassioned yet simplistic conversation, he found himself noticing the curve of her lips. He snapped his gaze away and stared out the windshield, nodding at appropriate points of the conversation where he felt some input from him was necessary.

"Do you think you can teach me how to… control what is going on?" he asked during a break in the conversation.

"We'll see," she replied cryptically.

He looked outside the car. They appeared to be on the outskirts of Brooklyn, though he had no clue how he recognized it. The Cranberries were playing on the car stereo, another memory he had no way of tracing. When had he first heard the band and why could he remember them, yet not recall anything about his own history? The unanswered questions swam and fought through his mind, curling back occasionally and snapping at him with razor-sharp fangs, warning that delving too deep could prove perilous.

"Where are you from?" he asked, more to make some semblance of conversation than anything else.

"South," she replied, as though that answered everything. He huffed softly and returned his gaze out the window. "I am originally from Guatemala."

Chance started at the added response and snapped his head around. Strangely, part of him yearned to apologize, as though he had somehow voiced the frustration flowing through his mind. Instead, he merely waited for her to explain further.

"My father was a United States ambassador stationed there, hence my lack of tan." Chance looked at her arm. Her skin tone looked pretty good to him. "My mother was working in the embassy as a cleaner. She rarely talks about what happened between the two of them, but there was some kind of scandal, and my father was recalled to the USA, but not before leaving my mama with a bun in her oven, so to speak." She glanced over her shoulder and changed lanes. A pensive expression flashed across her face. "When I was three, my mother managed to smuggle us across the US border. Two years later, she managed to earn enough money to travel to Washington and confront the man who had sired me. Apparently, the meeting ended… badly. My father never acknowledged me, and died of pancreatic cancer shortly after his fiftieth birthday."

"I'm sorry," Chance murmured.

She smiled, the expression lightening her face. "You might as well apologize for the death of a stranger on the other side of the world."

"No, I'm sorry for your hardship."

Bella shrugged. "It is what made me who I am." She glanced over at him. "It brought you and me together. Maybe directly, maybe indirectly. Perhaps without my painful upbringing, I would have been more satisfied with my station in life, and I would have ended up on my knees cleaning floors like my mother, always wondering what might have been. Knowing what I know has always driven me on; first in high school, then through college, and finally through my own studies."

Chance considered her words. "Fontaine isn't a South American name. Where did you acquire it?"

Again, she smiled, though this expression held less light. "It was my father's name; the one thing I was able to hang on to from him."

"I don't know. Maybe it's like you said, and you acquired more from his absence than you ever would have from his presence. Whatever the case, he sounds like a bit of a dick."

"Well, my mama thought so." Bella's laughter filled the car, and Chance felt himself reddening. Moments later, though, he joined in, feeling less daunted than he had for weeks.

They finally reached their apparent destination, and Bella parked the car.

"Is this the Bronx?" Chance asked.

"You know it?"

"I know *of* it." He glanced around nervously.

"It's not that bad," said Bella, climbing out of the car. "You know, once you get over all the burnt out cars and murders and stuff."

Chance followed her out of the car and looked around, half expecting gangs of thugs to emerge at any moment and demand his hospital slippers at gunpoint. For all appearances, though, this seemed a fairly typical residential neighborhood.

"Are you done?" Bella asked, cutting through his thoughts and making him jump slightly.

"Done what?"

"Done looking around like a rat in a house full of cats. Don't believe everything you hear, Mister Ripley. If this were the hellhole some people make it out to be, I would never have brought you all this way, would I?"

He thought about it as he followed her toward a tenement building. "Why do you live here, anyway?"

"Who said I live here?" She slipped her key into the front door and opened it. Without waiting to see if he followed, Bella strode into the building, allowing the door to swing closed behind her. Chance barely managed to slap his hand on the reinforced glass before the latch clicked shut.

As if he had a choice in the matter, Chance looked around. He heard children playing, but couldn't spy them anywhere. Their high-pitched giggling cut through his tension. With a sigh and a shake of his head, he walked into the building.

The inside hall held the generic hallmarks of every residence he had ever seen. Gray wallpaper contrasted slightly against the marginally lighter gray tiling. No pictures adorned the walls. Bella was waiting over by the only elevator, holding its door open.

"You look like a cat entering a new home. It's not that interesting, trust me."

Part of him did trust her, but another part screamed that this might be a trap. What kind of trap, he couldn't be certain, but Doctor Petrov's words rung through his mind, reminding him that the parapsychologist had held doubts about this woman, even fears. He looked at Bella, her patient smile coaxing him forward even as his instincts screamed at him to run. Nothing in this place appeared dangerous, and he had come to her, after all. After a moment, the feeling of foolishness overwhelmed his sense of disquiet, and he forced his feet to move forward. Eventually, he stepped into the elevator, and she allowed the doors to swish closed.

Pressing the button for the top floor, Bella began to chuckle darkly.

"Now you're mine."

Instinctively, Chance stepped back, smacking into the wall of the elevator. Bella's laughter changed to high peals, her mirth obvious. It took a moment, but he finally realized she had been making fun of his anxiety.

"That's not funny."

She shook her head. "That depends entirely on your perspective. Seriously, what's got you so wound up?"

"I thought Doctor Petrov told you about me?"

Bella slowly sobered, and she looked at him seriously. "She told me you were battling with incredibly powerful psychic abilities. She said you had managed to phantom walk on more than one occasion, without your control, and that you had displayed powerful telekinesis."

"So you don't know who I am?"

"No. Why would I?"

The elevator pinged, and the door slid open. Chance shook his head slightly while Bella held the door open.

"Maybe this is a mistake," he muttered.

"Who are you?"

He looked her dead in the eyes, his breath catching slightly as he did so. Part of him screamed to flee, but he yearned to trust this woman, to tell her all his secrets.

"I was committed to Mount Sinai Mental Refuge, a private institution for both the criminally insane and regular folks who slip off the rails of normality. Apparently, I was one of the former."

He held his breath, gritting his teeth while he waited for her reaction. This was the first step, and how she reacted to it would determine if he exited the elevator or departed the tenement to try to thwart Trinity on his own. The mere thought of the three killers made him dizzy. More than dizzy, in fact. He suddenly had to grip the wall of the elevator to stop himself from falling. Bella spoke to him, but the words were muffled, sounding as though they traveled down a long padded hallway.

An enormous bloodshot eye flashed directly into his mind. Chance cried out and stumbled backward, but the eye refused to release him. The iris burned with hatred, its wordless condemnation trapping him in the corner. He cowered there, soundless cries whimpering from his lips. He could feel Bella's hands on his arms, shaking him while she called out, but he could not snap free of the tormenting gaze. Something about it reminded him of Trinity, but this seemed more focused, powerful beyond imagination. Instinctively, part of him knew this was the mind behind the three killers, the architect for all the seemingly random killings.

An image of Special Agent Doug Broachford exploded into his mind. Agony etched the man's features, his lips contorted as he fought to let loose a howl from behind a duct-tape gag. As swiftly as it erupted, the vision faded.

Chance caught the scream even as it fought to break past his lips. His eyes bulged from his head, and he swallowed down the urge to weep. Bella's eyes widened at the trauma in his expression, and her face reflected deep concern.

"Are you all right?" she asked. "You look like you're about to faint."

He did indeed feel as though he were about to collapse. All concerns about Bella's trustworthiness faded in the wake of the overwhelming need to lie down.

"I need a glass of water."

Bella helped him walk down the corridor, stopping at the third door on the right. She produced her keyring and opened the door, helping a very dizzy Chance through. As the door clicked shut behind them, though, Chance's awareness kicked in, and he froze. This was not an apartment at all.

The first thought that sprang to mind was how clinical it all looked. The second thought was that he might have slipped back into the asylum without realizing it. The room was complete with a hospital bed, electronic equipment all around it. The walls of the room were white, and the floor was tiled with white squares.

"What is this?" he groaned, leaning on the wall.

"This is where I perform my research," Bella said. "Much cheaper than medical facilities, though the bed was a bother to move in. Come on, let's get you lying down."

He didn't want to, but the bed beckoned him. Part of him wondered if everything since stepping into Times Square had somehow been a dream, and this was reality calling him back to wakefulness. The steel of the bed felt too cold, though, and the sheets too coarse. The scent of cleaning products in the air seemed too perfect to be imaginary, and the warmth of Bella's hands on his arms made him hope none of it was a dream. Before he knew it, he had a pressure cuff on his upper arm and a pulse monitor on his index finger. The cuff tightened, and Bella marked his blood pressure down on a clipboard, nodding approvingly. She moved over and sat beside him on the edge of the bed.

"Well, it looks like you had one hell of a turn there. Do you mind telling me what happened?"

Chance looked around. His head was clearing, but his mouth still felt dry. "Could I please have a glass of water?"

"Of course." Bella moved to the bedside table, poured a glass of water from a jug, and handed it to Chance.

Chance took a deep sip, coughed slightly as the cold liquid slipped down the wrong pipe, and then drank some more.

When he looked down, the glass was empty. Bella took it and placed it on the bedside table, and then she sat back down, her thigh touching his hip.

"Can you talk now? I hate to pressure you, but it might be best to talk while the memory is still fresh in your mind."

Oh, it was fresh, all right. The image seemed burned into the backs of his corneas; every time he blinked he saw an echo of the horror that had glared into his soul. "Why do you have this place set up this way?" he asked, fighting to delay the conversation he felt sure would resurrect the hateful gaze.

Grimacing, Bella stood and walked over to the window. Chance couldn't see anything beyond it other than the red brick wall of the building next door. "My studies garner a lot of derision from among both the scientific and psychological communities. I am not accredited in anything. My experience lies in looking beyond the boundaries of what science believes is possible."

"So, you're not a doctor?"

She shook her head. "Does that concern you?"

"Are you some kind of professor?" Again, she shook her head. "Then why would Princeton allow you to lecture there? It seems kind of risky for their reputation."

"Not really. There was a strong online petition and support from a large sector of the student body. Young people are not as inflexible in their thought processes as those in the higher echelons of the education system, especially these days. I was granted allowances for a few lectures on the proviso that they didn't become recruitment seminars for future... people like me, I guess."

"And what *are* you?"

She peered at him intensely. "I heard a voice once."

The sudden change of subject caught Chance off guard. "Excuse me?"

"I was young, barely a teenager if I recall correctly. While lying in bed, I noticed my curtains swish, and I attempted to turn on my light. It refused to click on, so I sat in the darkness, terrified. And then something spoke to me."

"What did it say?" Chance whispered.

Bella shook her head. "That's not for you to know." She forced a smile onto her quivering lips. "Ever since that night, I have traveled and learned all that I can about the occult and the paranormal, alongside psychic ability and even religious theology. There is an answer I am desperate to unlock, and I will not waste time sitting through the rigmaroles of tertiary education, learning from people who know less than me simply to garner a piece of paper that ultimately means nothing."

The speech was startling. Not only for the information it divulged, but also for the transformation it created on the face of Bella Fontaine. Chance contemplated what to say. How could he follow up such a declaration?

"I phantom walked out of the asylum, and now I'm hunting three serial killers I believe might be siphoning off the psychic abilities of young women."

Saying it aloud evoked two emotions. On one hand, it felt great to get such a burden off his chest, but on the other, he realized how utterly insane that singular sentence sounded. It condensed everything he was going through, simplifying the entire scenario, but instead of relieving him, it only made him feel foolish. He waited for scorn from Bella, even though he sensed there probably wouldn't be any.

The look of concern on the young woman's face spoke louder than words. Chance half expected Bella to wrap him in an embrace, a prospect he didn't find undesirable. Instead, she stood up and walked away, over to the window, and stared through the glass at the wall opposite, as though she could see the answers of the universe etched in the red bricks.

After a moment of silent contemplation, she turned back. "So, if I am to guess correctly, you have no idea how you managed to phantom walk out of that place. True?" He nodded silently. Bella inclined her head. "The concept of siphoning psychic energy is an interesting one, but hardly original."

"Really?" asked Chance, surprised. "How so?"

"During the Second World War, the Nazis were known to conduct experiments on psychic abilities and paranormal entities. Their research was supposedly destroyed when they lost the war, but enough documented evidence remained to indicate they had a few minor breakthroughs. One such discovery was the ability to drain energy from a human mind. What they intended to do with such energy will likely remain a mystery, but one possible purpose could be exactly what you have suggested. The writings that I have read, and I warn you there aren't many, suggest that fear is the greatest creator of explosive electronic currents in the cerebral cortex. The cerebral cortex is the thin layer of tissue covering much of the brain, also referred to as gray matter. Such inducements could energize all of the brain in one hit, stimulating whatever part of the human mind they wanted without having to focus on specific components. Are you still following?"

"Barely," Chance admitted.

"Good. So, their experiments were looking for a way to tap spiritual or psychic energy. For what purpose? Who knows? Maybe they were making a massive soul bomb to… whatever." She looked invigorated, pacing back and forth as she spoke. "Do you think that might be what your killers are trying to do?" She looked at him eagerly, but then waved her hand. "No, scratch that. I know how stupid it sounds." She sighed. "If they aren't looking to craft something, what purpose could such energy possibly hold?"

"Could it be used by someone else to make their own power stronger?"

Bella looked up at him as though stung. "Such a concept is… horrifying."

"Trust me, it's been tried before." Chance recalled the shiny teeth of Howard Mason. "Maybe not on a psychic level, but consuming another human to absorb their strength has definitely been tried before."

"Of course!" Bella snapped, her eyes wide. "The Soul Eater!"

"Wait… what?"

She made a fumbling movement with her hands. "In some African folklore, there is a tale of the Soul Eater – basically, a person who can eat the soul of someone else. If my memory serves me correctly, it was most notably found among the Hausa people of West Africa. Tell me, do you know if any of these killers have a penchant for licking their victims?"

"Um… I did see one lick the cheek of a woman he'd stabbed in the eye."

Bella rounded on him. "What do you mean you *saw* it?"

"Well…." Chance paused, wondering how to explain it. Eventually, he simply shrugged and dove in. "I can sometimes see through the eyes of the victims. I enter their bodies and live through their murders. It hasn't happened for a while, though."

"Is that what caused you to collapse in the elevator?"

Chance shook his head, shuddering as he recalled the haunting eye. "No, that was something else."

"No wonder Doctor Petrov called me." Bella bit her lower lip, her expression thoughtful. "When I first met her, I came away with the impression I had overwhelmed her with my enthusiasm. She never followed up on anything I had suggested, nor did she answer any further correspondence from me." Bella stared at Chance, and he felt the hunger in her gaze. Not a physical hunger, more as if he were the answer she had been seeking for some time. "How many murders have you witnessed?"

He shook his head. "I'm not sure."

Her gaze narrowed. "Not sure because there are so many, or is there something else?"

"I'm suffering amnesia. I can only recall a few of the victims, but that's enough."

"I'm sure it is," she mused, nodding. "No doubt the trauma of such acts was sufficient to push your mind to reset itself, for want of a better term. At the risk of losing itself to complete insanity, your brain shut down and closed off that part of itself open to the harm." Her piercing eyes fixed upon his. "Which means all the answers might be hiding inside that beautiful head of yours."

"Hey, hang on."

"What?" she asked, frowning.

"You're not going to try to cut into my brain, are you?"

Bella laughed, the sound wondrous. "Even if I wanted to, there's no way I would risk what you can do. No, I'm thinking of something else entirely. Tell me, Chance, do you trust me?"

He wanted to say no. Wanted to tell her to leave him alone. All his instincts screamed at him to get up and run, flee from this strange room and this alluring woman.

"Yes," he whispered.

* * * *

The steady tick-tock of the musician's pendulum bounced back from the white walls. At first, it was an annoyance, breaking his concentration, but after a few moments, Chance found the sound sliding by the edge of his awareness. Bella's words, empty monotone murmurings, penetrated deep into his mind, drawing his attention away from all distractions. The words themselves meant nothing; she might have been reading off a grocery list for all their substance, but Chance found his mind drifting, much like in the brief seconds before an anesthesiologist's gas kicked in. He fought to retain his concentration, but time and again his mind wafted, until the compulsion to fight faded away completely.

"Can you hear me, Chance?"

"Yes." His voice sounded atonal. He didn't care.

"Where are you?"

"With Bella. In her… place."

That seemed to satisfy her. "I'm going to take you back, Chance. Back in time. Is that okay?"

He nodded. Words weren't necessary.

"Okay, so let's travel back to your time in the asylum." Chance drifted back, recalling his time in that place that seemed so much like Bella's. Looking over to his left, he saw the enormous bulk of Jarvis. At the foot of the bed stood Doctor Smith, analyzing his clipboard. "Are you there, Chance?" Bella's voice filled the air of the room.

He nodded slowly.

"What do you see?"

He told her.

"Do you feel comfortable?"

Chance shuffled down on the bed slightly. The mattress was hard. The plastic sheet underneath squeaked slightly. He told her.

"I mean the environment. Is there anything threatening there?"

"I'm all right," he murmured.

"Now let's travel to the time when you phantom walked out of there. Can you remember what happened?"

He shook his head.

Bella sighed softly. "What about the first night when you woke up, the first murders that you can recall after your amnesia? Can you remember that night?"

He nodded.

Think back to the first woman, but don't follow what happened to her. Take a step back, just a tiny one, and tell me what happened right before you fell asleep."

Immediately, he stiffened. "Someone's in the room."

"Do you know who?"

He shook his head wildly, snapping it back and forth on the pillow. "I can't see. The lights are out. But they're never fully out. There's always some light in here."

"Can you tell me anything about the person in the room with you? Is it perhaps a doctor or a nurse?"

"He has a pillow. I think he is about to –" Chance cut off, suddenly unable to breathe. His throat closed up, and his eyes bulged in his head. Strangled choking sounded from his mouth.

"You're no longer in the asylum," Bella snapped. "On the count of three, you will wake up."

The suffocating sensation continued. Chance was trapped in the vision, locked in the moment of attempted murder. The memory… but it wasn't a memory. Something about this was all too real. The attack was happening in his head.

At that moment, Chance knew who his attacker was. The bloodshot eye replaced the pillow, choking him with its power. He tried to fight it, but the wielder was too strong. Each moment saw Chance growing weaker. His throat closed so tightly, he couldn't even scream. It felt like feathers were being shoved directly into his esophagus. Somewhere off in the distance, he felt Bella shaking him. Her voice echoed as if journeying down a long corridor. Each moment saw the distance between them growing greater.

Panic roared through him, an unhindered beast of fire. It exploded out from his chest, a lion of mental energy. The building shook upon its foundations, and Bella flew from her feet, tumbling across the tiling. Every light in the place winked out, bare seconds before the bulbs exploded in showers of sparks.

The connection between Chance and his attacker severed in an instant. Part of him had the impression of the bleeding eye blowing back with all its force on its owner, launching Chance flying in the power vacuum. And suddenly the sensation was gone, leaving him disoriented and gasping for breath. The sheets upon which he laid were drenched with sweat, and the only light filling the room came from the cracked window.

Glass from the lights covered the floor. Both machines beside the bed had burned out; the room had become a technological wasteland, with nothing electronic functioning anymore. Looking down at the floor, he saw Bella staring up at him, her eyes wide, her mouth gaping.

"Are you okay?" he asked feebly.

Bella's mouth worked, but no sound emerged. The confidence she had shown in the university auditorium had fled in the wake of Chance's devastating display of power. From where he lay, she looked like a kitten dropped in the midst of a group of dogs.

"I don't think that was a good idea," Chance muttered, examining the devastation.

"You might be right," she finally breathed.

Chance climbed down from the bed and shoved aside a pile of glass with the toe of his shoe before stepping across the floor toward her. He held out his hand. After a moment's hesitation, she gripped it, and he lifted her easily to her feet.

"I never…." Bella trailed away, seemingly at a loss for what to say.

"I guess I should have warned you."

Her wide eyes focused slightly. "Has that happened before?'

"Never so strongly," he replied, and glanced around again. He shook his head in wonder. "Nowhere near as strongly. But I did break some lights once with Doctor Petrov. And then, when one of the Trinity killers attacked her in her home, I was able to project through her body and fling him away. Don't ask me how."

"That was going to be my very next question." She chewed on her thumbnail for a moment, and then seemed to realize what she was doing and lowered her hand back to her side. "You do realize how stunning this is, don't you."

"Stunning isn't the word I would use. Terrifying, maybe."

Bella nodded slowly, her eyes never leaving his face. "Yes, of course." She appeared to mull over something. "What brought that on? Was it the memory?"

Chance shook his head and self-consciously touched his throat. "I don't even know if that was a memory. Whatever just happened was occurring in the here and now. Somebody attacked me."

"Wait… how?"

"I can't be sure, but I think it was the person behind Trinity, the one pulling their strings. I don't believe they want me to know what went on before my memory loss. They attacked me… telepathically." Admitting such an implausible possibility chafed at Chance, but he could think of no other explanation. There was no way what he had experienced was a mere memory. "While the assault occurred primarily in my mind, it was like I could feel the pillow over my face, smothering me."

"What happened when you lashed out?"

Chance thought back. "I think whoever attacked me was flung away."

"Do you think you injured them?" Bella asked. She leaned forward, curious.

"I'm not sure." He looked up, meeting her gaze. "I hope so."

"You really need to tell me everything that is going on. If we're going to work together, you can't hold anything back."

Chance stared into her eyes, his heart skipping slightly. Did he want to work with her, to trust her with his innermost secrets?

The story began tumbling out of his mouth almost before he realized it.

CHAPTER XX

"I thought you were going to train me to use my… talent," Chance muttered.

Bella shook her head. "You need to learn control. I don't have the first clue what you are genuinely capable of; if your earlier display is any indication of what we're likely to be dealing with, you need to be able to feel when it's coming on and control it before you kill us both."

He glanced around at the cracks spiderwebbing the walls of the room and reluctantly nodded. If his mind had repelled any harder, chances were they would both be lying dead in a pile of rubble.

"So how does tea help me?"

"The tea itself is secondary. It's *making* the tea that helps focus your mind."

Chance looked at the ceramic tea set. Apparently, it was Japanese, for whatever that was worth. All he knew was that after setting up a folding table and two chairs beside the hospital bed, Bella had collected the set from the second room and placed it on the table, bidding him sit opposite her.

"Isn't there some kind of yoga we can do instead?" he asked.

"Yoga?" she seemed to contemplate the idea. "For your mind?"

"Well, yeah."

"Interesting concept. Now, make the tea."

Chance looked at the set. Shrugging, he picked up the box of loose tea.

"Wrong."

"This is shit," he muttered, throwing down the box.

"And that is why you can't focus. All you see is the task, not the purpose," she explained. "Everything has an order, whether you're making tea or working towards psychological strengthening. You cannot possibly hope to constrain instinctual emotions if you can't even make tea correctly. Now, try again."

Muttering inaudibly under his breath, Chance picked up the cup.

"Wrong."

With an effort, he placed the cup back down. "Why don't you just tell me what to do?"

"Learning doesn't work that way."

"So says the lecturer."

She smiled, ignoring the jibe. "What is the most important implement you will require for brewing the tea?"

"The tea."

Shaking her head, Bella said, "Try again."

Chance looked at the utensils on the table. The endeavor seemed pointless. "I don't know. The water?"

Bella clapped her hands and grinned. "Now tell me why."

Chance blew out a frustrated breath and looked at the teapot filled with steaming water. "I don't know. Because it cooks the leaves?"

"Close. Try again."

Her encouragement encouraged him. Furrowing his brows, he stared at the steam curling from the spout, but no answer came to him. Reaching out, he touched the side of the ceramic teapot, flinching as the heat stung his fingertips. Understanding slowly crept up within him.

"Too hot and it will burn the tea. Too cold and nothing will happen. Correct?"

Bella nodded. "That's right. Now, I won't expect you to go through trial and error to find the right temperature." Her voice lowered. "For the record, it's around one hundred and seventy-six degrees Fahrenheit."

"That's oddly specific," mused Chance.

"This is a specific craft," she replied. "What next?"

Chance licked his lips. "The tea?" he asked, raising a sarcastic eyebrow.

"You got it. How much?"

"How would I know that?" he protested.

"Think of it as your talent. What are the possible ramifications of being wrong?"

Chance looked around the room at the shattered glass they had swept into the corner and the cracks in the walls. Candles illuminated the room dimly.

"Chaos," he muttered.

"Put it into context with the tea."

"Too bitter or too weak."

"So, how much do you think you should put in?" Bella asked.

Chance shrugged. "How would I know something like that?"

"Exactly my point. Much like the water temperature, there is no way for you to know without either instruction or trial and error. I told you what temperature the water needed to be, and as such, you were able to move directly onto the next step. Therefore, without knowledge, you cannot learn, correct?"

"I have no idea what you are talking about," said Chance. "Are we still discussing tea?"

Bella peered at him across the table, her expression unreadable, but Chance still felt like a dolt. He chewed over all she had told him, searching for the answer to a question he felt he must have missed. But there remained no clue, and he shrugged wordlessly.

"How will you decide how much tea to use?" Bella asked.

"Either you tell me, or I guess."

She nodded. "So, how will you decide how much power to use?"

"Ah," he murmured, finally understanding. "But to continue your metaphor, if I use too much tea, it's not likely to kill us both, is it?"

"Hopefully not," Bella agreed. "Why don't you take a guess and find out?"

"Why don't you just tell me?" he countered.

She sighed. "Because the difference is, despite knowing how much tea is correct, I don't know how much power you have. You need to learn that on your own. This exercise is to help you understand the need for small steps, small increments to increase the flavor, if you will. That is the only way I can imagine you might be able to rein in the tumultuous power you displayed earlier."

"Well, the real problem is that I have no power unless I'm panicked."

"What about when you phantom walked. From what you said, there was nothing unpleasant happening at the time; how do you explain stepping across distances in an instant? And the instances of you stepping into those women's minds to witness their deaths? You weren't scared then, so what caused your talent to kick in?" She tapped her fingernail on the fold out table. "No, there is some other secret hiding in the shadows of your mind, some trigger other than fear, and we need to discover what it is. For now, however, we have tea. So, one spoon or two?"

Chance groaned inwardly and focused on the task.

* * * *

Chance gagged.

He spat the tea onto the floor and wiped his mouth with the back of his hand, fighting down the gag reflex trying to empty the full contents of his stomach. Sitting the teacup down on the table, he leaned back in his chair.

"I guess I used too much."

Bella leaned forward and sniffed the brew. Her nose wrinkled, and she leaned back in a rush. "I would tend to agree." She looked up into his eyes. "I'm glad it's only tea."

Chance nodded. "If we ever get to the point where I'm playing with actual telekinesis, I suggest we don't do it in a multi-story apartment building. I'm surprised the fire department hasn't turned up."

"Most of the people who live here will be away at work." She grimaced, looking at the damaged walls. "They're definitely in for a shock when they return home."

Chance picked up the teacup and sniffed it again, wincing at the odor. "I don't think much of your training technique."

"It's designed to open your mind to what you're facing. Similar techniques have been used by gurus for generations."

"It's opened my mind, all right. It has made me realize I have no intention of drinking tea ever again. Even if it's made by a master guru."

Bella giggled, the sound making him smile. "Fine, then. I have another technique you might find more appealing. Others have found it somewhat… awkward, but you need to learn this faster than most, so I guess we'll give it a shot."

Standing, she began to gather the utensils of the tea set. Chance offered to help, but she shook her head sharply and bid him remain seated. Walking to the adjoining room, she returned moments later carrying a simple board game. He recognized the box, though for the life of him he couldn't remember where from. He tried to read the lid, but Bella hid it from him.

"Have you ever heard of Kreskin?"

Chance shook his head.

"He's often called the Amazing Kreskin."

"Still no," he replied.

"He is, for want of a better title, an entertainer. During the seventies, he made several appearances on The Tonight Show and has since performed widely. He claims *not* to be a psychic, though his methods do display various levels of clairvoyance."

"What does any of this have to do with a board game?"

"Well, Kreskin developed this –"

Chance stood up from the table. "This is ridiculous. I'm not playing some kooky game from the seventies. People are dying, maybe even while we waste our time on this nonsense."

"What do you suggest we do, then?"

The question hit him like a slap in the face. "I… don't know. Maybe something a little more productive? I mean, what did we gain from making tea?"

"Are you saying you don't have a greater understanding of how tiny differences can affect the final process?"

Chance recalled the bitter swill he had sipped. "But it's only tea. What I'm dealing with is entirely different. I'm walking through walls and stepping into people's minds."

"And if you don't gain some modicum of skill, how long until you lose control and kill one of these hosts you've spoken about?"

He froze. "What are you saying?"

"What if you repel in the same way you did here while one of them is being attacked and collapse their house? You will go from being a witness to perpetrating manslaughter. And all because you were too impatient to partake in a few simple exercises."

The words ticked around inside his head for a moment, their significance seeping in as he felt his mouth go dry. He glanced around the room, imagining the walls caving in, the plaster raining down. Part of him relished the idea of taking down one of the Trinity killers with him, but the thought of an innocent paying the price for his actions made him quiver.

"Okay, so the tea is designed to make me appreciate how a tiny adjustment can create a massive difference in the end equation. I get it. I truly do. But how do I equate that with what is happening to me?"

"You shifted this building with your mind." She leaned in, uncomfortably close. "What if you moved the entire structure across the planet?"

The concept made Chance frown. He shook his head. "That's not possible."

"Everything is made up of matter. You have shown you can control that matter with your mind, albeit haphazardly. This talent is predominantly reactive, affected by fear. Your other abilities seem more latent, dragged out of you when extreme violence approaches." She thought about it for a moment, her face pensive. "Or.... What if fear is merely a byproduct of circumstances and has nothing to do with your talent? Maybe your mind is subliminally attuned to danger, attracted to it even, and you react differently depending on the scenario. As an observer, you simply watch, but when directly threatened, you act defensively."

Chance shook his head. "That makes no sense. When I am in the bodies of those women, I feel their fear. It's the most intense panic I can imagine. If I were ever to react, it would be then."

"Maybe you're getting stronger."

The thought made Chance grimace. If this building were any indication of what getting stronger entailed, he wasn't sure he wanted to see what happened when he hit his peak.

A knock came from the front door. The ensuing echo caused Chance to jump slightly. Even the typically composed Bella widened her eyes at the sound.

"Who could that be?" she murmured, turning toward the door.

"Wait," said Chance. He stared at the door, willing himself to sense who stood beyond it. After a moment, he released his breath and sighed. The tea lesson might have taught him the importance of portion control, but it hadn't taught him how to achieve it. The door remained a door, no matter how hard he strained.

"Let me get it," he suggested.

Walking to the entry, Chance peered through the peephole. A gray-haired woman stood on the other side, her face wrinkled and benign, her twinkling blue eyes staring blankly at the wood on the other side. She held what looked to be a platter in her hands, covered with a red dishcloth.

Cautiously, Chance turned the lock and cracked the door open, peeking out. The hall appeared empty apart from the old woman. He finally opened the door wide. Bella came and stood beside him.

"Can we help you?" asked Chance.

"I have a gift for you, Chance."

His blood ran cold at the mention of his name. "Who are you?"

"Oh, one of many," she replied, her voice doddering, yet warm. Her expression remained friendly, though her eyes appeared flinty. She nodded to the platter in her hands. "Aren't you going to look?"

He didn't want to, but the mysterious dishcloth beckoned. He had to know what lurked beneath it. Tentatively, he reached toward the red dishcloth, each moment expecting the woman to pull back, but she remained motionless, smiling widely. He gripped the cloth. It was wet. He pulled it away until he'd revealed what it hid. When he dropped the cloth, it landed with a splat. At that moment, he understood why the towel was wet, even as he realized the material wasn't naturally red. Blood had soaked through the fabric.

So much blood.

A hand lay on the wooden platter. Chance recognized the blue-stoned ring almost immediately. The stone had cracked down the middle as if the wearer had been fighting to his last breath. Everything in Chance screamed to slam the door shut and lock it, but he forced himself to stand firm. Beside him, Bella shrieked and stumbled backward. Chance met the flinty eyes of the old woman.

"Where is Broachford?"

She smiled sweetly. "Oh, you know. Around." She leaned in close, and her grin turned wicked, her tone conspiratorial. "He was delicious."

"Howard Mason sent you." It wasn't a question. The murderous bastard from Ward Alpha had promised this, and Jarvis had reiterated the warning, but never in a million years would Chance have envisioned the messenger looking like this sweet, old grandmother.

"You have a job you should be doing," the crone stated. All humor suddenly dropped from her face. "We are watching you."

Without waiting for a response, the old woman crouched, picked up the soaked dishcloth, and draped it once more over the severed hand. Nodding once, she doddered away down the hall. Chance glanced at the spatter of blood where the dishcloth had landed, momentarily saddened by the tragic loss of the agent. Nobody, not even Broachford, deserved to leave the world in such a way. Finally, he turned and closed the door, just in time to notice Bella lifting her cellphone to her ear.

In two strides, Chance crossed the floor and snatched the phone from her hand. He barely had time to see 911 on the screen before he ended the call. She looked ready to argue, but he cut her off with a curt shake of his head.

"No police. I'm a fugitive, remember?"

Bella cursed softly. "But that... what in the world *was* that?"

The normally composed woman appeared close to hysterics. Chance yearned to put her mind at ease, but he still felt too shaken by what had occurred to do much of anything.

"There are people," he began, his voice shaking slightly, "individuals who might seek to do me harm if I don't do something for the man they… follow."

"That old woman had a hand. A g*oddamn* hand. It was still bloody, which means whoever they cut it from was alive up until recently." She froze, her eyes suddenly snapping up to his. All panic fled as she became acutely focused. Chance longed to look away from her piercing gaze, but he held firm. "You saw it happening, didn't you? That was what made you ill when you first walked in here."

"I saw…." His voice cracked. "Broachford. Special Agent Broachford was helping me for a time. In the vision, he was being tortured. The image was gone in a flash, but it means... oh my God."

"What is it?"

"The two men who arrested Broachford outside Doctor Petrov's house. They took him into custody and another car drove him away. I naturally assumed they were all federal agents, but what if they were…?"

"Who do you think they were, Chance?"

He licked his lips. "I think Doctor Petrov is in danger. We need to get there now."

Without giving Bella a chance to question him further, Chance dashed from the apartment. He half-expected to pass the old woman while heading to the elevator, but it seemed she had vanished. The doors to the elevator opened with a ping, and he glanced back to see Bella fighting to pull the key out of the front door. She eventually managed and followed him briskly, scowling. The two finally stepped into the elevator, and Chance tapped hurriedly on the button for the ground floor.

"What is going on, Chance?"

"I never told you much about Howard Mason. He was a killer – *is* a killer, I guess. I made a deal with him while in the asylum. His son… well, there's no easy way to say it. One of Trinity is his son, and Mason wants him saved."

Bella's mouth hung slightly open. "How do you expect to do that?"

"No idea. But if I don't, apparently there's a whole fan club of Mason's out here in the real world who will do to me what they did to Broachford. What that old lady had on the platter –"

"Was just a reminder," Bella finished for him. "How can you be sure that was the agent's hand?"

"The ring. I noticed it when we first met. He used to tap it on objects when he was thinking."

The elevator doors opened, and Chance peeked out before leading the way. Bella strode alongside him, fishing the car keys from her purse as she went.

"You don't have to come with me," said Chance.

"I know."

Bella pushed through the front doors of the apartment building. Chance noted these now bore several cracks in their reinforced glass, meaning his reaction had reverberated all the way down to the ground floor. They had truly been lucky the entire building hadn't collapsed.

The drive to Doctor Petrov's house was slow, bogged down in afternoon traffic. Chance chomped at the bit, and several times sought within himself the power to step across distances, hoping to phantom walk into the doctor's home and warn her. His attempts bore all the satisfaction and effectiveness of screaming into a vacuum.

Eventually, they turned the corner, and Chance saw the house. Straight away, he recognized something was wrong. The front door of the house hung open, swinging in the light afternoon breeze like a broken jaw. He leaped out of the car as soon as Bella hit the brakes and sprinted up the porch steps. Part of him knew the house would be empty, but that didn't stop him from running room to room, calling out for the doctor. Eventually, he stumbled back to the front porch, defeated.

"Where could she have gone?" Bella asked.

"I have no idea. This was a witness protection house, apparently." He glared across the street toward the building where the agents had been housed. After what had happened to Broachford, he guessed it was folly to assume anyone was who they claimed to be anymore. "But they might know."

Chance stormed down the steps and across the road, ignoring Bella's queries as she ran to keep up. As he began to walk up the path toward the house, however, he felt her hand on his shoulder. She wrenched him to a halt and spun him back to face her.

"Stop. Think." She allowed a moment for the simple commands to sink in. "Who are these people?"

"She thought they were federal agents here to protect her."

Bella held her hands wide. "And you're just going to present yourself to them? You, the escaped mental patient?"

Chance chewed over her question, feeling his simmering ire beginning to abate. "They're the ones who arrested Broachford. If anything's happened to Doctor Petrov, they'll know where she is."

"Look at her house. Just look at it."

Chance peered across the street. "What am I looking for?"

"Does it look like an orderly exit? Do you think they walked in there, collected her, and then left without issue?"

"Well, no, but…."

"If she knew these people and believed they were there to protect her, wouldn't they have left everything in order? Think about it for a moment."

"But if they didn't take her, who did?"

Bella jabbed a finger at him. "That is exactly the right question." She glanced up the driveway beside the surveillance house. "The car is gone. In a hurry too, from the looks of those skid marks. At a guess, I would say someone else broke into Doctor Petrov's house, took her, and these men pursued them. It's probably the only reason we've been able to have this conversation on the sidewalk without anyone noticing us."

Chance's mind ticked over the logic of the assumption. "Do you think these men were truly FBI?"

"There's no way to know unless we contact the FBI directly," Bella replied. "But if they really were federal agents, whatever call they made would have been picked up by more than only the guys who turned up to cart Special Agent Whatever-his-name-is away. At a guess, I would say an elaborate ruse played out here, right from the time Doctor Petrov was attacked in her own home. I think they wanted to keep an eye on her, waiting for any indication of you appearing to help her."

"Jesus Christ." Chance rubbed his hand over his chin. "So who spirited her away, do you think?"

"I have no idea, but for now, we need to get away before someone returns to keep an eye on this place." She glanced at her watch. "We've already been standing around for too long."

Chance walked like a zombie back to the car and dropped into the passenger seat. The stresses of the day were building to a crescendo, and part of him feared he might soon shut down altogether. Had this been what it had felt like before his amnesia? He could imagine that the more pressure his mind came under, the harder it would be to function. Had he known what was going on, or had the early visions been enough to tip him over the edge?

They drove through the suburban streets in silence. At one point, Bella switched on the radio without Chance even noticing. He was too withdrawn into his own thoughts to pay much attention to what was going on around him. The memory of Broachford's hand on the platter returned to haunt him repeatedly. The smile of the platter-bearer morphed into the dangerous grin of an alligator. Part of him yearned for the simplicity of the asylum, for the routine it had provided, the high walls that might have offered some sort of protection.

The news came on the radio. Chance ignored it until the announcer mentioned the grisly murder of a woman in Manhattan the night before, strung up and executed in what authorities were claiming might have been a ritualistic torture. His mouth ran dry, and he leaned forward to snap the volume up. The details of the story were thin, but a part of him knew that Trinity had committed the sadistic deed. Which of the killers had performed the atrocity remained a mystery, but a deeper knowledge chilled him to the bones.

Chance asked Bella for her phone. Once it was in his grasp, he searched for similar murders committed within the past twenty-four hours. Several came up, but as he filtered the results, he discovered three similar ritualistic murders had occurred. One in Manhattan that he already knew about, one in Blackstone, Virginia, and the third in Pittsburg, Pennsylvania.

"They're getting closer," Chance murmured.

"What are?" asked Bella.

"The murders. They used to spread out across the country to keep them randomized. Now they are grouping them closer together." He looked up as realization hit. "They're heading here, to New York."

For a moment, Bella remained silent. Finally, she said. "What do you think they're coming here for?"

"My heart tells me it's for me," he replied. "But my mind says this is much bigger than one person. If they wanted me dead, they could have accomplished that a long time ago. I'm not sure what their ultimate plan is, but there's something that scares me just as much."

"What's that?"

"They know how to block me from seeing them. I'm blind."

* * * *

"Maybe it's not as dramatic as you're making out."

Chance looked at Bella across the table. They were in a small café on the outskirts of Brooklyn grabbing a bite to eat. He prodded his uneaten sandwich, and then decided to take a sip of juice instead.

"What do you mean?"

"Well...." Bella seemed to consider her words. "Perhaps you never had access to begin with. Maybe you only saw what they wanted you to see."

Frowning, he contemplated the possibility. "To what end?"

"Who knows? These people are crazy after all. No offense."

"None taken."

"Didn't you suggest they might have someone behind the scenes manipulating the situation? What if that person has an ultimate strategy?" She paused, peering directly into his eyes. "Maybe the killings aren't as random as you think. You've suggested they might be trying to siphon away psychic powers; what if there's even more to their strategy? Don't ask me what, because I have no idea. In the grand scheme of things, I'm a relative newcomer. A couple of hours ago, I knew nothing about Trinity or dead FBI agents or severed hands or any of it. Despite appearances, I'm struggling to keep up."

"You're doing a pretty good job, trust me." Chance picked up the tuna salad sandwich and took a small bite. After the incident with Broachford's hand, he couldn't bring himself to eat anything more carnivorous. He chewed the sandwich slowly and swallowed. "If this is you struggling, I'd love to see you in full form."

"Would you? I'll hold you to that."

Chance paused, unsure how to take the comment. After a moment, he decided to just move along. Now was not the time for fumbling around trying to understand a woman whose IQ was likely as large as his zip code. If he had a zip code. It troubled him that he could still remember nothing of his past, but he let that, too, fall by the wayside.

"I need to find out why they are moving closer to New York," Chance stated, placing the barely-eaten sandwich back down on his plate.

"You think the endgame is here?"

"Endgame? What is that?"

"It's the final move in chess, when a player has all their pieces in place and finally strikes to win."

Chance contemplated the statement and wondered what other pieces might have been moved into place. He imagined the entire United States as a chessboard, himself a lowly pawn, fumbling around with no idea of his ultimate function. Broachford had been another pawn, and Chance had seen what happened to pawns in this game. He looked at his hand, noticed it was shaking. He gripped it into a fist, and then placed it back on the table.

"Could all of this, including the threats and manipulation of Howard Mason, be driving toward a final purpose?" He shook his head in disbelief. "How could they know I would phantom walk out of the asylum?"

"Who is to say it was you who did that?"

The world seemed to freeze. "What are you talking about?"

"What if this great manipulator, the one behind the endgame, truly is siphoning off power from the women that Trinity is killing. Wouldn't it be possible that he – or she – is the one who broke you out of there? You said yourself that you had no idea how you managed to accomplish it."

"So you're saying I might not have any power?" The thought both excited and terrified him.

Bella shook her head. "No, we've both experienced the power you possess. What I am saying is that a master manipulator's ultimate skill lies in misdirection. Like a stage magician, they make you look at their right hand while their left does all the trickery. So, instead of focusing on what to do, you're too busy trying to find a way to execute skills you don't even possess."

"To what purpose?" Chance breathed.

"Who knows?" replied Bella with a shrug. "But there is something there, don't you think? The one thing we know you can do for certain is also possibly your most powerful weapon. If someone was looking to thwart you as an opponent, wouldn't they try to cloud that from you?" She paused, an expression of shock flitting across her features. "What if the amnesia came from this figure behind the scenes?"

Chance's heart thudded in his chest. "It's possible," he murmured. He picked up the half sandwich, trying to appear casual, but then placed it back down on its plate. "How do we stop them?"

"To stop them, you need to find them. Understand their influence or power over you, and seal yourself against it. The best way to do that would be to track down one of the Trinity killers, but at this point, such a strategy seems impossible." She paused, picked up her glass of soda and took a sip. "If your theory is correct, they are coming here to New York. We can't trust the FBI, because those people hunting Doctor Petrov might actually be involved with them, either directly or indirectly. But I do know a few regular NYPD cops I think might be trustworthy guys… and one girl. If I put feelers out, we might discover where Trinity is lurking."

"And what do we do when we find them?"

"That's something I'll leave up to you. In the meantime, you need to find a way to tap into your telekinesis. Focus all your energy on that, nothing else. If you get any other visions, assume this mysterious figure behind the scenes is projecting them to you for reasons connected to the endgame. Don't trust anything you don't directly manipulate or have control over."

"So, basically trust nothing."

Bella smiled sweetly and cupped his cheek. An electric thrill ran down Chance's spine, and goosebumps exploded across his skin.

"Only for now," she promised.

CHAPTER XXI

Dried blood cracked on his fingers as he clenched his hands into fists. He would need to wash them soon. How he had ever managed to fall asleep in such a manner remained a mystery. But that was always the way after a cleansing; such use of his talent sucked him dry to the point where he was lucky to make it to a place of relative safety to collapse into a near-comatose sleep.

The phone rang, jolting him fully awake. He wiped the drying blood from his right hand onto the sheet and answered. The giggling little voice on the other end of the phone instantly brought a smile to his lips.

"Hello, my girl," he murmured, his voice groggy. "How are you?"

"Where are you, Daddy?"

"I told you last time; I'm away on business."

"You're always away. When are you coming home?"

He sighed. "I don't know. But I promise it won't be long."

"You always promise." There was a pause. *"Mommy says you do it to make us money. Why can't you stay here and make money?"*

He stared at his hand, grimacing. "The work I do isn't like that, honey. I have to travel around for my employer. He tells me where to go."

"Is it like when you were in the army?"

"Similar. Hey, at least I'm not on the other side of the world, and you can call me every day. That's something, right?"

"I guess. Well, when you answer, anyway. We already tried three times today. Mommy says what you're doing is a big secret that even she doesn't know about. Are you like Jason Bourne?"

"What are you doing watching movies like that?" he chided. "Aren't you supposed to be watching Pokémon or something?"

He heard her sigh. *"I'm not six, Dad."*

"Oh no, eight is much more mature." He chuckled. "Listen, Pumpkin, can you put Mommy on the phone for me? I need to go and have a shower soon."

"Okay, Daddy. I love you."

"I love you too, Sweetie."

The phone went silent for a moment. *"Hello?"*

"Hi, Honey. How are you?"

"I would be a lot better if my husband was here to watch our little girl grow up. I swear she's taller every day."

"This is the last job. I promise." Climbing up from the bed, he walked to the bathroom. Glancing in the mirror, he grimaced at the bloody swipe across his cheek. Had he done that in his sleep, or had the woman smacked him while trying to fight him off? He checked the skin for gouges; the last thing he needed was to have left his DNA under her fingernails.

Nothing seemed apparent. "Once this is over, I can retire, and we'll move away to Tuscany like we've always planned."

"Do you mean it?"

"Of course I mean it. That villa is waiting for us, along with all the vineyards we can imagine. Soon we'll be swimming in our own wine."

"Ew. I don't think I like the idea of your sweat in the wine," she scolded.

The big man chuckled deeply. "No sweat, I promise." He stripped off his clothing, tucking the phone between his cheek and shoulder as he did so. "Well, maybe just a little. For flavor."

His wife laughed, and his heart lifted. Everything was going to be worth it in the end.

"Listen, Hon. I have to go. I love you, and I love our baby girl. One more job and that's it, I promise. Soon it will all be over, and we can start living the life we deserve."

"I love you."

"I love you too."

He hung up the phone and stared into the mirror once more. His right hand moved to his cheek, and he fingered the puckered scar tissue. The recollection of the IED in Afghanistan flashed through his mind. It had felt like he'd slipped into Hell for the few seconds it took to scorch his skin. The burns ran all the way across his chest and down both arms. Shaking his head, he placed the phone down and turned on the shower. With an effort, he pushed all thoughts of his wife and daughter away.

Bull stepped into the shower to wash off the blood of the woman he had murdered.

And felt nothing.

CHAPTER XXII

"Chance, wake up."

It felt like he was clawing out of a tunnel filled with spider webs strong enough to trap an elk. When his eyes finally cracked open, he saw Bella leaning over him, concern framing her features.

"What is it?" he grunted.

She glanced toward the motel window. "The police are outside."

The last lingering fragments of sleep vanished in an instant. Chance sat up in bed, his gaze flicking over to the curtained window. Blue and red lights flickered outside.

"Have they knocked on the door?' he whispered.

"No," Bella replied. "They only pulled in a few moments ago. I've been trying to get you to wake up."

"Sorry." He wasn't sorry at all. The dream had been a good one. "Any idea what they're doing?"

"In this motel? I'm guessing they could be here for any of the residents. It's not like we're at the Ritz Carlton."

"People in places like this tend to mind their own business." He had no idea how he might know such a fact.

Chance crept toward the window, pulled the edge of the curtain aside a fraction of an inch, and peeked out. Both officers remained inside the vehicle, one on the radio and the other checking the computer screen. At least the car wasn't parked directly outside; maybe the two cops *weren't* here for Chance.

"What are they doing?" Bella breathed into his ear.

In his fixated state, Chance hadn't noticed the woman sneak up beside him. She rested her hand on his back, and he felt his mouth go dry. For the briefest second, all thoughts of law enforcement bashing down the door vanished from his mind.

"They're getting out of the car," Bella hissed.

Chance let the curtain drop back into place and listened. Two car doors slammed, and he heard footsteps crunching on gravel, cutting off when they reached the concrete footpath. He stood up straight and turned his gaze toward the door. Bella's hand slipped from his back, and he grimaced, stepping in front of her. The footsteps scuffed right up to the door… and then continued by. He let out a soft sigh of relief. Loud banging sounded from the door to the next room, followed by muffled yelling. Several shouts and then the unmistakable buzz of a Taser. The crunch of a large body collapsing to the ground.

Cuffs snapped tight, and then both cops groaned as they hauled the offender to his feet. Chance risked peeking out the window once more and saw a bulky white man covered in tattoos smashed face down onto the hood of the patrol car.

The cops searched him, and then shoved him into the back of the patrol car none too gently.

"I wonder what he did," Bella murmured.

"Just be thankful it's not us."

A loud knocking came from the front door, and they froze. Chance glanced out through the window and saw only one cop outside, wiping his sweating forehead with a handkerchief.

"I think it's one of the cops," whispered Chance, pointing at the door.

"Get in the bathroom."

He followed Bella's order, softly closing the door behind him. The light remained switched off in case the cop asked to see the room's second occupant.

Chance heard the front door open. "Good evening, ma'am. Were you the one who called for police?"

"No, officer. What's going on?" Chance marveled at the anxiety Bella put into her voice.

"Nothing to be alarmed about, ma'am. Somebody called about an assault in the parking lot earlier. We have the perpetrator, but we're chasing up the original caller. Have you seen anything out of the ordinary?"

Chance sensed her shaking her head. "Nothing that I would call odd. Then again, this isn't the most seemly place to spend the night alone." A hint of allure drifted into her tone.

"You don't seem like the kind of person we usually see around here." Chance heard material scraping against wood and imagined the officer leaning casually against the doorframe. "Might I ask what a lady such as yourself is doing here… alone?"

Bella chuckled, and Chance hated the throatiness of the sound. "Let's just say I'm going to fire my travel agent." The officer laughed, a little too loudly.

The second cop called out, and Chance heard the officer's uniform scrape against the wood once more, the sound of the man suddenly straightening. The other cop must have been the senior officer.

"Well, ma'am. Here's my card. If you can think of anything at all, please call me on that number."

Bella tittered. "I'll be sure to keep you in mind."

The door closed, and Chance stepped out of the bathroom. "I thought I was going to be stuck in there until you two left on your honeymoon," he muttered.

A wide grin spread across Bella's face. "You sound jealous."

"No, I was…." Chance trailed away. "Have they left yet?"

Bella flicked the curtain wide open, and Chance almost dropped to the ground, catching himself at the last moment. "See for yourself," she said.

The parking lot was void of any police cars. Chance breathed a sigh of relief. "That wasn't funny," he muttered.

"Yes, it was." Bella let the curtain drop. "You need to smile more."

"I'll try to keep that in mind." He glanced at the bed. "Now, what do you want to do about the sleeping arrangements?"

"Well, I don't know about you, but I'm going to use the mattress. That floor looks way too grimy and hard for me, thanks."

"I guess I'll sleep in that chair, then," he said, nodding toward a sad, solitary padded chair in the corner, mottled in a print that might suit an ancient grandmother's taste. It looked horrendously uncomfortable. He might as well try to sleep on one of the wooden chairs beside the small dining table.

"I never took you for an idiot."

"What do you mean?" Chance asked defensively.

"This is a *double* bed. I'm sure we can both sleep on it."

Chance stared at the bed. "Well, there is that."

"You don't sound too confident. Would you prefer to cramp up in that awful thing? Because that's fine by me. I love to stretch out."

Chance found himself reddening. "No need to rub it in. I just… we need to keep this professional, is all."

Bella stepped close and cupped his cheeks in her hands, peering deep into his eyes. "I never asked you to screw me, Chance. Sleep is sleep."

"Oh." He had no idea what else to say. Bella grinned and released him.

"I'm going to have a shower in there with the cockroaches," she said. "And no, that's not an invitation to join me."

"Right."

As the bathroom door clicked shut, Chance shook his head and cursed softly. He felt like a twelve-year-old boy in the presence of his childhood crush. Sitting on the edge of the bed, he grimaced as a plume of dust blew up and the springs squeaked loudly.

"Yep. I'm going to get a lot of sleep," he muttered, sarcasm dripping from his tone.

* * * *

"Chance, wake up."

"What is it?" he murmured.

"He's coming."

Chance sat bolt upright in bed, bounced off the squeaky mattress, and raced over to the window. "Who?" he demanded.

"What?" asked Bella.

He glanced back toward the bed. "Who did you say is coming?"

Bella flicked on the bedside lamp and rubbed her bleary eyes. "What are you talking about?"

"You just… didn't you say someone was coming?"

"I was dreaming about dolphins. It was a nice dream. This? I have no idea what is going on."

"But I was sure," Chance murmured. Pulling aside the curtain, he peeked out. Nothing seemed amiss in the parking lot, but the feeling of oppression still hung over him. "I think we need to get out of here. Right now."

"Aren't you being a bit overly dramatic? You probably had a bad dream. Come back to bed and forget about it. It's only a few hours until dawn; we'll get going then." Bella laid down once more.

The door thundered.

"Move!" Chance demanded. Yanking on his hospital slippers, he for once felt grateful that he hadn't upgraded to proper shoes. He was also appreciative of the fact neither of them had undressed before getting into bed.

Something heavy hit the door for a second time. Hard.

"Into the bathroom," Chance urged, herding Bella ahead of him. He slammed the door shut behind them and glanced around. "We need to escape through that window." He pointed above the bathtub.

"Will you fit?" she asked.

"I have to fit."

A third bash on the door echoed, along with the cracking of timber around the doorframe. The imminent danger urged Bella and Chance into action. Bella stepped lightly into the tub and slid open the window.

"It's barred," she groaned.

"Stand aside."

Chance stepped in beside her and gripped the bars on the outside of the window. Rust clung thick on the steel, but had not eaten through the rods enough to allow Chance to bend or snap them. Another thud followed from the main room, causing his heart to pound in his chest.

"That door won't survive another hit," Bella warned him.

"I know. I know."

Frustrated, he slammed his palm against the metal shafts. A jolt not unlike an electric shock exploded down his arm, from his shoulder to fingertips. The bars, including their mounting frame, tore loose from the wall and hurtled away into the darkness.

"What the…?" he murmured, staring at his tingling palm.

Bella gaped at him for a moment, and then snapped into action. "Hurry up!"

Shaking his head, he helped lift her to the open window. Her lithe form slipped through quickly. When his turn came, however, things didn't go so smoothly. Chance managed to angle his shoulders through, but his belt caught on the aluminum window frame. A final boom echoed from the adjoining room, the door shattering into splinters.

"Get out of here!" Chance bellowed at Bella.

"Not a chance," she retorted.

Stepping back to the window, Bella gripped his forearms, braced one foot on the wall, and wrenched. For a moment, Chance felt like a prisoner on the rack. His shoulders screamed, but finally his waist tore through. The aluminum frame scraped his skin, but for the moment, Chance couldn't care less. He thudded to the ground, but bounced up, nodded at Bella, and began to run.

As they sprinted into the darkness, he glanced back at the tiny window. A face emerged, silhouetted against the light from the room beyond. Chance gasped and almost stumbled, but Bella held him upright. Nevertheless, the image of the intruder burned into his mind.

It was Nothingman.

* * * *

"You might be wrong."

Thankfully, they had left Bella's car around the corner from the motel. All the parking spaces had been occupied when they had pulled in, and avoiding any clear indication of their presence hadn't seemed a bad thing. A short sprint past some industrial trash cans and stray cats and they were zooming away, with Chance out of breath for reasons that had nothing to do with running.

"No, I'm not," Chance replied.

As swiftly as possible, he had explained the visionary dreams to Bella, telling her who he believed had just stormed into the motel room.

"What did he look like?"

Chance threw his hands in the air. "His name is Nothingman. He looked like… I don't know. A wispy shadow. A man made of smoke. Evil on legs. What do you want?"

"And you saw this. It wasn't just a hallucination?"

"You heard that door breaking down, Bella. The front doors in that motel were the sturdiest things about the whole building. Whoever owned the place was used to people breaking in, hence the bars on the windows. It would have taken a battering ram to smash the door down."

"Or a man made of smoke?"

"Listen, you're supposed to believe in this stuff. I shouldn't have to debate it with you. I saw what I saw." He clasped his hands together, trying to quash their shaking. "Trust me, I'm not happy about this either. It was bad enough when I saw him in my dreams. Seeing him here in the real world sucks a whole lot more."

"This girl you mentioned in the dreams." Bella hit the left indicator and turned down the street. They had no idea where they were going; Chance had just told her to keep driving. "Do you think she was Siren?"

Chance nodded. "I can't imagine who else it might be. She smelled…." He let the thought trail off. It sounded flimsy in his mind; voicing it wouldn't make it any less so.

"You know what that means, don't you?" Bella asked.

"I have no idea."

"She's been crying out to you for help. Whoever this Nothingman is, he's holding her under his sway."

Chance blew out a frustrated breath. It wasn't like the thought hadn't already occurred to him, but giving such a theory life made the complications it carried all the more tangible. "Maybe she's just trying to make me believe that," he argued.

"Maybe," Bella agreed with a shrug. For a time she remained silent. "What do you think it means that he appeared the way he did?"

"Excuse me?"

"I've been studying paranormal and psychic phenomena for years, and I've never heard anything like this outside of occult superstition. What you're talking about sounds like the boogeyman more than anything I've read about. These are the kinds of tales that get discounted as trash."

"I saw what I saw, Bella."

"I know. And I believe you." She paused, gathering her thoughts. "I think he was something else altogether."

"What?" Chance asked, turning to look at her.

"A disguise. Some sort of cloaking to keep him hidden. Or her. You never know, it might have been the girl you call Siren under all that smoke. They might be messing with your mind to make you doubt yourself. The more scared you become, the less of a threat you're certain to be."

"Threat?" Chance chuckled mirthlessly. "I'm running around without a clue, and they're going to consider me a threat? I highly doubt it."

"Don't sell yourself short." Bella slowed the car, stopping for a red light. She turned to face him. "You're closer to these killers than anyone else. For all we know, the police still haven't linked the murders. You have displayed the ability to hurt them across vast distances, and they aren't likely aware of how little you can control your talent. Look at what you did back at the motel. That grill flew out of the wall as if a truck had hit it. If you were my enemy, I'd certainly consider you a threat."

As the traffic light turned green and Bella drove on, Chance let her words sink in. They boosted him somewhat, while at the same time causing him to worry a little bit more. If Trinity saw him as a direct threat, what would they bring against him? Was that why they were all gathering in New York? And what of whoever hid behind the scenes, the mastermind?

He suddenly gasped. "What if Nothingman is their leader?"

Bella snapped around. "Is it possible?"

"How should I know? You're the expert. But it seems to make sense. I don't think it had anything to do with Howard Mason's followers, and from what we can tell, only one of the Trinity killers was close by. If Nothingman is the leader, that would explain why he masked his features. A man hiding in the background definitely wouldn't like to allow himself to be seen."

"Clouding his features like that, even only as he appears in your mind, would take immense psychic energy."

"Almost the same kind of energy it would take to transport my consciousness into the body of a murder victim, correct?"

Bella paled. "You might be right."

Chance rubbed his chin as though it might hold some answers. The deeper he crawled down this rabbit hole, the murkier it seemed to become. Never could he have imagined the murders he had initially witnessed would become the most ordinary part of this entire affair. Now, looking back, he wished for the naivety he had held back then. The more he knew, the less he wanted to know.

"Have you decided where you want to go yet?" asked Bella.

"Where do you suggest?"

She seemed to contemplate the possibilities for a moment. "I remember you talking about becoming lost in a crowd when you first arrived in Manhattan. It might not be such a bad idea."

"I'm not too sure…."

"No, listen. Sometimes psychic energy can become confused when buffered by so many thought processes. In a large city, a number of compressed minds in a small place can be like cotton wool to sound waves. No, a better comparison would be to say it's like trying to eavesdrop on someone in the midst of a rock concert."

"How can you be sure?"

"This is what I do, my boy," she replied with a chuckle.

"What about the people who threatened me? The ones who killed Broachford?"

All humor faded from Bella's face. "That's another problem. And not one I think we can work out right now."

"It's something we need to consider before we step into an area filled with people who might potentially eat us," snapped Chance. As the words slipped from his mouth, he realized his mistake.

"Eat us? What are you talking about?"

Chance sighed. "Howard Mason, the man these people follow, is the Billionaire Cannibal."

Bella stared at him for so long he feared they might run off the road. Eventually, she turned her face back to the street. "That is probably something you should have mentioned earlier." Her voice was deathly calm.

"I figured there was enough going on without you having to worry about that as well." He paused, and then decided to tell her everything. "I met him in the asylum. He threatened to have his followers hunt me if I didn't help his son. His son is one of the Trinity killers, the one called Pestilence."

"Are the people who threatened you cannibals, too?"

Chance nodded wearily.

"That means the hand the old woman showed you.... Did these people *eat* the rest of him?" Bella's generally stoic demeanor appeared close to cracking.

"I think so, yeah." No point in lying now. "They call themselves Masonites, apparently."

"Jesus Christ," she murmured. "Are they also linked with Trinity?"

Chance thought about it. "I have no idea. Nothing really indicates that they might be, but we can't presume anything. At this point, it seems like everyone is teamed up against us."

"You think?" she asked sarcastically.

"It's not too late for you to get off this ride," Chance suggested. Deep down, he feared Bella might take him up on the offer. Indeed, she glanced at him sideways, apparently considering the option. Finally, she shook her head.

"No, I need to see how this pans out. All of my research into the human condition might be explained in the next few days. If I back out now and miss my opportunity, I'll never forgive myself."

Chance almost breathed a sigh of relief, but somehow felt hollow. "Is that all?" he asked softly.

Bella pulled the car into a parking space and yanked on the parking brake before killing the ignition. "I think this will do."

It wasn't apparent whether she ignored the question or hadn't heard him. Either way, Chance felt too cowardly to open himself up again. Best to focus on their next step, keep moving ahead, eyes open for danger at every turn.

Looking out the windshield, Chance saw they were indeed on Manhattan Island. "Maybe I should have been paying more attention," he muttered.

"Maybe," Bella replied. "Look, the sun is rising over the inlet."

Chance looked toward the horizon, spotting Liberty Island almost directly ahead. A dark red glow shone beyond Lady Liberty, making the Upper Bay shimmer like blood. Were he to take such things seriously, he might consider it a dark omen. As it was, the silhouette of the woman holding aloft her torch lifted his spirits, as though an angel had smiled down upon him.

Chance grimaced. He needed all the help he could get.

"Why park here?" he asked.

"It's Manhattan," Bella replied, as though that were explanation enough. "You see a parking spot, you take it. Now, where do we go?"

Chance looked around, searching for inspiration, but nothing piqued his interest. "What would you suggest?"

"Well, I did have an idea of where we might be able to lay low for the day, but you might think it naïve."

"Speak up. At this stage, I'm willing to consider anything."

Bella turned and pointed toward the island. "We take a ferry out there."

Chance squinted, wondering if there were something hidden behind the Statue of Liberty that he couldn't see. "Liberty Island?" he asked uncertainly, sure he must have misunderstood her.

Nodding, Bella said, "They'll never think of looking for us there."

For a moment, silence fell between the two of them as Chance stared once more across the water. "It's also an excellent way to find ourselves trapped. Once we're there, we can't just wave down a jet ski and power away. Standard boats aren't allowed near Liberty Island."

"I know. That's what makes it so perfect. Ferry tickets to Liberty Island sell out weeks in advance. If the people chasing you don't have tickets, there is no way they can follow us there. Think about it; even now, someone might be watching us, like that old lady said. But out there, they can't follow."

"Right there is the snag in your plan," replied Chance. "We don't have tickets either."

Bella smiled, an expression Chance was beginning to associate with mischief. "I know someone who works on the ferries. He owes me a favor."

Staring at her, Chance weighed their options. Other possibilities flitted through his mind, each swiftly considered and discarded. The idea of secluding themselves on one of the most popular tourist sites in New York seemed ridiculous, but it also might work. It would give them time to think things through and plan in a place of relative safety. He peered out at the silhouetted statue, her right hand thrust aloft, clasping the torch meant to represent a sanctuary for those fleeing oppression and seeking safe haven.

"Fine," he muttered, still not entirely convinced, but unable to think of a better plan. "Make the call."

Two hours later, they sat aboard the slightly rocking ferry, the morning sunlight bathing them with warmth even as the sea breeze whipped icily around them. The salt in the air tasted like tears, and Chance stared toward the island, still uncertain whether they had made the right choice. Once on the island, they would be trapped. That singular thought repeated itself incessantly, to the point of making him nauseous. Despite all logic telling him their enemies couldn't reach them, experience had taught him not to take the abilities of those ranged against him for granted. For all he knew, he and Bella might be obeying some subliminal coaxing, luring them both into a trap from which there would be no escape.

A hand clasped his, and he glanced down, noticing Bella had interlaced her fingers with those of his left palm.

"Everything will be all right," she murmured.

He tried to smile, but felt it fall flat. "Am I so transparent?"

"Like a glass half-full of concern."

"Thank you for doing this," he said suddenly. "I mean all of it. Staying by my side and helping me, even when you know what we're going up against." His gaze dropped, and then he looked back up.

"What do you mean?" she asked, her expression quizzical.

"We're facing homicidal mysteries. I'm a freak." He held up a hand when she made to argue. "No matter how you twist it, nothing about me is normal. I mean, I'm a guy escaped from a crazy house, tormented by visions, who can apparently manipulate the world around us with my mind – though not altogether successfully, might I add."

"Oh, I don't know about that." Bella leaned back and stared at the newly risen sun. "You haven't killed us yet."

"The day is young," he murmured.

CHAPTER XXIII

After the ferry's constant rocking, the rock solidness of Liberty Island felt strange beneath Chance's feet. More than once, he stumbled into Bella; the walk down the jetty left him feeling like they were still swaying. He felt like a clod bumbling around with feet too large, but Bella only laughed at him, her glee taking any embarrassment from his clumsiness. By the time they stepped off the wooden dock, he was striding normally once more.

"How do you do that," Chance asked.

"Do what?"

"Laugh despite everything that's going on."

Bella shrugged. "The fact we're in danger doesn't take away from the fact you were walking like you were drunk. There's no risk here and now, so why should I tremble. I'm not some little princess who has lived in an ivory tower all her life, you know."

The statement made Chance realize how little he knew about the woman at his side. "Tell me about it. I mean, where did you grow up? What was your family like?"

Her face instantly clouded over. "Now isn't the time for that discussion." She cast her gaze out to the water.

Chance took the moment to look around. Liberty Island looked exactly as he had imagined it. The Statue of Liberty dominated the view, the iconic tarnished copper woman towering above a plinth of sandstone, trees and shrubbery spreading to one end of the island and lawn splayed out at the Lady's sandaled feet like a green carpet. The chilly breeze flowing into the inlet reminded him how close the ocean was, and he shivered slightly.

"Should we wander the grounds for a while, do you think?"

Bella glanced around. "I think we should use the time to our best advantage. Let's find somewhere to sit down and figure out some kind of strategy."

"Sounds good to me. I sure could use a coffee."

The coffee was so expensive that Chance initially thought the man behind the counter was joking. They searched for somewhere to take the weight off their feet, but other people already occupied the few tables they spotted. Eventually, the two sat atop a squat wall. Chance sipped his coffee, winced at the bitterness, and then turned to Bella.

"Right," he began.

Bella peered at him, waiting, but nothing else popped into his head. Chance knew that she expected him to have some tangible idea of what to do, but the sheer scope of their task seemed indomitable.

"You really have no ideas, do you?"

Chance shook his head and studied his coffee cup. "If I could control this talent…."

"You would what? Stride out to meet Trinity like a cowboy from the Old West? No offense, Chance, but that would be ridiculous. These people are killers; you would be dead in a heartbeat."

"Not if I threw a car at them."

"From what you've told me, they don't exactly approach their victims obviously. Weren't they rendering them insensible? How can you throw a car at them if you're unconscious?"

Chance licked his lips. "Okay, I concede your point. But you have to admit, I'd be a lot more efficient if I could at least fight them. When I hit Bull in Doctor Petrov's kitchen, he looked ready to pack his bags and flee the country."

"I'm sure that was satisfying, but you need to look at the bigger picture here. If three killers are coming for you, then in the time it would take for you to attack one, the other two would be on you, and you'd be dead."

"Not if I collapsed a building on their heads."

Bella picked up a twig. "Break this with your mind."

Chance huffed. "You know I can't."

She tossed the stick aside. "Then let's avoid talk of collapsing buildings. You almost did it before, but that had nothing to do with control and everything to do with panic. If you're panicked, chances are they'll kill you before you get a chance to fluff a pillow. What you need to do is outthink these people."

"Outthink people who might be able to see into my head, you mean?"

"I never said it would be easy."

Chance looked up and was about to speak when a figure striding down the dock caught his eye. He squinted against the early daylight, and then gasped.

"Run," he croaked.

Bella glanced toward where he was looking. "What is it?"

Chance stumbled to his feet. He grabbed Bella by the shoulders and stared straight into her eyes. "You need to get away. That looks like the last morning ferry heading back to the mainland; try to get aboard it. Bribe them, do whatever you can. But you have to get away."

"Why? What's going on?"

He looked over her shoulder. "Bull is here."

The massive figure was striding purposefully through the massing crowd, his scarred and puckered skin glowing red in the sunlight. Bella made to turn and look, but Chance stopped her.

"Don't let him see your face. He's here for me, but if he can use you against me, I'm sure he will."

"Maybe it's a coincidence."

Chance shook his head. "No, this is way too precise to be a coincidence."

"Come with me. We'll both get on the boat."

The thought teased him, but he pushed it aside. Bull was striding toward where they stood; he hadn't seen them yet, but Chance sensed the man was zeroing in on him somehow.

"No, you have to go alone. I'll give him the slip, and then meet you back at your car this evening."

"How will you give him the slip? It's an island!"

"Trust me. Now, go!" Chance released her.

For a moment, Bella looked torn, but then she turned and melded into the massing crowd, and Chance breathed a sigh of relief.

Glancing around, he realized how daunting his task was. The only large structure was the statue itself, with some sparse woods behind and to one side. He began walking casually toward the monolith, fighting the tearing urge to run like a fleeing animal. Strangely, the mass of his thoughts still lay with Bella, hoping she could escape the island safely. With difficulty, he pushed the issue aside and focused on the task at hand.

The entrance to the statue loomed ahead of him. A line of people snaked out from it like a long tongue. Chance pushed through the crowd, shoving his way to the front. Glancing behind, he couldn't see the killer anywhere.

Exasperated shouts followed him, but Chance ignored these in the hopes of gaining entry and perhaps hiding inside. The structure looked huge, and the downstairs museum promised plenty of nooks in which to conceal himself.

"Got you!"

A hand snatched at him, gripping his shoulder and spinning him around. Chance raised his hands, but froze as corpse-like features glared at him.

"Where do you think you're going?" hissed Pestilence.

Terror surged up within him, and Chance pushed the killer away. A pulse exploded from his palms at the point of contact, and the man suddenly blasted high into the air. With a startled cry, Pestilence soared over the crowd and landed with a dull thud on the concrete. His head hung at an acute angle, wide eyes staring at nothing as blood pooled out around his skull. People screamed and began running, clearing the way. Chance didn't waste the opportunity, knowing that the island's security forces or police would come running at any moment. He ran toward the turnstiles and leaped over them, sprinting into the foyer of the museum.

A figure crashed into him, tackling him to the ground. Chance smacked his head on the concrete floor, and the world above him began to spin. He fought to bring it under control as rough hands grabbed him and hauled him to his feet. Bull's horrific features glared at him.

"You're coming with us."

A knife glinted in the killer's hand, and Chance fought to step backward. Bull's grip held firm, however, and he couldn't break loose. With all his will, Chance sought the ability within him, but it remained obstinate, refusing to heed his call. He battered at Bull's thick chest, but the man merely laughed, the sound booming through Chance's dazed mind. With the strength of two men, the enormous killer hauled him back toward the open ground.

"No!" Chance shouted.

A blast of telekinetic power shot out from him, shifting the stones of the statue foundation with its might. Bull never stood a chance. Flung away like a doll, a sickening crunch sounded, as his bones impacted the wall, his body flopping to the ground. Curiously, two splattered blood stains marked the impact, but Chance didn't give them a thought. He turned and ran for all he was worth. If Pestilence and Bull were here, chances were Siren wouldn't be far behind. She would likely strike with much more discretion than the other two killers had.

Chance debated whether to continue into the museum, possibly heading up into the statue, or to retreat out into the open park once more. The idea of such exposure clawed at Chance, so much so that he eventually turned and fled farther into the structure. Soon, he met up with other visitors, people still ignorant of the chaos from which he fled. Such would not be the case for long, he thought.

As if in answer, alarms blared into life. Spinning lights on the walls flashed above fire exits, and people paused, confused expressions staring from their faces. Staff slowly began corralling them toward the exits, herding them back outside. For a moment, Chance contemplated merging with the crowd, trying to disappear within the mass, but his instincts screamed at him that to go outside was to die. He pushed through the people, ignoring the calls of staff as he shoved past.

His eyes flicked from face to face. Any moment now, he expected the beautiful features of Siren to leer at him, but only annoyed and concerned people shoved past him. It was like swimming up a river; each yard he gained felt more tiring than twenty out in the open. After an age of fighting against the stream of tourists, he finally spotted a set of stairs. These were not the stairs leading up into the statue itself; more likely, they headed to the top of the pedestal on which the Lady stood so majestically. But it was away from the open ground, and the longer he fled, the more chance he had of evading the final killer.

The crowd was almost nonexistent by the time he stepped out onto the plinth. Staff tried to halt him, but he shoved past them, muttering excuses about a lost son. No doubt, after the chaos he had created downstairs, police or security personnel would soon be heading up here after him, but all that drove him on was the need to flee. Even the accomplishment of defeating two of the Trinity killers paled in comparison to that all-encompassing need. His gaze turned skyward, looking up toward the crown adorning the Lady's head. Yes, there he would be safe.

Chance sprinted back into the structure and up the narrow stairs. The few remaining stragglers hugged the walls to avoid him crashing into them, many shouting curses that he ignored. After several flights, his wind gave out, forcing him to slow his pace. As he paused to lean against the handrail, he peered over it and down. Several darkly clad bodies flashed past his view and onto the stairwell, demanding people get out of their way. Police or security. No doubt they would be armed and prepared to shoot without warning after seeing the bodies downstairs.

Summoning his remaining stores of energy, Chance hurtled up the curling steel staircase once more. His feet clanged loudly on the metal steps, announcing his presence to those below, but there was nothing he could do about it. To move silently would be to move slowly, and to move slowly would mean capture.

Gasping and wheezing, Chance stumbled up the staircase. The crown seemed impossibly far away, but he fought on, determined to avoid arrest. Heading back to Mount Sinai would be as good as a death sentence, especially after having killed Howard Mason's son, Pestilence.

At one point, he stumbled and grazed his shin, the pain racing up his leg, causing him to swear loudly. Shouts from below responded, but he couldn't understand what they said. He doubted it was encouragement.

After what seemed like an eternity, Chance fell to the floor of the crown platform. His breath shuddered in and out of his tortured lungs, dribble oozing from the corners of his mouth. Placing his hands underneath him, he fought to rise, but his body failed to respond.

"No more running, Chance," murmured a voice. He recognized the sultry tone entirely too easily.

With dread, Chance lifted his head. Siren stood casually, leaning against one of the window apertures, smiling down at him wickedly. A curved dagger dangled carelessly from her right hand.

"What, no witty retort?" she murmured.

"Fuck off," Chance grunted.

"Tut tut, my dear. Is that any way to say hello?"

Chance pushed himself up into a sitting position and leaned against the wall of the chamber. "Kill me, and they'll catch you. There's no way out of here."

"Then why did you run up here?" Siren asked, her tone taunting.

"I...." Chance trailed away. For the life of him, all logic in fleeing into an enclosed place was now gone. It had made so much sense at the time. Now it seemed ridiculous. Like a rat knowingly fleeing into a corner while a cat hunted it. "They'll still catch you," he finally grunted.

"Who will?"

Chance leaned to his right and peered down the staircase. He strained to hear the banging steps that had pursued him so doggedly. Only silence greeted his ears.

"Are they gone?" she taunted. "That's odd."

With a groan, Chance stood. Breath still gasped in and out of his lungs, but the deadening of his limbs slowly faded. He flicked another glance at the staircase, wondering how fast Siren was. Could he stumble down without her catching him? He doubted it.

As if reading his mind, Siren said, "Not a good idea, Chancey. Not if you want your girlfriend to live."

His blood ran cold. "What are you talking about?"

"Come, have a look." She waved him over.

Cautiously, deathly aware of the knife in her hand, Chance staggered to the window farthest from Siren and glanced out. Crowds of people mingled around the edges of the island, in the footpaths leading to the dock, but that wasn't what drew Chance's eye. Directly in front of the statue stood three figures. One was Bella; the two Trinity killers he had thought he'd defeated downstairs framed her. Bull gripped her effortlessly.

Pestilence leaned in close and licked the length of her face salaciously. Bella kicked him between the legs, and the scrawny man fell to his knees. Bull's laughter boomed out, audible even from this height. Bella fought against him, but he slapped her over the back of the head, knocking her unconscious. He lifted her limp form and draped it over his shoulder. Nudging Pestilence, he began to walk toward a side jetty, away from the crowd of people. Pestilence slowly stood and limped after him.

"That can't be," Chance groaned. "I killed them."

"You killed someone," replied Siren with a snort. "But I doubt it was them."

"Who, then?"

She shrugged. "I've been up here all morning, waiting for you. But at a guess, I'd say it was somebody innocent. Probably a couple of guards."

"No," Chance moaned. He looked out the window in time to see the two killers board a small boat along with Bella. Moments later, the boat chugged away from the dock. The police boat bobbing nearby didn't even seem to notice its passing. "Where are they going?"

Siren glanced out. "Off to see the boss, I guess."

"Nothingman," Chance murmured.

All traces of humor vanished from her expression, and her face paled. "How do you know that name?"

He looked her dead in the eyes. "I think you told me. I dreamed of a pumpkin patch. We were both children."

Panic flared across her visage, and for a moment, Chance feared she might attack him. After a few seconds, the moment passed, but her mood for taunting had disappeared.

"I guess you never did go that far away, after all." Her tone was musing, her expression soft.

"What does that mean?" Chance snapped.

"You were one of us, Chance." She paused. "You're my brother."

The world seemed to crumple in around Chance's vision. For a moment, he reeled, fearing the statue itself was collapsing. A moment later, he slammed onto his butt on the cold steel floor, and the dizziness faded.

"You're lying," he whispered, though his voice lacked conviction.

"Before you fled, before we called ourselves Trinity, we were four. But you left us… you left me. The next thing I knew –" She suddenly froze. All tenderness vanished from her face, and her features became etched in stone once more. "Yes, I understand. He apparently knows nothing. I'll bring him to you." The woman moved forward and threatened Chance with the dagger. "Get on your feet."

"Who were you talking to?" he asked, rising.

"Someone you're going to meet very soon."

"Nothingman," he murmured, his voice edged with dread.

Nudging him with the knife, Siren – his sister – motioned toward the staircase. Still stunned by what she had told him, Chance stumbled down the stairs. Part of him wanted to lash out, to fight against her, but when he reached the museum lobby, all thoughts of retaliation fled. Two blood smears still stained the wall, but their origin was now horrifically apparent. The victim was not Bull. Now, warped and crushed, two uniformed guards lay in a heap of broken bones and pooling blood.

"What…?" Chance murmured.

"He can make you see whatever he wants you to see." She pricked Chance in the back with her blade, forcing him into motion once more. Outside the ticketing area, however, he froze once more. A tiny body lay broken on the ground.

"No. That was Pestilence."

Siren shook her head. "Seems you killed a ticketing girl." She giggled, but the sound seemed absent of any kind of mirth. "Still think you have free will?"

"What are you talking about?"

"That's all you would prattle on about before you vanished. You would tell me how we all had a choice not to listen to him, how you and I could be free." She motioned toward the dead girl. "There's your freedom." Siren snorted derisively. "What did you think she was? A cop? A demon, maybe? A fluffy-haired clown? None of it matters. We've always been his playthings. That will never change, no matter how much you try to fight it."

"I don't remember," Chance murmured.

"Of course you don't." She directed him through a mass of tourists being held back by island security. Not one person even looked in their direction. Onlookers' eyes seemingly peered through them, staring horror-struck toward the scene of the murders; not a single gaze latched onto the pair. What kind of power would it take to do such a thing? Hundreds of people stood around, but nobody saw a thing. "That was your grand plan, after all. You figured if you had no memory, he wouldn't be able to find you. I didn't think you could go through with it, but you proved me wrong. Proved us all wrong."

"Wait," said Chance, pausing. "I didn't have amnesia until weeks after they admitted me. It had something to do with the medication."

Siren shook her head and jabbed him once more. "That's what he wanted you to think." She stared hard at his profile. "You really have no idea how powerful he is, do you?"

"But Doctor Smith. The patients."

"People believe what he makes them believe. Look around you. I'm walking across one of the most sacred monuments in the United States with a knife at your back, and nobody even notices. There are hundreds of people here, and I could kill you without a single person knowing. By the time your body appeared, I would be at home sipping on a margarita. Even you, the strongest of us, could never stand up to his manipulations."

"But I escaped."

"Did you?" she asked. "Do you think anything you have done isn't part of his plan? Did you actually see those murders all on your own? And what about your breakout from the asylum? Was that just magic?" She laughed bitterly. "There's no escaping Nothingman. I told you that, but you refused to believe me. Now you're going to pay the price."

"What price?"

"That's up to him. I'm just the delivery person."

Chance searched within himself for some semblance of power, but not even a spark emerged. He felt drained, either from his earlier displays, the run up the statue, or something else. He contemplated fighting Siren hand-to-hand, but she had far too much experience wielding a knife for him to last more than a second, and he knew it.

Slowly, she led him to the same side jetty Bull and Pestilence had departed from with Bella.

"What is your name?" Chance croaked, desperate to divert his mind from what he had done.

Siren appeared surprised. "I'm... Christine."

"Chance and Christine," he muttered. "We're twins, right?"

She nodded. "That's right."

"What about...?" His voice cracked, but he forced himself to continue. "What about our father? Is what I heard about him also true?"

She looked away. "I don't want to talk about him."

Chance spun around in an instant, his flailing hands grasping for Siren's knife. A look of surprise flashed across her face, but she recovered swiftly. Before Chance knew it, she hip-tossed him. The wind exploded out of his lungs as his body thudded heavily upon the concrete. A cold blade dug into the skin of his throat. Christine crouched above him like a spider, peering down at him coldly.

"Don't be stupid, Chance," she whispered. She spoke the words casually, not an ounce of tension in her being. At that moment, he knew that if the order came down, this woman would not hesitate to kill him. Whatever loyalty to one another they might have once had was gone like smoke in the face of a hurricane. A hurricane named Nothingman. "Now, get up."

She didn't offer him a hand. Chance groaned as he lifted his bruised body from the cold stone. "What now?" he asked.

"The boat is returning," she said, indicating offshore.

Chance looked, noticing the same boat that had taken Bella away. His heart plunged when he saw Bull and Pestilence riding in the aft of the vessel. Bella was nowhere to be seen. The small boat pulled into the dock, its engine revving as the driver forced it into reverse. It barely kissed the rubber fenders.

"Get on board," Christine ordered. Somehow, thinking of her as Christine made her more human, less likely to plunge the knife into his back. Then he recalled her icy expression when the blade had rested against his throat. Christine might be human, but Siren wouldn't hesitate.

The man piloting the boat seemed as blind to their presence as the multitude back near the statue. His face lay slack, his eyes slightly glazed. A soft ditty mumbled from his lips, wisps of it reaching Chance's ears over the thrum of the engine and the slaps of the waves against the dock.

"Welcome back, traitor," grunted Bull as he stepped aboard. The huge man gripped his upper arm and shoved him into one of the seats. Chance ignored him.

Pestilence leered over Bull's shoulder. As Chance looked up at him, he wondered at the remarkable similarity between son and father. Apart from age, the two could have been identical twins.

"Your father says hello." Chance uttered the words softly, casually, but their effect was instantaneous. The leer fell from the cadaverous young man's face, and he turned even paler than his already ashen skin.

"What did you say?" The words rose from his throat as a hollow wheeze.

"Your father. Howard Mason. I met him in Mount Sinai."

Pestilence flashed forward. Before Chance knew it, he was choking. The steely grip of the wiry killer cut off his air as surely as a noose. "What the fuck did you say about my father?"

Bull grabbed the writhing killer and hauled him back. "We need to bring him in alive. You know that."

"He said he saw my father," Pestilence spat. "Everyone knows he was executed."

"Maybe he's just trying to get a rise out of you. You remember how much of an asshole Chance could be."

Chance rubbed at his bruised throat and coughed. Christine slid down next to him and chuckled. "That was dumb," she murmured. "You know how sensitive he is about daddy."

Chance nodded. "I do now."

She stared at him strangely. "Why did you leave?"

"You people are psychopaths. You're killing innocent women to… what? Steal their psychic abilities? Is that even possible?"

Her expression hardly changed, but an edge of softness seemed to creep in. "How do you think he is able to do the things he does?" Her voice became softer. "How do you think you're able to do the things *you* do?"

"What?"

"You were the strongest of us. I think he found out you had been leeching for yourself, harvesting their energies for your own ends. That's why he hates you so much."

"For myself? You mean I was killing women?"

"I always knew you weren't as dumb as you looked," rumbled Bull with a chuckle. "You killed three times as many as the rest of us combined, I reckon."

"He did not," hissed Christine, though her voice lacked conviction.

"It's not possible," Chance mumbled.

"Anything is possible," she replied, her voice wistful. Chance glanced at her and saw deep sadness in her visage.

"Are you really my sister, or is that all a lie?"

She smiled, but the humor failed to thaw the coldness in her eyes. "If we wanted you to believe a lie, we would have left you alone."

"What does Nothingman want from me?"

At mention of the name, all three killers stilled. Christine looked up at Bull and Pestilence. "Yes, he knows the name."

"How does he know that?" hissed Pestilence.

"I know a lot of stuff," snarled Chance. "For instance, I know that if you two have hurt Bella, I'm going to kill you."

Bull appeared unimpressed. Pestilence's eyes flashed with anger.

"If you could hurt us, you would have done something by now," said Bull.

"I thought I'd killed you both once already. Doing it again won't be too hard." The words were spoken with a bravado Chance didn't honestly feel.

"You killed people *he* let you kill," Bull grunted, his scarred face pulling one side of his mouth up in a mock grin. "Everything you've done is because *he* let you do it. Nothing here has been random; your entire course was set from the moment you opened your eyes."

Chance scowled up at the big man. "All of it?"

Bull refused to answer, looking away toward the shore instead. Pestilence grinned maniacally, and his tongue flicked out like that of a snake. A shiver ran down Chance's spine, and his flesh exploded in goosebumps. How could he have been one of these people? Siren seemed most untouched by malice, but at the same time, he had seen her kill with relish. Had he once loved to murder as much as these people, or was he, even now, being duped?

The boat bumped against a dock, and Siren stepped off alongside Pestilence. Bull lifted Chance quickly from his seat and placed him on the jetty. With a nudge in his back, they started moving toward a pair of black cars with heavily tinted windows. Similarly to the island, nobody seemed to notice their presence, and they navigated New York's waterfront bustle without incident.

As they approached the cars, the passenger door on the rear vehicle opened and a familiar figure stepped out. Chance froze. Trinity looked at him in near unison, initially not noticing who had stepped out of the car. When they did, however, Chance spotted a frown flit across Christine's brow.

This wasn't part of their plan.

"Who are you?" she asked.

The little old lady who had visited Chance bearing Broachford's hand smiled widely. "We're not here for you." She pointed a shaky finger at Pestilence. "We've come for him."

The scene seemed to freeze around them. For a moment, the three killers didn't seem to comprehend what was happening. Chance, however, understood the old woman implicitly. He glanced around, noting the mass of people who had previously ignored the four figures, but now looked directly at them. He also noticed the blood smears on the windshield of the lead car, along with the tiny trail of crimson dribbling from the corner of the old lady's mouth.

"We need to run," he hissed at Christine.

"Who are they?"

"Cannibals," he replied with dread.

At mention of the word, Pestilence spun to face him. "You weren't lying. My father truly is alive?"

"He said he wanted me to keep you safe. To lead you from the path you had taken."

"Hardly!" the killer spat the word and drew a blade from his belt. "I stole something from him, and now he wants it back."

Dozens of people surrounded them now. Christine and Bull had also drawn knives and looked ready to defend against the horde.

"Can you give it to them?" asked Christine.

"It was a life, one he yearned for." Pestilence shook his head. "The only way they can retrieve it, is to bring me to him alive." He glanced accusingly at Chance. "They used you to find me."

"Hey, don't blame me. I'm the one *you* came after, remember?" For the moment, Chance couldn't decide who he feared more; Trinity, or Howard Mason's crazed followers, his Masonites.

Three more Masonites climbed out of the two cars, their long knives dripping blood. Whomever Trinity had assigned to watch the cars was definitely no longer going to be of assistance. The semicircle threatening them pulled tighter, edging them back toward the dock. They seemed like everyday Joes. Nothing about them indicated they were fanatics. The housewife to his left bearing a cleaver, for instance, didn't wear an unblinking Hannibal Lecter leer. The middle-aged man with half-moon spectacles didn't bear a Charles Manson swastika on his forehead. These were ordinary people from all appearances, but not for a minute did Chance think he could plead with them for his life. Their gazes were focused, their expressions intense. The brutal reality of such an unreal circumstance almost froze him to the spot.

"I don't suppose any of you brought guns," Chance asked.

"This isn't our typical quarry," replied Christine.

"What about Nothingman? Why can't he manipulate them?"

Siren glanced left and right, her blade pointing threateningly toward the horde. "I don't know. This isn't supposed to be happening."

A towering giant, almost as large as Bull, suddenly lurched toward them with a strangled yell. The large man wore a black leather jacket and jeans that bulged with the thickness of his thighs. In his right hand, raised high, he bore a long machete, ready to chop down.

Without pause, Bull stepped in to meet him, the fluidity of the scarred giant's movements almost dancer-like. Chance didn't see the killing blow. One moment the Masonite was standing, the next he fell, disemboweled, to the ground, leaving Chance stunned at the swiftness of the kill. He gawped at the body, twitching on the grass, blood flowing from his severed intestines, soaking into the soil. After a moment, the twitching ceased.

"You've grown soft, brother," growled Christine. "There was a time when you would have found such a scene amusing."

"I must have been an asshole."

"Yes," hissed Pestilence.

The death of their comrade didn't cause the gathering to pause. They continued to tighten the noose, forcing the group back toward the water.

"The boat!" Chance yelled, turning. The dock was empty, and he blinked several times before spinning back. "Where did it go?"

"The driver probably fled once Nothingman's control vanished," Christine advised him, her gaze narrow.

"So he wasn't with you?"

"The only people with us are us." She flipped the knife to an underhanded grip, ready to plunge it into the first person within striking distance.

Chance peered around. There seemed no escape from the fanatics. Part of him yearned to beg them to let him go, to take Pestilence and be done with it. But he knew they wouldn't let him survive. These weren't the live and let live kind of people. They would carve him up and leave him to bleed out on the grass beside their fallen colleague. Either that or carve him up and take his corpse home to fill their freezers.

Neither prospect held much appeal.

A skinny woman wearing a tattered dress lunged toward Chance with a filleting knife. He barely felt it dig into his forearm. When the pain registered, however, he flung out his hand to ward her off. A silent explosion erupted from his fingertips. The woman hurtled through the air to crash to the grass. Without thinking, Chance sprinted through the gap in the semicircle. The footfalls of Trinity pounded close behind him, making him run all the faster. Whatever illusory comradeship had formed in those few moments of impending death had now vanished. All he wanted was to escape all the psychopaths.

Unfortunately, they had other ideas.

As he made it across the street, Chance felt a slim hand on his shoulder, a blade pricking his ribs in the same moment. Siren angled him toward one of the tourist buses, a bright red double-decker with an open roof. The four of them made it onboard just as the bus began to pull out from the curb. The door swished closed behind them; the driver didn't even glance in their direction. Another *gift* from Nothingman, Chance guessed. The horde pounded on the doors, and several tourists looked around, concerned, but the driver paid the commotion no heed and drove away.

"Upstairs," Christine hissed.

Chance trudged his way up the stairs. Once there, he spun and tried to shove Bull using his powers, but it felt like he was hitting a cement wall. The large man didn't budge. Instead, the impact sent tremors up Chance's arm to his elbow, and he winced.

"Well, that was stupid," grunted the killer. Bull grabbed Chance and shoved him down into one of the seats, bustling in behind him. Christine sat beside him, and Pestilence slithered into the seat in front.

Christine peered at him for some time before asking, "Why can't you use it all the time anymore?"

"I have no idea."

She looked around, the wind blowing her hair as though they were in a shampoo commercial. When she looked back, her gaze was thoughtful. "You used to be more in control. There were things you could do, amazing things. That's what made you so dangerous, so unpredictable." She leaned in closer, uncomfortably so. "It's like you're an entirely different person."

"Good. I don't think I would like the guy I used to be."

"Not many did," grunted Pestilence. He was cleaning his fingernails with his knife.

Chance turned his attention back to Christine. "How did I get away?"

His sister smiled ruefully. "Looking for tips?" She sighed. "The truth is, we don't know. One day you were there, the next you were gone. The first we knew of your reemergence, you were in that damn psychiatric ward."

Chance thought about it for a while, finally giving in to the urge for more information. "A woman told me I killed our father. She said that was how I ended up in there."

Christine snorted. "That is highly unlikely."

He waited for her to elaborate, but she remained silent on the subject. "So how did I end up in Mount Sinai?"

"Chasing squirrels, perhaps?"

The suggestion rang a chord deep within him, but Chance couldn't place where he'd heard it before.

"Where are you taking me now?" he asked.

"To see him."

"But where is he? I mean, we're on a tourist bus circling Manhattan. Does it stop nearby?"

She grinned humorlessly. "It will if he wants it to. You still have no concept of how potent he has become, do you? All those lives siphoned into his own mind, making him more than just a man."

"You make him sound like a god."

"Maybe he is," she said. A shiver seemed to pass through her skin. "Or the Devil."

"He scares you?"

"Of course he does. Anyone with half a brain is scared of... him."

Chance noted the pause, but could think of no reason for it. He glanced behind them, half expecting to see a horde of Howard Mason's supporters following the bus. The street remained clear of them. For now.

"They won't give up, you know," he assured her.

"It won't matter soon."

"What do you think they want from him?" Chance asked, nodding toward Pestilence. His attention seemed to be on the midday crowds strolling the pavement.

"How should I know?"

"Aren't you all linked? You know, psychically?"

Christine shook her head disappointedly. "I thought you were smarter than that."

"What do you mean?"

"Well, you've had a taste of it. Can you turn it on and off at will? Can you read what I'm thinking right now? No? And why is that?"

"I could never see into your minds," Chance argued. "Only the minds of your victims."

"What if I wanted to kill that woman there?" She pointed at a dark-skinned woman standing at a crosswalk. "Could you simply leap into her mind?"

"You know I can't."

Siren leaned back in the seat with a huff. "And now you know how much control we have. We communicate because *he* wants us to. I doubt we have any real power anymore. We did once, but he's probably sucked us dry." She chuckled dryly. "That's what he does."

"Why don't you leave him?"

She glared at him. "And go where? Do what? Look at you. You tried it and ended up in that fucking asylum. God only knows what happened to you before you woke up in there." Her gaze pierced deeply into him. "And you were the strongest of us."

"You keep saying that."

"But you're still not listening."

The bus suddenly shuddered to a halt. Traffic behind started blaring horns and yelling, but the vehicle remained motionless.

"Guess this is our stop," said Christine. She stood up and nodded to Bull, who hauled Chance to his feet as effortlessly as a mountain lion lifting a kitten. Christine glanced around the street. "Seems clear to me."

The moment the four figures stepped off the bus, it lurched into motion as if they had never existed. Chance felt Bull guide him gently but firmly to the pavement, and then nudge him to the right.

The crack of a rifle parted the air, and Bull toppled into Chance. The huge man's weight drove Chance to his knees, but then Bull tumbled off, leaving Chance peering down at his stunned face. Blood pooled out beneath the scarred giant, and his mouth gasped for air.

"Tiffany," he whimpered. His body stiffened, and then went limp.

"Get up," Christine snarled at Chance, grabbing him by the shoulder. "Move!"

Chance stumbled to his feet and fell into a lurching run. Pestilence led the way, sprinting into a nearby department store. As Christine shoved Chance inside, a second bullet ricocheted from the stone frontage, spraying Chance with shards of concrete. Christine swore and threw him through, following closely. Chance stumbled, but maintained his footing. He ran after Pestilence, who cleared the crowd in front of them with maniacal shrieks. A store security guard ran forward, fumbling for his gun. Pestilence gutted the man swiftly, economically, and swept up his sidearm. He gripped the gun in his right hand, the bloody knife in his other.

Movement from their left caused Chance to turn rapidly. A dozen people sprinted toward them, fanaticism glowing in their expressions. Pestilence fired off a single shot, dropping the lead male to the ground, but the rest of the horde didn't pause. This group held guns, and two fired off shots that whizzed over Chance's head. Angry shouts followed, and suddenly the gunfire ceased. But the crowd still surged forward.

Chance ran for all he was worth. He wasn't sure why, but he stayed with the remnants of Trinity. There was no time to think, only to flee. Perhaps it was the hope of safety in numbers. Maybe he thought they might be able to protect him from a group that, if he were honest with himself, terrified him beyond belief. These were ordinary people literally baying for his blood. In the end, it didn't matter why he stayed with Christine and Pestilence. All that mattered was getting away.

Pestilence led them to a fire exit and banged open the door. They entered a stairwell and sprinted down. Part of Chance worried what might happen if they arrived at the bottom and found the doors there locked, but he had no time to second-guess the decision. All his focus remained on not tumbling down the steep concrete stairs.

When they arrived at the basement level, Pestilence kicked the fire door, and it flung open, banging loudly on the wall as it swung around. The trio ran through, into a parking lot lit by buzzing fluorescent tubes. Pestilence didn't pause, didn't look around to see if Chance and Christine were following, he simply sprinted away.

"Follow him," Christine grunted.

Something in Siren's tone made Chance look at her. Pain racked her expression. He glanced down and saw blood seeping from a wound in her leg.

"You're hurt," he said, somewhat unnecessarily.

"One of their bullets grazed me. I'll be fine." She threatened him with her knife. "Hurry up."

"Would you actually kill your own brother?"

"After what you did?" Christine leaned in close and snarled, "In a fucking heartbeat. Get moving."

Chance began jogging after Pestilence. The scrawny man darted between parked cars, momentarily vanishing behind a van before re-emerging once more. His face appeared flushed, his expression panicked. Chance supposed if anyone knew what the followers of Howard Mason were capable of it was his son.

The fire door behind them banged open. A horde of Masonites surged out like termites from a smoking mound. Pestilence shot the gun, dropping one of them, but the group poured forth without pause.

Pestilence turned and fled.

Chance and Christine followed; her hobbling slightly and trailing blood. Part of Chance screamed that now was the time to give her the slip, but she was his sister. He knew this, deep in his bones. Some kind of kinship had rekindled upon their reunion, and while it might not be seamless, the bond was definitely there. Logic dictated that it might all be an illusion put in place by Nothingman, but the idea of leaving his sister to fend off the Masonites left him torn.

"Hurry up," he muttered.

Dropping back, Chance flung Christine's left arm around his shoulders and hugged her tight at the waist. She grunted in pain, but did not pull away. Together, the two hobbled through the parked cars at a markedly faster pace than she had been managing on her own.

Barely ahead of the trailing horde, the three fleeing figures raced toward the exit ramp, heading back to street level. Chance worried that once they arrived there, the unseen sniper would pick them off one at a time, like Bull. However, the imminent threat of cannibals on their heels pushed him on.

Panic rushed through him, and he yearned to focus his fear, to hurl the Masonites away with his mind, but not even an inkling of power flickered through him. It was like living in a desert and turning on a faucet, to find only dust emerged.

A hurled knife flew past his left arm. The sting of a wound flared a fraction of a second later. He glanced down, noting that the material of his shirt and the flesh beneath had parted in a straight line. Blood began to well. However, that was all the consideration he could give the situation. The injury wasn't going to kill him so it could wait.

The Masonites neither cried out nor fired shots. The only sounds of pursuit were the slapping footfalls echoing from the concrete driveway. In a way, their silent haranguing made the chase all the worse. It felt to Chance like they were fleeing through a forest with soundless wolves shadowing them. The wolves didn't want to catch them, merely tire them out, so that when the final attack came, they would be too exhausted to do anything other than die.

The exit ramp beckoned. Sunlight illuminated the pavement like a torch from God. But with it came the knowledge they would be running out into exposure. The wolves would still dog their heels, but they might also be attacked by eagles from on high. Eagles with high-powered sniper rifles.

As he stepped from shadow into light, Chance reflexively cowered, as if that might make a difference. When no stinging bullet knocked him to the ground, he increased his pace.

"Help us!" he called out to Pestilence.

The cadaverous form ignored him and continued running. Several bystanders saw the weapons in his hands and leaped out of the way, shrieking. It would only be a matter of time before police sirens wailed.

Unless the seemingly omnipotent Nothingman intervened, of course.

"We have to hide," he hissed to Christine.

"No," she snarled, and he felt the dagger in her hand curl around to press against his carotid artery. "We continue on together."

"He doesn't even care about you," argued Chance, nodding toward Pestilence. The thin form was creating a greater gap between them with every passing moment.

"It's not about him."

"What if they're not even chasing you and me?" Chance contended. "I mean, they claimed to only want him. That's probably why he's running so fast."

"If we separate, we will die. I don't expect you to understand. After all, you left us once already. What's to stop you doing it again?"

Unable to answer, Chance reluctantly continued hauling Siren along as swiftly as he could. She wasn't a dead weight, but the farther they ran, the more she drooped onto his shoulders. Before long, he would be exhausted. Would the Masonites bypass them in their pursuit of Pestilence, or would they pause to carve off a few snacks for the journey?

The thought fortified him. He hauled Christine up higher and sprinted for all he was worth. She groaned softly in his ear, but he ignored her pain, recalling the minds of those women whom Trinity had slain.

Part of him called out to let Siren go, to drop her in the street and flee. He ignored the voice, knowing that to do so would make him no better than Trinity. The awareness that he had once been one of them gnawed at him; he didn't need to reinforce the fact by acting like one of them.

Pestilence ducked down a side alley, and Chance followed. Moments later, he heard the killer curse. When he looked up, he saw the reason; the alleyway ended abruptly, blocking them in and trapping them. Chance turned to retreat, but the first of Howard Mason's zealous followers slipped into the alley, slowing when they saw their quarry was cornered.

Cold metal pressed against the base of Chance's skull. It took him a moment to realize it was the muzzle of a gun.

"Get rid of them," Pestilence snarled.

"How do you propose I do that?" Chance demanded.

"I've seen what you can do. Do it to them."

Chance cursed and blew out a frustrated breath. He felt nothing that indicated he might be able to do as Pestilence asked. Slowly, cautiously, he lowered Christine to the ground. Her knife scraped against his throat as her hand pulled away, but it did not cut the skin. Propping her up against the wall, he straightened and looked sideways at Pestilence. The murderer licked his lips and glanced toward the entrance of the alley. More and more Masonites filled the passage, each possessed by the same blank look in their eyes.

He closed his eyes.

Breathe. Just breathe.

Control slipped over him like a sheet made of ice. With it came the knowledge of what he needed to do, how to manipulate the power within him. It was a part of him, had always been a part of him.

Snapping his eyes open, he grasped Pestilence with his mind. The cadaverous figure squeezed the trigger. The bullet shot wide, cracking into the brickwork of the wall beside Chance. With a flick of his head, Chance tossed the killer into the midst of the crowd.

Eager hands, dozens of them, grasped the flailing form. Screams erupted from Pestilence, along with several gunshots. Soon, however, his ammunition ran out, and his screams turned into choked shrieks. The sound of rending flesh emerged from the mass, and Chance cringed.

The power within him fled as swiftly as it had arisen. With its departure vanished the momentary understanding of how to control it. What had seemed so simple a moment before slipped away into the fog of his mind, becoming little more than an echo of knowledge. It was gone, but he sensed it hadn't retreated completely. Not yet, anyway.

Eventually, the horrific sounds faded. The crowd looked toward Chance, unsated hunger evident in their eyes, and he prepared to fight his last fight. He threw a swift glance down at Christine and contemplated leaving her there and fleeing. Her face was pale from blood loss, and he knew she would not be able to stop him, but something made him pause. It wasn't the likelihood that she would bleed out without his help, nor even that she might suffer a fate similar to that of Pestilence. Something firmer held him in place, refusing to let him abandon her.

Charging footfalls echoed from the walls of the alleyway. Chance's head snapped up to see scores of Masonites hurtling down the alleyway. Blades glinted in their hands, knives and hatchets, machetes and cleavers. Some even clutched broken bottles and shards of mirror. Their approach was haunting. No war cries preceded them, no threats or screams. In a way, this made their assault even more terrifying.

Chance had no time to think. Cringing back, he threw his hands up in a warding motion.

An implosion of power caused the walls of the buildings on either side to collapse into the alley like mini avalanches. Tons of rubble toppled down onto the Masonites, quashing their forward rush in an instant. Not even a shriek escaped from the dust.

"Whoa," Christine murmured, her voice weak.

"I didn't mean to do that," Chance's wide eyes stared at the dust pluming from the collapsed walls. Not a single limb twitched. No voice called out for help. "Jesus Christ," he breathed. He looked to the damaged building to his left. Several startled faces peered out from the collapsed office building, but nobody appeared to move. "Let's go through here."

Hauling Christine to her feet, he helped her climb up the mound of rubble and into the building. The loose bricks slid beneath their feet like sand on a dune, but they managed to scramble into the second floor of the ruined structure. Several office workers stared at them silently, their eyes wide, but Chance ignored them. He headed for the rear of the building, hoping there was an exit out to an entirely different street.

At the back of the building, he found a staircase leading down to the ground floor. He was able to push open a fire door, leading them out to another alley. Before allowing the door to swing shut, he peered around for any indication of more Masonites. When nobody appeared, he stepped away, Christine's arm still draped across his shoulders. The door banged shut with booming finality, and he grimaced.

"I need to get you to a hospital," he stated.

Christine shook her head. "He'll kill us."

"If I don't, you're going to bleed to death."

Once they made their way to the main street, Chance hailed a Yellow Cab. The driver didn't notice Christine's bleeding as Chance hauled her into the rear seat and demanded they be taken to the nearest hospital. The Pakistani driver set off into the morning traffic with barely a disgruntled huff.

Christine slumped down in the seat, and Chance peered out the side window, searching with wide eyes for a sign of more zealots. No manic gazes met his, but that didn't leave him feeling confident.

As the cab pulled away, he saw pedestrians glancing at the mountainous pile of rubble, but none paused for more than a moment of curiosity. Was this New Yorkers' natural disdain for involving themselves in issues not directly affecting them, or had Nothingman become involved once more?

Chance fell back into the seat of the cab, feeling sweat prickling the skin of his forehead. He glanced sideways at Christine, wondering if she were going to live or die in the back of a cab, leaving him to explain her bullet wound to cops who might or might not care.

As the taxi passed the third block, Chance heard sirens. Twisting around, he peered through the rear window and spotted flashing lights back where the walls had crumbled… or more precisely, where he had collapsed them onto dozens of people. He couldn't tell if the sirens belonged to the police, fire department, or an ambulance, but a part of him felt relief that the sane world hadn't frozen completely.

As they pulled into the hospital, Chance jumped out and raced around to Christine's side, calling for assistance. A nurse ran forward with a wheelchair and helped him load Christine into it. He turned back toward the cabbie, readying an excuse for non-payment, but the man simply drove away, leaving him staring at the trunk of the yellow car in amazement.

Turning back, Chance saw the nurse was already wheeling Christine inside. He jogged to catch up, but the woman was swift, and Chance was still tired from the day's frenzied pace. The woman ducked down corridors, almost at a run. Chance called out for her to wait, but she ignored him. He barely caught sight of her entering an elevator before the doors swished closed, cutting him off.

"What the hell?" he muttered.

Watching the flashing numbers, he frowned as the elevator descended two floors to the second basement. He checked the floor plan next to the elevator, noting that the emergency ward was on the ground floor. Why had the nurse gone downstairs? The directory mentioned nothing about the second basement floor, stating only that it was for long-term storage.

He pressed the call button and waited, his stomach churning. Once the doors opened, he entered and pressed the B2 button.

Nothing happened.

Frowning, Chance stabbed the button with his index finger once again. The doors closed, but the elevator remained motionless. Chance was about to tap on the button again when he noticed the security swipe and cursed. He needed a card to access the lower levels of the hospital. As he was leaning forward to press the door open button, they swished apart, and a man in a white coat entered. The man didn't even look at Chance, but swiped the card reader and pressed the B2 button. He then stepped out once more, leaving Chance alone. The doors closed.

"What going on?" Chance murmured.

Once on the lowest floor, the doors opened with a soft ping. Chance peered out, searching for signs of a trap, but all he saw was an empty corridor. The whiteness of the walls was blinding. Directly across from the elevator doors was a sign bearing two arrows pointing in opposite directions. Chance swallowed and stepped forward, pausing in the doorway, refusing to let the elevator depart. The arrow pointing left indicated the morgue; the one stabbing to the right stated that administration was down that way. He looked each way; both directions looked the same.

Chance frowned, recalling that the floor plan upstairs had stated that B2 was designated for storage. Surely the morgue and administration were important enough to be listed. He sighed, contemplating stepping back into the elevator and leaving this place. Christine had claimed to be his sister, but that didn't mean they were bound together. Surely the hospital would give her the care she needed. His presence was hardly necessary.

What about Bella?

The thought popped into his head without warning. His only link to Bella was Trinity, only one of whom remained alive. And she was somewhere down here.

Chance stepped clear of the elevator doors. They snapped shut like the jaws of a bear trap. He glanced around, sure the movement had been unnatural. The only sight to greet his gaze was a set of stainless steel doors. A flashing light indicated the lift was climbing to higher floors. Rubbing his chin, he flicked his stare back to the sign, pondering which direction to go. Administration seemed the logical choice. Christine wasn't dead, so there seemed no reason for the nurse to take her to the morgue. At least in administration, there might be someone with who could tell him where to go. The morgue conjured images of sallow-eyed monosyllabic workers who spent more time with the dead than the living.

The corridor reminded him of Mount Sinai. The stark whiteness of the walls combined with the pungent scent of antiseptic brought with it memories of the asylum he had so recently escaped from. The linoleum squeaked beneath the soles of his feet, conjuring further reminisces, but he pushed them away. He turned right around the corner.

Chance stopped so suddenly that he almost toppled forwards. Before him was not a continuation of the corridor; it was Betsy's room back at Mount Sinai. She still lay motionless on the bed, beeping machines helping her to breathe, monitoring her pulse.

He spun around. A door had materialized behind him.

It was closed.

Breathing heavily, Chance slowly turned back to Betsy. Was this an illusion? The entire scene appeared horrifically real; he couldn't discern any dreamlike blurriness or oddities. No unicorns pranced about the room, no giant hazy figures standing in the midst of a pumpkin patch. Grimacing, he stepped forward until he stood beside the bed.

"Betsy?" he whispered.

Chance wasn't sure if he expected a response, but his body definitely felt tense, ready to flee at a moment's notice. Slowly, tentatively, he reached out and touched her hand.

Nothing happened.

Gripping it tighter, Chance frowned down at Betsy. A whisper caressed his mind, and he tilted his head as if to hear it better.

B...are.

"I can't understand you," he said softly.

Betsy's eyes suddenly flared open. "THIS ISN'T REAL!"

Chance threw himself backward, stumbled, and then fell. Instead of hitting the solidity of the linoleum floor, tentacles wrapped around him, groping across his face, hugging him tighter than a bear. There seemed to be dozens of them, their suckers puckering and pulling against the skin of his cheeks. Welts swelled up in the wake of their passing. A scream tried to force its way past his lips, but the moment his mouth opened to release it, a tentacle slithered down his throat. Thrashing wildly, he felt the slimy sluglike thing push down his windpipe, choking away all breath. The room began to fade, grainy clouds pushing in from the edges of his vision.

Power surged up from within. The moment it exploded out from his chest, however, the scene changed. He flashed from Betsy's room back to the subbasement corridor. The tentacles vanished in the moment of transition, but it was too late to call back the explosion.

Walls cracked, and plaster fell. A large chunk of concrete tumbled from the ceiling, crashing down onto the floor beside him, barely missing his head. Sucking in a huge gasp, Chance controlled the shriek fighting to break loose. For some time, he remained prone on the floor, too terrified to stand lest the tentacles reemerge.

"Get up," he whispered.

Slowly, a trembling Chance rose upon unsteady legs. He blew out a breath, and then glanced around to ensure he was, in fact, standing back in the hospital and not the asylum. It took another moment to get his legs moving, but eventually he was shuffling along once more, albeit with much more caution.

A doorway beckoned on his left. He paused, cutting wide on the hallway, trying to get a glimpse inside, but the corridor was too narrow. What he did see, though, was the sign posted beside the doorway.

MORGUE

It was a simple sign. Black lettering on a white plaque.

"What the...?"

Chance had headed toward the administration section. He felt sure of it. So how had he ended up so turned around?

Turning on his heel, he jogged back down the corridor, pausing at the elevator to check the signage, and then running on toward the administration. Within moments, he was staring at the morgue's sign once more.

For a short time, he stared at the sign, grinding his teeth. Whatever was happening was beyond his understanding. Christine had hinted at the Nothingman's prowess; could this be another indication of his capabilities? Had he flung Chance, albeit briefly, back into the asylum? If so, what was his plan? Was he solely trying to wear Chance down, making him second-guess himself? The questions were endless, and he sensed the only way to find answers was to walk through the double-doors into the morgue.

Straightening his back, Chance flicked a glance back at the chunk of concrete that had barely missed his head. The walls on both sides of the corridor seemed to have bulged out like sand pushed away by a bubble. The thought that such power had come from within him bolstered Chance, allowing him to step toward the mysterious door.

The plain white door had no window in it, strange considering what Chance had seen in other hospitals. Such panes revealed if anyone were pushing a stretcher or wheelchair through from the other side, although in this case, it might be more of a cart or trolley. Maybe in some instances, it was a wheelbarrow. He reached out tentatively and brushed his fingers against the wood.

"Come in, Chance."

The voice was male. Sure and resonant. Full of power. It would not take much for the request to twist into an order, Chance sensed. If such a thing occurred, would he be able to resist? He sighed, dark knowledge seeping into his mind. If he had been able to resist, there was a good chance he would now be standing in front of an administration desk instead of this door.

Pushing open the door, Chance stepped inside. He stood tall, walking with confidence, determined to face whoever lurked within the morgue with confiden –

Chance froze. Every muscle in his body tightened in an instant, cording to the point he thought they might snap. A soft breath escaped his lips. Looking forward, his eyes widened, and his heart began to pound. The shadowy figure from the pumpkin patch stood casually beside a wheelchair. Dark smoke swirled around his features, obscuring any details.

"Nothingman," Chance hissed.

The figure appeared to smile, though expressions were difficult to gauge within the murk of his face. Chance looked down at the wheelchair, noticing for the first time that it wasn't Christine sitting in it, but the nurse who had so vehemently rushed down here with the Siren. The woman's neck was twisted at a horrific angle, and her blank eyes stared at the ceiling. Christine was nowhere to be seen. Neither was Bella.

"Where are they?" Chance demanded through clenched teeth. His jaw felt close to shattering with the pressure coiled in his tensed muscles.

"They are… about. This moment is solely for you and me. I don't want any distractions."

The swirling void where Nothingman's mouth should have been stretched wide like a horizontal tornado. It enlarged ever more until Chance feared it would touch the ceiling. He tried to take a step backward, but his clenched muscles refused to yield an inch. Nothingman stepped closer until his chasm of a mouth swirled mere feet away from Chance's face.

Like a tickle in the back of his throat, the trembling began small, coalescing into a massive internal quake. It vibrated from his core outward, tingling his ribs, spreading down his shoulders and hips, rushing to his fingertips. Eventually, energy exploded out of Chance and smashed into Nothingman. He expected the smoky figure to be flung away, but the power vanished down into the vortex, leaving Nothingman untouched.

Chance's heart dropped. Enough telekinetic power had erupted from within him to demolish a small house. All for naught.

Nothingman stepped closer. Tendrils of smoke flicked against Chance's cheek like probing fingers, but he battled to ignore them. Instead, he cast a glance upward. Hope surged within him at what he saw. A desperate plan formed in his mind in an instant. With no time to consider the consequences, he unleashed another blast of energy, this time into the ceiling.

Concrete fractured. For a second, the roof held, but then the entire floor above came raining down. Tons of artificial stone collapsed onto Nothingman, and he crumpled under its weight. The tornado of smoke disappeared in an instant. The bonds holding Chance vanished.

Leaping backward as more stone pounded down, Chance turned and lunged out through the door. Thunder rumbled behind him, but he continued running, sprinting down the corridor for all he was worth. Concrete pebbles smacked against the backs of his calves, some flicking up to hit him in the buttocks, spurring him onward. It seemed the entire hospital was collapsing, and he desperately searched for some kind of escape.

Rushing around the corridor, he spotted the elevator. The steel doors remained closed to him, however, and he brushed aside the notion of pausing to wait for the carriage. Lungs burning, he continued fleeing the building avalanche. Larger rocks were pelting him now, and he could feel the heavy exhalation of tumbling concrete blowing against his spine. Any moment now, and the collapse would overtake him. He would die, crushed beneath the irony of a building designed to save people crumbling on top of him.

A door appeared on the left of the corridor. Chance sprinted forward and flung himself through, tripping as he crossed the threshold. He sprawled on the cold linoleum, and then scrambled to gather himself to continue fleeing.

"Hello, Chance."

He looked up from the floor. The rumbling had ceased, cut off as if with a knife. Nothingman stood before him, his swirling form betraying nothing. Looking around, Chance realized he was back in the morgue… or had he never left? Nothing seemed damaged. Not even a hairline crack marred the white paint.

"What's going on?" he breathed, rising slowly to his feet. He could still feel the dust of the crumbling concrete at the back of his throat.

Nothingman scrutinized him, his glower overwhelming.

In an instant, Chance was gone.

One moment, he was standing in the hospital morgue, the next he was within Howard Mason's underground cell. Everything appeared as opulent as his last visit, but now a monotone beep sounded endlessly from the machine beside the murderer's bed. Mason himself dangled half-out of the bed. One arm had flung wide as if trying to defend himself in the last moments of life. But he had failed. The Billionaire Cannibal's bodyguard stood nearby, his eyes wide, staring at the blood on his hands. Upon Chance's appearance, his gaze lifted, but there seemed no hope in those eyes, only bewilderment.

"I did not do this thing," he murmured.

Booted feet stomped down the corridor beyond the barred cell door. The hospital staff wore rubber-soled shoes, so whoever was coming was either security or police. They would have weapons, and Chance remained an escaped prisoner. He glanced around, searching for somewhere to hide. There was nowhere.

The boots thudded closer. Just outside the cell.

The scene flashed, and Chance found himself somewhere else. Looking around, he recognized the scene as the safe house of Doctor Petrov, but someone had trashed the place. He tried to recall what it had looked like when he had last seen it, but pushed the issue aside. Whatever had transpired here had occurred since he and Bella had last stepped through the door. Within the living room, he saw a large body.

Doctor Petrov. Dead.

Whether it had been the Trinity killers or the imposters posing as the FBI would remain a mystery. Her body was as much a mess as the house around her. Whoever had carved her up had certainly enjoyed what they had done… or been made to do. The bodyguard of Howard Mason's whispered plea from only moments before echoed in Chance's ears.

"I did not do this thing."

For a moment, Chance considered that it might have been Masonites, but despite the carnage rendered to Doctor Petrov's body, no flesh appeared to be missing. Cannibals would never leave such a succulent carcass untouched.

The morgue materialized back into his view. There was no blurring of vision or cloudy transition. Each change was as sudden as a blink of his eyes. He glared at Nothingman, hate burning deep within.

"Why did you kill Doctor Petrov?"

A harsh, barking laugh. "She was nourishment, nothing more. Granted, I did not receive as much from her as I would have if I had used one of my Trinity, but you use the tools at hand."

"Nourishment for what?" Chance snarled. "What are you hoping to achieve?"

After contemplating the question for a moment, Nothingman silently stepped forward. Despite himself, Chance took a step backward. The shadowy figure seemed to grin, though it was impossible to be certain within the shadows miring his visage.

"I want it all," Nothingman stated softly. The words thrummed with power.

"What do you mean?"

The figure shook its head. "You still don't understand, do you, Chance? You never could grasp what I envisioned. This is why you turned against me, I think." He paused. "Did you think suppressing your memories would hide you from me? It took less than nothing to find you. After that, implanting you in the asylum was simple." He chuckled darkly. "Where better for you to be rehabilitated?"

Chance's world seemed to crumble slightly. "You put me in there?" His thoughts buzzed. "But how could you keep an eye on me? How did you know things were going the way you wanted?"

Nothingman took another step forward. This time Chance held himself firm.

"It's simple, Chance. I was with you the whole time."

Chance visibly staggered. His mind rushed through the possibilities of who this monster might have been. "You were Betsy," he said finally.

Nothingman barked another caustic laugh. "What point would there be in hiding within a husk? Try again."

The possibilities seemed endless. So many questions crowded in, battling for supremacy.

"Time is wasting, Chance. You need to hurry."

That caught his attention. "Why? What happens if I don't?"

"Look around you. You asked before where Bella and Christine are. Well, imagine the two of them are in a room together, and only one of them is allowed to walk out. How long until your sister guts the woman you gaze at so moonily?"

Chance's throat tightened. "Christine has been shot."

Nothingman shrugged. "She's been shot before. And stabbed. It never stopped her from fulfilling her part of the bargain. She knows the alternative is far from pleasant."

"What alternative?"

Chance dropped through the floor. Or at least it felt like he did. The next thing he felt was pain. No, pain was far too sedate a word for what tore through his body. Was he in Hell? Darkness surrounded him, but within that darkness was a fire that created no light. Tongues of flame lashed at his skin, searing his flesh. Chance opened his mouth to scream, but could suck in no air. The blaze sucked all oxygen from the atmosphere.

In a flash, the fire and darkness were gone, and Chance had returned to the morgue. He let out a long wail and collapsed to his knees. Holding his arms out before him, he examined the skin, expecting only strips of scorched flesh to remain, but the limbs appeared intact and whole.

"Imagine that torment forever, Chance. Or at least eternity in your mind. That is what Christine faced, and it is why she remains so loyal. The other two had different prices, but both were acceptable." He paused, and even though Chance couldn't see his eyes, he sensed Nothingman glared at him hatefully. "You, however, were always the hardest to control. Threats and promises didn't work on you, and I always knew that eventually there would be a reckoning." Nothingman sighed heavily. "You could have stood by my side as I conquered the world. Instead, you chose to become a shell without memory, an empty vessel of what you once had been. But I always knew there was power still inside you, more than you had ever known. Hidden wells resided within your blank slate, and all I needed were the right triggers to bring your talent into the light where I could consume it."

A chill rushed down Chance's spine. He looked up from his knees at the shadowy figure and understanding bloomed. All of this, his torments and tests, were pushing him to his limits. And what happened each time he reached his limits? His power became evident. Perhaps that was what Nothingman needed from him; to reach his absolute threshold, to implode with telekinetic energy.

"You finally figured it out." Nothingman clapped his hands slowly, theatrically, the sound hollow and muted, as if Chance's ears were stuffed with cotton.

"You can read my thoughts."

"I can do far more than that, my boy."

Chance scowled. "What did you call me?"

Nothingman seemed to huff, and Chance wondered if the shadowy figure had let something slip he had meant to keep secret. "I guess the time for charades is over. You probably deserve to know the truth."

"What truth?"

The shroud of shadows vanished in an instant. Chance gasped.

Nothingman stood clad in a black suit, a light gray silk shirt underneath. A red silk tie completed the ensemble. His beard and hair were immaculately trimmed, and while he still looked enormous, now his bulk was sculpted and in different areas.

"Jarvis?" Chance whispered.

"The one and only," the big man chuckled. Whereas the Jarvis Chance had known in the asylum had appeared obese, the real version looked capable of crippling Bull without breaking a sweat. "Now, why not give me a hug?"

Chance's jaw hung limp, and he closed his mouth with a conscious effort. The scene didn't seem to make any sense. Part of him screamed that this was merely another illusion, while –

"No illusion, I promise," Jarvis cut into his thoughts. "It's me. The one and only."

"But you…."

Jarvis chuckled and walked over to one of the mortician slabs. With a mighty heave, he launched himself up to sit on the cold steel. "I escaped, remember? But it wasn't out through the sewers. I walked straight through the front gate. Nobody even noticed. And nobody remembered a patient named Jarvis, either. Well, nobody except that son of a bitch, Mason. Something about him refused to be manipulated, no matter what I did. Luckily for me, his bodyguard wasn't so rigid."

"What were you even doing in there?"

"I was keeping an eye on you, my boy." He rubbed his hands together gleefully. "You thought you could escape me by wiping your mind clean. An unusual plan, but one that theoretically could have worked. I mean, if *you* didn't know who you were, surely there was no way *I* could find you, right? And I'll admit, it did take me a while to locate you. But when I did, I figured you might as well add to my own growing list of powers." Jarvis adjusted his tie and brushed a fleck of dust from his jacket. "No matter where I searched, I could never find anyone with anything close to your level of telekinesis. It's absolutely astounding. Therefore, I tried to take it from you forcibly. However," he held up a single finger, "here I discovered the real genius of what you had done to yourself. In wiping your memories, you had also denied yourself access to your talent. And so I set out to break down those walls."

"You put those images into my mind," Chance confirmed, his voice shaking. "The visions of the women being killed."

Jarvis grinned widely. "I always knew you were a smart cookie. Yes, I figured the best way to lead you back to yourself was to link you with Trinity. If you recalled what they were doing, I thought your memories might return." He sighed. "But in this I erred. I went into it thinking you had simply covered up your memories, when in truth you had wiped them forever. The old you is gone, never to be retrieved, sadly. That takes commitment, I'll give you that." He nodded, as though he had just offered the greatest compliment. "And so the manipulation began. It wasn't easy, let me tell you, but you're my son, so –"

"Wait!" Chance cried. "What?"

Jarvis frowned. "Your sister never told you." He rubbed his chin. "Maybe she's more like you than I thought. No matter, you're here now, and the fact I have been able to mentally fling you around like a rag doll has shown me that you're more than pliable enough for what I need to do."

Chance was still reeling. "And what is that?"

Jarvis smiled. It was almost a sad expression; at least it would have been if not for the hunger glinting in his eyes. "I'm going to kill you, Chance."

Spinning on his heel, Chance bolted. The door to the morgue was closed, but Chance smashed it open and hurled himself through, only to freeze on the other side. Jarvis sat on the mortician slab directly in front of him, blocking his path. The large man hopped down and brushed his hands on his dark slacks. "Are you done?"

Chance spun again and dove for the door. Wrenching it open, he paused, seeing Jarvis in front of him once more. Looking over his shoulder, he saw an identical scene behind him. He let the door swing shut.

"What the hell is going on?" he grunted.

"You can't escape your own mind, Chance," replied Jarvis. He reached up and tapped his own temple with his forefinger. "And I'm always in here."

"So none of this is real?"

"I never said that. To explain it, however, would take far too long." The big man looked around at his handiwork. "Cool, huh?"

"No, that most definitely is not cool." Chance peered around for some kind of escape, all the while willing his mind to remain blank. He wasn't sure how much of his thought processes Jarvis could pick up, but he'd already shown at least a modicum of ability in that regard. What he really needed was a way to delay things. "You claim you're my father. I was told I had killed my father. That was why I was committed to Mount Sinai."

Jarvis shrugged. "Best way to fool you, I figured. I couldn't have you learning the whole plot too soon, could I?" He smoothed down the hair of his beard. "The idea was to feed you snippets, but keep you constantly on guard."

"Was Howard Mason part of your plan?"

"Mostly. I mean, after all, it was me who led you to him, wasn't it. But in that, I nearly made a mistake. His followers were too fanatical for me to influence, and they almost killed you all out there."

"Shame about Bull and Pestilence."

Jarvis grinned coldly. "No, it isn't. Bull was a mercenary, someone I paid. He cost me a fortune, but he got the job done. Pestilence, or rather Howard Mason Junior, was a pain in my ass. A disgusting little prick, but as long as I kept the victims flowing, he didn't really care."

"And your own daughter?"

"Sacrifices need to be made, Chance." He grimaced. "That was something you never really understood, was it? You and your pretentious sense of right and wrong. A few dead bitches and you ran for the hills." Jarvis leaned in closer. "We could have been gods, you and I. Now look at you; you can't even escape the basement of a hospital." Jarvis took a step forward. "We can do this the easy way or the hard way. It's totally up to you."

Looking beyond Jarvis, Chance murmured, "The hard way."

Jarvis paused, frowning. The mortician slab behind him suddenly wrenched free from the rivets holding it to the floor and slammed hard into his spine. Chance barely caught a glimpse of the startled expression on Jarvis's faced before both the slab and the large man careened past him and out the door through which Chance had entered.

Without pausing, Chance sprinted toward the single door at the far end of the room. He yearned to believe that the collision had finished Jarvis, or at least knocked him out cold, but after everything he had witnessed in the last hour, he knew better than to accept what his eyes told him.

As he ran, his gaze flicked left and right, searching for some kind of advantage, but every time something caught his eye, he recalled the building collapse from earlier. The demolition had been entirely in his mind, but it still seemed too real, too fresh, to be ignored. Any replication of what he had done could result in similar devastation. Perhaps that was why Jarvis had designated this as their ultimate place of confrontation. It definitely put Chance at a disadvantage, even with the tenuous grip he managed to retain on the power flowing through him.

Cutting left around a corner, a sledgehammer-like fist knocked him flying. Chance skidded across the floor like a fallen ice skater, desperately clinging to his consciousness as the world around him faded in and out in fuzzy shades of gray. Looking up from the floor, he saw Jarvis standing over him, chuckling. Not a crease marred his immaculate suit. Not a scratch blemished his face. Not a ruffle tarnished his hair.

"You almost got me, I'll admit it," said Jarvis, staring at his ham-sized fist. "But your eyes gave you away. Now, where were we?" He stepped forward.

With a wrench of his mind, Chance tore loose an entire section of the wall and slammed it into Jarvis. Without looking to see the result, he scrambled to his feet and began to run again. He had no idea where he was going; all that burned through his terrified mind were thoughts of escape.

The next attack almost broke his leg.

He had no idea what had hit him, but as he tumbled headlong across the linoleum, agony shot from his thigh all the way up his spine. When he finally stopped rolling, he let out a low groan.

Jarvis stepped into view once more. He still appeared unruffled. "You're really starting to piss me off, Chance."

A mental blast sent the large man hurtling through the air to crash heavily into the far wall. The concrete crumpled beneath the force of the impact, and Jarvis slowly slid from the wall to the floor. He looked up, dazed, and then collapsed face-first onto the floor.

"Don't trust what you see," Chance breathed to himself. "Get up."

With a yelp of pain, Chance managed to regain his feet. Leaning against the wall, he battled on, desperate to escape the labyrinthine corridors. Once clear, he would focus on finding Bella; she had to be in here somewhere. Failing at that, he would settle with finding Christine. His sister would likely know where Bella was hidden. Nothing Jarvis had mentioned hinted that Bella was gone for good, and Chance refused to allow himself to think along those lines.

The more he moved, the better his leg felt. As he navigated the hall, the feeling began to flow back into the rigid muscles, and the pain slowly ebbed and shrank from his bones. By the end of the corridor, he was almost walking normally.

Turning right at the corner, Chance paused. He almost cried out in joy. The hall before him looked completely different to the one previous, with no sign of a morgue door in sight. Hobbling along, he lurched toward the desk with a homely woman sitting behind it. Dangling above the desk was a sign.

ADMINISTRATION

"Please, you have to help me."

"What do you need, my boy?" the homely woman asked.

Chance froze. "What did you call me?"

She grinned. The smile widened. Widened even more. Eventually, the skin split and fell away like peeling paint, exposing shadowy features. The woman stood, knocking over her chair, and the desk crumbled into ash. The air around her swirled, becoming shadows.

Chance groaned as Nothingman swelled tall. His head scraped against the ceiling, and his long arms became tipped with smoky claws.

"You are mine," Nothingman hissed.

The gargantuan shadow leaped forward. Chance barely had time to lift his hands before darkness engulfed him.

CHAPTER XXIV

The wheelchair squeaked.

Christine snapped her head back and looked around. Despite the haze fogging her head, she noticed something was wrong. For a start, this looked nothing like any hospital she had ever been in before. In fact, the place looked more like a junkyard than a building. As she peered around, the haze began to lift even more. Blue sky shone through the fogginess, and piles of trash surrounded her.

"Where am I?"

The last thing she recalled was sitting in the cab, trying to stem the bleeding in her leg. But had it been a cab? Something about the memory seemed wrong.

Bull and Pestilence were dead.

The memory stabbed into her, seeking substance in which to thrive, but she found she didn't actually care. They had been her companions in their combined task, but the three could never be considered close. Nothingman had promised them each something different to secure their loyalty, but he had exacted a high price. Well, the two men had given their lives for him. Would he be satisfied?

She knew he wouldn't be. All the deaths in the world would not sate his appetite. He would suck them all dry, and then forage elsewhere. The only way to avoid his hunger-filled gaze was to do his killing for him. Each death brought with it an individual stay of execution.

Things had definitely worsened since Chance's escape. Her brother's desertion had stabbed deep into the heart of Nothingman. Not in the way a father might feel betrayed from the loss of his son. No, this was in the way God might feel betrayed by a priest who chose to renounce his faith.

Nothingman had become obsessed. Not only with whatever objective he had originally planned, but with dragging Chance back into the fray, making him beg for mercy. So much had gone into the planning of her brother's recapture, more even than Christine knew about, she felt sure. Looking around at the colossal maze she sat within, she realized how much she had remained ignorant to.

It was not as if she and her father were exactly chummy these days. Christine did what he told her, and that was all. His intention to enter the asylum beside Chance wasn't even something he had discussed with Trinity, nor was his plan to open her brother's spiritual eyes to the women they culled. Everything was a game to her father, but not one to be enjoyed. It became an objective that needed to be won at all costs, and damn anyone who stepped in his way.

For herself, Christine could barely look in the mirror. Nothingman was everywhere. He was everything. Endless nightmares cemented in her a terror she felt sure nobody would ever understand… until Chance had somehow appeared within one.

At first, she could not believe the Chance in her dream had been real. She assumed he appeared as a figment of her tormented mind or a projection from Nothingman, there only to plague her, to amplify her desperation to please him. But the essence of peace Chance had left in his wake slowly convinced her that the childlike version of the brother she saw in her dreams was indeed a projection from Chance's subconscious. He was reaching out to her… or perhaps she was reaching out to him.

Twins were close. Much closer than normal siblings. Maybe it was spending so much time together in a womb that linked them, or perhaps it was part of the horrendous legacy they each had inherited from Nothingman.

Chance had learned early in life to control objects with his mind. At first, it had been nothing more than peanuts on a Monopoly board, but as his teenage years had kicked in, the telekinesis became more and more forceful. Sometimes he would manipulate objects without even noticing. Flicking on a light switch or changing the television dial became second nature to her talented brother. Christine, on the other hand, seemed to have inherited her father's ability to manipulate people's thoughts. Nowhere near the scale of what Nothingman could do, but influential enough to coerce strangers to her side, to imprint on them memories of events that had never happened, or wipe out ones that had. A side effect of this was the ability to see through some of Nothingman's illusions.

Like now.

She sat in a rusted wheelchair in the midst of a dump.

Whoever the cab driver had been – hell, he might have truly been a taxi driver, but one controlled by Nothingman – he had not driven them to the hospital as Chance requested.

Looking back, she wondered at the length of the car ride. At the time, it had not seemed long. She still suffered light-headedness and weakness in her limbs: both signs of substantial blood loss, an odd thing from such a minor wound. The drive must have been extensive, possibly lasting more than an hour, for her to lose so much lifeblood. Nothingman knew she could see through his illusions, and as such would have focused hard to fool her. Now his attention seemed fixated elsewhere, allowing her a modicum of freedom.

If sitting near death in a rusted wheelchair could be called freedom.

Christine examined the bullet wound in her thigh. The bleeding seemed to have almost stopped; the clotting was thick, indicating she had been sitting here for some time. The blood had pooled in the seat of the wheelchair, soaking into her jeans, a period from hell. With a grunt, she tore loose a strip of cloth from the bottom of her shirt, exposing her abdomen. She used the makeshift bandage to field dress the wound, stopping any further blood loss.

She stood up, initially unsteady on her feet, but finding she was able to remain upright without major issue. The world around her spun, snapping back only when she focused her thoughts intensely. There was nothing psychic about what she accomplished, merely force of will.

"Where to?" she wondered.

Nothingman had deserted her. Whoever had posed as the nurse was undoubtedly long gone, possibly retaining only a headache as evidence of the incident. The woman would walk away with no memory, no knowledge she had been mentally invaded, molested as surely as if she'd been raped. As a result, Christine could not even seek the woman out in the hopes of interrogating her for answers.

The piles of trash around her weren't common household refuse, she noticed. No stinky piles of rotting food or discarded nachos containers. There were mountains of heavy appliances: dishwashers, fridges, washers, dryers, freezers. Other mounds contained smaller electronics, some so new they looked barely unboxed, whereas others appeared positively archaic. In one stash, she saw a washing machine with what looked to be a linen roller attached. She had only seen such a device in magazine images or articles on the internet and wondered briefly at its utility.

Was this a collection of some sort? Some morbid hoarding of a person who yearned for the serenity of steel? She discarded the notion. If it were, the owner would have cared for the appliances better. Searching within herself, Christine also sensed this wasn't an illusion, at least not one she could discern. It wouldn't be beyond the scope of Nothingman to throw her into such a scenario simply to see how she reacted, but her instincts told her his attention was focused elsewhere.

Reaching behind her back, Christine checked to find her first knife still tucked into her waistband. The bone handle seemed to stretch out toward her grip, but she left it in its sheath for the moment. Her second blade was snug on the inside of her right boot; she could feel the toughened leather case through her sock, rubbing against her ankle. She leaned back against a top-loading washing machine and sighed.

Chance's face flashed into her mind. Poor, naïve Chance. There had been a time when she would have thought her brother was perhaps the only person capable of standing up to Nothingman, but those days were gone, along with his memory. He still displayed erratic spurts of the power he had once so confidently operated, but now it was like a toddler wielding an assault rifle. Her brother was as likely to kill himself as achieve anything of worth. Added to this was the fact he could no longer shield himself from Nothingman's machinations. He would be as defenseless as a puppy before a firing squad.

Christine knew she should flee. Whatever this place was, it wasn't somewhere she wanted to be when all hell broke loose. She sensed the piles of equipment had nothing much to do with Nothingman's reasoning for luring Chance here. In all likelihood, they were far beyond the edges of the city, somewhere they weren't likely to be disturbed. Anything urban would probably draw focus from residents or businesses. And such focus would mean police. And police carried guns.

The last thing her father would want while toying with Chance was a group of unknowns stumbling through his playground, holding his potential demise in their hands. He was a planner, and such an outcome would have been high on his list of things to avoid.

Despite all his assertions to the contrary, Nothingman was still mortal, even if his mind ascended beyond human limits. If he were battling Chance, all his concentration would be drawn towards overpowering his son. The fact Christine had broken free of his illusions within her weakened state showed how much focus Chance was drawing.

Seizing this knowledge, Christine ascertained they were likely in the middle of nowhere within a maze of trashed appliances. Not a huge leap of intuition there. She had never heard of anywhere like that, but then again, she wasn't from New York. Maybe it was a common thing to dispose of your appliances at the slightest hiccup. Whatever the reason, she needed to escape from here, and quickly.

A soft cry sounded through the air. Christine paused. The shriek had been feminine, she felt sure of it. Over the past few years, she had heard enough screams from terrified women to recognize the anguished shriek lingering in the still air.

The girl dogging her brother's heels, what had her name been? Bessy? Maybe Bella, or something similar. Chance certainly had seemed taken with the woman. Judging from looks alone, Christine could understand, but something more had connected the two, something that had allowed him to be taken when little else could have stopped him.

Christine's eyes narrowed. Was her brother smitten? Such a concept seemed odd considering the sibling she had once known. But Chance had changed. Some vital part of him seemed to have been burned out along with his memories. The mire that had once clung to his soul was absent, leaving a purer version of the Chance she had known so long ago.

The thought raised a tantalizing possibility. Could Christine cleanse her past in a similar fashion? Was there a way for her to expunge her sordid history and begin anew? This was a prospect she had never before considered. Now, like a swift bird released from a cage, the idea seemed impossible to haul back. As she imagined it, Christine realized it might be something she didn't *want* to haul back.

She began walking toward where the shriek had emanated from, a fragile plan forming slowly in her mind. There was a possibility Chance might show her how he had cleansed his past, but to succeed she first needed to return the one thing he cared about, the one thing he had risked his life to save.

* * * *

Debris erupted everywhere.

Nothingman leered before Chance, his hollow laughter booming. The more Chance battled, the easier the telekinesis flowed. With it grew the knowledge that this is what Nothingman wanted, to bring him to his full potential, thus making him a riper peach to pluck. No matter what he threw at his father, the shadowy figure flung his efforts aside like a cougar attacked by a kitten.

Gone now was any pretense of Jarvis's mortal form. The halls of the hospital basement filled with the haunting figure seemingly comprised of smoke and shadows. Chance blew apart walls, tore down ceilings, anything he could imagine that might slow the inexorable pursuit of Nothingman, but nothing proved fruitful. Apart from tearing down the entire building, Chance had no idea what he might be able to do. Nothingman seemed everywhere and nowhere at once. A nightmare made of mist, lingering in Chance's mind and yet tormenting his flesh.

The maze repeated itself eternally. Every now and then, a glimmer of hope appeared before Chance like an oasis in the desert, only to morph into yet another mirage. One moment there was a contingent of police rushing to his aid, the next, Nothingman was tumbling to his death through a rupture in the floor. Frustratingly, each illusion snapped back to reality with horrific sharpness. At least what he thought was reality. The bonds holding Chance's tenuous sanity together seemed to be stretching, becoming more insubstantial. It felt like they might snap altogether at any moment, leaving him flailing and at the mercy of his oppressor.

A scream sounded. It was faint, barely audible, but Chance recognized it… or thought he did. The tone had sounded like Bella's voice. The softness had not been a matter of distance, more a muffled quality, as though he had been hearing it through a pillow. Without pause, Chance sucked in a huge breath and began running in the direction of the sound.

Nothingman's voice taunted him. A ghostly hand scraped down his spine. The walls turned to ash and corpses flew at him from all sides, only to turn to powder as Chance blasted them asunder. The walls snapped back to their pristine white, and then suddenly bulged with the maws of wraithlike hellhounds, gnashing and snapping at him as he ran past.

A nurse suddenly stepped around the corner, focused down at her clipboard, oblivious to Chance. Too late to halt or swerve, Chance crashed headlong into the woman. They both tumbled to the ground, her clipboard smacking the wall loudly and cracking. Out of habit, Chance gasped an apology. The woman's head turned slowly toward him.

It was Bella.

For a moment, the world around them seemed to freeze. Bella smiled widely, recognizing him. He sighed and smiled in return, only to pause, and then frown. Bella's smile continued to grow, eventually splitting the skin of her cheeks, tearing from the corners of her lips up toward her ears. Skeletal fingers grasped at him, but Chance scurried away, swiftly gathering his feet beneath him and hurtling away down the corridor once more.

Turning another corner, he skidded to a halt. Hundreds of Bella forms, all in white nurse's uniforms, complete with white caps adorned with red crosses, lurched toward him. They called out his name like a murder of crows. A cacophony of haunting voices.

"Chance."

"Chance."

"*Chance.*"

They held out their arms, evil parodies of the embrace he yearned for. His name bounced from the walls, and for several moments, Chance had no idea what to do.

Scuffing footsteps behind made him spin. A second horde of Nurse Bellas lurched around the corner, similarly calling out his name and reaching toward him.

With a strangled cry, Chance let loose an explosion of power. It ripped through the illusions, tearing them apart like rotted fabric. All that fluttered to the floor of the corridor were wisps of charred paper.

He knew they weren't real, yet a choked sob still escaped his lips. The scraping footfalls from behind motivated him into action, and he jogged away. Gone was the frenetic energy that panic had lent him for so long. Now all that remained was a trickling flow that allowed him to move slightly faster than that which followed him.

Part of his mind wondered what would happen if he allowed the horde of illusions to swamp him. Would they vanish into mist, or would they consume his mind completely? Perhaps that was how Nothingman hoped to overwhelm him. Maybe only abject surrender would allow his father to absorb the power entwined within him.

Chance struggled along.

* * * *

A dull booming snapped Christine's head around to the left. She waited, breathless, but no further noise came. She tried to guess how far away the thud had been, but within the junkyard, with its high mounds of electrical appliances, it remained impossible to judge.

Turning back, she released tiny tendrils of spiritual energy once more. Nothingman had taught her this hunting technique to aid in tracking down their more elusive quarry. Usually, such tactics were ridiculously effective, but here, within the walls of steel and wire, her signals seemed muted and turned around. She could sense the presence of the woman she assumed was Bella, but it flitted around like an angered wasp. One moment she seemed directly in front of Christine, and then the signal snapped around to the right faster than any human could move. An instant later, the presence would be behind her, but only for a half-breath, before returning to its original position.

As frustrating as it was, Christine was unwilling to let go the one talent that might prove the difference. Part of her wondered if this was the reason Nothingman had chosen this man-made maze as his final stalking ground for Chance. Did he fear his son so much, even now with the greater part of her brother's talents wiped away? It would seem so.

Another weak cry sounded from ahead and to the right. Christine wondered if she might be able to climb to the top of the junk heap to peer around, but the tons of steel appeared too tenuous to risk. No, she would refrain from such a tactic unless it remained her only option.

Over the years, she had developed into a skilled huntress. Patience was always a virtue, especially when stalking prey. To rush in could prove fatal. Thrust aside emotions and release them only in controlled levels when necessary, or not at all. They were tools for the hunt, nothing more. But here, all her training threatened to tear apart. Fear battled within her for supremacy.

What if Nothingman discovered her intent?

What if everything around her was an illusion, and she had been fooled into believing she was in control?

The terrors stacked up, each one weighing heavier on her mind, confusing her. But she was better than that. She knew it.

She breathed in. Her pulse became a controlled beast, a raging stallion controlled within a pen, but ready to break loose at any given moment. She breathed out. Sweat glistened faintly upon her brow.

With little energy to spare, Christine held herself together, knowing that to unravel now would surely hasten death. Or worse.

And then she rounded a corner and her mind shattered.

Nothingman glared down at her. Towering as tall as the mountains of steel on either side, his shadows unfurled like demonic wings, ready to twist around her and snatch her from her feet.

She snapped to the right, her blade in her hand, preparing to hurl it into the dark face, but she held back. At the last moment, before she had slid to the side, past the sanctuary of the corner, she had noticed Nothingman was not focused on her at all. His eyes, or whatever could pass for eyes within that miasmic abyss, glowered down the trash corridor beyond her.

Slowly, fighting hard to control her pounding pulse, she turned and looked. Chance stood there, gasping for breath, his eyes fixed on the towering shadowman. He seemed not to even notice Christine, and as she exhaled, she understood why. He was trapped within an illusion, an illusion that didn't include her.

Chance's face glared at Nothingman, and Christine cursed. She recognized that expression and knew what was coming next. Her brother was about to attack. She looked around frantically for somewhere to hide, but apart from scrambling up the precariously balanced trash, she had nowhere to flee.

The pulse of psychic energy knocked her flying. Thankfully, it had not been directed at her. Even so, when she landed catlike on the dirt, it left her mind buzzing. The reality of her blood loss returned, its effects still lingering, crashing over her in a wave of dizziness. For a moment, she saw Nothingman hurtle down the trash corridor past her, but then the illusion shattered into flecks of light, each smaller than a dust mote. She gasped, stunned at the authenticity of the deception. To be able to trick her when she was not the intended recipient would have taken monstrous amounts of power and control. No wonder Nothingman had released her from the delusion. He had no choice.

When she looked back, Chance was gone.

For a moment, Christine considered pursuing her brother, but she feared it might draw the attention of the real Nothingman. Besides, she knew it would be for naught. He was trapped. As surely as this maze confined them both, Chance was held secure in his own mind. Christine had experienced similar horrors over the years, and she didn't envy what he was going through. Nothingman would taunt and exhaust Chance until he finally surrendered. The reaping of his soul would be utter, leaving nothing but an empty husk behind.

"Hold on," she murmured, unsure if she spoke the words to herself or her brother.

* * * *

Ice trapped Chance's feet.

Rubble rained down upon him, large chunks of concrete smashing to shards in clouds of destruction. Dust filled the air… or was that smoke? He could no longer tell. All his senses seemed turned about, and his brain felt like mush. The power practically sizzled within him now, but everything he focused it on turned to shadows and ash.

He fought on.

The ice shattered, and he stumbled away, beyond the reach of the concrete avalanche. He wondered how the building was suffering under the onslaught of his powers; would it topple in reality soon? How would he even know he was dying? The nightmares assaulting him were so real he could no longer differentiate truth from imagination. Perhaps those slabs of concrete had not been part of the illusion after all. Perhaps they were.

As if in answer, an entire wall collapsed, blocking the corridor. Chance contemplated blasting it to dust, such an effort would be easy now. Instead, he honed the energy thrumming through him. This was a much more focused use of the telekinetic power, and one that required infinitely more concentration: the difference between kicking a football and stitching up the laces.

Sweat dripped down his forehead, stinging his eyes. He reminded himself that if this barrier were truly one of the supporting walls, detonating it might collapse the entire building. With infinite care, he slipped the concrete back into place, held it there until he felt sure it wouldn't move, and then ran past. Looking back, he noticed there was no seam, no evidence of damage, and he cursed.

The entire thing had been an illusion.

Chance pushed aside the sense of looming despair. He had wasted so much time and energy on something that did not even exist, resources better utilized trying to escape this hellish place. But what choice did he have?

He shook his head. No, this wasn't Hell. This was Purgatory.

There were no answers here, no final revelations; only questions through which he needed to battle. Chance wanted to scream at the walls, to demand they answer him, but knew it would avail him nothing.

The ground disappeared beneath him. Once again, he found himself sprawling onto the floor of Doctor Smith's office. This had been the third… no, fourth… time he had visited this place. Straps materialized from the ground, snapping around his wrists, ankles, and throat. He struggled to break loose, to tear the leather apart with the power of his mind, but it seemed to have vanished.

A nurse approached the bed upon which he reclined.

When did I get on a bed?

The nurse held a syringe the size of his forearm. The needle looked like a rapier, green ooze dripping from its sharpened tip. The liquid hissed and spat like oil in a frying pan as it hit the floor.

"You might feel a small prick," wheezed the nurse.

Chance looked to her face and gasped. The visage of Howard Mason grinned wickedly.

"You're not real," Chance insisted, struggling harder.

Nurse Mason chuckled hollowly and raised the immense syringe. He thrust it like a spear into the center of Chance's chest, and Chance howled. The Billionaire Cannibal chuckled wheezily as he jammed down the plunger. Green ooze spurted around the edges of the wound, but Chance could feel much more emptying into his chest cavity. He choked, hot liquid bubbling up from within his lungs. All the while, it ate through his internal organs and muscles.

Screams hit his ears, and it took a moment to realize the tormented cries fled from his own lips.

* * * *

Christine heard shrieking. This was not a woman. After a moment, she recognized Chance's tortured voice.

They were the cries of a man close to death.

But he wasn't finished yet. Whatever Chance was suffering, it was only happening to his mind. If Nothingman had actually defeated him, Christine knew there would be no sound at all as the light of his life snuffed out.

Indecision plagued her. One part wanted to run to her brother, to try to aid him somehow, but she knew there remained little she could do against the might of Nothingman. No, better for her to continue searching for the woman, Bella.

If she kept her safe, perhaps that would allow Chance enough focus to escape the mental bonds under which his father chained him.

The screaming stopped. Christine sighed, knowing it indicated not release, but another angle of attack. There would be no escape, not until Chance broke himself free of whatever nightmares lashed him. There was a time when she had believed he might have been powerful enough to defeat Nothingman, but that had been before the latest list of victims. Nothingman's endless hunger had grown in volumes, but so had his power.

Pausing, Christine tightened the makeshift bandage around her thigh, wincing as the material pulled tight. No hiss escaped her lips, though, and she lifted her gaze back up. Sending out her wisps of psychic energy once more, she combed the nearby area. The person she believed was Bella slipped away as she reached for traces of her, but Christine felt confident she had drawn closer. Biting her lip, she crept on through the wreckage.

The pulse in her target was potent; Bella's psychic energy seemed higher than normal, though that might have been interference from the white walls around her. Christine fought to hold onto the connection, despite it flitting in all directions. After waiting several moments, she found she could estimate the approximate direction where the woman hid.

Looking above the mound of dead machines, Christine almost gasped. Soaring high into the sky was a pyramid of debris twice as tall as the walls of the labyrinth through which

Christine stalked. What better place to keep a captive than upon such a sky prison? To attempt escape would risk upsetting the entire mound, tons of scrap metal ready to rain down upon the hapless escapee. Surely this alone would not be enough to stop the woman from trying, though. No doubt Nothingman had placed other safeguards in place. Who knew, perhaps this Bella woman even now imagined her platform floated a mile above the ground. Such an illusion would be simple for Nothingman to hold in place, taking almost no concentration.

Grimacing, Christine set off toward the tower.

* * * *

Chance choked back a sob.

Despair assailed him like tiny birds pecking at his soul. Each challenge he vanquished seemed to open the doors for something even greater.

Nurse Mason had torn Chance's beating heart from his melting chest and dangled it in front of his eyes before devouring it with jaws that expanded like those of a snake. The sight had pushed Chance's panic to a whole new degree, allowing him to overwhelm the bonds controlling his mind. The scene had shattered the moment he had torn loose from his mental restraints, but had left Chance anguished and desperate.

"WHERE ARE YOU?" he screamed furiously.

He paused for a moment. Who exactly was he calling out to? Was he even looking for Bella anymore? What about Christine; did she still live? Did he care? Part of him knew he should, but another part, one so hungering for escape he knew he would chew off his own fingers if such an act could guarantee his release, understood that he would give up anything to flee this endless nightmare.

How long had he been here? It seemed like weeks since he had blundered so willingly into Nothingman's snare. If only he could see outside; the sky and light might bolster his spirits, allowing him to know that the real world still existed beyond these walls. But there was nothing, only endless white walls and ceilings interspersed with fluorescent tubing.

Not for the first time, he pondered whether he was still locked inside Mount Sinai. Perhaps everything he had experienced had been nothing more than a complete psychotic break. Nobody could move things with their mind. No one had the ability to create the visions he was suffering.

That was it. He wasn't special. Nothing about him was special. He was just another loon in a basket full of crazies. Right now, they probably had him tied to his bed, spooning baby food between his flabby gums, ignoring him as he mumbled about Nothingman and telekinesis.

On the other hand, he might be strapped tight in a straight jacket, screaming endless iterations into the padding of a secure cell. Perhaps the surgeon was even now readying his instruments, preparing to remove that tiny portion of his brain causing all his distress. Did Chance want to end up a vegetable, all because of stubbornness?

Accept your fate, a little voice told him. *Give up and let reality seep back in. The asylum wasn't so bad, was it? Better than this incessant nightmare, surely?*

"No," Chance grunted. He blinked several times, slowly finding the determination to battle on.

Looking around as if waking from a dream, Chance wondered at which point he had sunk to his knees. Slowly, he stood and sucked in a deep breath. A demonic figure with smoldering-coal eyes lurched up from the floor, and Chance flicked his head to the side casually. The body flew sideways, crashing heavily into the concrete and slumping to the floor. Chance stepped over it calmly and walked down the corridor.

* * * *

The pyramid of junk loomed high above her.

Grimacing, Christine tried to see what lay atop the flat wooden platform at its peak, but the angle prohibited her seeing anything beyond the Electrolux vacuum teetering near its edge. All of the thousands of appliances, in fact, looked ready to tumble at the first misstep.

"I can't believe I'm about to try this," she muttered.

With great caution, Christine placed her right foot on the side of a dented freezer. The metal groaned as she lifted her weight, and the steel plating caved in further, but a thousand tons of refuse didn't collapse on her head, and for that, she remained grateful.

Slowly, inexorably, she crept up the pile. A toaster tumbled away to her left, clattering down the side, its guts gradually separating themselves. She froze, waiting for the entire mound to shift. Thankfully, the rest of the debris seemed more compact, and after a few groans, silence returned. Christine resumed climbing.

Her right foot landed on a serving tray, which skittered away underneath her. Her legs split, and Christine threw herself face forward onto the mound, her hands desperately grabbing anything more substantial than a power cord or camera tripod. The entire section under her right leg shunted a full foot down the slope. Christine held her breath, waiting for the avalanche to begin, but again the mound held firm. She blew out a soft sigh of relief.

"I hope Chance is doing better than me," she muttered.

* * * *

Chance hurtled headlong down the corridor.

The cut in his leg bled profusely. He tried to tell himself that the wild boar was not real, that it was all part of his imagination, but the pain definitely felt real. As he ran, he fought to bring his emotions under control, to focus enough to defend himself, but he could hear the beast grunting directly behind him, its breath hot on his calves. To pause, even to glance behind, might see him gored once more.

A corner loomed. Chance ducked around it and spun. The boar roared around the turn, and he hit it with a mind blast. Instead of throwing it backward, however, he lifted the beast, intending to smash it into the concrete ceiling. The creature rose up… and up… and…

The ceiling vanished. For an instant, Chance glimpsed blue sky. All around him were not hospital walls, but piles of electrical products. His breath caught in his throat, but before he could fathom what was happening, the image was gone, replaced once more with the antiseptic walls of the hospital.

What was real, the blue sky or corridors?

Chance reached out and touched the wall. It certainly felt real. Looking down, he saw that the wound in his leg was gone, though the memory if its throb remained.

Glancing left and right to ensure the hall was clear of threats, Chance pulsed against the wall. It wasn't a savage explosion of mental will, more a probing to see what might happen. For a moment, the slightest fraction of a second, he felt the wall depress slightly, like a sponge being squeezed. It snapped back out, pushing Chance away a step.

"What the hell?" he murmured.

Checking the corridor once more, Chance stared hard at the point he had pushed in and focused his energy. He smashed into the wall with his mind, focusing on a space about a foot in diameter. The concrete caved in, but quickly returned to its original form. Looking around, Chance cursed softly.

"None of it is real," he whispered. This entire structure was nothing more than a mental projection. Looking at the ground, he stomped his foot. The slap of his rubber sole against the linoleum definitely felt real, but so had the wound from the boar. His eyes lifted toward the ceiling, focusing on the fluorescent tube buzzing within its bracket.

Chance released a burst of power at the light, and then immediately spun and hurled a pulse toward the same section of wall he had already probed. The illusion flickered for the briefest moment, and he saw the sky, the mounds of discarded appliances returning to his view. The second burst hit the electrical appliances, and they exploded outward.

The illusion shattered.

Chance gasped and stepped back as reality blasted into view. Sunlight, vastly unlike the false illumination of the imaginary halls, made him squint, but not before he noticed the trash embankment teetering toward him. Unsure if it was real or an illusion, and unwilling to take the risk, Chance dove to the side. Tons of fridges and tumble dryers crashed down where he had been standing. A clothes iron smacked the edge of a computer tower and hurtled toward his face. At the last moment, Chance snapped his head aside. The cord whipped across his chest, and he swore.

Eventually, the mass of appliances settled, and Chance breathed out a sigh of relief. The relief faded, however, as he peered around. Mountains of electronic devices soared above him, all lined up in rows, walls so sheer they were almost vertical. No wonder one had toppled so effortlessly. How had he wandered through these masked halls, blasting away at imaginary foes, without managing to crush himself beneath tons of rubble?

The possibility remained that the rusty knolls were all illusion, but these held a subtlety and intricacy he doubted Nothingman could project. Every wire, every cracked glass pane, every mottled cord design was there for him to see in all its minute detail. Despite not knowing his father well, Chance sensed the man was used to a more direct approach. A swinging hammer could not paint porcelain.

Rising to his feet, Chance glanced left and right. Despite the change in scene, his plight seemed identical. Whatever had snapped Nothinman's hospital illusion was unlikely to be permanent. At any moment, these walls could turn into anything. He searched for indications of an exit, but the walls were too high. The only edifice that stood higher than the walls was a towering pyramid of junk away to his right. Its walls were less steep, and Chance felt he might be able to scale them. From such a vantage point, he would be able to view the entire maze and plan how best to tackle his escape.

Bella's face flashed into his mind. Scowling, Chance knew that he could never leave without her. Now that the incessant assaults on his mind had ceased, or at least paused, he knew that if he tried to flee without her, he would forever condemn himself. No, that wasn't an option.

Looking toward the pyramid once more, its four angled sides reaching a broad wooden platform set at the top, he came to a decision. That was his target, no matter what. From there, he could detect where Bella was, and possibly even his sister, though she was a secondary objective.

The plan seemed flimsy, but it was better than what he had been enduring. At least now he had a focus, something to concentrate on. If the illusions returned – or perhaps he should say *when* – he at least knew how to combat them. Hopefully, he could replicate the feat should the need arise.

Hopefully....

* * * *

Christine threw herself flat against the pile.

This time, however, it was not to combat sliding appliances. A figure moving above had snatched her attention, and not the person she had expected to see. Even now, she could hear him cursing.

"Where did that son of a bitch go?" the figure muttered. "How the hell did he shatter my illusion?"

Even if she hadn't recognized his form, Christine knew that voice. She would never forget it, not in a million years.

"Nothingman," she murmured.

Glancing over her shoulder, she wondered if it were possible to retreat without garnering notice. From the sounds of it, things were not going to Nothingman's liking. Maybe, if she were cautious, she could withdraw quietly enough to escape discovery.

She paused. A ridiculous thought flashed into her head. Christine disregarded it almost instantly, but it returned, lingering like a bug at a light. It tapped at her mind the way a bug might batter against the glass of a bulb, unremitting and relentless. Again, she pushed it away, attempting to take a step down, but even as she did, her leg froze, almost against her will.

She looked up. He still hadn't noticed her.

Could she?

Chance dared oppose him. Why couldn't she?

Years of indoctrination swarmed on Christine, arguing against rebellion, against even *thinking* about rebellion. But the bug kept on tapping.

The decision, when it came, brought with it a wave of unexpected relief. One way or another, her ordeal would end.

Gripping her knife in her right hand, Christine crept high. At the lip of the platform, she paused and peeked over.

Nothingman glared down into the maze, searching for something.

Searching for Chance.

Christine surged up. At the same time, the television beneath her right foot gave way with a crash. Rubble collapsed beneath her. The avalanche she had feared finally gripped the electrical slope. Nothingman spun around, surprise erupting across his features.

All her years of training kicked in. Without thought, she leaped toward her father. In his face, she saw a moment's hesitation. That was all she needed.

Panther fast, she darted low and pounced high. Almost of its own volition, the blade drove down into the triangle of soft flesh between Nothingman's collarbone and trapezius. She felt the six-inch blade dig deep, like a hungry fang, and a rush of euphoric satisfaction washed over her.

Nothingman backhanded her, hurling her backward. Catlike, she snapped to her feet and drew the second blade from her boot.

A lion leaped from her right. The beast was gigantic, a huge mane surrounding a snarling head the size of an engine block. The creature smashed into her with the power of a freight train. She knew it wasn't real, but the weight of the imaginary lion still crushed her down as its claws dug deep into her flesh. With all her strength, both of mind and body, she held the lion's jaws away from her throat.

"You… *bitch!*" screamed Nothingman. "You betrayed me!"

Closing her eyes, Christine battled to extinguish the powerful hallucination of the lion. After a moment, she felt the weight vanish. Cautiously, she opened her eyes.

Her father stood, panting and sweating, barely able to remain on his feet. Whatever battle of wills he had endured with Chance had exhausted the giant man. Dark circles hung under his eyes. His beard glistened with rivulets of sweat. His bulk seemed to weigh him down, and he appeared too weak to pull loose the knife from his flesh.

Without waiting for him to recover, Christine darted in for another attack. The huge man swung at her, but she ducked under his sweeping blow. Her right hand drew back, and then snapped forward, aiming her knife directly into his groin. A second blow cartwheeled her backward, tearing the blade from her grip.

Slipping back to her feet, she eyed him warily. Her movements feline, she slunk low to the ground. At the first opportunity, she would feint for his neck and then –

A thousand bats suddenly buffeted her, knocking her off her feet. In an instant, Nothingman was upon her, his crushing weight driving her to the platform.

"Did you want this?" the huge man hissed. With a massive wrench, he finally dragged the knife from above his clavicle. A gout of blood spurted forth, but he ignored it.

Without pause, Nothingman stabbed the blade into her ribs. He glared into her eyes, hunger glinting within his gaze, and she knew he intended to feed on her as he had all those others. For the first time, Christine understood their fear; it rattled through her bones. If the pain in her chest had so allowed, she would have screamed to the heavens.

"Get off my sister, you fat son of a bitch, or I'll tear you apart."

The words were spoken calmly, though Christine could sense the deep well of anger thrumming within them. Within her bleeding chest, her heart leaped.

Her brother had arrived to save her.

The world started to fade, the gray edges of her vision creeping in until there was barely more than a nickel of light at the end of the tunnel.

* * * *

Chance yearned to fling Jarvis high into the air, to spear him with a hundred shards of broken glass, to tear him limb from limb and hurl his body toward the four points of the compass. But to do so would be to risk the safety of Christine.

Jarvis chuckled, the sound hoarse within his throat. Slowly, he rose from Christine's form, his hands raised high in the air. "Chance. My boy. What are you doing here? I stopped her for you."

Tendrils of mist crept into Chance's mind, and he frowned. "What…?" He glanced around, fighting for cognitive control. "What are you… talking about?"

"She was the one fooling you with all those hallucinations."

Chance glanced at Christine. Through the fog, Jarvis's words suddenly made sense. An inner voice tried to argue with the logic, but a broad hand brushed the feeble arguments aside with a sweeping blow.

Christine had been behind all the machinations, all the murders. Jarvis was his friend. He had been his friend all the way from the asylum. They had shared a room there, for God's sake!

Smiling, Chance shook his head, amazed he had been about to accuse his friend of such a travesty. "I'm sorry, Jarvis. I don't know what came over me."

"Not a problem, my boy. Come here and give me a hug."

Chance took a step forward, and then stopped. Sweat gleamed across Jarvis's forehead, and his face scowled with strain. At first, Chance thought it must have been from the big man's injuries, but this seemed different. Jarvis was glaring at Chance, concentrating hard, his eyes barely blinking. His breath was coming in ragged pants, and Chance noticed his hands were clenched into rigid fists so tightly they were shaking.

"Why are you sweating so much, Jarvis?"

"Don't worry about that," the big man grunted through clenched teeth. "Come here."

Chance looked down, staring hard at Christine. She was his sister. He looked back up at the giant figure sweating and straining. Jarvis was his father, but he was also more. Fighting through the fog, traveling down its mental paths back to its source, Chance gasped at the image of a towering figure in the midst of a pumpkin field.

With the image, Jarvis's mental assault snapped. The huge man visibly sagged, eventually dropping to his knees.

"You killed all those women," Chance murmured.

"No!" Jarvis snarled. He stabbed a meaty finger toward Chance's chest. "You killed them." He turned and jabbed the same finger down at Christine. "And she killed them." He held up his palms and grinned manically. "My hands are clean, Chance. They always have been."

"You enslaved us," Chance growled.

With a flick of his head, he wrenched Jarvis's arms wide. He lifted the man who had been his friend, his father, his tormentor, high into the air, dangling him from his wrists. Pain etched his father's face, a silent howl stretching his mouth. Chance swung him high above the platform.

"Test me now, Jarvis. Throw one of your illusions into my mind; see whether you can invade my brain before I fling you off this platform."

"I am your father," Jarvis managed to cry.

Chance shook his head. "You might have seeded me, but you most certainly are not my father." He glanced down at Christine. Dead eyes stared back at him, and he gritted his teeth. "A father wouldn't do that to his child."

"I was defending myself."

Chance felt spirit fingers scraping against his mind like a hundred octopus tentacles, probing for a way in, a way to override his control. Grimly, he shut the walls of his psyche against the invasion. It felt like he had squashed a bug beneath his shoe. Jarvis cried out in pain.

"So sorry," said Chance with a tight smile. "I was defending myself."

A gunshot split the tension wide. Nothingman's head snapped back, and then flopped forward, a gaping wound torn through his eye socket. Chance dropped the body and snapped around. Bella stood unsteadily on the slope, a handgun gripped in her shaking palms.

"Bella! What are you doing?"

She nodded toward the space behind him. A man stood there, dressed in a set of grimy overalls and work boots. He was old, possibly sixty or even seventy, bewilderment clouding his features. In his hands, he gripped a long-handled shovel, the blade upraised like an ax, as if to swat Chance.

"What's going on?" the old man asked, his voice barely above a whisper.

"Who are you?" Chance demanded.

"I'm Henry. I'm the…." He appeared battling to recall. "I'm the custodian of this place." Slowly, he let the shovel droop and peered around. "Who built this damn tower? More importantly, who's going to help me put it right?" The old man looked at Bella. "Is that my gun?"

Bella clambered up the rest of the pile and stood beside Chance. She looked at the gun in her hand. “I found it in the little shack beyond the piles of scrap.” She grinned sheepishly at Chance, though he saw the echoes of her actions lingering within her gaze. Her eyes flicked toward Jarvis’s body. “Kind of lucky I did.”

Trembling, she dropped the handgun. It landed with a clatter on the wooden platform. Chance embraced her, smelling her hair, feeling the tangible reality of her body against his, praying none of *this* was an illusion.

Surveying the hectares of labyrinthine corridors, Chance grew reflective, “I don’t know if you can ever put a place like this right.”

Henry shook his head, peering off the edge of the platform bewildered. “Who could do such a thing?”

Chance glanced down at Jarvis’s corpse.

“Nobody of worth. A Nothingman.”

EPILOGUE

Chance awoke with the ghost of a scream on his lips.

Jerking up in bed, he found himself drenched in sweat. The room was dark, darker than midnight, darker than the soul of Howard Mason. Panting, he battled for control, fighting down the roiling emotions yearning to break loose.

"Another dream?" asked a voice in the night.

Chance reached over and flicked on the light. Bella squeezed her eyes tight but elbowed up in the bed.

"Was it the same as the others?" she asked.

Again, Chance nodded. "He'll never leave me alone."

"Not until you let yourself be free."

This time, Chance shook his head slightly. No matter how close the two of them became, she still couldn't understand, perhaps would never understand. Bella was surely the smartest person he had ever met, but she struggled to comprehend the extent of the horror that still gripped him. She simply didn't see what she didn't want to see.

Chance stood, his body as naked as his soul, and moved to the window. Moonlight on snow greeted his vision. Snow on rooftops, on cars, on trees. Quebec seemed impossibly beautiful at this time of year.

A cracked remembrance flashed through his mind, and he visibly winced. If Bella saw the reaction, she let it go. A shuddering breath escaped through his gritted teeth.

"It's been a year. You would think that would be long enough, wouldn't you?"

Bella came and stood beside him. He saw her naked reflection in the glass and smiled despite himself. She hugged his arm and rested her head on his shoulder.

"I don't think it will ever end," she admitted softly. "It might simply be a thing you need to learn to live with. Whatever he did to you, both before and after Mount Sinai, went far deeper than any psychological treatment I know of could hope to carve out." Chance groaned, and she continued. "But that doesn't mean such a treatment doesn't exist."

"I see their faces. So many faces. More than just the ones I thought I knew about. There were hundreds." Chance shook his head and wiped a hand across his mouth. "He must have been killing them for years. Decades. How much evil did he pass on to me?" He paused. "How much did I impart unto myself?"

"That wasn't you. And even if it were, the fact your previous self fought against your father shows that you weren't inherently evil. You sought to escape, did everything in your power to do so, even to the point of somehow erasing your entire personality. You effectively killed yourself in the hopes of protecting future victims. Whatever you were, whatever you did, let that sink in for a moment."

"Yeah, I guess." He dwelled in the silence for a moment. Finally, he said, "I wish I could have saved her, though."

"Maybe you did."

"How so?" he asked, turning toward her.

"Well, from what you said, Christine was trying to kill Nothingman when you happened upon them. Who else but you could have had that influence on her?"

Chance scowled. "I always assumed they had some kind of falling out."

"After all those years of dominance merely to fall out right when you come on the scene?" Bella shook her head. "Too much of a coincidence. No, I think something in you reached out to her. Twins are always close; perhaps reuniting transferred some of the good in you into her."

Chance's eyes became distant. "That's a nice thought."

She drew away from him and then walked seductively over to the bed. "Why don't you come over here and let me help you forget those dreams."

A grin drifted across Chance's lips, but then faded. The idea was attractive, if somewhat dubious. With each passing day, he heard Nothingman's booming laughter sounding louder in his mind. Along with it came a hunger that reminded him all too vividly of his father's ravenous appetite for power. How long until that hunger became his own?

Focusing hard, Chance brushed aside the concern, scattering his angst. Perhaps good memories could wipe out the bad.

He drifted over to the bed and fell into her embrace.

Made in the USA
Monee, IL
29 December 2019

19643593R00286